More Praise for the
Gus Parker & Alex Mills

"With *Valley of Shadows,* Steven Cooper has pulled off a neat trick. He's written a tightly-plotted police procedural that somehow manages to subvert genre expectations and offer something brand new. Think you know what to expect from a detective teaming up with a psychic? Better think again. Long live Detective Alex Mills and his reluctant psychic sidekick, Gus Parker."

Hank Early, award winning author of
Heaven's Crooked Finger

"Beneath the endless money, the gorgeous mountain homes, and the perfectly-ordered lives of Phoenix high society lies a seething, malignant obsession with power and wealth that feeds on the ambitions and insecurities of the members of a cultish religion. In *Valley of Shadows,* Steven Cooper thrusts Alex Mills and Gus Parker into the middle of their most hair-raising investigation yet."

Roger Johns, award-winning author of
the Wallace Hartman Mysteries

"Along with the authentic police procedural detail, Cooper provides quirky and vivid characters, smart and snarky social observations, and challenging but fulfilling personal relationships. This is first-rate entertainment."

Publishers Weekly Starred Review

"Cooper continues to blend solid investigative work, psychological insight, and personal touches to create a broadly appealing series. . . ."

Kirkus Reviews

VALLEY OF SHADOWS

ALSO BY STEVEN COOPER

Desert Remains
Dig Your Grave

A GUS PARKER AND ALEX MILLS NOVEL

VALLEY OF SHADOWS

STEVEN COOPER

SEVENTH
STREET
BOOKS®

Published 2019 by Seventh Street Books®

Cover image © Shutterstock
Cover design by Jennifer Do
Cover design © Start Science Fiction

Inquiries should be addressed to
Start Science Fiction
101 Hudson Street, 37th Floor, Suite 3705
Jersey City, New Jersey 07302
PHONE: 212-620-5700
WWW.SEVENTHSTREETBOOKS.COM

10 9 8 7 6 5 4 3 2 1

ISBN 978-1-64506-000-0 (paperback) | ISBN 978-1-64506-006-2 (ebook)

Printed in the United States of America

To
Paul Milliken and Nancy Sciore
24/7

1

It's hot as fuck. But this is Arizona, so it's a dry fuck.

Even still. At 114 degrees, it's an oven.

Homicide Detective Alex Mills is on his hands and knees in the backyard of Viveca Canning's ample home. While Mills conducts his search under a blazing sky, Ms. Canning remains coolly inside her air-conditioned house waiting for the Office of the Medical Examiner to arrive. Relatively speaking, there's no hurry. Ms. Canning is dead. Shot twice in the head, it would seem, and cold, indeed. The crime scene specialists have spread throughout the house searching for evidence while scene investigator Jan Powell supervises. Out here, in the yard, Mills and one of the specialists scour for footprints in the gravel; they should be easy to spot, but they're not. Someone had kicked enough gravel around, apparently on purpose, to almost certainly render footprints useless. But fuck, it's hot. This is what happens during a Phoenix summer: every five to seven minutes you remind yourself how fucking hot it is.

And, yes, you sweat, despite the dry heat. A Colorado River of perspiration meanders from Mills's neck to the small of his back, threatening the Continental Divide of his ass. He's in the backyard here with the tech because it was obvious upon eyeballing the inside of the house that the perpetrator had entered through the rear by kicking in a glass door between the dining room and the swimming pool. The backyard is a resort, which is common if you live in the Valley of the Sun and you have money. The pool is one of those lazy, shapeless ones, surrounded by boulders and succulents, with a gushing waterfall at one end and a swim-up bar at another. Mills would like to tumble in now, sink to the bottom of the pool; it's tempting but he wipes his brow and shakes his head. There's a tennis court. And a small putting green. He gets up, his hands and knees chewed up a bit by the stones of desert landscaping. Immediately he hears a distant fluttering in the wind. A coming percussion. Then a roar. He looks to the sky, fully knowing what approaches. There they are, the metal vultures of the media, swooping in, sniffing around for the carrion. But he's done. The news choppers won't see anything out here except the immaculate indulgences of yet another wealthy Phoenician.

He leaves his colleague behind to do her measurements of all things measureable, and there's a shitload to measure; most people don't realize how meticulously a crime scene is recreated on paper. He heads back inside, runs into Detective Morton Myers in the doorway. Mills, who was assigned by the sergeant to be case agent, has asked Myers to be the notetaker. Myers is good with notes.

"Preston checked the garage for a car," Myers tells him. Ken Preston is probably the oldest, wisest detective at the crime scene. "It's empty."

"OK," Mills says. "Any indication that others lived here?"

"I found a stack of bills. All addressed to the victim. Nothing indicating a marriage. Preston is talking to neighbors now."

"Good."

"Mind if I go out back?"

"Go where you need to."

Mills brushes past him and finds Detective Jan Powell in what poses as a library. Mills considers it posing because people don't read enough anymore to require a personal library; they just want to look like they do, and rich people just want to show that their houses are big enough to accommodate a mahogany room exclusively for books. Phoenix, Scottsdale, and Paradise Valley have become, in recent years, magnets for the pretentious bullshitters who get more for their conspicuous wealth here than they can in LA. Plus the air quality is better, but not by much. He lingers here in the library because he still loves a good book. For some reason, probably back to that English Lit major he dated in college, he knows no better Zen than reading. He reads every night in bed. Can't get to sleep without escaping first between the pages of literature. He prefers the classics, but he's started reading contemporary novels too. He likens a good book to a grand detour, as if he's driving down an everyday, unremarkable highway and suddenly veers left onto a road that doesn't exist on a map. That sharp left turn takes him into another world, gets him out of his. Kelly, his insanely perfect wife, sometimes calls him a nerd. He finds that charming. There's a great-looking edition of *Don Quixote* on a lower shelf of Viveca Canning's home library. Mills is tempted to remove it and sift. Instead, he turns to Powell and says, "Nothing in here."

"It's about the only room on this side of the house that wasn't touched."

And she's right. He returns to the victim. Ms. Canning, in a silk dress, the clinging kind that Kelly would call a "cocktail dress," lies sprawled on the floor in the next room, a formal room with a fireplace and area rugs, marble tables, and leather upholstery. He drifts in there with Powell at his heels. He studies the room again. There's a wall of floor to ceiling shelves and cabinets. The cabinets are open and the contents—CDs, records, DVDs—are tossed everywhere on the floor. He turns to the adjacent bedroom where drawers of Viveca Canning's life clutter the floor, extracted like teeth from the bureaus. Closet doors stand agape, revealing a tumble of jewelry and a landslide of gowns that speak volumes in the silence.

"We have a lot to go through," Powell tells him in a reverent whisper.

"Yeah."

"The other bedroom across the hall looks the same," she says.

"I saw."

They return to the living room where Viveca Canning rests. Mills really wishes he could channel his good friend Gus Parker right about now; the psychic would have a fucking field day here at the crime scene. But Gus is out of town. He's out of town a lot these days, costarring, as he is, in the life of rock 'n' roll star Billie Welch, who lives in LA and tours the world. Today, however, the psychic is burying his father in Seattle. Mills thinks he has the day right, can't quite remember. But in Gus's absence Mills is left wishing he had some of the man's psychic gifts, which he doesn't and never will, but he does have good instincts, he tells himself, as he stares at the entry wounds in Viveca Canning's head. He rethinks the shattered glass, the back door, the sign of forced entry. He doesn't think she was robbed, despite the material carnage.

Too many jewels were left behind. He had noticed pearls on the floor of the bedroom. He had eyed a diamond watch perched on a nightstand. Mills inventories the walls of fine art. Nothing taken, with one exception. One space on the wall is empty; a lone nail and a perfect square, a shade darker than the faded surrounding walls, perfectly mark the site where one painting evacuated. But everything else is intact, and these aren't prints, to the best of Mills's estimation. He reads the signatures: Lichtenstein; Pollock; Chagall. Mills doesn't know much about art, but the collection seems eclectic and original. This is not a woman who peddled in replicas.

"Here's what I'm thinking," he tells Powell, backing away from the techs, "this was made to look like a general robbery, but the missing painting tells me whoever did this came for one item and one item alone."

"And killed our victim to get it?"

"Absolutely."

"It must be worth a lot of money," Powell says.

"The diamonds and the pearls are worth a lot of money," Mills reminds her. "And they weren't taken."

"I noticed an emerald too," she whispers. "And I'm almost sure the brooch on the bathroom floor is ruby."

"Right. So the painting, I'm guessing, is worth more than money to someone."

Powell nods. Mills goes back to the body, sinks to his knees. The blood from the victim's head is barely a tributary. A tech, Roni Gates, hands him a fresh pair of gloves. "We found the shell casings," she says.

"Well, it's obvious she's been shot twice."

"At close range," Roni says. "Probably within two feet away. I've noted the compact stippling around the entry wounds."

"Exit wounds?"

Roni nods and says she's just recovered a spent bullet, then points to an exit wound behind the victim's ear. "It's consistent, I think, with the bruising under her eye. The bullet apparently exited and hit the wall. It's got significant deformation."

"So, we're assuming the other bullet is lodged somewhere inside her squash here," Mills speculates.

"Correct," Roni says. Then she looks at him with a beaming smile. That's her trademark. He can never be certain whom he'll run into at a crime scene, but when it's Roni Gates he's always greeted with a radiance, as if she has unearthed the secret to happiness in an unhappy world. She is, after all, kneeling over the body of a homicide victim. And smiling.

There's no weapon in sight. Clearly not a suicide. And again, that empty square on the wall. He looks at it once more, trying to peer through it, as if the answer is just beyond the drywall. He shakes his head.

"We'll know more after the ME x-rays for the other bullet," Roni says.

"Yeah. Assuming the bullet didn't fall apart in her skull."

"You guys didn't find a weapon anywhere? Out back? Other part of the house?" she asks. "It's a big place."

"We've been through it as best as we can on plain sight. There are a few locked cabinets and drawers we're going to have to break open once we get a judge to sign off," he tells her, "but I suspect our perp came here with a gun and left with a gun."

Roni Gates nods and, again, smiles. In that moment, as Mills hovers over the body of Viveca Canning, with her exquisite coif of silver hair, her bluish face, and a bullet nesting in her brain, Mills can honestly say, as long as Roni is smiling, the world still bends toward the light.

2

The priest's words fall absently. They don't resonate with him at all. Gus is not a churchgoer. To many at the church service, Gus is the antichurch. The anti-Christ to some, of course, what with their hostility toward him, their ignorance about his gift. This is what he contends with in Seattle: the curious stares, the outright scorn, the indignation that he'd have the gall to return even now. They don't care that he's burying his father. He's a heathen! A fortuneteller! A soothsayer! Mrs. McConnell over there has a UTI; it's just a sudden vibe he gets. His vibes always got him in trouble as a child. That's why his parents banished his blasphemous soul from Seattle. Together his parents, Meg and Warren Parker, equaled one Piper Laurie.

He rides to the cemetery with his sister, Nicole, and her lawyer-turned-preacher husband, an irritable man named Mack (short for Mackleroy).

"See, church isn't so bad," Nicole says, a placid smile resting on her pale white face. She could be Amish, but she's not. A sister wife, but she doesn't share. A cover model for *Preacher's Wife Monthly*, but she has a lazy eye.

"But it's not so good either," Gus tells her.

Mackelroy clears his throat.

"I'm sorry, Mack. Didn't mean to offend. But I have a problem with a family using religion to disown a child."

"You weren't exactly disowned," Nicole scoffs.

"Mom and Dad threw me out of the house because they thought my visions were the work of the devil. What would you call it?"

"They loved the sinner, hated the sin," Mack says.

"Oh please. Who's to say that a little psychic hobby is a sin?"

"Hobby!" Mack says with a snort. "You make it sound so innocent."

"It is. And it wasn't a choice. You don't choose to be psychic. In fact, I never refer to myself as psychic. You know that, Nicole. I'm too neurotic to trust most of my visions. The ones that come true always rattle me."

"Whatever," his sister says.

"You don't seem too sad that Dad is gone."

She turns to him. "Of course I am."

"You've been smiling all morning."

"It's my faith," she says. Her preacher husband puts his arm around her. "You're the one who doesn't seem so sad."

"I'm not happy. But for the past twenty-five years or so, he's been mostly a stranger to me. So I don't really feel much at all."

"You're so cold," she tells him. Then the limo driver swings open her door and guides her out.

As they walk toward the gravesite, Mrs. McConnell approaches and tugs at Gus's arm. "Gus? A word?" She has a throaty, growling voice, the kind that crawls out of a pack of cigarettes. "You mind?"

"Uh, no. I guess. Don't want to hold up the service, but okay . . ."

They step aside, stopping by the grave of Lillian Hemingway (1921–1998, Beloved Wife and Mother). "I can't say I'm speaking for all of your parents' friends, Gus, but I suspect I am when I say it's shocking to see you here."

"Shocking?"

"You know how protective your parents were of the church."

"Yes. Something like that."

"And yet here you are defiling it again in your father's name."

He looks at her vacantly. He guesses she's in her early seventies, the same generation as his parents. She has a scrimshaw of smokers' wrinkles around her mouth but nowhere else. For a woman of her age, she has remarkable posture. There she is standing tall and indignant in her black pillbox hat and veil.

"I'm here out of respect for my father," he tells her. "What happened between him and me is a private matter."

First she rolls her head to register her outrage. Then she says, "Are you telling me to mind my own business?"

He nods. "Pretty much. And I mean no offense."

"Your being here is an offense, Gus Parker."

He locks eyes on hers. He bores into her. "If you're so concerned about defiling the church, Mrs. McConnell, perhaps you should reconsider being here yourself."

"How dare you?"

He speaks slowly, quietly. "Does Mr. McConnell know that you have been engaging alternately in vaginal and anal intercourse with the retired professor who lives at the end of your cul de sac?"

"What?" she shrieks.

"Your UTI, Mrs. McConnell. It's speaking to me."

She nearly trips as she turns on her heels and makes a mad dash. Gus can hear her screaming, "Heathen, Soothsayer, Fortuneteller, Anti-Christ," her hands wringing the air, all the way to Warren Parker's gravesite.

That's pretty much how the funeral went. He had no reason to stay in Seattle afterward, not even to visit Georgetown or the International District, the only neighborhoods where he fits in, so he's off to SEATAC for his flight to Los Angeles. He won't stay long; it's just a drop-in on his crazy relationship with Billie Welch (knowing the ugliness he'd be greeted with in Seattle, he begged her not to come to the funeral). His rock 'n' roll girlfriend finished touring after almost a year (they rendezvoused in Miami, Cleveland, New Orleans, London, and Paris, and took a few weeks last summer to vacation in Italy), and now they're returning to their completely abnormal normal life. He lives in Phoenix. She lives in LA. They commute back and forth. Her music is waiting for her in California. His clients are waiting for him in Arizona. And his job. He still works as a tech at Valley Imaging. Whether with a client for a psychic consultation or with a patient for an MRI, he really does like seeing stuff no one else sees. Unless the images disturb him. Which they often do these days.

He and Billie walk along the beach. They go to a party. They sit on the deck watching the sea. And they make love in her third-floor bedroom overlooking the endless ocean. They are all over each other like twenty-year-olds, though Gus, admittedly, could be a bit harder, but he's hard enough; it seems to take him longer to get there, and for her too, but it still works for them, he at forty-seven, she at fifty-seven. She still bites at his neck, his little vampire woman. She still scratches his back with her fierce nails, her guitar-strumming nails, and she still grabs at his ass just the way he likes it. Sometimes when he's with Billie he thinks she is simply a manifestation of one of his visions. As if he has dreamed her up too. As if she's not really real. And sometimes he thinks they dwell inside this vision and that his late uncle Ivan, who bestowed upon him his otherworldly gifts, is smiling down on them from heaven.

He has a plane to catch.

"This visit was too quick, Gus," Billie says, as they wrap up breakfast on the deck, the ocean roaring in front of them.

"It just seemed that way."

"No. It was too quick. Come back next weekend."

"I'll see."

As she clears the table, she stops behind Gus, wraps her arms around his neck, holds him close and says, "I love you, you know."

He knows. "I love you." Then he looks out to admire the waves but, as he squints against the sun, he sees an apparition of many faces rising from the water. Out there, beyond the waves, a small population is surfacing. He blinks and they're gone.

CalAir Flight 1212 departs Burbank at 3:59 p.m. He's among the first to board because he flies the route so frequently he's earned some kind of Diamond Status privilege pomposity. It's a single aisle aircraft, three-and-three, the typical sardine can of flying these days. No matter the Diamond Status privilege, his knees will be in his throat and his elbows will press on his kidneys (or the kidneys of his seatmate) all the way to Phoenix. Thankfully it's not a long flight. He's in a window seat. The takeoff is uneventful, though the path out of the Burbank airport always looks a bit challenging, surrounded as it is by mountains. He's never quite sure the planes will clear the peaks. The light turbulence lulls him into a cushiony nap. For about five minutes. Then the cabin crew zips through with a beverage service and a special brand of impatience. "Flight time is only forty-seven minutes," a flight attendant reminds the person in 7C who, apparently, can't decide what he wants to drink.

"This is an express service!" another attendant scolds.

Billie once told him to drink eight ounces of water for every hour of flight (she insisted on thirteen servings of H2O when they flew home from Rome). So he orders water to stay hydrated and compliant. In between sips he rests his head and turns to the window. Out there, the sky's aglow. A perfect stripe of orange and a perfect stripe of blue rest atop a wedding dress of clouds. The shadow of another plane glides across the layers of fabric, the shadow first, then the aircraft, itself, swooping into view. Had it bisected his flight's path? Had it come from overhead? Was it too close? It's a big plane, a bulbous jumbo jet, in rich, colorful livery. TRANSCONTINENTAL AIRLINES A380. The graceful ship banks a sharp left, like a salute to its smaller cousin, Gus's plane, but nobody except Gus seems to notice the huge interloper out the window. He says, "Look at that," to the person sitting beside him, and she says, "Beautiful sky," but nothing more. Perplexed, Gus presses his face against the window, really screws his nose into the plastic so he can watch Transcontinental and assess its intentions. This must be too close. He can see the pilots waving from the cockpit window. The pilots bring the nose up, then down, then up again, like a dolphin saying hello. He can see the passengers now. The passengers! His oval window becomes a portal to the other plane and his face dissolves right through. He's aboard now. The aircraft is brand-new. Polished. Fragrant. Crisp. He's sitting on the upper deck in a window seat. He tries but he can't see the CalAir flight anywhere. He sees the ocean, which means he's no longer headed for Phoenix. This worries him but someone hands him a hot towel and a pair of slippers. "Your seat fully reclines to a flat bed," she tells him. "When you're sleeping we won't disturb you." She's dark and lovely, a princess, a goddess, Polynesian, he suspects. As she wanders off, the plane does a slight shimmy and wobble, and then the huge beast lets out a howl, a scream, and Gus sits up straight and grips both sides of his seat. Everything goes quiet for a moment, a palpable absence of sound, and it is here, in the silence, that Gus knows he's headed for disaster. The plane screeches again, a grinding noise, a deafening grinding noise, and it banks so sharply the angle defies logic. At its breaking point, it stalls, then dives toward the sea.

Gus watches from the window, and watches from the window, and watches from the window, as people around him cry and holler, wail and screech, and the cabin becomes a pinball machine of flying objects. He watches from the window.

His face against the fuselage.

His nose screwed to the plastic.

The oval a portal.

CalAir Flight 1212. A single aisle, three-and-three, mundane and crowded jet. He's back on the flight bound for Phoenix. And yet Transcontinental is still out there diving, at first hesitant, then fully committed, nose down, spiraling at cataclysmic speed, through layers upon layers of the wedding dress. The contrails of the A380, so beautiful out there, so perfect and white, rise from the impending doom like pillars to heaven. Gus watches, shaking his head, willing the other plane to steady, but it doesn't recover from its tailspin. The jumbo jet plunges through a final layer of cloud, presumably to the enormous ocean waiting below. But Gus can't see. TRANSCONTINENTAL AIRLINES simply disappears.

"Ladies and Gentlemen, we are on final approach to Sky Harbor International Airport. Please be sure your seat backs and tray tables are in their upright and locked positions, and that all carry-on items are safely stowed at this time. We will be landing momentarily."

Gus comes to. He's sweating all over. He's lightheaded and can't catch his breath.

3

At this point in Detective Ken Preston's career, he's a fixture. At sixty-six years old, he's been on the force for almost as long as Alex Mills has been alive. As far as Mills knows, the older colleague never put in for a promotion, never got a promotion. He's just happy to do what he does. And he does it well. The guy's a fucking reference book for crime. More than forty years of busting lowlifes will do that. With no mandatory retirement age, Preston will probably work until he croaks. And he'll probably croak while reading Miranda to some toothless methhead who just sliced off a neighbor's head in the west valley. Here, in Viveca Canning's enclave of privilege, however, there are no headless neighbors, and Preston has availed himself of that advantage by wandering the community and coaxing information from people behind closed doors. He's great at this. He knows how to handle people and get them to talk. He knows how to open doors. Mills is not surprised that Preston comes back with a wealth (ahem) of knowledge.

"Looks like our victim lived in this house for about fifteen years," Preston reports. "Her husband died five years ago. It was a tragedy but Viveca Canning was left with a handsome inheritance."

"Stop right there," Mills tells him. "What kind of tragedy? How did her husband die?"

They're standing in the victim's driveway, under the porte cochere to stay out of the sun.

"Not sure. Most neighbors speculated it was a heart attack. Nothing newsworthy, if that's what you're asking."

"Of course that's what I'm asking," Mills says as he turns to Myers.

"Make a note of that anyway, Morty. We need to check into her husband's death."

"The neighbors say she was a socialite," Preston continues. "The kind who chaired charity balls and galas. You know the type: gowns, hair, shoes, the see-and-be-seen crowd. According to neighbors, if you open any Phoenix magazine you're going to find her pictures splashed across the pages. Apparently, there's not a month that goes by when she's not holding a fundraiser for the arts, or spina bifida, or whatever, at the Phoenician or the Sanctuary. Like I said, you know the type."

"Children?" Mills asks.

"As far as I can tell, two. Both probably in their mid-to-late twenties."

"We have to find the kids," Mills says.

"They stand to inherit a fortune now that Mom is out of the way," Preston says. "If you know what I mean."

Mills knows what he means and signals so with a jaded scoff. "Yeah, so let's find them. If for no other reason than to notify them. 'Cause I'm going to want to release her name as soon as possible, hoping it might generate some leads."

Preston rubs his chin. "The neighbors say they don't know the kids personally, so they can't help there."

"Names?" Myers asks.

"Nope," Preston replies.

Mills gives them a nod and says he'll be back. He drifts out to the street and around the bend. In the distance he can see the media parked outside the gates of the community. Sergeant Jake Woods and the department's public information officer, Josh Grady, will handle the reporters once they get the latest from Mills, even if the latest is thin on detail. He studies the gates separating him from them. The subdivision is called Copper Palace Estates, whatever the hell that means—this kind of wealth is the type of wealth that flaunts.

To enter Copper Palace, the perp would have had to be cleared by someone in the guardhouse. There would be a log, a name (perhaps falsified), probably a license plate. Unless Viveca Canning brought someone home with her last night and the two of them drove in through the residents' lane. But, if that were true, how did the perp leave the scene? In whose car? Was there a car missing from the garage? Was the killer driving off with a large painting? Mills shakes his head as he visualizes the list of unanswered questions, a kind of receipt of items he doesn't recognize he bought. But he owns the whole thing now. Yeah. This again. It's like the beginning of any case when he realizes a case is a case and there's no turning back. Often the realization is met with the mental equivalent of fanfare, a charge of adrenalin; other times, it's met with the heavy thud of dread, a lead fist to his stomach. But something propels him forward. It must be the adrenalin. He's making a sudden beeline for the guardhouse, his instincts, alone, paving the way. The media sees him coming. The reporters think he's coming for them. The crowd excites. It throbs to life. The amoebae move in pantsuits and khakis, hairdos and microphones, closer to the gate. The reporters shout questions. He only hears their noise, the collective voice of the amoebae, but he can't hear what they're asking and that's fine with him, just a mechanism at work. Mills reaches the guardhouse, speaks to a uniformed woman named Florence who lets him see the log from last night. She has a tiny old mouth, but as big of a smile as the mouth can muster. She looks at him like a mother looks at a son, or like a cougar looks at her prey. He can't be sure. His eyes run up and down the columns of the log: VISITOR; VISITING. No one for Viveca Canning.

"It doesn't look like she had company last night," Florence says. "At least not through the visitor lane."

"Do the guards here keep an eye on the residents' lane?"

Again, the smile. "That depends, Detective. If the visitors' lane is slow, then sure, we'll be watching for residents. We like to wave, you know."

"So it's possible someone saw Ms. Canning come home last night?"

"Oh sure," she says. "But it's harder to see at night. So sometimes we just wave at a dark window. But our company knows who comes and goes just by the signal from the residents' remotes. Plus we have cameras."

"I'll need the contact information for your management, ma'am."

"No problem."

She retreats into the booth and returns moments later with a sticky note. "Here. If you need anything else, you just let me know, Detective."

"And if those reporters start bothering you, you let me know."

"Okey dokey," she says with a wink he can't infer. The silver-haired woman either wants to feed him or fuck him.

Mills reconvenes with his colleagues in the leathery and gilded library of Viveca Canning's home. "No one signed in as a guest in the past twenty-four hours," he tells them. "Has anyone recovered a cell phone?"

"Yep," Powell tells him. "It's bagged."

"Anything else in plain sight?" he asks.

"Just all the jewels that snuck out of their boxes last night to have a party," she says.

"We need to check her social accounts," Preston says. "If she's a socialite, she's gotta be on social media."

"At her age?" Mills asks.

"Yes," Preston replies. "These dames love the attention of being socialites. Give 'em a new platform, and they're on it."

"Did you just say 'dames'?" Mills asks.

"I did. I'm an old man. What do you want?"

Mills laughs and grabs the guy by the shoulder. "I want you and Myers to work on a warrant for her computer, laptop, iPad, whatever."

"Yes, sir."

The doorbell rings. "Was anyone expecting a pizza?" Mills asks his squad.

They all laugh, except Myers who says, "Pizza? What kind?"

Mills, followed by Preston, heads to the front door. There they find a gum-chewing patrol officer snapping and popping away. He looks stunned when caught in midbubble. "Yes?" Mills asks him.

"Got a visitor."

"Oh?"

"Says he needs to get in the house, and wants to know why all the cop cars are here."

"Does he have a name?" Preston asks the officer.

"Bennett Canning."

Mills looks to the street and sees a gleaming Mercedes. Out of the car steps a man behind a pair of mirrored sunglasses. Bennett Canning, for all the mystery behind the lenses, has the posture of an impatient, inconvenienced child. Mills says, "Let's go" to Preston, and they move down the lawn. Seeing them approach, the man meets them at the curb.

"Can someone please tell me why I can't get into my own house?" He's tanned and athletic-looking, his hair purposely tousled, as if he swung by the hair salon on his way to Copper Palace. "What's happening here? What's with all the cops?"

"Who are you?" Mills asks.

"Bennett Canning. You can call me Ben."

"Ben, I'm Alex Mills, homicide detective with the Phoenix PD. This is my partner Ken Preston."

The man almost loses his footing. "Homicide?"

Mills explains.

Bennett Canning puts his head in his hands. He turns away and utters a strangled scream, like he can't breathe. Neighbors turn to look. All eyes are on the man in the linen blazer and deck shoes as he gasps for air. "He's hyperventilating," Preston shouts to the ogling crowd. "Someone get me a paper bag!"

Preston lightly takes the young man's arm, but Ben Canning stumbles backward. Mills steadies him.

"I want to see her," Ben says. "Take me to see her."

"We can't do that quite yet," Mills tells him. "The scene needs to be completely processed."

A neighbor rushes forward with a brown lunch bag. Preston puts it over Ben's mouth and says, "Come on, now, just breathe normally. Just breathe."

It takes a few breaths for the gasps to subside.

"Do you live here?" Mills asks him.

"No."

"But you referred to the house as your own," Preston reminds him.

"Form of speech," he says. "I mean, you don't have to be a Princeton grad like me to understand that."

"What is your relationship to Viveca Canning?" Mills asks.

"Jesus, did you guys even get your GEDs? She's my mother. Isn't it fucking obvious?"

Mills would like to punch this brat in the face. Instead he says, "It isn't until you tell us. We deal in facts and facts only, Ben. What may appear obvious to others, doesn't necessarily mean shit to us."

Preston nudges him.

"I need to see her," Bennett Canning pleads.

"I know you do," Mills concedes, "but we can't have you contaminating the scene. That might compromise our investigation, and we're sure you want us to find the person who killed your mother sooner than later."

"Killed?"

Mills squints at the man behind the shades. "Yeah. I told you what happened here."

"I know you did. But you can't possibly be right about that. No one would do that to my mother."

"Precisely our first question for you," Mills says. "Are you aware of anybody who'd want to harm your mother?"

Tears fall symmetrically to the corners of his mouth. He wipes them away and says, "No. Quite the opposite."

"The opposite?" Preston asks.

"Yeah. She was loved by everyone, even by people she never met. She did more for the valley than all the organizations combined. I mean, come on, I'm sure you've heard of her, of our family. We're huge in philanthropy."

Having to say you're huge in philanthropy, Mills suspects, suggests the philanthropy is not completely about the philanthropy. He keeps that assessment to himself. But if there is such a thing as nouveau riche philanthropy (giving simply to show how much cash you have to give), this must be it. "So she had no enemies, no rivals, nobody who had ill will toward her?"

"Of course not," Bennett says with a spit. "She's practically a saint."

"Practically a saint," Preston repeats. "But even saints have enemies."

Again, a wrenching wail from the kid. Then, "Obviously it was a break-in or a robbery, or something. I mean, if you're looking for a motive, someone probably thought they could break in here, steal a fortune, and get away."

Mills nods. "Of course we're considering that." Now he folds his arms across his chest. "But I'm not sure how somebody would get past the guardhouse."

"Good point," Bennett says. "Unless it was an inside job."

"A neighbor?" Preston asks.

"Worth considering."

"For sure," Mills says. "Everyone's a suspect." He hands Bennett Canning his card, but asks the guy to stick around. "We'll have more questions for you."

The kid nods, then lowers his head as he drifts toward his automobile and slips into the lap of Mercedes luxury. Mills tells the gum-chewing officer to keep an eye on the dead woman's son, to not let him leave.

4

CalAir Flight 1212 dips into Sky Harbor and chews up the waiting runway as the plane grinds to a stop. All of a sudden, inertia. Earth, not sea. Air, not water. Alive, not entombed at the bottom of the ocean. Still, his stomach is in knots. The vision of Transcontinental Airlines going down was one of the most vivid in recent memory. One of the most disturbing. The first vision ever that foresaw massive death. He'll need to talk to Beatrice about this. The vision is too big for one psychic.

"Hope you had a nice flight," the attendant says as Gus files toward the exit. "Buh-bye now."

They still say "Buh-bye."

Later, at home, Gus drops his luggage in the front hall and makes a mad dash for his office, where he powers up his computer and tries to recall every single detail of that doomed flight. He creates a file called "Transcontinental" and it looks something like this:

TRANSCONTINENTAL
(unknown flight number)
Possible departure point: LAX
Possible destination: Australia, New Zealand, Fiji

Wide body. Twin aisle. Upstairs 2x2x2. Downstairs 3x4x3. 450 passengers. New plane. Fresh scent. Chemicals. Floral. Sweet. Blue sky. A white mattress of clouds. A mostly white interior. Nose up. Soaring. Seats of sky blue fabric, abstract lime green stitching. TRANSCONTINENTAL. Bright. Promising. Smiling cabin attendants, accents from somewhere in

Oceania. Adventure, luxury, the beauty, the beauty, the beauty, all of it palpable. Dinner simmers in a nearby galley. Carts jostling, rolling, braking. White gloves, linen cloths. More smiles. A flutter of turbulence. A rolling tremor. A tug-of-war from wing to wing. The plane, with a burst, escapes the bad air and steadies at a higher altitude. The relief is short-lasting. The turbulence has followed, stalking TRANSCONTI-NENTAL and tugging it by the tail. People gripping the armrests. The bounce of heads. The turning of faces. Alarmed. Then everything pushes forward, like a rear collision, like a tremendous weight and people scream. Attendants tumble in the aisles. Overhead bins burst open. Oxygen masks drop. Dangling masks. A constant scream, a constant wailing. Attendants cry, "Brace, Brace, Brace." Nose down. Nose down and spinning. A spiral of seats and heads and meticulously arranged oval windows. There are no shades, just wide-eyed witnesses and imminent death.

"What the fuck? If I do say so myself," says Beatrice Vossenheimer after lunch, reclining on her brocade fainting couch in the living room of her Paradise Valley home, she and Gus in a cube of glass that takes in a view of Camelback Mountain and the spread of the valley beyond it. She's been dog sitting for Ivy, Gus's devoted golden retriever.

"I know! Crazy. I have no clue," Gus confesses. He's lying on the floor with Ivy on top of him, all sixty pounds of her.

"We can work on this," Beatrice assures him. "Don't worry."

He shakes his head. "Yeah, but this isn't going to resolve overnight no matter how much work we do. My gut says this will be difficult to completely unfold. I see it as a long, protracted test. I don't feel up to a test."

Beatrice purrs for a moment and then says, "I'm with you, hon. We'll figure it out."

"And in the meantime, a plane goes down."

"No," she says with a resolve that pitches Gus forward. "No. My vibes tell me this incident is not imminent. It feels months away, Gus. Distant. Out there on the horizon."

He sits up, nudges Ivy aside. "I don't know. My vibes tell me to warn someone."

"Who?"

"The FAA? The TSA? The NTSB? The FBI?"

"Let me know when you get off the acronym train," she says with a laugh. "And I'll tell you to do none of the above."

"L-O-L."

"Not really an acronym, darling. And besides we are not LOLers. We're not those people. And we're not people foolish enough to go the government with this kind of warning. Next thing we'd know, we'd be on the No-Fly List."

"What's that?"

"Are you kidding me? Have you been living under a rock?"

"Mostly."

"It's a list of potentially dangerous passengers forbidden to fly."

"Well, you would know. You're in the air more than you're on the ground for this book tour of yours," he says. Then, "Oh, God . . ."

"What?"

"What if it's *your* plane going down? Jesus . . ."

"Oh, please," she scoffs. "You're not seeing my plane going down because I'm not seeing my plane going down, and I'm not headed across the Pacific any time soon. But I have to tell you something."

"Okay . . ."

She leans forward. "Would you like some more wine?"

"No. I'm good." Still on the floor, he scoots to the side of the couch and rests his arm there, facing her.

"I just want to say you walked in my house tonight a lonely man."

"Lonely?"

"Yes. What do you think that's about?"

"It's my disposition," he says.

She tsks. "No, it's not, Gus. Don't be silly. I can always tell the single people from the partnered ones. People with love in their life have an energy beside them at all times. I can see it, sense it, feel it. It's a light, a bubble of light, with a kind of prism inside. You have the bubble. No prism."

"Suddenly?"

"I've been doubting your prism for a long time."

"So, what are you saying?"

She drifts off, her face toward the mountain outside, toward the great beast whose only movement in centuries can be measured in tectonic inches. She scans the blurry horizon and nods. He waits and watches. She tents her hands in front of her face as if she's a doctor about to prognosticate. "Ask Billie where she sees this going . . ."

"Where she sees this going? What do you mean?"

"I mean the future, for the two of you."

"We've been together for over two years. Where do you think it's going?"

"You don't know. Do you? It's a mystery to you. Are you content to live in that mystery?"

He smiles. "You mean, am I content not to label our relationship? Yeah, I am."

"Neither of you wants to commit. She thinks love is too fragile. And you think she's too strong to let you get any closer."

"Are you getting this from her music?"

She gives him a light kick. "Did you forget I'm psychic? I see you lonely and so I wonder if you could be seeking more commitment from her."

"Here's what I'm seeing about what you're seeing, psychic to psychic: She's older than me by ten years. She may go before I go. And then I'll be lonely for her. Then her energy might be missing from my side."

Beatrice doesn't say anything for a moment. He listens to her hum softly. She has a violin hum. "When she goes, her energy will never be missing from your side. Love doesn't die like that. I tell this to everyone.

But yes, I might be seeing you in those later years without her. And still I sense that a little clarification now goes a long way."

"Duly noted."

"Have you lost your keys?"

He feels for his pockets. "Uh, no," he says. "My mind, maybe, not my keys."

"Oh, never mind. I just had a weird vibe about your keys. Or my keys, maybe. Or somebody's keys."

"Maybe you're telling me to go home."

She laughs. "You can stay as long as you'd like, but I'm ready for a siesta. The wine, you know. Hang around if you'd like."

But he doesn't. As Beatrice drifts off into the dainty snoring phase of her nap, Gus and Ivy slip out of the house and into the car.

5

Well, if it isn't the ultracool Calvin Cloke. Cloke is Mills's favorite medical examiner in Maricopa County. Most of the doctors assigned to the OME don't turn up at the crime scenes. They send the examiners, the civilians. But Dr. Cloke is all in. He loves this shit. A one-armed Gulf War vet with awful skin but an overcompensating smile, Cloke always gives prompt, precise, and cheerful service to the PD. Mills has never seen the guy have a bad day despite the consequences of battle. Cloke is not bitter about the war. In fact he remembers it fondly as the time he, personally, put Saddam Hussein on notice. If his arm were collateral damage, he'd tell people, it was a price he was willing to pay. And yet, he's not a crazy war hawk looking to shoot down every news chopper he sees, which puts him on opposite sides of that argument with Mills.

"Dude!" Cloke shouts.

"Dude!"

"Don't they kick people like you out of places like this?"

"Yeah," Mills says. "But now that you're here, finally, I can blend in with your elegance."

"Finally?"

"Well . . ."

"Come on, man, I was right in the middle of a shrimp quesadilla when I got the call."

Mills explains the demise of Viveca Canning. "I'm confident you'll find at least one bullet in her brain."

"First place I'll look," the ME tells him.

"If only the brain could reveal those last few minutes of life," Mills says. "If only you could download the memory. You know?"

"Sounds like a job for your psychic."

"He's not *my* psychic," Mills says.

"So he's everyone's psychic. Thanks for sharing."

"Powell's in the house. She's scene investigator. Have fun."

As Cloke's hulking frame passes through the front door, Mills reaches for his phone and dials Gus Parker.

"Hi, this is Gus Parker. Don't bother leaving your name or number," the recording says. "I know who you are and how to reach you. Just kidding. I'm not as psychic as you think I am."

Mills shakes his head. "Your new message is supremely douchey," he says after the beep. "Call me."

Then he heads back to the street to deal with the son of Viveca Canning. He does another quick study of the man's face, looking for a nuance, any nuance, which might suggest a lingering emotion. Gus Parker has told him to look beyond the obvious emotion, to see little flickers of truth that would otherwise be hiding beneath the surface. Watch the last syllable of a smile for a wince, Gus says. Watch for wickedness running through the shadows of grief. The corner of the mouth. The glint in the eye. Gus tells him the lingering emotion is the first step to intuit the rest, and Mills can't argue because it's really part of his repertoire anyway; their work is not so different in this regard. In every other regard, Gus is in another world.

The chiseled Bennett Canning, still leaning against his precious automobile, his arms folded across his chest, yields very little beyond the cocksure posture and the Hollywood hair. Mills knows his searching gaze is making the guy uncomfortable, but he doesn't care. He lets it hang there until the slightest tremble crosses Canning's bottom lip. Mills offers a thoughtful nod as if to encourage more divulgence. The slick scion could be playing him, however. He could be onto Mills. The tremble of the kid's lip, even in its microscopic brevity, could be a ruse. Then Canning exhales a deep sigh and rolls his shoulders. "You okay?" Mills asks him.

"I don't know," Canning replies. "You tell me."

"What would you like me to tell you?"

"I'd like you tell me who killed my mother."

"I'm afraid it's too soon to know that."

"Right, of course."

"If you'd be more comfortable, we can continue our conversation back at headquarters," Mills suggests. The suggestion is not a threat of any kind. It's a genuine offer.

The kid shakes his head. "No. I'm fine here," he says. "I'm staying here as long as my mother's here."

And that's fine. Restrained by the yellow tape, the gawkers can't hear what they're saying. There's a fair degree of privacy out here in the open.

"How well do you know the neighbors?" Mills asks him.

"Like I told you, I don't live here. Never have. My parents bought the house after I went to Andover."

"Andover?"

"Prep school in Massachusetts. You never heard of it?" Canning asks, his inflection preppy and presumptuous.

"No."

"Well, that's where I lived for high school, except summers, and then I went to tennis camp. And then I went off to college. You know how it goes."

"How it goes . . . of course."

Canning removes his sunglasses, bats his eyes against the glare, and says, "Are you sure it's her?"

"She matches the faces in the photos throughout the house," Mills says. "You can confirm it's her if you want to. But we're not quite done yet."

"Yes. I want to see her."

Mills takes one step closer. "You have a sister? The neighbors tell us you have a sister."

"I do. A younger sister. I just called her with the news."

"Name, age, place of residence?"

"Her name is Jillian. She's twenty-seven, lives in San Francisco. Well, Berkeley, actually."

"What does she do there?"

"She's a lesbian."

Mills shakes his head. "Okay, but that's not what she's doing, Ben. I'm asking what she does for work."

"Oh." His shifts his eyes back and forth, up and down. "Something with film. I think she's a film editor."

"You're not close?"

"We both have busy lives."

"What's your line of work?" Mills asks him.

"I'm between jobs."

"Doing?"

The cocksure posture returns, the arms across his chest. "Are you interrogating me?"

"Of course not," Mills lies. "It's just really important for us to know as much as we can about the people surrounding the victim. Let's say you angered someone in your line of work. Maybe this is revenge." *Or maybe you're in between jobs and need a shortcut to your inheritance, Bennett Canning.*

"I don't think so. I don't anger people in my line of work. I'm a tennis pro."

Of course you are. "Where?"

"Most recently The Cliffs Resort and Spa."

"And why aren't you there anymore?"

"That's really none of your business."

"That's okay. We can find out."

"I assure you my mother's murder had nothing to do with The Cliffs."

Mills smiles mischievously. "Unless a jealous husband caught you doing more than training his wife on the court."

Canning groans. "Oh, come on, Detective, you've been watching too many Lifetime movies."

"Never," Mills says. "Follow me."

Just inside the foyer Mills grabs a pair of booties and instructs the son of Viveca Canning to slip them on. The man's eyes widen, fear and doubt lodged there now, as he takes in a foreign scene before him in an otherwise familiar place. The cops, the techs, the people are crawling everywhere. There are specimen kits. There are gloved hands all over the family's treasures. There are voices uttering a language he can't possibly understand. And then he gasps, almost stumbles backward. His mother's body on the floor. Dead.

Mills watches the whole thing unfold across Bennett's face.

The kid covers his mouth, utters, "Oh God."

Mills says, "You okay?"

"Oh my God," Bennett chants, without acknowledging the question. "Oh my God."

Mills gently tugs at the guy's shoulder. "You can't get any closer. I'm sorry, but we have to stay back."

The dead woman's son nods slowly. He seems unable to blink. Mills recognizes shock setting in, so he guides the man away from the body.

"Tell me, Ben, how old is your mom?"

"Sixty-four."

"Looks like she was an art lover," Mills says, gesturing to the walls.

"A collector, yes."

Then Mills points to the obvious empty space between paintings. "You know what hung there?"

"I'm pretty sure it was a Dali. An original," Canning replies. "Where is it?"

"That's what we'd like to know," Mills tells him.

"It was the most valuable one she'd display."

"Do you know how valuable?"

"Not really. But probably a million or more," Canning replies. "She'd rotate it, all of them, actually, in and out of the vault."

"What vault?"

"She has a collector's vault in one of the galleries in Scottsdale," he replies. Then after a moment of consideration, he says, "You think it was stolen? You think maybe she interrupted a burglary?"

"You're ahead of us, I'm afraid."

"But it's possible, no?"

"Of course," Mills says.

"Someone came looking for that painting specifically." It's not a question.

"That's a reasonable theory, assuming it was stolen. We don't know that. Your mother could have been in the process of rotating it out, as you say."

The guy glares at the wall, shakes his head. "I know who you should talk to," he says bitterly. "My aunt Phoebe. Phoebe Canning Bickford. She fought like hell for that painting."

Finally, the first glimmer of a lead. "I'd sure like to know why and with whom," Mills says.

"With my mother, of course. Phoebe is my dad's older sister. She gave the Dali to him for his sixtieth birthday," Canning explains. "It came from her collection so she figured it was hers, not my mom's, after my dad died. They've been feuding about it ever since, like five years."

"Technically I think the law would grant it to your mother," Mills tells him, "but that's a moot point now. Does the painting have a name?"

"I don't remember," Canning replies. "It might be an untitled work. You can ask my aunt."

"And where can we find," Mills says, looking down at his notes, "Phoebe Canning Bickford these days?"

"Here. In Phoenix. She lives up on Camelback. If you give me your number, I'll text you the address. It's up on Hawkeye Ridge. I just don't know the street number off hand."

Mills tells him not to worry about the address, that someone back at the PD will nail it down. "But what about close friends?" he asks. "To whom would your mother have confided if she was scared, worried, or threatened?"

Canning stands there and mulls for a moment, his eyes shifting to the right, then the left. "I guess any of the ladies in her social circle, her gala crowd. But probably the church."

"Your mother was a religious woman?"

The guy laughs. "Very," he says. "She and my dad supported the church. They practically built it."

"Which church?"

"Angels Rising."

"Where?"

"Here in Phoenix."

Mills scribbles a few notes, nods, and leads the man from the house. "I'll need your phone number . . ."

Canning recites the number.

"And your address . . ."

"Which one?" Canning asks.

"Which one?"

"Yeah. The house in Arcadia or the pied-à-terre?"

"The what?"

"I also have a condo near the Biltmore."

Mills doesn't hide the eye roll. "I'll need both."

Bennett Canning looks beyond Mills to his dead mother's house, as if he's staring at the incomprehensible, and absently lists his two addresses.

"Thanks, Bennett," Mills says. "Two things you should know. First, the house is off-limits until we release it to the family. It's still a crime scene. And, second, don't be surprised to hear from us again. We'll likely have more questions."

"That's fine," Canning says. "I have nothing to hide."

Of course he does, Mills knows. Everyone has something to hide. Everyone. Fact of life.

6

Later that afternoon Grady and Woods hold a press conference outside the gates to Viveca Canning's subdivision. They've conferred with Mills and are releasing only surface details for now.

"Not going to the media circus?" Powell asks him.

He shakes his head and feels a smile emerge. "No. I have a fear of clowns."

"One of these days you're going to find a reporter you actually like," she says.

"I like Sally Tobin from *The Republic*, but she's about to retire."

They've gathered again under the porte cochere where they're sheltered from the blistering sun. Lower in the driveway, Preston emerges from his car. He's carrying his tablet. He steps into the square of shade and says, "Just a simple Google search tells quite a story about Viveca Canning."

Mills looks over his shoulder as Preston reads from various headlines. Seems the Internet is gushing about her. Praise for her philanthropy, her kindness, her compassion. Last year she went with church leaders to Africa to pray for children suffering a famine. She's building a clinic in Bangladesh, another in Haiti. She's featured in magazine articles and TV stories. She has a Twitter and a Facebook account. Her Facebook feed is a Who's Who of gala life and gowns galore. Nothing about her family, Mills notices. Her tweets feature the See and Be Seen nonsense, as well, but ever since she created the Twitter account two years ago, she's also been tweeting regularly about her church along with photos of functions and outreach; there's a post about a church dinner at a homeless shelter; she sent a series of tweets from a literacy event where her church donated five thousand books. She tweeted a photo of her pastor shaking hands with one of the U.S. senators from Arizona.

> Thanks to @SenWayneGooding for helping @CAR with our #AbstinenceforTeens campaign. A #righteous effort. #Purity #Chastity #Elevate

"Okay . . ." Powell says. "Looks like we have a holy roller on our hands."

Mills just stares at the screen and says nothing for a moment. The holy roller thing is obvious, and while he doesn't want to overlook the obvious, he also doesn't want to neglect that which hides beneath. He remembers the days before social media when virtually everything hid beneath. There was no immediate window into anyone's life, no gaping wide window, no selfies. And yet, even in this era of oversharing, Mills is mindful that social media only shows what people want it to show; it's the Greatest Hits of someone's life, the Profile of a Winner, the Resume of a Star, the Happiest Family on Earth. And dogs. Dogs that are never quite as entertaining as their owners think. The only person in the world he knows without a Facebook or Twitter account is Gus Parker. But that doesn't surprise him. Mills, himself, is on social media. If you can call one post every two months a social media presence. And it's mostly dedicated to his son, Trevor, winning games at U of A. "If you notice," he tells the gang, "she stopped tweeting about church sometime in May. It's August now. Does church go on summer break?"

"No, but apparently she did," Preston says, scrolling down. "Looks like she was having a busy summer of travel. There are all kinds of photos here from Greece, the Canary Islands, Norway, Sweden, Switzerland . . ."

"Maybe she just got home," Powell says. "Which would explain why her shit's all over the place. Maybe this isn't about someone trying to make it look like a robbery. Maybe she just got home from summer vacation and dumped everything everywhere."

Mills shrugs, indicating he's not convinced one way or another. He asks Preston to go back to Google and search the son's name. He watches as the other detective types in V-i-v-e-c-a by mistake, and before Mills has a chance to stop him, Preston hits "search." A page of bright blue headlines appear. Bright blue and brand new.

VALLEY SOCIALITE FOUND DEAD IN HER PHOENIX HOME

"Wow, that was fucking fast," Powell says.

POLICE SAY SOCIALITE'S DEATH LIKELY HOMICIDE

The press conference hasn't even ended and reporters are already pumping out news copy.

WHO KILLED VIVECA CANNING? THE FAMOUS PHOENICIAN GUNNED DOWN

Three stories from an ongoing press conference and it won't stop there. Reporters are now primed to post from the scene, tweet from the yellow tape, and Instagram the instacrime. The competition is as hot as a fever. In the old days Alex Mills was not affected by the competition. But now his boss expects him to be faster than an iPhone because technology, after all, has reset the speed of society. Now, not later. This second, not this minute. Yesterday, what the hell is that? Yeah, he gets it. If the average person can find all the answers in less than .46 seconds on Google, surely we can solve cases faster. "At least that's the expectation," Sergeant Woods had warned him a few years ago. "People don't understand the concept of waiting anymore."

Yeah, he gets it. The case of dead valley darling Viveca Canning will spin exponentially into a shitstorm before he even leaves the scene.

His jaw aches from grinding his teeth.

7

Now that Beatrice's book, *Memoir of a Psychic: I Told You So*, has been sitting on the bestseller list for almost a year (in it she references Gus too many times for his liking, his modesty, and his privacy), her phone doesn't stop ringing. Everybody wants to meet Beatrice, know Beatrice, ask Beatrice, and tell Beatrice, and that doesn't even include the media. The media is relentless. Everybody wants a piece of her. She's doing a media tour but that's only resulted in more requests for consultations from prospective clients. Beatrice's assistant, Hannah, a sweet and misty-eyed lady of eighty-eight, can't keep up with all the requests. So, when people can't book with Beatrice they ask for Gus. Which would explain why his client list is growing rapidly and almost uncontrollably, and why his phone is ringing at 7:00 a.m. with a chirping Hannah who needs to refer a client.

"The woman sounded urgent, Gus. She says she needs to see someone soon. Like today!" Hannah gushes. "She actually requested you, said she read about you in the book and remembers your name from a case on the news."

Gus feels the first twist of a headache in his skull. He had begged Alex to keep his name out of the news, but more than once the detective had dropped Gus's name to give Gus credit he had not asked for and, no doubt, to give the chief and the sergeant the chagrin Alex had thought they deserved for being pricks. Mentioning the psychic always gave the brass the grief of dubious inquiries from a skeptical public.

"I don't go back to my real job until tomorrow," he tells Hannah. "So have her come by at 10:15."

She offers him a *mwah* and disconnects.

So he dashes into the shower and then into the kitchen, puts on the coffee and lets it brew while he takes Ivy for her morning walk. She's in good shape, this dog, still rushing and yelping at the birds, still inclined to leap at Gus just because she can't get enough of play. She's seven years old. The vet says she's one of the healthiest golden retrievers he's ever seen, and he says Gus gets all the credit. Again, the credit! Gus doesn't understand all the clamor about credit. Who really gives a shit? He remembers his old days on the beach, meeting a Buddhist surfer dude who told him the difference between the biggest wave and the best wave; the biggest wave was for the ego while the best wave was for the soul. The ego needs the credit for attempting the biggest wave, but ego surfers often miss waves of enlightenment that rise around them all day long. They were both a little stoned at the time, but Gus remembers the beauty of being in the moment with any wave he chose, closing his eyes as he rode the crest, being there, alone with the sun, being there, drowning in the golden light that seeped through his lids, being there, if only for a moment without a single thought, without a single word, without a memory or a plan. He sailed in transcendental bliss. He learned Surfing as Meditation from this Buddhist buddy who one day gave him a hug for no reason and a soaking wet slap on the back, and never returned to the beach. He simply vanished from Gus's life. Gus wonders if he ever truly existed, or whether he'd been a visitor from Gus's imagination, or a vision, or a bit of both. It was more than twenty years ago. He can't remember, through the haze of those days, the name of that Buddhist surfer.

Her name is Aaliyah. "Two 'A's at the beginning, one at the end," she tells him. She's punctual, arriving precisely at his door at 10:15. He's on his second cup of coffee. He offers to brew more for her but she declines. They sit in his office and Gus observes her impossible face. He knows nothing about makeup and can't infer anything about cosmetics but assumes the flawlessness of her skin is natural. Her brown eyes are lighter than Billie's; instead of dark moons, they're orange flames. Like a tiger. She smiles and Gus is in that light again, on that wave, drowning for a moment. Aaliyah Jones is a messenger. Gus can see it. He knows it. She is here for answers but she comes with answers. She crosses her legs, her long, thin legs. She's a foal. With turquoise-beaded anklets.

"Welcome," he says.

"Do you always do the once-over of your clients?" she asks.

"I'm sorry?"

"You undressed me with your eyes."

Gus feels the color drain in a whoosh from his face. "Oh no," he begs, "no, no, no. I promise I wasn't doing that. I'm sorry if that felt like undressing, but you're a new client."

"I don't understand."

"I was trying to read you. And I guess that feels like undressing. I apologize for making you uncomfortable."

She laughs, like the joke's on him. "Never mind. It takes a lot to make me uncomfortable."

Gus nods, allowing the blood to return. "I see," he mutters to buy another moment. "What brings you here this morning?"

"It's important," she says, sitting up, squaring her shoulders, ballet-like. "I might know something about a murder."

That lands like a big box of surprise. Gus swallows hard and looks at the box between them. It's wrapped and bowed. Like a gift, but not. *Unexpected gifts.*

"What are you looking at?" the woman asks.

"Nothing. Everything. I see things differently than you," he tells her. "That's why you're here. Tell me about the murder."

"It's been all over the news. The socialite who was shot in her home, did you see it?"

"I've been traveling for a couple of weeks. Just got home, so no . . ."

She leans forward, her athletic arms folding, elbows to her knees. "Oh. I'm a news reporter. On TV, Channel 4."

"Wow. You *are* a messenger," Gus chants.

She tilts her perfect face. "What is that supposed to mean? Have you never seen a black reporter before?"

Oh God. Gus puts his head in his hands and groans. "Of course

I have. I'm sorry you misunderstood. I just got a vibe about you when you first sat down. I sensed you were full of knowledge, or information, or something materially important. It would make sense that you're a journalist."

"Really?"

He looks up. "Yeah. Really. Maybe we should start over."

She laughs, again at his expense. "It's okay. I was half-kidding."

"Half?"

"There are more Circle Ks in the valley than black people," she says. "We do sometimes feel alien."

"Ah, I see. Of course."

"Just so you know, I didn't cover the murder. I was working on something else. But some of my colleagues did. All the stations and newspapers did. She was kind of well-known."

"And you think you know why she died?"

"I think I might know some background that others might not consider," she says. "I don't know what to do."

She's a tough one. Aaliyah Jones may be a messenger, all right, but her vibe is an otherwise complicated mix of danger and thrill he can't quite fathom. It's too soon. They've only just met.

"I'm not sure what you should do either," he concedes. "Do you want me to visualize what you should do? Or do you want to tell me what you know, and I can try to intuit whether it's really linked to the murder you're talking about?"

"The latter would be perfect, but I can't tell you what I know, at least not yet. I just can't," she tells him. "So, maybe the first thing. Maybe you should just visualize what it would look like for me to go to the cops."

He sits back. "Okay, but first I have some basic questions about you."

She sits back, as well, apparently sensing Gus's ease. "I'm ready."

He asks how many years she's been a reporter. Seven. Has she always worked in Phoenix? No. Where has she worked before? Jacksonville, Florida. Albany, New York. He asks if she's from Phoenix originally.

"No," she says. "I came here for the job three years ago. I was born and raised in Atlanta."

"And your family is still there . . ."

"Wow, you really are psychic."

"Uh, no. Just a good guess."

"I know," she says.

She knows. She's messing with him. Powerful woman. She's all electric around him, like a storm. She's thunder and lightning and a swirling sea.

He takes a deep breath, exhales, and says, "What's stopping you from going to the cops with your information?"

She narrows her eyes and says, "Journalistic ethics. I'm not against helping the police. Reporters will informally coordinate with cops from time to time. But I'm not sure if I can reveal what I know to them because it could reveal my sources, and these sources fear for their lives."

"Fear for their lives . . ." Gus nods as he tries to conjure up a vibe. He shakes his head. "I think you need to wait a few days before you do anything, because the law, the investigation, moves much more slowly than you see on *Law & Order*. And you need to see what information becomes public. What becomes public could relieve you of your need to come forward. Also, I fear for your sources," he tells her. "I'm getting a strong vibe about that."

Even as she goes, as she rises to her feet later and moves to the door, the ballet of her arms as wispy as reeds of Ocotillo in a crisp desert wind, even as she retreats down the driveway and slides into her car, even as she disappears around the corner, Gus is standing there, still standing there, sensing strong vibes about a dangerous wave that's coming for people who are nowhere near the sea.

8

To no avail, Mills has been trying to reach Viveca Canning's daughter all morning. Jillian is her name. Bennett had given Mills his sister's contact information, but Mills had sensed a certain estrangement, so for all he knows the info is outdated. And so he has sent Powell and Myers back to the scene while he and Preston pore through details about the victim's associates, mostly gained through social media, some from magazine and news stories. Viveca Canning has been profiled by the valley's big glossy magazines (particularly the ones that dwell on luxe life and privilege) a dozen times (no exaggeration), and with every article comes soaring praise from her friends/fellow socialites as well as the recipients of her charity. Mills and Preston are gathering names. Contacting most.

First they meet with Dina Hallandale, a Scottsdale woman who runs a dating service. "I'm in those fancy magazines too, I assure you. A lot, in fact. But I also have a business to run."

Mills just nods.

"I'm not one of those ladies who just sits around all day planning benefits," she continues. "That's not meant as a dig toward Viveca. She was lovely. Truly lovely."

"So you've said on Facebook and Twitter," Preston reminds her. "Were you close friends?"

"Oh no," she says without hesitation, almost swatting the question away as if it were a fly. "Our social circles overlapped. We might have worked on a few functions together, but most people of our echelon make a big deal about our endless cadre of friends, when really we have lots superficially, and only a few that are very close."

"Wow. That's some explanation," Mills tells her.

She smiles and bats her eyes. She's probably Viveca's age, maybe late fifties at the youngest. Her hair has that frosted kind of blondeness befitting her profession, and facial muscles that defy movement. Mills has seen this before. A recent case had him searching for the killer of a plastic surgeon, so he's come across his fair share of Botox. "When your charity work intersected, Ms. Hallandale, do you ever remember Viveca discussing any kind of problem or trouble she was facing?"

The woman, sitting behind an ornate desk, one of those old French ones that's supposed to be in a palace or something, searches the room with narrow eyes and pursed lips. So dramatic. Mills wants to laugh but he doesn't. "Gosh, no," Dina says. "I mean, of course, she faced her share of problems when her husband passed. I mean, who wouldn't? But I don't remember her talking about anything, you know, suspicious. You should talk to Liz Livingston. She really was Viveca's closest confidante."

Livingston is on Mills's list. He had made contact with her earlier in the morning. They thank Dina Hallandale for her time. And now she rises and follows them to the door. "Are either of you single?" she asks.

Mills says no. Preston says, "I'm widowed. But I have a special someone now."

"Lovely," she says. "But if either of you ever find yourself single, absolutely call me. I'm the best in the business. My clients are normally high earners, but I'd certainly make an exception for you boys!"

Mills turns around before the woman can see the expression on his face. Preston just laughs out loud.

"Not terribly upset by Viveca Canning's death," Preston says as they get in the car.

"Like she said, superficial friends," Mills reminds him. "And clearly that woman specializes in the superficial."

From the office of Dina Hallandale, they drive to the home of Liz Livingston. She lives in Paradise Valley, off McDonald. Camelback looms large behind the house, a home that blends into the mountain like so many do with their humble shades of beige and brown, a home, like so many, that even in its expanse is dwarfed by the mountain, taking some of the show out of the picture. Liz Livingston answers the door in a tight black bodysuit, as if they've interrupted her warrior pose, something Mills suspects only because Kelly has taken up yoga and moved her practice mats into the third bedroom where the treadmill and stationary bike are collecting cobwebs. Ms. Livingston's hair is as black as her bodysuit and it falls to her shoulders. Her skin is creamy white, her lips ruby red, and her smile placid. "I'm glad you called ahead," she tells them. "I wouldn't have answered the door otherwise."

"Because?"

And then, as if on cue, the woman sobs. She covers her face with her hands, weeps modestly, turns her back, and Mills can see her shake with each spasm of grief. He wants to reach out to her, gently touch her shoulder, her arm, anything, but not these days. What would have been an innocent gesture a few years ago could become an impeachable offense today. He thinks he understands the whole sexual harassment thing (at least he's mastered the training about harassment in the workplace), but he knows he has a lot to learn. Kelly is patient. She tells him it's wider spread than he can possibly imagine. She's right. He can't quite imagine. Finally, Ms. Livingston turns to them, wiping her eyes.

"I'm sorry," she says. "Not a great introduction. I'm Liz. I can't shake your hands because they're soaked."

"We understand," Mills says. "I'm Detective Alex Mills. This is my colleague, Detective Ken Preston."

She leads them through a foyer of fine art and sculpture to a room that borrows, if not steals, from the designs of Frank Lloyd Wright. Glass and beams. Wood and windows. And leather seats. They sit opposite her. A giant glass slab in the middle hosts a battlefield of Kachina warriors. The woman catches Mills admiring the dolls. "They're real," she tells him. "Bought them directly from the artist. I collect."

"They're great specimens," Preston gives her.

"So, according to some sources, you're Viveca Canning's closest friend," Mills says.

"What sources?"

"That's how Dina Hallandale describes you," Mills tells her.

The woman laughs bitterly. "Oh, Dina. Of course. The social secretary of the valley. She'll never chair a ball, of course, but she'll help out on the sidelines, just close enough to hear the gossip." Livingston reaches toward a side table for a tissue and dabs her eyes. "But yes, I would consider Viveca and I the closest of friends."

Mills watches the woman's chin quiver. "What can you tell us about her?"

The woman hides her face again and begins to weep. "Oh, I'm so sorry," she says between gulps of tears. "This is why I wouldn't have answered the door. I've been in my bed all morning curled up in a ball. I can't. I just can't . . ."

"Maybe we should come back," Mills suggests.

"No," she says. "I want to do whatever I can to help you. I owe it to her."

"Do you need a minute?" Preston asks.

"No." She dabs again at her eyes, soaking through a tissue. With a sniffle she says, "I'm fine." She says she met Viveca Canning about fifteen years ago while working on a benefit for the Arizona Heart Center. Viveca had recruited her through friends at the hospital where Liz's husband is chief surgeon. "Ever since then we've been like two peas in a fundraising pod."

"But your friendship extended beyond fundraising, no?" Mills asks.

"Absolutely." She recounts vacations together, with and without the husbands. Golf outings, tennis outings, theater, museums. She tells a strange tale about a girls-only trip to Italy and an incident there when Viveca had come out of a museum, she thinks it was someplace called the Galleria dell' Accademia, in tears. When Liz asked her why she was crying, Viveca would only say she wished she could live life as a statue.

"What did that mean?" Mills asks.

"I have no idea," Liz says. "And then her husband died. And that was hard on her."

"What about her relationship with her kids?" Mills asks.

The woman smiles. "She loved her kids, treasured them. But, at the same time, she could only take so much of them. I mean, I can relate, you know, because my kids are about the same age. Adults who don't want to fully own their adulthood."

"Bennett Canning. A man who hasn't quite decided to grow up?" Mills asks.

"Oh Bennett! You've met Bennett?"

"Yes. At the house yesterday," Mills replies.

"Of course. And, yes, you nailed him. Not quite ready for the big world, as they say. But a sweet boy, nonetheless. And full of charisma!"

"What about the daughter?"

"Oh, Jillian is fine too. She's had her disagreements with her parents, but she's a fine young woman. More of an adult than her brother. Moved away for the sake of all of them."

"What does that mean?" Mills asks.

"They clashed a lot, that's all," the woman says, a veil coming down, like a shadow covering her face. She looks away.

"Were you a member of the same church?"

The woman looks back, horrified. "Oh, God no!"

"Stated like a true atheist," Preston says.

"My husband's an atheist. I'm just a lapsed Catholic. No church for me."

"Was Viveca's church a Catholic church?"

"I don't think so," Liz says. "I'm not sure. We didn't talk religion. That's the only thing she was very private about. But I do know she was very, very devoted to her church."

Mills leans as far forward as he can without prompting a Kachina uprising and says, "I need you to think about this very carefully and very thoroughly. Is there anyone, anyone whatsoever who'd want to hurt Viveca Canning? She confided in you. Think about anything she said that might have indicated her concern, her fear even. Were there any run-ins with adversaries? Jealousy, gossip. Anything related to her late husband. Her children?"

He lets the weight and complexity of his question settle. He understands how the layers of these questions can suffocate a person; he imposes these layers on himself all the time. And so he waits and he watches as the woman scrambles her brain, almost visibly, as her eyes search the room like eyes always do, how she begins to speak, but hesitates, rethinks a thought, begins again, but sighs. It's all there. The whole ritual. Down to the tissue crumpling in her hands right before she sighs again and says, "That's the whole thing. I've been racking my brain all morning trying to think why anyone would want to hurt her. I mean, I've tried to think about all the unpleasant people in our lives, and even they aren't unpleasant enough to kill someone. She never mentioned feeling threatened or abused or anything like that. She never mentioned being scared that I can remember. I'm sorry."

"I don't suppose you can provide us a list of all those unpleasant people in your lives," Preston says.

She narrows her eyes. "Are you kidding? I was speaking rhetorically, Detective. When I say unpleasant, I really mean annoying."

"What about jealousies?" Mills asks.

She shrugs. "Everybody's jealous of something. But this isn't the *Real Housewives of Phoenix*, if that's what you're asking."

Mills gets up. Preston follows. "Okay. I think we've taken enough of your time today. I'll give you my card. Please call if you think of anything."

Liz takes the card from Mills and walks them toward the door, back through the foyer of fine art.

"Oh, one more thing," Mills says, stopping just short of the front door. "I notice you're quite the art lover. So was Viveca Canning."

"I know that. Of course," Liz says. "It was one of the many things we have, had, in common."

She begins to fight back tears again, but Mills has to probe further. "Were you familiar with her art collection?"

"Uh, yes. As a matter of fact I was. Mostly," she says. "I mean, I lose track of my own, so I wouldn't be able to account for all of Viveca's."

"Of course not," Mills concedes. "But I need to ask you about one particular work of art that appears to be missing. Her son says it's a Dali."

The woman makes a sudden gasp. For a moment it's as if she can't talk, alarm in her eyes.

"Ma'am?" Mills asks.

Finally she exhales with a gust and says, "Oh my! I'm sorry. It's just that I'm shocked. That's her beloved Dali. Of course I know it. I was there when she pulled it from the vault to go back on display. It's g-g-gone?"

Mills nods.

Liz sobs. She sniffles, and sobs, and wipes at her tears. "I'm sorry. But it's like two deaths now. A double murder. Oh lord, what has happened?"

"Ma'am, are you okay?" Preston asks her.

"I don't know. I don't know," she replies. "But I do know this. If that painting is not back in her vault, I know where it is."

"Where?"

"Phoebe has it. Her sister-in-law. That bitch!"

"Ma'am, I thought you said she had no adversaries . . ." Mills reminds her.

"I know. I'm sorry. I mean, Phoebe's a nemesis, but I don't think she'd murder Viveca."

"Not even to get the Dali?" Mills asks.

"She doesn't need the money."

"Not even to make a point?"

"Maybe to make a point," the woman says.

"What can you tell us about the painting?" Mills asks.

"What do you want to know?"

"The name of it. The value. The subject matter, I guess."

"I'm pretty sure it's untitled. But I know for sure it's an original, so it's worth a lot of money. It's surrealist, of course."

"Of course," Mills says, if for no other reason than to sound informed.

"Something like dancers in a dream," she adds. "Hallucinatory."

Hallucinatory? *I'm sure as shit not going down that rabbit hole.* "Guess we better go talk to Phoebe," he says.

"I'd check with the gallery first," she tells them. "Do you have the address?"

Mills assures her they do. Then the men shake her hand and thank her for her time.

The Carmichael and Finn Gallery on Scottsdale Road is a seven-minute drive away.

"You need a cup of coffee first?" Mills asks.

"No. Let's not break the rhythm," Preston says.

Mills laughs. "Amazing that someone your age still has any rhythm at all."

"Well, you can go fuck yourself," Preston says with a smile. "This old man has no plans to retire. They'd have to shoot me first."

"You know I'm messing with you," Mills tells him. "Still it surprises me that you don't want a life of leisure. You know, travel, hobbies, family."

"Overrated, overrated, see 'em on weekends."

Mills laughs again, then the car goes quiet until they reach the gallery.

An assistant fetches the gallery owner who enters from a back room with a beauty pageant strut, her arms and hands extended just so, kind of teapot-like, her hips making curves with every step. She introduces herself as Jacqueline Carmichael and offers a wide-eyed, blood red smile as if she's waiting to be enlightened.

"I'm Detective Alex Mills with the Phoenix Police Department.

This is my partner Detective Ken Preston. We're investigating the death of Viveca Canning," Mills tells her.

"I see," the woman says. "A tragedy. I hardly slept last night."

There is not a sign of fatigue on the woman's face. A bun of hair sits on her head buttressed by a ring of two thick braids. She wears a flowing thing, a caftan, Mills has heard these things called. She looks like the famous Italian actress, what's her name.

"Were you a close friend of Viveca's?" Preston asks.

"No, but she's been a client here for almost twenty years," the woman replies. "We didn't socialize, so to speak, but we were more than acquaintances."

"Did she ever talk about family with you? Business? Her charity work?"

The woman looks to the floor, clasps her hands. "I think we should continue this in my office."

Mills and Preston follow her and her gyrating hips to an office in the back of the building. It's an L-shaped room, with modern art paintings (the splotch and splatter type that Mills doesn't understand) leaning on the walls as if they're auditioning for the gallery. She sits behind a large chunk of glass that rests on two marble pillars. Her assistant corrals two chairs for the men. Again, her smile. Her ogling eyes. Mills is tempted to ogle back. Instead, he reminds her why they're there. "Whatever you can tell us about Ms. Canning would be very helpful."

"I can tell you mostly about her art. Like I said, we weren't social. She talked about her charity work every so often, and I actually attended some of those events over the years. But not because of her, necessarily. My gallery has sponsored some fundraisers that she was associated with."

"That's fine," Mills tells her. "We're here to talk about her art. Can you show us her collection?"

The woman raises an eyebrow. Actually her whole face seems affronted by Mills. "Her collection is in the vault, gentlemen."

"Would it be a hardship to have us look around?" Preston asks her.

"Normally, I'd need consent from the owner," the woman says. "But I'm afraid since Viveca's . . . gone . . . that leaves me in a quandary."

"But we're officers of the law, ma'am, investigating the owner's murder," Mills reminds her.

"I understand," she says. "But at very least I'd need to call security to accompany—"

Then she stops suddenly and lets out a howl of laugher. Her whole body seems to jiggle. "Why would I need security, when the two of you are the police? How silly of me."

She leads them down a dimly lit hallway and around a corner. A heavy perfume, as cloying as a room deodorizer, swirls in the woman's wake. It could be coming from a deodorizer plugged in somewhere, but Mills thinks it's her. She presses a code into a keypad and, after a series of beeps, she enters another code. The door makes a hydraulic kind of sucking sound, reminiscent of the doors that open to a cell-block and, *thud*, they're in. Carmichael leads them down another dim hallway past a series of doors. At the second from the last door the woman enters a key and turns the knob. She flips a switch and the room goes from black to reddish to yellow gold. Spotlights from the ceiling land on various canvases.

"Did Ms. Canning normally lend her art out to museums or galleries?" Mills asks the woman.

"Yes. Of course."

"To individuals?"

"No," she replies. "Actually, I can't recall."

"Had she discussed the Dali with you lately?" Mills asks.

"Which one?"

"Which one? I don't know the name. Was there more than one?"

Jacqueline Carmichael narrows her eyes, puts a finger to her lips, thinking. "As a matter of fact, there are three," she whispers, as if this vault, this chamber, deserves some kind of reverence. "I believe she only kept one in her home. The others are on loan, I think. She treasured them all. But of course, who wouldn't?"

"Of course," Preston allows her. "Has anyone been in here asking about them? Friends? Family? Strangers? Anyone?"

She shakes her head. "I can't recall," she says. "But yes, I have a vague recollection. Maybe. Oh, dear, I must sound old and senile. May I be excused for a moment? We log all our visitors. I know if I run down the log, it will trigger something."

"That's fine," Mills tells her.

"How far do I need to look back?"

"Three to five weeks will be fine," he says. "Besides, you could receive a subpoena for the log as part of the ongoing investigation."

Jacqueline Carmichael gulps on that remark as if it's a slice of Octavia Spencer's shit pie. Then with a spit she says, "Oh lord, a subpoena! I hope not!"

She turns to the doorway. "I'll leave you boys here, but remember there are security cameras."

"We're cops. Remember?" Preston says.

She clutches the doorframe and flashes a smile. "You just have to forgive me. I'm not used to this drama every day."

Of course you are, Mills thinks as she disappears. Her departure gives Mills the opportunity to check in with the OME. He gets Calvin Cloke on the phone, who tells him that he's up to his elbow in guts. "I don't mean that figuratively, Detective."

"I'm aware, Calvin."

"If you're calling about your lady with the bullet holes, I can almost certainly say that the gunshots to her head killed her," Cloke tells him. "But I can't say anything for sure until toxicology comes back."

"Also aware, Calvin," Mills says. "But I'm wondering about the integrity of the bullets. Have you gone digging through her brain matter?"

"Not yet, buddy. We're kinda busy here. There's a queue."

"Got it. You'll hit me up as soon as you can tell me something?"

"As always," he says and disconnects.

Mills and Preston exchange glances. The two of them, in this mortuary of a room, scanning the artwork, don't have the aptitude for this kind of legacy. Mills is confused by the garish furniture in the corner. He knows this is not his wheelhouse, that he couldn't tell the difference between an original and a print, a Renoir and a Rembrandt, a fucking Dali and a fucking deli. Well, that's not entirely true. He does know where to get the best corned beef sandwich in Phoenix (Miracle Mile, maybe Goldman's in Scottsdale) and, man, is he getting hungry.

She returns. She glides into the room with a sigh. "Yes," she says. "After an exhaustive search, I did find something. Not a visitor. But a call we logged in about three weeks ago. From Viveca's sister-in-law, Phoebe. Phoebe Canning Bickford."

"What was she calling about?" Mills asks

"The note only said she wanted to know if her Dali was in storage, or whether it had been loaned out."

"Hers?"

"I think she meant the one she gifted to Clark Canning."

"Did you take the call?" Preston asks.

"I must have. My initials are in the log."

"Do you remember what you told Mrs. Bickford?" Mills asks her.

"I've been trying and trying to recall that conversation. The only thing remarkable was that she was upset. Very upset. When I told her the piece was actually in Viveca's house, Phoebe started stuttering or sputtering, or whatever you call it. But I didn't ask for details," Carmichael explains. "This is a highly confidential business we work in, you must understand. Most things are none of our business."

"Understood," Mills tells her. "Do you mind explaining to me what the furniture is doing in here?"

Carmichael puffs up and says, "It's art." She pitches her nose at just the right incline to peer down at the detectives. "I assume you gentlemen don't have much appreciation for the masters."

"That would be a safe assumption," Preston tells her. "Is the furniture something that she'd loan out for exhibits?"

"She has."

"Would she ever put it in her home?" Mills asks.

Carmichael laughs. "Oh, heavens no. This isn't home décor,

Detective. They're priceless heirlooms. Not to mention they simply wouldn't 'go' with today's modern furnishings."

Mills studies the ornate, gaudy pieces. "What would you call that style?"

"Rococo. Eighteenth-century French, some Italian."

"Damn, even the style sounds pretentious," Preston whispers.

Carmichael tsks. "It doesn't suit everyone. But it suited Viveca. She knew her art. And her collection's worth a fortune, if you ask me."

"I'd like to ask you what happens with it now," Mills says.

"That would depend on her estate. But she once confided in me that the collection would be divided between her heirs and her church."

"Do you know the value of the untitled Dali?" Mills asks her.

"I think they were all untitled pieces," she says.

"The one gifted to Clark Canning . . ."

"I think you're better off asking Mrs. Bickford."

Preston points to the far corner of the room, beyond the elaborate table and the desk, behind the chair drooling with ornamentation, at a lone wooden chest, decidedly not Rococo, more rustic; Pier 1 Imports meets *Pirates of the Caribbean*. "What's that?" his colleague asks.

"That chest is another heirloom," Carmichael tells them. "It's Moorish, 1400s. She bought it from a dealer in Kentucky."

"Kentucky? I was thinking maybe Spain or Morocco," Mills says. "That much I know."

"Well, of course that's where it originated from, but it has changed hands quite a few times since the Moorish centuries."

"What's in it?" Mills asks her.

Carmichael, again, bristles at his ignorance. "Nothing, to my knowledge. It's not functional at this point. It's art."

Mills points to a large gold padlock hanging from two handles on the chest. "But that looks like a modern lock," he says. "May we investigate?"

She nods and leads them closer to the piece.

"Beautiful," Preston says.

They both admire the dark wood and the faded inlaid design, a fable, Mills imagines, scribbled out in the penmanship of a faraway language.

"But I don't think the lock was designed by the Moors," Preston adds. He points to the engraving on the padlock that says S-C-H-L-A-G-E. "Any idea why Viveca would keep this locked?"

"No idea," Carmichael says, her voice now betraying her impatience.

"Do you have the key?" Preston asks.

"No."

"Who would?" Mills asks her.

"The only one to my knowledge would be Viveca."

Preston scoffs. "Great. The dead woman has the key."

Mills shoots him a look.

"Like I said, the piece is not used for storage," the woman reminds them. "I don't recall her ever opening it."

Mills backs away toward the exit. "All right. I think we're good," he tells her. "But don't be surprised if you're served with a search warrant. It's just business as usual. Standard procedure in case we need to enter something into evidence."

"But you've already searched . . ."

"No, ma'am, we've looked. Thanks to your willingness. But a search warrant would allow us to seize items we think are helpful to the investigation," Mills explains. "Again, thanks. You've been great about this."

A half-truth he can live with if it lubricates this woman for next time.

Sophia Loren! That's the Italian actress she resembles.

It's, once again, hot as fuck today. August will never end. He and Preston both use the cotton fabric of their polo shirts to grasp the door handles of the car. Not doing so risks third degree burns. The steering wheel sizzles. No window tinting in the world can prevent a car from becoming an oven of hell during a Phoenix summer. As the A/C stirs to life, Mills listens to his voice mail. Two messages. One from Kelly saying it's too hot to cook tonight. "Salad or we're going out." He's fine with either option. Her voice in the middle of the day is a sudden, cool breeze. The next message begins with an unfamiliar voice. "Hi Sergeant . . . or is it Detective Mills? Or both? My name is Jillian Canning. Sorry I missed your calls. I'm at the airport in San Francisco. I'll be in Phoenix early tonight . . . staying with my aunt. I want to see my mother . . ." She pauses, takes a deep breath, then Mills hears her shivery exhale. "I want to see her if that's even possible. Can you call me tomorrow? Thanks."

Speaking of Jillian Canning's aunt, and Mills assumes she means her aunt Phoebe Canning Bickford, the men buckle up and head south on Scottsdale Road to Camelback, en route to the lady who lives on the mountain.

High up on Hawkeye Ridge multi-layered homes climb the belly of the camel and the sight pisses Mills off. He shakes his head the whole way up. Yeah, people have a right to the beautiful view, but at what cost? He doesn't begrudge these privileged folks their four million, eight million, twelve million, sixteen million dollar homes, but he doesn't think money should be able to buy public scenery and make it private. Besides, part of the allure of Camelback is seeing her from afar. And that view has changed forever. As development continues to carve into the beautiful beast—this icon, this landmark, this compass of the valley—Mills wouldn't blame the animal if it rose on its haunches and ran away.

He recognizes the ledge. It's familiar, too familiar. A few years back a psychopath dumped a body here; his victim was a young tourist who he'd lured up here to see the view. The killer had taunted everyone, especially Mills, in a case that still inflicts embarrassment. He'd rather forget. But he can't forget. Not now as he approaches the ledge where he and his squad found the body stuffed into a shallow cave. And yet, the ledge is all but gone, the cave nowhere in sight. Instead, this is Phoebe Canning Bickford's address. A big, fat box of a home protruding from the mountain. He rolls through the open gate and up the driveway.

They ring twice before someone comes to the door.

"Can I help you?" The uniformed woman is young and Asian and, clearly, not Phoebe.

"We're here to see Mrs. Bickford," Mills tells her.

"Is she expecting you?"

"Not necessarily, though we have tried calling her," Mills explains. He introduces himself and Preston.

"I'll just be a minute," the woman says. "Come in out of the heat." She asks them to wait in the foyer, a two-story vestibule of glass and bronze. Sculpture and other multidimensional art hang from the walls and the ceiling. The sun splashes everywhere.

"Any chance we'll be dropping by any middle class homes today?" Preston asks.

"Doubtful. Unless you'd like to drop by mine."

They stand quietly for a few minutes before footsteps return, a shuffle in the distance, and then more discernable, the woman rounding a corner and reappearing in the hallway. She calls to them. "Come this way."

They're led to a box within the box. The room has a wall of glass overlooking an infinity pool and the expansive view of Phoenix, a view that regularly drew Phoenicians and their visitors to see spectacular sunsets before the ledge was displaced by Phoebe Canning Bickford's home. The other walls are lined with shelves and bookcases and cabinets unified in a light-colored wood, probably teak, and all the chairs in the room face outward as if the only thing that matters is the view. There's a nautical quality to the space, with the blue and white fabrics, the sailboat images, an enormous area rug that is a rough rendition of a compass and a mast. And then Mills gets it. This room is meant to represent the inside of a yacht, a stateroom, maybe. A private verandah, perhaps. It's confirmed when Phoebe Canning Bickford appears in her docksiders and Mills almost laughs. He bites his tongue, not figuratively. She's wearing those pants that stop just below the knee, exposing tan calves and a diamond anklet on her left leg. She's salon blonde. Mrs. Bickford is probably in her late sixties, but looks younger, thanks to her glowing skin and, perhaps, a scalpel. She doesn't introduce herself. She waits for the men to make the effort. And once they do, she stands there staring at them as if they haven't done enough to make her care.

"Do you mind if we have a seat and talk?" Preston asks.

"Of course. Don't mind me," she says. "I was just trying to figure out what Jasmine can whip up for you boys."

"Oh no," Mills says. "That's very kind. But we won't be needing anything. We won't be here that long."

She sits and they do likewise. "At least let me get you something cold to drink. Jasmine can do a nice refreshing daiquiri or, if you'd prefer, we have all kinds of imported beers."

"No, ma'am, we don't drink on duty," Preston tells her.

She crumples. "Well, then fresh squeezed lemonade it will be!" She pulls out her phone and texts, presumably an order for the lemonade to Jasmine. "I received your messages, but I'm afraid things have been tossed around like a ship at sea these past twenty-four hours," she says as if she's intent on dramatizing the nautical theme.

"I understand. Nobody saw this coming," Mills says. "Or did they?"

"I haven't a clue," the woman says. Her skin is a seafaring bronze, an even brown tan spreading across her chest, up her neck, flawlessly covering her face, making the whites of her eyes and her teeth look so much brighter, the diamond P hanging from her neck more dazzling. "I don't know why anyone would want to hurt her, if that's what you're asking."

"That's one of the questions we're asking," Preston confirms.

She shakes her head, puts her hands palms up. "You got me."

"She wouldn't have confided in you if she were in trouble or threatened?"

Phoebe tightens her chin and again shakes her head. "No. We weren't close. We couldn't be close."

"How come?" Mills asks her.

"Viveca wanted my brother all to herself. She didn't want anyone or anything standing in the way."

"Were you standing in the way?" Preston asks.

She utters a single laugh. "Only to some of the fortune. Viveca didn't come into the marriage poor. She was the daughter of money. So I would never describe her as a gold digger. I abhor that term. But she was very protective of my brother's wealth."

"Wasn't his wealth her wealth?" Preston prods.

"Much, yes, from his own business, but some of it was Canning family wealth."

"And that's where you get involved," Mills says. "Did she feel threatened by you?"

She smiles oddly and searches the room with her eyes, hums blithely for a moment, then says, "Probably. But that doesn't mean I ever threatened her."

Mills is listening and nodding. Nodding just to keep her talking, but listening to every phrasing of every answer, because sometimes it's in the phrasing that people reveal themselves. Their choice of words. Their choice not necessarily conscious. Phoebe Canning Bickford is sitting here in this replica of her yacht describing herself as an adversary, whether she knows it or not, whether she means it or not. "I think we should probably discuss the Dali."

Phoebe blanches through the tan. "What about it?"

"We understand that you'd been feuding about it with your sister-in-law . . ."

She crosses her legs, folds her hands around a kneecap, and says, "I don't mean to be patronizing, but *that's* no secret."

Mills would argue that she does mean to be patronizing, but he wouldn't argue it aloud. Instead, he says, "You do know the Dali is missing."

She nods heavily. "My nephew told me."

"Do you have it?" Mills asks her.

"No. I don't."

"Do you know where it is?"

"No, I don't."

"Do you believe it belongs to you?" Preston asks.

"Yes. I purchased it for my brother. And, as you can imagine I paid an inordinate amount of money for it. I don't believe it belongs in their estate."

"I think the law would disagree with you, ma'am," Mills tells her.

"Which is why I chose not to sue her for it," Phoebe says. "I thought she'd just be sane enough to give it back."

"You said you paid an inordinate amount for it," Mills says. "How much?"

The woman bristles. "I don't like discussing money, and I don't remember the exact figure. But it was just north of a million."

"Do you have a photograph of it?" Preston asks.

"No," she replies. "Why would I?"

Preston says, "I don't know. I don't know much about the art world."

"If you're thinking about a catalogue, then yes, there are photos of it in catalogues," she says. "I'll see what I can do to find one."

Jasmine arrives with the lemonade. Phoebe is all smiles again as her maid/cook/whatever pours the drinks into highball glasses and passes them around. The ice cubes tinkle as if they're sharing a private joke. And this seems to please Phoebe Canning Bickford, convinced, perhaps, that this is a party, after all. "I hope you enjoy it. It's fresh squeezed. Did you know it's good for the kidneys?"

"No, ma'am. I didn't," Preston tells her. "I get kidney stones, so that's good to know."

"Ah, yes, stones," she says. "My husband gets them and his urologist recommends frequent consumption of lemonade."

"Duly noted," Preston says.

"Would you mind if we searched the premises?" Mills asks.

His question is the pin to the party's balloon.

"Absolutely, I would mind," she says, the muscles of her neck and face tightening. "Is this where you tell me I'm a suspect?"

"Everyone's a suspect," Mills says. "This is where I tell you that we can eliminate you as a suspect by letting us search the house."

She's up on her feet. "Good luck getting a warrant for that," she says. Her eyes are jewels of fury. "Even I know enough about the law to know you have no cause."

Mills rises slowly. "Look, there's no need for this to get contentious. We came here to ask questions, not to search the house. If that were the case, we would have had a search warrant in hand. But now, since we're here, it just seemed a reasonable request to make. I apologize if offense was taken."

"I didn't kill her," the woman says.

"Thank you for your time. The lemonade was delicious," Mills tells her. "Especially on a day like today."

He can see the tears filling her eyes.

Preston stands and walks to the wall of glass. Staring out at the pool and the valley beyond, he says, "The view is a work of art itself. On permanent display. Where do you store your collection, Mrs. Bickford?"

"What do you mean?" she asks.

"I mean, do you store your pieces off-site, like in a gallery, as your sister-in-law did?"

Not a single tear has spilled. She raises her chin and says, "My lawyer's name is Carson Huntley. He can answer those kinds of questions."

"Thank you, ma'am," Mills says. He half-turns to leave, then conjures up some drama of his own. "There used to be a cave up here, Mrs. Bickford. What happened to it when you built the house?"

She looks at him, confused. Then she folds her arms across her chest, the snaking together of her limbs alone an invitation to them to go fuck themselves. "I know all about the protests, Detective. Nobody wanted us to build here. Old story."

"It's not that, ma'am," Mills says. "I just wondered whatever happened to the cave."

She smiles. "We were clever. We built the house into the mountain and annexed the cave."

"Annexed the cave?" Preston asks.

"Yes. We attached the house and preserved the cave," she says gleefully. "It's our wine cellar. Didn't you read about it in all the magazines?"

"Oh," Mills says. "We found a dead body in there a few years ago."

"A what?" she cries.

"Dead body," Mills repeats. "Didn't you read about it in all the newspapers? See it on TV?"

"Let's go," Preston says. "Thanks for your time," he tells the woman, who stands there stiffened, chilled. The glee on her beautifully bronzed face gives way to a ghostly white.

9

Gus slept well. He dreamed of surfing and dolphins. That's usually a sign that everything's fine. That's what he's taken it to mean over the years, this reoccurring dream of the ocean and his frequent companions. He's still getting his Phoenix feet back, still absorbing some of the culture shock he gets when he comes home from Seattle, this visit somewhat more complicated because of its implications, finality, and all that, but somehow it was also a voyage into outer space, into the true unknown, because despite Gus's gifts, he cannot fathom his father's whereabouts. He can't see that. Though his gut does tell him that Warren Parker has boarded some kind of vessel that's sailing toward the gaseous neighborhood of our constellations. His father was a difficult, uncompromising man, but Gus doesn't think the man's character was so flawed that Warren Parker might be denied entry into his religiously informed version of Heaven. That's all Gus knows. Gus doesn't think of Heaven as a place. He thinks of it as a state of mind, here and thereafter.

The LA visit with Billie feels like a blur, but a blur that still prickles his skin. He gets up, makes coffee. He has about an hour and a half to get to work. He considers doing a load of laundry, but as he assesses the pile the phone rings.

It's his new client. The woman who came yesterday.

"I'm sorry to bother you so early, Mr. Parker."

"No worries. I'm up and about. And you can call me Gus."

"I haven't been completely honest with you, Gus."

"Haven't you?"

A silence. Then, a stuttering, "I'm sorry."

There's another hyphen of silence, in which Gus waits for her to compose her story, because this is what the call is all about. He knows this. He sees her through the phone struggling but adroit, reticent but strident. The contrasts are her morning workout. That's what he gathers in her vibe-inducing silence until she speaks again. "I'm sorry," she reprises. "I'm in the business of truth. Truth is my currency. All this nonsense lately about fake news is ridiculous. If you're a real reporter, and I am, you are the truth of your stories. And I'm the truth of mine."

"Did you lie to me, Ms. Jones?"

"No," she replies. "But I omitted some information. Do you have any time today?"

"I'm sorry but I'm working a full shift at my day job."

"Tonight?"

He apologizes again. "Probably not. What about tomorrow? I only work until three. I can see you at four."

"Okay," she says. "And I'm the one who's sorry, Gus."

Heading to work later he contemplates all the sorrys of the morning. We live in a world full of apologies. So many regrets. There's the half-empty glass of mistakes. And there's the half-full glass of forgiveness. And if you're lucky you live closer to forgiveness on the spectrum. He wonders if he can call this a retroactive epiphany. Something about that trip to Seattle, about finally traversing the line between then and now. There's a severance, for better or worse, and he knows, as he drives toward the expanse of the morning sky, that with severance comes the tugging of reconciliation, like an undertow. And that's fine. Just fine. He aims for the exit ramp, hits the blinker, checks his rearview mirror. Staring back at him in the mirror is the face of Aaliyah Jones. In her eyes she's haunted. The oval of her mouth articulates a fear Gus can't comprehend.

Kelly got out of bed this morning carrying an inordinate weight of misery on her shoulders. Mills could see it on her face, in her trudging gait, those deserted eyes. This is the first day of a case she dreads. She's defending Trey Robert Shinner, the valley's serial thief, trespasser, stalker, vandal, drunk, ghoul. The forty-two-year-old man is infamous for his petty crimes and his colorful rantings that sound like demented poetry. As a child, Shinner suffered a brain injury of unknown origins and has been a ward of the state ever since. He bounces from one halfway house to another, haunting neighborhoods in Metro Phoenix like a clown who escaped Stephen King's bottom drawer. Trey Robert Shinner is funny/scary, harmful/harmless, a man, a child, and now he's on trial for stealing cars at the ballpark, particularly Jeeps and pickups, and joyriding off road in the desert. He posed nude in the stolen vehicles and, for whatever reason, sent the photos to the addresses on the auto registration. This is the first time Kelly's been assigned to a Shinner case. She had not even made opening arguments and she looked weakened; Mills tried to give her a transfusion of vigor this morning by holding her extra close, promising to cook dinner, promising to do the laundry, to book her into a fancy spa when the trial is done. She smiled and left.

"Oh Jesus, Shinner. What a freaking mess," Jan Powell says. "Why can't they get him off the streets once and for all?"

"Petty crimes."

"Probation violations."

"The judges don't want to do it because of his diminished capacity."

"Then why don't they commit him?"

"Because they have no balls, I guess."

They're driving up to Hawkeye Ridge to meet with Jillian Canning. Mills has warned Powell about the reception they'll get from Aunt Phoebe, but Powell just shrugged off the apprehension. "Did you know they built a house up there on the ledge?" he asks her.

"Yeah, I heard," Powell says.

"If you haven't been up here for a while you won't believe how much of the mountain is fenced off for construction."

Powell nods. "We can't fight all the battles, Alex."

Mills has never liked the resignation of human nature. But he doesn't say anything. Not another word until they're parked up the steep driveway, until they're at the front door and Jasmine is standing there with her doleful eyes and placid smile. "Hello, Detective."

"We have an appointment with Jillian," he tells her.

"She's expecting you."

Jillian Canning meets them in a room that appears to be only a room, not a replica of Phoebe's seafaring lifestyle. They're surrounded by adobe walls, potted cacti, and other desert flora. Native American art hangs from the wall; some of its creatures, their faces turned away or hiding, seem almost embarrassed by the Canning-Bickford wealth. The leather sofas have earthy hides. They sit.

"I don't know what I can tell you," Jillian says. "I live far away. I didn't know much about my mother's daily life."

A preemptive strike, Mills notes to himself. Jillian Canning is very quick to distance herself from the crime scene. He studies her. He sees the redness in her eyes and the puffiness that surrounds them. She's not crying now, presumably because she's all cried out. Her auburn hair is pulled back tight into a ponytail. She's wearing a t-shirt and wide pants that tighten at the ankle; they look like pjs or the bottom half of a belly dancer's ensemble, colorful, with a pattern of elephants spiraling in all directions. He smiles.

"That's fine," he assures her. "What was your relationship like with your mother?"

She lowers her head, studies her hands. "It was getting better."

"Better?" Powell asks.

"Yeah. We weren't close for a long time. I don't know if my brother told you, I'm gay."

"He did," Mills says. "And your mother didn't approve of your lifestyle?"

"It's not a lifestyle, Detective Mills," she tells him. "Unless you're born with a lifestyle."

Powell laughs.

"Oh no, I'm sorry," Mills says. "I guess I'm not that great with the terminology. But I get it. Of course. I hope you'll excuse me."

The woman nods and smiles. "No offense taken, but yes, it was a source of tension in the family. But my relationship with my mother was definitely improving after my father died."

"Can you imagine anyone wanting to harm your mother?" Mills asks her.

She hesitates, either considering or avoiding the question. Then she shakes her head and says, "No. I've been going over scenarios in my head all night, but nothing makes sense."

"Do you think she would have told you if she were concerned or afraid, now that you two were getting closer?" Powell asks.

"I don't know," the woman replies, gazing just a bit deeper into Powell's eyes than she had into Mills's. As if they're exchanging a secret code. "You should really talk to her pastor. They were very close. I'm sure my mother would have told him if she'd been threatened by anyone or felt unsafe."

"Your mother obviously was a very religious woman," Mills says.

"She did a lot for her church," Jillian says almost with no inflection. "She's on the board of directors. Was, I mean."

"Can we get the name of your mom's pastor?" Powell asks.

"Gleason Norwood."

"Wait," Mills says, then clears his throat. "Gleason Norwood? *That* Gleason Norwood?"

A crinkle of confusion curls up Jillian Canning's face. "Uh, yes," she says, stretching the words. "I thought my brother mentioned it to you."

"No, he didn't," Mills says. "And I don't believe I asked. I remember a reference to the Church of Angels Rising, but I guess I didn't make the connection."

Gleason Norwood has made himself memorable for so many reasons, in so many ways, most of them controversial. His shadow looms large over the valley, as if he were a governor, a titan of business, or a king. As the founder and head pastor of the Church of Angels

Rising, he's all three and then some. He sports a catatonic smile and million dollar teeth that are as synonymous with the church as any scripture. He's got a sixty million dollar cathedral and an equally rich TV ministry. He's everywhere for the faithful and nowhere to be found by mostly everyone else, including the IRS and the *Arizona Republic*, particularly Sally Tobin, who has been after him for decades. Now it occurs to Mills that the church was tagged in a few of Viveca's social media posts.

"So, are you a member of the church as well?" Mills asks her daughter.

The woman scoffs and says, "No. I was raised in the church, but when it was clear they couldn't cure me I was asked to leave."

"Cure you?" Powell asks.

"Get the lesbian out of me, like an exorcism."

"There are rumors that once you leave Church of Angels Rising you're pretty much cut off," Mills says. "True?"

"Absolutely," Jillian says. "My parents were forced to erase me. That's what they call it, 'erasing.' My father did it perfectly. He never spoke to me again. But not my mother. She could never fully let go. And that became a huge, really huge conflict in their marriage. He went to his grave with it."

"Five years ago, your brother said?"

"Yeah, I think so."

"And how did he die?" Mills asks.

"Heart attack. He dropped dead one night after a dinner party, or something, with friends."

Jillian Canning folds her arms across her chest, hugging herself or hugging a memory, bracing herself for some kind of hurt, it seems. She's doe-eyed and suddenly not a woman, but a girl, a bit lost and a bit frightened. He wants to reach for her and say that she was never wrong, that she's been through enough, but what the hell does he know? Somehow, at a place in his career when he should be comfortably jaded, he's more often caught in a cloying web of compassion. Empathy overwhelms him and he gets a glaring reminder that being a cop has always meant rescuing strangers in one way or another, and that, yes, he inherited the righteousness of his father, the legendary county attorney who died young battling every demon of the valley. Lyle Mills fought ferociously for justice, his passion ticking away, ticking all day, ticking at home through family dinner, late into the night in his library, ticking through trials, through victories and tumultuous defeats, ticking until it finally exploded.

Jillian Canning fidgets in the silence. Powell clears her throat.

"Well, I think that's enough for today," Mills says. "How long will you be in Phoenix?"

She smiles bitterly. "I don't know. We have to make arrangements for the funeral. We probably have to go sit with the lawyers and figure out what to do with the house. Like I said, I don't know. There's so much to take care of."

"Of course there is," Mills says. "But would you mind if we checked in with you again? I think we'll probably have more questions."

"That's fine," Jillian tells him. "Do you have any idea when my mother will be turned over to us? You know, her body?"

Mills hesitates but says, "I would think in a few days, no more than a week. I can check with the Office of the Medical Examiner, if you'd like."

She stands. "If you could, that would be great. You know how to reach me."

Mills assures her he does.

On the way back to headquarters, Mills senses his father's presence with him, in the front seat, appropriating Powell's space. He sees the valley differently on this drive. It's not a grid of streets and avenues and intersections. It's not block after block of commerce and concrete buildings and strip malls and gas stations. The whole valley is in front of them. It's all a panorama. And they're chasing phantoms.

10

"**G**uess who I'm going to visit today?" Mills asks his wife the following morning when they convene in the kitchen, post showers, over coffee.

She gives him a sleepy smile and says, "Too early for trick questions. Who?"

"Gleason Norwood."

"Who?"

"Gleason Norwood. You know, Church of Angels Rising."

With an eye roll she says, "Oh, God. Why?"

"He was a good friend to my victim. From what I'm learning, they were confidants."

"Was she a member? Or do I even have to ask?"

He holds his cup in midair. "Oh, yes she was. On the board of directors, or something like that."

Kelly seems to mull this over, or mull something over, maybe just the day that lies ahead. Then, her voice percolating with sarcasm, she says, "I want you to be careful, Alex. It's a cult. I'd hate to see you brainwashed."

He laughs, sips, and says, "No chance of that, hon. I'm already brainwashed by the church of Kelly Mills."

"Oh, how sweet," she tells him. "After court today I have a quick doctor's appointment, then I'm all yours. And by 'all yours,' I mean, let's have sex. A lot of sex. All night."

He almost spits out his coffee. "On a school night?"

"One of the perks of having our kid away at college."

True. It's a perk. Trevor's at University of Arizona on a football scholarship. Despite his arrest a few years ago for selling pot, a twisted mess that tugged alternately at the parental coils of fury and forgiveness, maybe even love and hate, Trevor turned out to be an amazing kid. More amazing now that his parents can have sex with abandon, not that as a couple they're up to it so much, but they talk about it a lot. As if talking about it keeps the craving alive. And how can you not crave her? At forty-six, she's a creature who defies age. She defies everything. She captures you with her gleaming eyes. She pulls you in with her lips. She holds you to her hips and she's gravitational. She redefines the universe for him every day. When it comes to her, Mills is a sucker for hyperbole.

When Mills rolls into headquarters he's intercepted in the hallway outside his office by Jan Powell, who tells him she's secured a search warrant for Viveca Canning's house. It's a necessary formality for them to legally search and seize beyond what's in plain sight.

"And I got a call from the lab," Powell tells him. "They have prints that don't belong to our victim."

"Fresh?"

"It would seem so."

They drift into his office, followed almost immediately by Sergeant Jake Woods, who stops the door from closing. He's crisp and cologned, his shirt so heavily starched it crunches when he moves. "No pressure," he says, which always means pressure, "but Hurley's been inquiring . . ."

Scott Hurley is the squeaky clean mayor of Phoenix, the one who defines himself by how many "lowest crime" lists the city makes in one year. Murders. Rapes. Drugs. And gangs. He's got the pie charts in his head, the spreadsheets on the wall behind his desk. If it can be measured, Scott Hurley will measure it and put it in Excel.

"He doesn't want Viveca Canning to be emblematic," Woods tells them.

"Emblematic?" Mills asks.

"His word not mine. Hurley doesn't want the valley defined by dead socialites."

"The body is barely cold," Powell groans.

"I know," the sergeant says. "He's jumping to conclusions. You know how he is. 'I keep Phoenix as safe as I keep my family. We are meticulous with crime.' He just wants to be sure we're being meticulous."

Mills laughs. Not ha-ha funny. More like what-an-asshole funny. "And you really needed to tell us this?"

"Yeah," Woods says. "Because Hurley wants to know that this is an isolated case."

"At this point there's no reason to believe it isn't," Mills says.

"And it doesn't look random. Does it?" Woods asks him.

"We can't say for sure," Mills replies. "But it looks like she was probably targeted. You know this already."

"I do," his boss concedes. "I'm just fielding a lot of questions from reporters. Grady and I will probably have to do another press conference soon. No pressure."

Mills plants himself squarely, firmly, takes Woods in from an angle and says, "No pressure inferred, Jake."

Confusion crosses the sergeant's face, like he doesn't know how to respond, and then, awkwardly retreating, he offers the detectives two thumbs up.

At the home of Viveca Canning, Mills and Powell supervise the orderly upheaval of the place. Officers come and go with computers and phones, notebooks, a Rolodex, folders and documents, bank boxes full of paper. Myers is here taking notes. Preston is logging the items collected. Most of the jewels are gone. Not stolen—there's no sign of a secondary break—just swooped up, probably, by the vacuuming hands of an heir or heiress.

He dials.

"Bennett Canning? This is Detective Mills. I'm the one working your mother's death."

"Right. I remember. What's up?"

"I just need you to confirm that you removed the rest of the jewelry from your mother's house, you know, the stuff we left behind."

"I thought you took all the jewelry that was laying around."

"We did," Mills says. "But we had observed jewelry boxes and cases all over the house, even a cabinet. It's all gone."

Dead silence. Then the kid clears his throat and says, "I have everything."

"Bad move, Mr. Canning."

"I was just securing her stuff," he argues. "I have a right to protect the family's investments, don't I?"

"I could arrest you for disturbing a crime scene."

"But you're not going to do that are you?"

"That depends. We'll need to see where you've stored the jewelry, and we'll need to inventory every piece."

"That's easy," Canning says.

"And if we need to take some of it, or all of it, we have a warrant. So don't get creative."

Then he hangs up before the kid can say another word. He studies the empty space on the wall in front of him, the Dali territory, and wishes he knew more about fine art. There has to be a reason. Or a symbol. That painting has to be a symbol of something to someone. It occurs to him to reach out to ASU and get with a professor of fine arts, or maybe to call the Heard and get with a curator or whatever they call the experts over there. He and Kelly don't have expensive art around the house. Not on their salaries. They have some decorative stuff they picked up at Z Gallerie, but that's about it, except for Kelly's new obsession with pottery. They have a lot of pottery, particularly pots for plants that sit empty without plants. She's been living among pottery of the American Southwest all her life and now, all of a sudden, she's a collector. He turns when he hears his name. It's Powell approaching.

"Check your email," she tells him. "We heard from the OME. They retrieved the bullet from the brain. Same as the bullet found at the scene. One gun, two bullets. Analysis by Firearms shows it was a 9 millimeter. A Smith and Wesson—"

"M and P Shield."

"Most probably."

"I shoulda bought stock."

The ride to the Church of Angels Rising Cathedral, or C-ARC as it's known locally, takes him just under fifteen minutes from the Canning home. The monstrosity of glass and brick sits in a nest of land just off the Hohokam on the approach to Sky Harbor. You can't miss it. He turns onto 44th Street, drives a block or two before turning into the gaping acreage that becomes church property. C-ARC made news, and enemies with its closest neighbors, when it purchased several surrounding buildings and had them bulldozed. The result is huge unpaved parking lots, the size of football fields, on all sides of the C-ARC; the church leaders argued they wanted to expand the perimeter around the cathedral to give their members a greater sense of privacy and sanctity in their worship. To many Phoenicians that argument had the hollow ring of a cult calling its members to the Kool-Aid fountain. The Phoenix City Council, itself a home to several religious lunatics, ruled in C-ARC's favor, however, and now has an eyesore to commemorate its unpopular decision. C-ARC never groomed the lots it annexed. Its immediate grounds are a botanist's dream, but the surrounding football fields are empty stretches of clayish dirt and rocks. They didn't even plant a fucking palm tree. Or a cactus. On windy days the lots swirl to the sky in menacing dust devils, blowing debris on nearby cars, pedestrians, and businesses. Preston is waiting in his car when Mills arrives. Mills pulls up beside him. Both men emerge into the blistering sunlight.

"Shit, it has to be over a hundred and it's not even noon," Preston says.

"And you've lived in the valley how long?"

"All my life. But it never gets easier."

Mills nods, but he disagrees. He hates the heat, but it's not disabling.

As if reading Mills's mind, Preston says, "Just wait to you get to be my age. It's different."

"Well, let's get you inside, then."

Inside the huge atrium of the cathedral, Mills takes in the expanse of soaring glass. There are supposedly a thousand windowpanes throughout the building; that's what he's heard on the news. It's not like he's going to count, but Mills has never been in the cathedral, and the lobby alone is a pyramid of crystal.

"King Tut meets Liberace," Preston says.

"What's Liberace?"

"You're pathetic," Preston says.

Mills just shrugs and approaches the receptionist who's sitting against the far wall, a slab of granite serving as her desk. She looks up, wide-eyed and ingratiating. "How can I help you?"

"We're here to see Gleason Norwood, ma'am."

Her lipstick matches her fingernails, Merlot.

"Is this about membership?" she asks with that catatonic smile most often associated with Gleason Norwood.

Mills pulls out his badge. "No, ma'am. We're with the Phoenix Police Department. We need to speak to him about a case."

She folds her diamond-encrusted fingers and winces. "Without an appointment?"

"Yes, without an appointment," Mills tells her. "Is there some problem?"

She adjusts the cuffs of her sleeves. Her blouse is silky, her skirt, from what he can see, tight. "He may still be taping his show. And any visits need to be cleared with his publicist."

Mills leans against her desk and smiles. She smiles back. And the smiles just hang there outdoing each other. It's like a staring contest with teeth. Mills is the first to break when he says, "ma'am, this is not an optional meeting. We're officers of the law. If he's on the premises, please let him know we're waiting."

She hops off her stool and lands on heels that give her a six-inch lift. Her legs are what old Hollywood would call "nice gams," and they're perfect for her elongated strut as she disappears behind the two doors to the left of the lobby.

"Are you staring at her ass?" Preston asks.

Mills bristles. "What? No, of course not. You know I don't do that."

"How could you help it?"

"I can help it, Ken. I don't do that."

"Your eyes were all over her."

"Yeah. I admit that. But not lasciviously. I'm just a bit surprised to see such a, what would you call it, skimpy skirt in a place like this."

"Skimpy is an understatement."

"See what I mean?"

"Oh, I saw it, Alex. If it were any shorter, I'd have to go to confession."

Mills laughs. "I know. I just find it odd in a place like this. What would Jesus think?"

"Oh, I don't think there's a whole lot of Jesus here."

"No?"

"No. I don't think it's that kind of religion," Preston tells him.

"Right. If rumors are to be believed it's a cu—"

They hear footsteps approaching. Mills turns and sees the receptionist coming through those same two doors followed by the church's illustrious leader, Gleason Norwood, his championship smile nearly five steps ahead of them both.

Mills shakes the man's hand and introduces himself. "And this is my colleague, Detective Ken Preston."

"Your smile precedes you," Preston says to the preacher.

Mills steps back and surreptitiously pushes an elbow into his partner's belly. Meanwhile Gleason Norwood unleashes a fit of laughter and says, "Oh yes. I've been told my smile is more famous than my church!"

"We're here to talk to you about Viveca Canning," Mills tells him.

"Ah, yes, I knew you'd be coming by," Norwood says.

"You did?" Preston asks.

"Of course. Viveca is a member of our board, has been for years. We want to help in any way we can."

There's more to the man than his teeth. Like his leggy receptionist, he's wearing miniature cathedrals of diamonds on his fingers. His hair swoops back from his forehead and dovetails to the nape of his neck, actually below the nape, longer than Mills would expect from a man of the cloth, but Gleason Norwood appears more a man of fashion than religion. His suits are perfectly tailored to outline his athletic body. His shoes have that made-in-Milan cachet. Norwood stands just shy of six feet, Mills estimates, with a spray tan covering nearly every inch.

"It was her children who suggested we reach out to you," Mills tells him.

"They surely would. Viveca and I were very close. I'm grieving," Norwood says. "Let me assure you the whole congregation is grieving."

And yet he's still brandishing that fucking smile.

"Is there someplace we can talk privately?" Mills asks him.

"Oh sure. Of course. Follow me."

They follow Gleason Norwood through a set of doors recessed into the back wall to the right of the reception desk. Mills hears the clack of heels. "We'll be fine," Mills tells the woman, who stops short and almost falls off her stilettos. Her arms are swinging a bit as she tries to maintain her balance; her eyes roll with a kind of adolescent indignation. Seeing this, the preacher offers her a few quick affirming nods and says, "I'll let you know if I need anything, Valentine. This shouldn't take too long."

Her name is Valentine.

Norwood escorts them down a hallway, glass on one side, offices on the other, then through another set of doors that open to a circular vestibule ringed by Greek columns and statuary, all festooned with tropical flowers. The floor is marble, an inlaid star at the center, each point stretching to the base of a column. Everything is splashed with white paint and sunlight, just like Greece itself. The flowers pop.

"This will lead us to my office," the preacher says, pointing toward the sloping marble ramp.

The office is palatial. Probably the size of a modest Phoenix home. There's a kitchen and a dining area. From there, the flow goes into a formal dining room with an elegantly carved table and ten chairs. At another end of the office, television screens hang from the ceiling, below them a fully stocked mahogany bar with five stools of matching wood. A wide spiral staircase twists toward an upper level. Mills eyes the winding ascent and finds that it ends in a dome of light. "If you'd rather talk up there, that's fine," Norwood says. "It leads to my balcony overlooking the stadium."

"Stadium?" Preston asks.

"Sanctuary, I mean, but it's as big as some stadiums."

"We're fine here," Mills tells him. "I was just admiring the architecture."

"But if you'd be more comfortable, I also have a living room on the other side of the bar."

"I said we're fine here."

The man settles in and sits, indicating the others should do the same. Then he pulls in closer, rests his elbows on his desk, clasping his hands to his chin. He exhales a mournful sigh. "We're doing a memorial service for Viveca next Monday night. You're welcome to come of course. I'll introduce you to the rest of the board and some of her closest friends."

"I'll keep that in mind," Mills tells him. "But Ms. Canning's daughter says Viveca would likely confide in you, first and foremost, if she were in trouble or in harm's way . . ."

The man considers a far corner of the room, then the ceiling. As he brings his eyes back to Mills, he says, "I don't know if I'd say first and foremost, but she would certainly come to me if something was bothering her."

"And did she? Lately?"

"She did not," Norwood replies. "I know she would have said

something if she thought her life was in danger." His eyes begin to fill. He wipes a brimming tear and smiles.

"Her children weren't members of the church," Preston says, a question embedded.

"Not true. Her son is a faithful member," Norwood says. "Her daughter defected. A source of much sadness for Viveca."

"Defected?" Preston asks.

"Just the angels talking, sorry. She *left* the church."

"Did Viveca tell you why?" Preston persists.

"Well, you know with her lifestyle . . . We love the sinner, but hate the sin."

"Because she teaches yoga?"

Good one, Preston.

"Because of her identification as a member of the gay movement," Norwood replies, seething through the panels of his Colgate smile. "It's just not compatible with what I teach at the church."

"And that makes you judge and jury?" Preston continues.

Norwood looks at his Rolex, a diamond per minute. "I don't have a lot of time, gentlemen, and this is not relevant to Viveca's death. Why don't we stick to that?"

Mills leans forward, rests his elbows at the edge of the desk. "We have to consider everyone and all motives. Perhaps Jillian wanted her mother dead. Perhaps it was retaliation."

"Retaliation for what?" the preacher asks, his eyes narrowing.

"For being ousted from the church."

"We did not *oust* her," Norwood says defiantly. "She left the church."

"Her choice?" Mills asks.

"She could have chosen to renounce her lifestyle. But she chose to leave the church instead."

"But she couldn't stay and be her true self?" Preston asks.

Norwood laughs. "Not *that* true self."

"We understand," Mills tells him. "She was banished. Excommunicated. Ousted. It's all semantics. But whatever you call it, Jillian

Canning might have had a motive, after all."

"Are you asking if the Cannings cut their daughter off financially?"

Mills shakes his head. "No. That's not what we're asking. But did they?"

The preacher's hands go palms up. "I have no knowledge of the family's finances."

"Except how much of their finances they donated to this church," Preston says like a cross-examining attorney, which momentarily reminds Mills of his wife and her promise of outstanding posttrial sex tonight.

"Again," the preacher says. "Relevance?"

This line of questioning is testing the limits of Norwood's smile. And perhaps the limits of the Botox (not much has moved on Gleason Norwood's face, certainly not a furrowed brow). "No relevance if you know nothing of the Canning's finances," Mills tells him.

"I don't," Norwood says, rising from his desk. "But I really must be going. I have a meeting."

Mills and Preston take his cue and stand. "Thank you for your time," Preston says.

"No, thank *you*. I certainly appreciate you coming by. And I certainly appreciate you pursuing this. We're devastated. And I'm at a complete loss at how this could have happened."

Mills shakes his hand. "I'm sure you are. It's a shock."

"Don't hesitate to call me if you need anything. And the memorial service will begin at seven, Monday," he reminds them.

They silently retrace their steps to the front atrium. Another round of handshakes and, as Mills and Preston are about to turn to the front door, Norwood says in a low murmur, "I do think you should look into their finances. Their wealth was no secret. And money breeds trouble, I'm afraid."

"You say that as a moneyed person, yourself," Mills says.

"Yes," Norwood concedes, his eyes brimming again with grief.

11

At precisely four o'clock, Gus hears a knock at the door. He finds Aaliyah Jones standing there and escorts her to his office. He offers something to drink.

"I don't want to trouble you," she says.

"No trouble."

"You're very kind." She looks at him in a fetching way and it throws him a curve.

"Iced tea? Water?" he stutters.

"Water."

He heads to the fridge trying to intuit a distant vibe, too distant, vexing. He fills a glass with ice and water and returns to the office. "Sorry," he tells the reporter. "I don't do bottled water anymore. I'm trying to save the planet."

She laughs.

"I'm serious," he insists.

"I'm sure you are."

"What did you want to see me about?" he asks her. He sees a lion approaching. He sees Aaliyah taming it to a sudden deference. The animal goes down on all fours, purring mightily but submissively to this woman who dances across the plains like strikes of lightning.

"As I said, I was not completely honest with you the other day. I failed to admit that I sought you out specifically because I know you work with the detective investigating the Viveca Canning case."

"I see you do your homework."

She smiles weakly. "It's no secret, with Beatrice Vossenheimer's book, and a simple Internet search. I guess I was hoping you'd be my bridge to Detective Mills," she explains. "If I gave you information, maybe you could give it to him. That would keep me out of it."

Gus listens to her, then to the silence that follows, then to the immediate voice of his that says, *no*. It's one of the swiftest chimes of intuition he's ever had. No. Of course not.

"Alex doesn't really work that way," Gus says. "He needs what you might call a chain of custody of information, not hearsay. He'll respect your privacy, Aaliyah. You can probably make the conditions. But you'll need to contact him yourself."

She settles back. She studies Gus. She nods, understanding. In her eyes, a migration of angels, both dark and light, move across the horizon. "Could you make the introduction?"

"Yes," he tells her. "I'd be willing to do that."

She's gone a few minutes later, and Gus stands at his open front door searching her wake for necessary clues.

A wall rises in the distance. It billows in towers of pink and beige. It's a moving mountain range, building before his eyes, as it crawls toward him from the southwest corner of the valley. Mills is only a quarter mile from headquarters; he'll probably make it back before the dust storm reaches him. But he can hear the first flourish of pebbles under his car. And then comes the no-see-ums of dirt, the splatter of tiny specks of sand against the windshield, a familiar warning. In minutes all visibility might be gone. He steps on the gas as he watches the behemoth grow. From here, the wall cloud seems to dwarf the skyscrapers of the Central Corridor. He calls Kelly but gets no answer. He tries the landline at home. No answer there either. He then remembers her doctor's appointment, takes a deep breath. This will be over by the time she's done. She won't get caught up in the pestering storm. The faster he drives, the more he hears the commotion of dirt outside. By the time he reaches the parking lot, the wind is rocking the car. On his way inside, he pushes against the force of the storm, leaning in, and shields his eyes.

He runs into Preston in the elevator.

"We got out of that church just in time," Preston says.

"How do you mean?"

"The dirt lots out there. Our cars would be buried."

When they reach the third floor, they find just about everyone at the windows watching the tsunami of debris that's swallowing the valley, the view peppered with excited expletives. But not Morton Myers. Myers is leaning on a cubicle outside Mills's office, waiting. Unlike him to ignore a crowd or a spectacle. "What's up?" Mills asks him.

"We're barely into her computers," Myers says. "But I knew where to look first."

"Of course you did," Mills says, waving him in. Preston follows. The men sit at his desk, opposite him.

"I just searched for her will and there it was in a file 'Will.' Easy peasy," Myers explains. "Don't know if it's up to date or the final thing, you know, but she left everything to the church."

"Not a total shock," Mills says. "Some people do that. I've seen it before." Preston nods soberly. Like a grandfather.

"Yeah, well, maybe this will shock you," Myers says. "Her estate is worth over three hundred million dollars."

"It says that in the will?" Mills asks him.

"No. There was another file called 'Assets.' Again, she made it easy for me," he says with a snorting laugh.

"I imagine the artwork is worth probably half of that," Preston says.

"The three hundred million doesn't include her artwork," Myers tells them. "She left all of that to the Heard."

Mills almost gulps.

"Toldya it would shock you," Myers says.

"I'll need those files," Mills tells him.

"No problem," Myers says. "I guess this eliminates the kids if we're looking at inheritance as a motive."

"Assuming they knew the money was going to the church," Preston interjects. "If they didn't know, they're still in play and so is a motive."

"Same goes for the church," Mills says. "There's motive there, too, if the victim made her wishes public. We've got to dig in, boys. Make a bunch of people nervous."

He hears a roar outside. He turns to the window.

"Jesus Christ!" Myers screeches.

Preston gets up, moves to the glass.

The three of them stare out as pillars of dust round the corners of downtown and join on the street below, merging in perfect collaboration. In an instant, the invigorated storm hides the building across the street. It just disappears. Mills can't see a thing. Dust whirls and slaps against the window. And then, the grand entrance and grand exit in one salutation, the *haboob*, as some weather geeks like to call it, leaves almost as fast as it came.

12

Mills has tried to reach Bennett Canning for two days now. He's left messages. He's texted the guy. He's tried to get his attention on Twitter, for Christ's sake, and Mills avoids social media the way most people avoid the sun on a 111-degree day in Phoenix (which it is outside presently). Yeah, social media is a necessary evil, eh, not so evil, when it comes to tracking people down; it helps, and it has really become an asset for cops, but man, the shit you have to weed through can pretty much knock your brain out of commission. Really numbing, all the minutiae people care about. And the pets! Jesus, the pets! He's got nothing against animals, but come on, do you really, really think your cat can lip synch the words to "Dancing Queen?" Or should? Really?

He can't put it off any longer. He pushes himself from his desk, and it's out into the oven of Phoenix. Midday, no less. Preston joins him for the drive out to The Cliffs Resort and Spa. It's far north in Scottsdale, abutting Thompson peak. But it might as well be anywhere. With its sun-splashed paint job, its tile roof, the palm trees and brick thoroughfares, the place looks cut from the very same cookie mold as so many other resorts in the valley. There are fountains everywhere cascading over Mexican tile and sculpture, as if water were as plentiful here as zinc oxide. Handsome and stately palms line the driveway to the check-in lobby and valet where Ferraris and Maseratis and one social-climbing BMW wait for their owners. At the front desk, they're asked to wait for a hotel manager. Mills observes the guests and members come and go. It's the low season, but judging by the business suits, capitalism can take the heat. Lots of tans and jewelry. A woman approaches. "I'm Nicole Harper," she says. "I hear you've been asking about an employee."

"Former employee," Mills tells her. "Bennett Canning."

"Right. Mr. Canning no longer works here."

Mills introduces himself, then Preston. She seems disinterested to know them. Her eyes and the tightness of her face suggest she's already onto the next meeting in Outlook, as if she's about to charge into a conference room and cut ten percent of the staff.

"Care to tell us the circumstances of his departure from the Cliffs?" Mills ask her.

"I'm sure you know that's confidential."

"Sorry. We thought you'd might want to cooperate with the law."

She smile-frowns and clasps her hands in front of her waist. "All I can say is that Mr. Canning's work ethic was not compatible with our policies and priorities here at the Cliffs."

"Can you give us an example, or three?" Preston asks.

"No," she says, batting her eyelashes, her annoyance well-crafted and implied. "I'm not at liberty to do that. If you wish, you can contact our legal team."

"I don't think that will be necessary," Mills tells her. "We'd just like to know more about him. I'm sure we can find some of his former colleagues who might be more forthcoming. Unless, of course, you have some kind of corporate gag order."

"We don't. That's ridiculous."

"What's ridiculous is that we're trying to find out who killed Bennett's mother and you seem unwilling to help us," Preston says.

"Like I said, you're welcome to contact our legal team if you want access to Bennett Canning's employment records." She predicates her thought with a double cough, the suggestive, mocking kind.

"I see where you're coming from," Mills assures her. "We'll be on our way."

"Can I treat you two to lunch?" she asks.

Mills says thanks, but no thanks, and offers the woman a cordial handshake.

Out in the car, the air-conditioning blasting, Mills says, "Let's go find Bennett. He gave us two addresses. What do you think? The Biltmore condo or the house in Arcadia?"

"He has a house in Arcadia?"

"Gus's neighborhood," Mills says. "I don't see Bennett there. I don't know why. But it's too adult. He's a high-rise condo kind of guy. Floor to ceiling windows. Wears his sunglasses inside."

Preston belts out a laugh. "I think you nailed him! To the condos we go."

At the condos, a cluster of midrise buildings of unimaginative steel and glass, they find nothing except for a cheery concierge and cheery foliage in the lobby. And, of course, a fountain, floor to ceiling, sucking even more water from the Colorado River. They take the elevator to the eleventh floor. The hallway smells perfumed. Mills knocks. A woman answers the door, wide-eyed, her mouth agape, as if she's never answered a door in her life. Kind of bunker looking. Agoraphobia lurking on her face. Mills guesses she's in her early twenties. Five-three. Maybe five-four. No makeup. Long, limp blonde hair. Beautiful in her simplicity, striking even. Mills flashes his badge and asks if Bennett Canning's at home.

"No," she says. "He doesn't live here, really."

"Do you know him?" Mills asks.

"I know Bennett," she says. "But he doesn't live here. He lives in Arcadia."

"What's your name, ma'am?" Mills asks her.

"Ashley. Ashley Pepper. Opposite of salt."

Mills doesn't have the heart to tell her that pepper, technically, is not the opposite of anything. Instead, he introduces himself and asks her how she knows Bennett Canning.

"We dated for a while. He got me this place. His parents didn't approve of us living together at his house."

"But you lived together here?" Mills asks.

"No. I told you he lives in Arcadia. That's not to say he didn't spend many nights here. I'm not going to lie."

"So, I take it you're no longer dating?" Preston asks.

She leans into the doorframe. It's only now Mills realizes she's standing there in a camisole and panties. It strikes him, not because of her stage of undress and her lithe physique, but because he hadn't noticed, because she was, ultimately, just another face at another door among the blur of thousands of faces he's seen and thousands of doors he's knocked on.

"Why are you interrogating me?" she asks.

"We're not interrogating you," Mills says. "I'm sorry if we made you feel that way. That wasn't our intention."

"I don't know why we broke up. I just think it wasn't working. And I also think that he's a player. You know, the minute he settles down with you he's already on to someone else."

"Understood," says Preston. "How did you meet?"

"At church."

"Church of Angels Rising?" Preston asks.

"That's the one."

Preston asks if she'd give them her phone number, says he might want to follow up with her later. She recites it and both men enter it into their phones, thanking her. "So sorry to disturb you, ma'am," Preston says.

The Lady of GPS directs them to Bennett Canning's address in Arcadia. This is the swanky part of Arcadia, not Gus's part of Arcadia, which is more Arcadia Light than anything (modest, older homes, with great vegetation but outdated façades, respectable but certainly not luxurious); this part of Arcadia, however, is where money goes to relax against the mountain, Camelback, to be specific, not far from Aunt Phoebe, but not high up there intruding on the beast. This is what Gus Parker calls "the lap of the camel." In the lap sit modern ranch homes behind walls and the occasional gate. Big windows gaze up to the mountain. Slanted roofs at clean angles salute the sun, commemorating the work of Frank Lloyd Wright. Completing the tribute are decks and railings and the tendency for these homes to sort of disappear into the terrain. Except they don't fully disappear. The owners make concessions to their own vanity and make sure the walls aren't too high. What's the point of making all this money if you can't show it off? Sure enough, Bennett Canning's Mercedes, as gleaming as it ever was, sits in the circular driveway at his Arcadia address. Mills can hear movement inside the house after they ring the bell. The movement is distant, but it's there. He rings again. The sound from within comes closer. There are footsteps and then the door swings open, revealing a diminutive woman with dark eyes and a hesitant smile. She's wearing an apron.

"We're here to see Mr. Canning," Mills tells her.

"Mr. Canning? I believe he's still sleeping."

Mills looks at his watch. Twelve-forty-five.

"And you are?" Mills asks her.

"Juanita. I'm Mr. Canning's housekeeper."

He flashes his badge and she blanches. He identifies himself, mentions Preston.

"I see," she whispers. "Well, I'm making his breakfast. I was planning on waking him soon."

"Could you wake him now?"

"Yes, of course," she says. She bows her head. "Please wait here."

She closes the door and Mills turns to Preston and says, "Must be nice to sleep past noon on a weekday."

"Well, his mom did just croak," Preston reminds him, to which Mills responds with a shrug.

They wait a while. A while longer than Mills would have expected. It's not such a large house. How long can it take to get someone out of bed? When Bennett Canning appears in the doorway, Mills gets his answer. It could take a long time to drag this deadbeat scarecrow from slumber and bring him back to life. Black circles surround his eyes like bruises. His hair is straw and matted. The insignia of sleep stretches across his face in the form of sheet and pillow lines. His lips are chapped. His breath is atrocious when he opens his mouth and says, "What are you doing here so early?"

Mills can't help himself. He laughs. "Seriously, Bennett. It's past noon."

"Thought you might be out job hunting," Preston says.

The guy drops his head to his chest, rolls it from one shoulder to another, and blows out another torrent of sewer breath. "You'd expect me to be looking for a job at a time like this? I mean cut me some slack."

"No, that's not what we'd expect," Mills assures him, fully aware that this overindulged scarecrow has been given a lifetime of slack. "We need to follow up on something, Bennett. May we come in?"

Bennett leads them in and asks them to wait in the sunken living room, a square of chrome, glass, and leather befitting a gigolo. It's all image for Bennett Canning, an aspiring *GQ*er, who obviously uses this room itself as part of his seduction. But today he's not seducing anyone; he smells like he hasn't showered since last summer. "You mind if I clean up a bit? It'll only take me a minute."

Mills suspects it will take longer than a minute for the scarecrow to transform himself into the Mercedes-driving, tennis-pro ladies' man, but he says, "Fine."

The magazines under the coffee table: *Men's Journal, Architectural Digest, Town & Country, Condé Nast Traveler*, and, aha, *GQ*. The art on the walls is big and abstract, the kind that Mills has seen in museums but doesn't understand. What is it about a small purple circle on a big white canvas that makes this thing art? Or the one where the painter apparently tripped over her can of paint and decided the accident, like colorful blood spatter, was a masterpiece?

The housekeeper reappears and asks if the men would like some iced tea, maybe, or even a cocktail. The men decline. Bennett returns. He's sprayed down his hair with something and he's slicked it back. His tight t-shirt, emblazoned with an image from *The Walking Dead* (so appropriate, but probably lost on Bennett Canning), shows off his trim waist and bulging pecs and biceps. "Rough night?" Preston asks him.

"No. I'm mourning. Remember?"

"So, you haven't left the house?" Mills asks.

"I didn't say that," Bennett replies, taking a seat on a slender leather recliner. "Why don't you tell me why you're here?"

"I've been calling and texting you," Mills says. "But you never replied. So I had no choice but to show up."

The guy nods but says nothing.

"We're here to follow up on a few things," Mills tells him. "First, the jewels."

"I told you. I took them," Bennett says. "I couldn't just leave them in the house with all your people picking over her stuff like it was some kind of garage sale."

"That's what we do," Preston says. "We pick over stuff. It's called a homicide investigation, young man."

Bennett leans forward, shaking his head. He utters a laugh, then says, "Rule number one, don't condescend to me. OK?"

Mills leans forward as well to neutralize the space and says, "As far as the investigation into your mother's death goes, my friend, we make the rules. Now why don't you tell us where the jewels are?"

"In a safe deposit box," he says with a scoff.

"You're going to need to give us access so we can take appropriate inventory," Mills says.

Bennett Canning laughs again. "What? You think I'm selling them? How could you be so cold?" Then he sniffles, like he's on the edge of tears, and clears his throat. Mills can't tell whether he's witnessing bullshit artistry as it unfolds, or whether the kid is just in over his slicked-back head. "Those jewels were her treasures! Our treasures! Part of the family fortune. I couldn't just leave them there. I wasn't so worried about your people pocketing a brooch or two as I was scared that someone would break into the house and steal everything . . ."

"Break into the house?" Preston asks.

"Everyone knows she's dead," Bennett says. "And any criminal with half a brain has to know that the house might be unoccupied and full of valuables. I mean, come on, think about it from my perspective. You can't say this wouldn't have occurred to you."

Mills looks at him. He says nothing, but he just looks at the guy who's sitting here in the lap of his parents' luxury, his whole fucking house a designer man cave, uttering lamentations about brooches and treasures and fortunes. It's a fucking soap opera. He shifts his gaze away from Bennett Canning and toward the built-in bookcases across the room that house macho novels of espionage and shadow governments. Big, thick, bestselling thrillers of international intrigue. Not a classic among the collection. Without looking at Bennett, Mills says, "Your mother has some very valuable books in her library. Why didn't you take them?"

"Like what?"

"Leather bound editions of the classics, some first editions. And there's at least two shelves of ancient texts behind glass. What about those?"

"Yeah, she said she had some expensive books. You know, collectibles, I guess. But they're not my thing. And who would steal books, anyway?"

Mills laughs. "You're right. Who would steal books? Nobody reads anymore," he says, mocking the kid. "You disturbed a crime scene."

"So arrest me," Bennett says, folding his arms across his chest.

"Don't tempt me," Mills says. He sees a sixteen-year-old Trevor in this twenty-nine-year-old asswipe. Apparently, money stunts your growth.

Preston gets up, walks to the bookcases, removes a book, and turns back. He's holding *Tinker, Tailor, Soldier, Spy*, which, if asked, Mills would concede is a classic in its own right. "You read this?" Preston asks Bennett. "You like Le Carré?"

"I don't know," Bennett says with a shrug.

"You don't know if you read it?" Mills asks. "Le Carré is a master!"

"Or is this whole book collection just an image thing for you?" Preston persists.

"I answered your questions about the jewelry," Bennett says. "My book collection is irrelevant. If you have any more questions you can talk to my attorney. His name is Darren Styles, in Central Phoenix."

The guy stands up, as if he's prompting them to leave, but Mills stays planted on the couch. Preston returns to the couch and sits as well. You work with someone long enough, you learn how to choreograph on the fly, and this choreography seems to infuriate Bennett Canning, who throws his arms out wide and cups the air. His face turns a raging crimson. "I said you could call my lawyer if you have any more questions." His voice is crisp, imploring.

The men say nothing. They stare at him.

"What the fuck do you want from me?"

The men look at each other, then at him again. But they remain silent.

"Oh my God," Bennett cries. "Don't I have the right to ask you to leave?"

"Please sit down, Bennett," Mills says finally. "Please. We won't be a bother much longer. I promise."

Bennett complies, returns to his recliner. "Just tell me what you want."

"Look," Preston says. "We're here to help. We know it doesn't seem that way but, ultimately, we're the best friends you can have right now."

Bennett scoffs.

"I'm serious," Preston insists. "We're going to nail whoever did this to your mother. That's our job. Sure, we're intrusive, and we're pests. We know that. But you want us to be intrusive and you want us to be pests, because that's the only way we're going to bring the killer or killers to justice."

"Wait," the kid says. "You think there could be more than one killer?"

"I was speaking rhetorically," Preston says. "Anything's possible."

Bennett exhales an enormous sigh, as if, maybe, he's reconciled to the cops being in his face.

"What was your relationship with your mother like?" Mills asks him.

The guy shrugs and says, "I don't know. What do you mean?"

"Were you close?" Mills asks.

"I guess . . . I mean, she was a good woman and a good mother and obviously," he says, waving his hands around, "very generous."

"Obviously," Mills says. "Did you know she left everything to the church?"

Bennett hesitates. He fidgets. Then he curls his lip and says, "How did you know that?"

Mills explains that his team has started combing through Viveca's computer, that they found the will.

"For real?" Bennett asks, a warble of doubt in his throat. "I mean, it was a running joke in the family, but . . . are you sure?"

"As sure as the will itself," Mills tells him.

"It may not be her final will," Bennett says. "That's definitely something you should talk to the lawyer about."

"We plan to," Preston assures him.

The kid puts his head in his hands. And Mills allows him the gathering of grief and confusion, a particularly daunting mix of emotions. There might even be remorse. Mills can't be sure. There's a part of Bennett Canning that always remains aloof, as if the detachment is a learned skill, something to master. But these silences are important. They're always important. Sometimes they yield nothing, but oftentimes they drag up a wide net of details. Silence makes some people nervous. Nervous is good. Nervous people talk.

Bennett, however, is not talking. He's breathing heavy, but he's not saying a word. Mills can hear the guy's sniffling again and suspects that, now, the grief is authentic, not for show. "So you were unaware that your mother had left her money to the church?" he asks.

Bennett doesn't look up. But he shakes his head. "I was not aware," he says.

"Does this upset you?" Preston asks.

"What do you think?" Finally, Bennett shows his face. "It was her choice to do what she wanted with the money, but I don't know why she wouldn't take care of my sister and me. It's confusing."

"I'm sure it is," Mills tells him. "Do you think she was brainwashed?"

"Huh? Brainwashed?"

"Yeah. By someone at the church? Or threatened? It's a rather large bequest," Mills says.

The kid nods absently. Then he asks, "How much do you know about the church?"

"Only what we've read in the paper, seen on TV," Mills says. "Some people call it a cult."

Bennett laughs. It's a big belly laugh followed by a "sheesh!"

"What's so funny?" Preston asks him.

"The whole cult thing. I've been a member of the church all my life, guys. It's not a cult," he says. "Yes, we've all heard the whispers around town and such, but the truth is we're just private people worshipping in a private, humble way."

Now Mills is close to a belly laugh and a "sheesh!" but he tightens his core and restrains himself. "Yeah, well, with a cathedral that ginormous, it's hard for a megachurch to stay humble. Don't you think?"

"We attract many people to our faith," he says, his voice cool, the rest of him aloof again. "We've grown to accommodate the faithful."

"When you say 'we,' are you suggesting you have some kind of leadership role in the church?" Preston asks.

"No," he replies. "It's a form of speech. My mom was on the board of directors for many years. She would say 'we' all the time."

"What role do you play in the church?" Preston persists.

"I hope to be an elder someday. But I'm really not at liberty to talk about church business. The Church of Angels Rising rarely does interviews."

Mills clears his throat. "This isn't an interview, Bennett. This is an investigation."

"Then maybe you should talk to Gleason Norwood."

"We did," Mills tells him.

"You did?"

"Yes," Mills replies. "You sound surprised."

"You think maybe he should have warned you?" Preston asks.

"Warned me? What do you mean?"

"Never mind," Preston tells him. "It does strike me odd because from what we know of your mother, she doesn't seem to fit the profile of a cult member . . ."

Bennett stands again, abruptly. "It's not a cult. I don't like the implication, gentlemen. In fact, it was never her idea to join the church. All my life I was told it was my father's plan. Or rather, demand. He's the one who brought us to the church and insisted we worship there. My dad was kind of a nutcase, but not my mother."

"A nutcase with a brain for making money," Mills says, getting up.

"A lot of wealthy, powerful people are psychopaths," Bennett says.

"We're aware," Preston tells him, then rises as well.

As the men drift to the front door, Mills turns to the young scion-of-nothing and says, "One more question, Bennett. Were your parents separated before your father's death?"

"No. Why do you ask?"

"Just curious. That's all. I wasn't sure what kind of stress might have led to his heart attack."

"I have no idea. I didn't ask questions. I'm not even sure it was stress."

"Thanks for your time," Mills says.

Bennett Canning says nothing. He shakes his head, disgusted, lips tightening and curling inward. A stray wad of slicked hair comes loose and dangles over his forehead. His posture collapses. The kid's on the verge of tears. He'll completely buckle once the door is closed. That's a privacy Mills can afford him. And so he ushers Preston out quickly, giving Bennett the right to grieve in his own space. Besides, Mills has to make a call.

He's in the car Googling "Darren Styles, Attorney, Phoenix," when his phone rings. It's Gus Parker.

"Gus Parker!"

"Hey, Alex."

"How the fuck are you?"

"I'm fine."

"We're in your neighborhood! You must be psychic!"

Gus laughs. "Yeah, that's what they tell me."

Mills lowers his shades and cranks the A/C. "Hey, I'm sorry we couldn't make it to Seattle for the funeral, man."

"I told you it wasn't necessary, Alex."

"Yeah, I know. But still," Mills says as clumsy as a shy date. "Hey, you free for dinner tonight?"

"I get off work at 5:30."

"Rosita's Place? 6:30?"

"Sure," Gus says. "But this isn't just a social call. I have some business to discuss."

"Oh?"

"Yeah. I have someone who wants to meet you."

"I'm happily married," Mills says, fawning over his own humor.

"Right. Never seen a happier couple," Gus tells him. "But this isn't a hookup, dude. Just someone who might know something about an investigation you're working on."

"I'm intrigued," Mills admits. "The Viveca Canning case?"

Gus replies affirmatively.

"Intrigued, Dr. Psycho, but I got some important calls to make now," Mills tells him. "Can we pick this up at Rosita's?"

"Sure," Gus says. "See ya' later."

As soon as Mills is off the phone, Preston hands him his tablet with the home page of Styles, Styles, Styles, and Berman loaded on the screen. Mills calls, can't reach any of the Styleses, or the Berman, for that matter, so he leaves a message for Darren Styles with a polite receptionist who says she'll do her very best (not just her best) to get Mr. Styles the message by the end of the day.

13

They know Gus by name here. All the waitresses in their puffed out uniforms, gliding by with mountains of food balanced on their shoulders, all of them bend in and smile, which feels like a kiss, feels like an embrace, feels like love, their faces mothering and accommodating. "Hello!" one cries, bumping the table. "Nice to see you again, Gus. How *are* you, my friend?"

"Just fine."

Another approaches. "Oh, *hijo*, you're back! You good, baby?"

"Very good. Thanks."

The air carries the crispy fried grease right to his nose. Delicious. But he knows better. But still, delicious. He recognizes all of them, the waitresses, they've been here forever, which might explain why this place feels like someone's house, not a restaurant, and why from the roadside it looks like a dive in a dive neighborhood, but inside it's your Aunt Rosita's kitchen. He admires the woodwork of the tables and chairs. Thick, pale carvings, built for a hearty meal.

"Gusto! My baby! You alone?" It's Irena, a sixty-something-year-old original with a wide face and huge oval eyes. Almost wrinkle free, her golden skin sheens from a busy night. Like most of the other servers, she wears her hair pulled back. She speaks in what Gus calls a Mexicali accent. A little Mexico, a little Southern California. A border town voice. Not uncommon in the Southwest.

"No, I'm expecting two others."

She strokes his shoulder. "Your detective friend, huh?"

"Yes."

"Good. Good. You want your margarita."

"Sure," he says, and just then he sees Alex and Kelly passing by the front window. In a moment, they're in the lobby and Gus waves them over. He gets up and gives Alex a brotherly hug. Kelly kisses him hard on the cheek.

"We've missed you," she says.

"Likewise," he tells her. They all sit and Gus looks at his detective friend and sees that Alex is looking good. Happy, healthy, busy, devoted. There's something about this couple, Gus thinks. Their admiration for each other is obvious; they talk about it all the time. They're demonstrative. But there's something that doesn't say a word, that doesn't have a gesture, which simply resides between them. It's nothing new. It's a vibe Gus gets when he's with them. Maybe it's an aura-for-two he sees. But he senses a powerful, completely magnetic devotion between them.

Irena returns with his drink. Alex and Kelly order the same for themselves.

"I'm enlisting you on the Viveca Canning case," Alex tells him. "Unofficially."

"As opposed to . . ."

"You just need to stay under the radar," Mills explains. "You've impressed my sergeant. He thinks you're kind of amazing and kind of crazy, which is pretty much what everyone thinks, especially when you get it right. Are you available, say, Monday morning?"

Gus nods. "As you know, I prefer to fly under the radar, so, yeah, I'm happy to help, so long as you don't mention me in your interviews with the press."

"I hope to hell not to be doing interviews," Alex tells him. "You know I avoid the media like the plague."

"Then I don't suppose you'll be too thrilled with the news I bring tonight."

The rest of the margaritas arrive, and they all hoist for a toast and clink. "Here's to old friends, new cases, and a sergeant who pretty much lets me do what I want," says Alex.

They order their dinner. As soon as Irena retreats into the kitchen,

Gus leans forward, plants urgency in his eyes. "I told you I have someone who wants to meet you," he says. "Someone who might have information on the case. She's a news reporter."

Alex shakes his head and scowls. "You're right. I'm not thrilled."

"She's a TV reporter."

"Even worse."

"No," Gus says more sternly than he had intended, "it's not like that. She's for real. None of that beauty queen nonsense. I got a very good vibe from her."

"What kind of vibe?" Alex asks him.

"Solid. Truth. And, I don't know, some kind of mystery."

"You have *me* intrigued," Kelly says.

The dinner arrives with a bit of fanfare thanks to the sizzle of Alex's fajitas. They dig in, not a fried meal between them. Spanish music plays faintly. Noisy families indulge all around them, most of them immersed in boisterous Spanish conversation. A few of the children shriek, but they're gorgeous to Gus, those eyes, those smiles. He wouldn't admit it here, maybe only to Billie, but the children break his heart.

"I don't know why you never adopted," Kelly says.

"Is it that obvious?" Gus asks, feeling his cheeks blush.

"Yeah," Kelly replies. "Anytime I see you around children."

"Even now—" Alex says.

"Even now," Kelly interrupts. "Years after we learned about your sperm count."

Gus turns to Alex and, at the very moment the music stops playing, says, "She knows about my sperm count?"

Then, looking up and surveying the room, Gus sees the entire restaurant staring back at him.

Kelly squeezes his knee.

Alex instantly erupts in a heap of laughter. He's clutching his stomach. There are tears in his eyes. He won't stop laughing.

"I think I should go," Gus whispers.

Kelly pulls him close, her arm nudging his shoulder. "Oh, I am so sorry, Gus. I'm so sorry. I mean, we tell each other everything, Alex and I, always have. I had no idea it was still a fresh wound for you. I would never—"

"I wouldn't call it a fresh wound."

The music resumes.

"Great timing," Gus says.

"Finish your dinner," Kelly tells him. "You're not going anywhere. You think these people never heard of, you know, your issue before. It's a fact of life."

"OK," Gus says. "OK. Maybe we should change the subject."

Kelly releases him with a tap on the shoulder. "That's my boy. Go on tell us about this reporter who has you so ensnared . . ."

"Oh come on. Please don't," Alex begs.

"I don't know why you're always so hostile toward the media," Gus tells him. "Your job is not much more popular than theirs. You've said so yourself."

"I know. But a lot of them like to pretend they're detectives. It just gets under my skin."

"But she's not looking for information from you," Gus says. "I think she's looking to give you information."

"What kind of information?" Alex asks.

"I guess she has sources who are telling her stuff about your victim. They might know something about who murdered her or why she was murdered."

"She said that? Your reporter friend?"

"In so many words she said that. And she's not my friend. She's a client."

"Right," Alex says. "A client. I'll accept any and all leads," he says with a smile.

"So I can give her your number?"

Alex is attacking his plate now, gobbling up the food like it's the last carcass on earth. In midchew he says, "Yuh, sure," without looking up, without slowing down.

While Alex plunders the table, Gus turns to Kelly and says, "You look cold."

"In this weather? With my hormones? I'm sweating."

"Oh."

"Why?"

"I don't know. I sensed a chill in you. Or a chilly draft inside you."

Gus's signals are getting crossed. He can tell. Vibes everywhere. The room expands. He hears a siren. Then an ambulance comes wailing down the street, its whirling lights reflecting in the restaurant window. Rings of blue and red spin around the room. "No, I'm good," Kelly says. "How are things with Billie?"

"Fine," he says, swallowing another bite of dinner. "Just saw her on the way back to Phoenix. She's working on a new album. Or what she thinks will become an album. The music industry has changed so much."

"I bet."

"But she's a prolific writer, you know. I don't think retirement is even a possibility for her."

"And the long-distance thing?" Kelly asks. "That's working okay?"

He shrugs. "I guess. It's not ideal. But it works for us right now."

And then he shakes his head because the truth is he doesn't know. And he doesn't know when he's going to know. And as long as he can stay distracted, then, maybe this thing will figure itself out. To that end, he's thinking about taking up knitting, or BASE jumping. He scoops up another forkful of the enchilada verde and right then, right as he takes a bite, he feels the G-force of a jumbo jet going down. The bottom is falling out. The plane tilts, it's almost vertical, descending now at hysterical speed. He's spinning. Nobody can see him. And he can see no one as he fully disappears into the darkness of a heavy sea.

14

The weekend flew by, as weekends do when you most need them to idle. They did finally make good on Kelly's promise to have constant, crazy sex, a delayed gratification because Kelly had not been up to the activity after trial proceedings all week, as it turns out. And as it turns out the sex was not exactly crazy; it was a bit frantic, but not crazy. It was good, but Kelly was apologetic. "I'm sorry if I'm not that into it," she said. And his dick immediately took it personally. It had to be him, he was certain of it. His dick has a fragile ego. They were athletic in their lovemaking but not Olympians. She tired out quickly. She seemed pleased, but not devastated by her orgasm. They kissed for quite a while afterward. Which made up for everything. Because when Mills kisses his wife, really kisses her, he's thankful for his entire life. It's like a drug. It's the best high in the world.

They made pancakes.

And then the weekend was over.

Detective Ken Preston comes in Monday morning sporting a face wide with satisfaction. Kind of like the face of somebody who'd spent the weekend, euphemistically, as an Olympian. But no, Preston spent the weekend researching the Church of Angels Rising.

"They try to quash all press," Preston says, taking a seat in Mills's office. "But the few stories that get out are not flattering."

"So, are the rumors true? Is it a cult?"

Preston takes a sip of coffee, tilts his head back and forth, and says, "Seems to be. The experts on cults think so. *Time* magazine did an article on the church about five years ago. You should read it. Makes the church look like a corporate cult."

"A corporate cult?"

"They have a bizarre fee structure for membership. They intimidate people into giving more and more money after they join. It's major intimidation, sometimes physical, if the accounts in the article are to be believed. And they have crazy policies regarding people who leave the church."

"How so?"

"Well, we've already heard they force families to erase any loved ones who leave the church. They can have no contact whatsoever. In essence, the person who leaves is no longer related. They're not just banished, it's like they never existed."

"Jesus . . . that's fucked up," Mills says, bringing a coffee cup to his mouth.

"Speaking of Jesus, the church has been sued twice by the federal government over its tax-exempt status. The government says the Church of Angels is not a true religion."

"Hmm. That's kind of dicey. Who's to say what a true religion is?"

"When it comes to taxes, the government."

Mills supposes he's right.

"I'll send you the articles," Preston tells him. "I'm not sure how relevant they are to the case, but since Viveca left all that money to the church, I thought it was appropriate to take a look."

Mills gives an emphatic nod and says, "Absolutely. Thanks for this, Ken."

"Did somebody say money?"

It's a jaunty Morton Myers standing in the doorway. He's all nervous energy and smiles, as if he's ingested more caffeine than Preston and Mills combined.

"Yes, Morty," Mills replies. "We were just talking about Viveca Canning's church."

"Well, would you like to know a little more about Viveca Canning's money?"

Mills gives him a smile, waves him in. "Pull up a chair, Detective. And spill it!"

In spilling it, Myers describes how Viveca Canning had with-drawn a huge sum of money from some of her accounts and transferred it to a real estate holding company in French Polynesia. "I did a Google search for the company," he says. "It's in the middle of nowhere. But it looks like paradise."

"French Polynesia," Preston says. "I wonder why. Could the church have property there?"

"How much money?" Mills asks.

"Almost three million dollars."

"That's a drop in the bucket," Mills says, "if you consider the value of her entire estate."

"True," Preston says. "But who has three million dollars in a bank account?"

Myers pulls his chair closer. "She withdrew money from a few dif-ferent accounts to come up with that amount. And it looks like she took most of it from some kind of trust."

"OK," Mills says, "let's not get too much into the weeds with this. Morty, I want you to dig a little deeper into the real estate company, but I also need you to stay on top of every, and I mean every, other detail forensics pulls from her computers. You need to go through every file, and if you need help, I'll get you help. I'm very curious about that church. Anything on those computers about the church or church business needs to be flagged."

"Got it," Myers says with a bounce from his chair. "We'll talk later."

As he exits, Preston turns back to Mills and says, "Our little boy is growing up."

"He's pushing forty. 'Bout time."

Mills's computer dings three times, a perfect two-second interval between each ding.

"It's me," Preston says. "Just sent you the articles from my phone. Enjoy! I'll catch up with you later."

Mills gives him a wave, but doesn't look up. He opens the first file.

I DIDN'T LEAVE THE CHURCH, I ESCAPED
A College Student Tells All about the
Church of Angels Rising

Celia Drake
Metro Correspondent

Twenty-year-old Jeremy Withers, dressed in baggy jeans and a Lakers sweatshirt, looks like any other college student making his way across the UCLA campus. To hear Jeremy tell it, however, his story is far from typical for a college senior.

"I can't believe I made it this far," he said on a sunny morning outside the Student Union. "I went from third grade into a cult. I never saw a real schoolteacher again. And then at sixteen, I realized what was happening. I risked my life and escaped."

Jeremy is one of very few people who've left the controversial Church of Angels Rising to come forward and share his story publicly. It's a story filled with terrifying allegations of abuse and intimidation, of power run amok, of a church leadership that worships money, and, perhaps most disturbing, of people who disappear.

"This is a business for the Norwood family," Withers alleged. "It's not a church. Gleason Norwood thinks of himself as a ruthless CEO. And he acts like one. Instead of layoffs, there are places people are sent to for remediation."

While the LA Monitor has not been able to corroborate Withers's allegations, the college student spoke about a work camp in Sedona, Arizona for children who are raised in the church where corporal punishment is a daily activity. He said the so-called camp was also a place where the church would send undesirables.

"Anybody who threatened the church in any way, in speech, in writing, or behavior would be sent to Sedona,"

Withers said. "And you might think Sedona is a beautiful place to be imprisoned, but the undesirables hardly ever see the light of day. Some of them just simply disappear. Nobody knows where they end up."

The camp, according to Withers, served as a home for up to 100 children at a time and a detention center for up to 50 adults.

A spokesperson for the Arizona Department of Family and Children would not comment for this story, declining to say whether it has ever investigated accusations of abuse against the so-called camp in Sedona . . .

His phone rings, startling him for a second.

It's Gus Parker. "Hey man, I'm ready."

"Oh, right, yes . . ."

"Is this a bad time?" the psychic asks.

His eyes still fixed on the screen, he hesitates a moment, then says, "No. No, I'm good. You ready?"

"Just said I was. I'm on my way. See you there."

Mills hangs up. He says, "See you there" to the empty room in front of him. He's in somewhat of a trance, thinking but not thinking, seeing but not seeing, a detective's miasma of suspicion and doubt. Then he downloads the article and logs off the computer.

The weather guy on KPHO said the thermometer would hit 117 degrees today. He would not be made a liar. Gus can feel the city simmer all around him; coils of heat rise from the pavement, and waves of it broil in the distance like apparitions. Somewhere someone is frying an egg on the sidewalk just because. There has to be some-place cooler to escape to. Like the Sahara. But last he heard flights are delayed at Sky Harbor because the temperature has reached the point where it's too hot for planes to safely take off. It's days like today, dusty and brown, when Gus remembers how barren the desert is. The mountains lose their reddish hue to a jaundiced version of themselves. Gone are the hikers. Hiking would be suicide.

He arrives before Alex. The guards at Copper Palace won't let him in. "You'll have to wait for the detective," one of them says, pointing to a small parking area. "Just pull in there."

Gus complies and glides into a space that sits just below a mesquite tree, which affords slices of shade. He studies the entrance to the enclave of mansions and wonders how people can live like this. It's all too much with the constant indulgences and the constant pressure to keep up. There's no Zen whatsoever for the people here (he gets a potent vibe about this right now), save for the spa visits and the yoga studios and the meditation classes that don't count if you don't strip your soul. You have to strip your soul. These people don't strip their souls for anything but their profit margins and their Maseratis. He's intimately aware of wealth because of Billie. How could he not be? She immerses him in luxury. Her rock 'n' roll stardom has been paved in gold. But there's a difference. She's an artist. She's a songwriter. She's in the music industry (and he's come to know this about the core of her being) because of the music, not because of the money. She's tried to explain it to him so many different ways, but he's told her no explanation is needed. He gets it. She's stripping her soul for her muse and nothing else. She doesn't live like these people. She doesn't care what the neighbors think. She doesn't care about the external stuff. She lives in a mansion, but her mansion is not her home; it's her house. Her music is her home.

A rap at the window, and a strong one at that.

"Hey, Gus! Follow me in."

It's Alex. Gus gives him a nod and waits for the gate to open.

On the way to the front door, Alex grabs Gus by the elbow and says, "Any vibe whatsoever, speak up. No vibe is too small."

"So, in other words, you have no leads at all."

Alex play punches him in the arm. "That's not what I said."

"Sorry. That was my gut, not my vibe," Gus says.

"Whatever it was, forget it. We have some leads, but they're preliminary."

They enter and Alex leads him to a room.

"Don't say a word. Don't influence me."

"I know how it works, buddy," Alex says. "So, just stand here for a minute. See what you can gather. Don't touch anything."

Alex drifts into a hallway. Gus admires the room. It's a library, one of those stately ones with the leather-bound books and floor-to-ceiling shelving. There's even a ladder that hangs from the top shelves and glides the length of the room. Gus wonders if the woman of the house ever used this library, ever sat in here ensconced in the hearty leather furniture, the fireplace raging, and read a book. Or whether this was just another trapping of wealth on the Copper Palace Parade of Homes. His eyes are drawn to a small writing desk in the corner. He inspects it more closely, gazing over the top. Under a sheet of glass, one of those gilded old-world maps covers the entire desk. He navigates there and finds only the pretense of a wealthy family, nothing of merit in their conceit of globetrotting. Likely, the gold is nothing more than ink. And yet, he's pulled back, beckoned, summoned to the Pacific Ocean on the map. He stares at the wide expanse of sea, depicted here with artistic ripples, with lines suggesting longitude and latitude, and with renditions of medieval ships exploring. His eyes bore in and slip beyond the creamy parchment, underneath where the sea is swelling, and it's night, a purple night, and the moon is but a sliver and the stars have turned their backs, and the only light, the only steady light is the one that looks, at first, like a shooting star, the way it seems to soar across the sky and then plummet to the horizon. It's a bright light coming at him, at a seventy-five degree angle, rushing at him, really, growing larger and larger and more determined in its path, like the moon's been pushed from its axis, a plunging moon; then Gus can see the wings, and the tail, falling so fast, so instantly fast, it's over in seconds. The jet enters the water and disappears without making a sound.

"Jesus," Gus mutters.

"What is it?" Alex is back. "See anything?"

"I've been having a reoccurring vision. But it started before I knew anything about this case, so, no, I don't think I have anything relevant yet."

"Come with me."

Alex leads him down the hallway and around the corner to a living room area, or some kind of sitting room. Alex tells him to stand at the perimeter. "I can't let you in the room, so just hang back and see what you get. The victim's body was found here."

"By whom?" Gus asks.

"By the maid."

"It's always the maid," Gus says with a laugh.

Nothing from Alex.

"No crime scene humor today?" Gus asks him.

The man just winces and says, "Sorry. I'm just really distracted. The usual pressure and everything."

"Don't worry, Alex. You guys will be fine."

Alex looks at him curiously. "What is that supposed to mean?"

"I'm not sure myself. I just said it because it came to me."

"Out of nowhere?"

"Out of nowhere."

The vibe in here is prickly, if not downright hostile. Gus doesn't understand so he tries to psychically disassociate. He watches Alex turn away to another side of the house. Then Gus turns back to the room. Despite the furniture and despite the paintings on the walls, the room is emptier than empty. It's emptier than death. There is nothing here but an echo of life, and even the echo is fading into the woodwork. And yet he feels her. He feels the stirring of Viveca Canning. Gus closes his eyes and he can see the victim's face, her charitable smile, and her coral-colored lipstick. She wears eyeliner, too, or mascara—he's never sure which is which—but there's also color around her eyes, a kind of frosty green. Eye shadow. His eyes remain closed, but his feet begin to move. His steps are tentative as he follows the presence of

Viveca Canning. He doesn't see ghosts, doesn't talk to dead people, but he never intuits more deeply than when his footsteps intersect with the path of a spirit. It just happens. She may only be present in a vision, but because she occupied this room in life and in death, she's here. And so he follows her, his arm outstretched like a blind person, just in case. She's wearing chiffon. They must be at a party. A big festive gathering. A blur of celebrants fills the room. The music swings and the crowd begins to dance, their laughter soaring to the ceilings. But she stops now, not quite at the precipice of the party. She stares at a wall. Ignoring the clamor around her, she stands there dutifully and stares. She clenches her fists, her white-gloved fists, in front of her. Her whole body trembles, supplicating as it is to something holy before her eyes. She turns to Gus, points to the wall, and waits for Gus to acknowledge the masterpiece. Before he can, she's gone. He sees her rush to her husband's side, knocking a drink from the man's hand, the glass shattering on the floor. The shards go flying, like bullets, and there's blood everywhere. People gasp, the music stops, everything is quiet except the trickle of death.

Gus's eyes bolt open, as if from a fever dream.

"What's up?" Alex is standing there. "Didn't want to bother you. Looked like you were in one of your trances."

"Yep. I was getting a visual."

Mills smiles, satisfied. He likes when Gus performs. Gus knows this. Gus used to feel a bit like one ring of a three-ring circus, but he doesn't anymore. He welcomes the encouragement. "You found an interesting place to stop," Mills tells him. "But I told you not to enter the room."

"I couldn't help it. I had my eyes closed. Indulge me, dude."

"Consider yourself indulged. Dude."

Gus takes it in. He's in front of a blank wall, or at least a blank part of the wall, an artistic impasse in the collection. The paintings on either side witnessed everything but say nothing. But there was a crime. A very simple crime. He points to the wall and says, "Stolen."

"Jeez, Gus, your instincts are superhuman today."

Gus smirks. "No need to be a dick, dick. Just confirming. Can I touch the wall?"

"If you must, put on some gloves," Alex tells him. "The place has already been processed for prints, but you never know."

"I always worry the latex will get in the way of a vibe, like filter stuff out."

"Has it ever?"

Gus's uncertainty brings a twist to his mouth. "That's hard to know if I'm always wearing the gloves. But I bet my clues would be more consequential. Maybe they'd add up faster to the truth. I don't know. It's not an exact science."

"It's not a science," Mills says. "Here. Put on the gloves."

Without another word, Gus takes the latex gloves from Alex and pulls them on his hands. He stretches and curls his fingers for a snug fit. Then he puts his hand on the wall, runs it the length and width of the absent painting's outline; it's an area of trespass, a place of abduction, this square of wall that has barely seen the light. The square is a dark, squinting anomaly. He can see the artist squinting in his studio. The sun enters from above and the artist must shift his easel to get the light out of his eyes. The artist is a master, a fiend, a brilliant interpreter. He lives his life in the abstract. The artist dominates Gus's vibe; what Gus cannot see, cannot feel, is the person or persons who came to this wall with malevolent hands. *Damn.* There is something here. But it's not the painting. It's not the subject of the painting. It's not the artist who matters. The vibe is deductive, not inductive.

"The painting is pivotal," Gus says.

"Another superhuman instinct. Is that all you're getting?"

"Sorry to disappoint you, man. Could I spend the night?"

"What?"

"I bet if I slept here tonight I'd be overrun with visions."

Alex puts his hands on his hips and shakes his head. "What are you smokin' these days, Gus? You can't spend the night here. You probably shouldn't even be here now."

"But—"

"It's not going to happen. As much I'd like to give you the keys, my friend, I can't. And you know it."

Gus steps forward and put his face inches from Alex's and says, "That painting is the key. To the murder and so much more. We have to find it."

Alex leads him out of the house. Crossing the lawn he stops Gus and says, "Obviously we need to find the painting if we want to find our killer. But are you sensing there's more to the painting than that?"

"I know there is."

"Like maybe the painting was purchased on the black market?"

"Something like that."

"Well, it was a gift to Viveca Canning's husband."

"Doesn't matter. Who knows how many times it's changed hands? Maybe there's some symbolism in the painting itself. What was the name of it?"

"It's an untitled Dali."

Gus nods.

"What?" Alex asks him.

"Nothing. But I think the artist in my vision looked a little like Dali."

"You know what Dali looks like?"

Gus scoffs. "Not exactly. But in my mind I conjured up a face that's probably not too far off, I don't know . . . what I'd imagine Dali to look like."

"There could be all kinds of messages in the painting but I don't have time to take an art history class," Alex says.

"One of my clients works at the Heard. Maybe he can help."

Then Alex asks him if he'd be free to go to a memorial tonight for the victim. "Her body won't be there. We still have it. But I bet you'll pick up all kinds of vibes. It's at her church. She was on the board of directors. We're doing a little surveillance."

Gus checks his calendar on his phone, making sure he doesn't have a client and, finding no appointments, he gives Alex half a shrug and says, "Sure."

"Meet me at 6:45 at the C-ARC," Alex tells him. "You need directions?"

He can feel the bulbs of his eyes almost pop. "What?"

"I asked if you needed directions."

"No, no. I thought for a moment you said the C-ARC. You couldn't have said the C-ARC. Could you?"

"I did."

"Jesus."

"Don't know if he'll be there. Somehow I doubt it."

Gus gets in his car, throws a wave in Alex's direction, and peels out. Imagine me, he thinks, at the Church of Angels Rising cathedral! All that effing glass will shatter the minute I walk in. There will be blood everywhere. Just like the party at Viveca Canning's house.

Back at headquarters, Mills is forking his way through a homemade salad when Calvin Cloke from the OME calls. He doesn't stop eating. He and Cal have a talking-while-chewing relationship. Cal tells him that, as suspected, Viveca Canning was shot at close range, that the second bullet, not the first, was the one that killed her. The first entered below her eye and exited behind her ear. But the second bullet killed her instantly. She had alcohol in her system. She wasn't drunk, but she had been drinking. Nothing excessive. She had Premarin in her system, a common menopause treatment that's also used for osteoarthritis and breast cancer. She definitely had arthritis, but no signs of cancer. She was also taking Diclofenac, a nonopioid painkiller, Lyrica, and traces of Valium.

"Lyrica is for nerve pain, and fibromyalgia," Cal says.

"When you say traces of Valium, what does that mean? Like a dose she took a long time ago, or a small dose she took closer to her death?"

"I'd go with the latter," Cal replies. "We still have a few more tests ongoing. I'll be in touch. OK?"

"Sounds good."

"And next time invite me for lunch if you're going to chew in my ear."

With a friendly "eat me," Mills hangs up.

He's no sooner off the phone when it rings again. He's studying his notes: Premarin, Diclofenac, Lyrica, Valium. He puts a circle around Valium, then picks up the call. The caller introduces herself as Aaliyah Jones, a reporter for Channel 4. "I'm calling about the Viveca Canning case. Your sergeant transferred me. I figured it would be best to go through him first so it's all above board."

"I'm not used to reporters being so conscientious," Mills tells her.

"You've been dealing with the wrong reporters."

Her voice is as sharp and clear as a figure skate on ice, or whatever image might cool him off on a 117-degree day. "I don't deal with reporters, Ms. Jones. That's why we have public information officers. You should know that."

"I do," she assures him. "But I have information that I don't want to go public with. Hence, my fear of the 'P' in the 'PIO.' I've met with Gus Parker. He suggested I contact you."

"I know. He already told me. Look, I'm busy right now. Can you come by tomorrow?"

"Yes."

"And can you give me a hint about what you have?"

A hesitation from her end of the line. All he hears is white noise. The sound of empty. "ma'am?"

"I'm sorry," she says with a fluster. "I can't. I can't give you any hints. I'm afraid someone might be listening in."

"Listening in?"

"Tapping my phone."

"Are you serious?"

"Yes," she says. "It's all about tactics."

He rolls his eyes. "Whose tactics?"

"I can't say any more. I'm sorry."

"Okay," Mills says, elasticizing the word. "You better not be indulging me in some crazy fantasy of yours, Ms. Jones. I don't have time to be led down some half-baked path to nowhere."

"I can assure you I'm not, Detective. I'm not some anonymous tipster. I'm a reporter."

Before he knows it, before he can control it, Mills laughs out loud.

"Maybe you think this is funny, but when you hear what I have to say you won't be laughing."

He closes his eyes and shakes his head, both ashamed and annoyed. At her. At himself. At the heat. At the fucking world. "Hey, I'm sorry. I shouldn't have laughed. But my experiences with reporters have, frankly, sucked. But I'm sorry. Why don't you swing by around four o'clock tomorrow afternoon? Ask for me at the front desk."

She tells him she'll be there. Then she asks if he has a favorite kind of doughnut.

He laughs and hangs up. But touché, Aaliyah Jones. Touché.

A few hours later he races home and shoves dinner down his throat. Kelly comes in as he's scrubbing a pot. "What time is the service?" she asks. She's trudging. She tosses her briefcase on a chair, flings it, really, like a case dismissed.

"The squad is meeting me at 6:45," he says. "I gotta leave in ten minutes. You okay?"

"Define OK."

"Kelly..." He goes to her. He pulls her close. "You look exhausted."

"This trial is a fucking grind."

"I can tell. It's written all over your face." Something has stolen the glimmer from her eyes.

"Thanks, Alex. Not what I needed to hear."

He kisses her cheek. "You know what I mean. You'll always be the most beautiful woman in the world. Past. Present. And future."

She laughs. He's been saying that for years. He laughs too. They stand there, still in the embrace, laughing until Kelly begins to weep. "Oh, Alex . . . I need some time off."

He pulls back, holding her arms tight, consuming her with his eyes and says, "And you will get it. I promise you. As soon as this case is over and your trial is done, we're taking off. OK? Wherever you want to go . . ."

"Right now I'd settle for a spa day at the Phoenician."

"Don't give me any ideas."

She brushes away and he follows her to the bedroom, where he gets changed for the service. "How were the leftovers?" she asks.

"I have no idea. I ate so fast I wasn't paying attention," he tells her. "There's still more in the fridge."

He says goodbye as she's stepping into the shower.

The sun has drifted westward and the valley to the east has turned into a city of gold, as it always does at this hour. The mountains are gilded like masterpieces, a fleeting but reliable beauty complete with the diamonds of waning light shining in the vast windows of those fortunate homes in the foothills. Dusk is an illusion, Mills knows. It paints a deceptive picture. Everything, from those jewels in the mountains to the streets below, everything glitters, even while crime, grime, and despair crawl in the underbelly. For about an hour a day, it's a respite. He's thinking too much. He looks to the west now, where the sun is sinking behind blood orange coils of clouds, several layers of coils stretching to the horizon. And he's nearing the cathedral. He can see the glass prism from the highway. It's on fire. Not fire department fire. Sunset fire. A confusion of rays in the prism creates the illusion of flames. He pulls into the long driveway, recognizes his colleagues as he swings into the parking lot. Powell waves. Preston nods.

Gus arrives a few minutes later and Mills leads all of them to the church's lobby, where they're promptly stopped by security guards. These are ex-marine types in tight fitting suits, expensive looking suits, wearing earpieces as if they're Secret Service, which they're not. They're bald, all four of them. A dress code, Mills guesses. "This is a private function," one of the bouncers says.

"Right," Mills says back. "And we've been invited."

"The church emailed invitations to its members and guests that must be presented here at the door," another brawny guard tells them. "Do you have one to show us?"

"No," Mills says. "I don't think we were on the email list. But we were invited by Pastor Norwood. Personally."

"Do you have any identification?" the first guard asks.

Mills ceremoniously, and he's entirely conscious of the ceremony, displays his badge. As does Powell. As does Preston.

The guards look at each other emptily, like they're as stupid as they are massive. Like they're massively stupid. Then a fifth guard pokes his head into the mix and says, "Who's this?" pointing to Gus.

"He's with us," Mills says. "Maybe if you alert the pastor that we're here, everything will be cleared up and you'll be free to harass some other guests."

Two of the guards turn away. The remaining three fold their arms across their chests and attempt to stare down Mills and his entourage. The pomp and formality must be out of some Rent-a-Cop training manual, Mills guesses, right down to the synchronized arm folding, so he lets it go. Powell clears her throat. With her, that can only mean one thing. She's about to launch into a laughing fit. He turns to her and glares. "Don't," he mutters like a ventriloquist. She bows her head. Her back begins to rattle. Very nice. Decorum, not her strong suit. Gus is staring off into nowhere, his eyes lost in the prism. Motley crew, that's how they must look, with grandfather Preston ignoring them all, as grandfathers do. Suddenly a flourish. Like the arrival of a Saudi Prince, Gleason Norwood, flanked by the two security officers, marches toward them, six heels clicking in precision, a giant cape billowing behind him.

A cape.

"Mr. Norwood, I'm sorry if there's some confusion," Mills says, extending a hand. "But I thought you had invited us."

The preacher laughs uncomfortably. "Didn't know you were bringing a whole posse," he says. "But of course, you're all welcome here."

Norwood makes a magnanimous gesture with his hands. His cape is elaborately embroidered, its edges gold. It's not a prayer shawl. It's not a robe. It's a damn cape, like a superhero's, words all but hidden in the tapestry of it all, words vaguely stitched within the winding fields of color. Arabic, or something from that part of the world. It's Gleason and his Amazing Technicolor Dreamcoat. Powell, who had looked up, has lowered her head again.

"Is the event open to the public tonight?" Mills asks.

Norwood puts his hands together like he's praying. "We have many nonmembers on the invite list. We wanted to open the cathedral to her friends who might not be Angels."

"Angels?" Gus asks.

"We call the members of our church Angels. You know, Church of Angels Rising . . ."

"I did not know," Gus says.

"Neither did I," Mills says, then makes introductions all around.

"As I'm sure you know, Viveca had a large presence in the valley," Norwood says. "She had many friends who worship elsewhere, and that's OK with us."

Okay with you?

"I had heard that the church is otherwise very private," Mills says. "That you don't, in fact, welcome strangers."

Norwood scoffs with glee. "That's nonsense. We welcome new-comers every day. But yes, our most holy days, Saturdays and Sundays, are off-limits to nonmembers. Now, why don't we get you situated . . ."

From the belly of the cathedral an organ begins to moan. Out here the music echoes against the glass, sending shivers down the prism's spine. Mills can feel it in his fingertips. Ushers call for the throngs of visitors to form orderly lines before entering the sanctuary. There's a scurry of footsteps as the music reaches a climax.

"We'd like to keep your presence as subtle as possible," the preacher says. "Wouldn't want to worry the congregants."

"Of course not," Mills says. "You'll notice we're not in uniforms."

The preacher nods. "I'll have you escorted to one of the skyboxes by these fine gentlemen," he says, indicating the jarheads surrounding him. "You should be comfortable up there."

"Are we free to roam?" Powell asks, sporting a straight face at last.

"If you must," Norwood replies. "But, again, the word of the night is 'subtle.'"

"Subtle," she repeats.

"I promised to find some key people to talk to you about Viveca, and I have. They'll be available after the service," Norwood tells them. "That said, I must ask you to not solicit information from random people tonight. That would make people nervous."

Mills gives him a tacit agreement with a nod.

15

Norwood's security team has placed Mills's group in the skybox above the preacher's office. Like the office, the skybox is a marble and leather showplace. It looks out to a stadium-sized arena with floor seating of easily thirty rows, thirty across, surrounded by two levels of balconies and, topping it all, this nose-bleeding strip of skyboxes. They're perched above midfield, Mills guesses, with a decent view of the stage, a mammoth platform with a pie section for the orchestra, now tuning up, and risers for the choir, now filing in. Dressing the stage are flags with symbols unfamiliar to Mills, and Corinthian columns. Mills doesn't get the columns, thinks they're gratuitous. Suspended high above the stage from a daunting network of rafters are stacks of loudspeakers and spotlights. "We're in for a fucking rock concert," Mills says.

Powell kicks him. "Have some respect. We're in a house of worship."

"Hell if I know what they're worshipping," Mills retorts.

The stadium goes dark. The audience goes reverently silent. Then, piercing through the darkness comes a Jedi-like battle of laser lights and a massive ooh and aah from the bedazzled crowd. Next, the choir lifts its voice in a trembling harmony of awe. A cymbal crashes, followed by another, and another, and another. The suspense of the music is no accident. In the murky darkness Mills can see people on the edge of their seats. Then comes something that Mills could not have expected: an army of dancers storms the stage as the music escalates to a thudding beat. They're dressed like warriors of ancient Egypt, the men in bronze chest plates, the women in sheer gowns and Cleopatra headdresses. All of them wear sandals with straps that serpentine high to the knees. They're flying, tumbling, twirling. The men spin the woman overhead, and Mills can't watch because the whole thing is giving him vertigo this high up. "It's like a fucking Madonna concert," Powell says to him.

"What happened to respecting a house of worship?" he asks, smirking.

And then the music hushes as a booming voice rises. It has the effect of a bass drum, vibrating in Mills's stomach. "And now," it says, "please welcome, the one and only, Pastor Gleason Norwood!!!"

The choir exhales a soaring crescendo. A small circle at center stage opens, and up from below, on some kind of hydraulic platform, rises the man himself. In his cape.

"Like Beyoncé," Powell yells into his ear.

"Sorry, I get an 'F' in pop culture."

"Ladies and gentlemen," Gleason says, as his oval elevator stops flush with the stage. "Welcome to this very special night. Tonight is not a night of worship. No. Tonight we open our doors to the public to honor a woman who transformed our church and our community for the better. Tonight we say goodbye to Viveca Canning . . ."

A flourish of "ahhhs" from the choir.

"She was a rare angel," Gleason gushes. "We all know that. She made us better. She set an example. She taught so many of us how to fly. She loved her church. But she loved her valley just as much. And gave so much to help those less fortunate. She touched so many lives. Because she was truly on an angel's mission."

More "ahhhs."

Mills winces. This memorial service has all the qualities of a *Saturday Night Live* parody.

"Tonight, we'll hear from some of her beneficiaries, from some of the lesser angels here in the church who came under her wings, and from our friends out in the living world, as well, whose organizations were enabled to do great things because of Viveca Canning's generosity."

A stadium-sized round of applause.

Mills mostly tunes out during the endless parade of tributes that comes next. Powell nudges him a few times. He knows he should be listening to every word, because in every word there could be a clue. But the words are dripping in the fat and grease of lavish praise, and his colleagues are better with that sort of thing, so instead he studies the faces in the crowd. He can't see many of them, of course, in this darkened arena where all the lights favor the stage, but Mills can easily determine a commonality among those seated in the middle floor section. No one has an expression. Not a smile. Not a frown. Not a movement. Eyes stoic and unblinking. No one laughs. No one sobs. They simply watch. And watch. And barely breathe. They are not guests here. This is the congregation. They are members, angels hoping to rise. How fucking weird. There will be no communion, Mills suspects; there will be Kool-Aid. The rest of the crowd, the ones up in the balconies, are clearly the guests. He can spot emotion in those balconies, despite the arena's unreliable light.

The drums rattle. The cymbals crash. And the invisible voice emerges again. "Ladies and Gentlemen, now a special appearance from Viveca Canning's own rising angel himself. Please welcome the bereaved but blessed Bennett Canning . . ."

Applause, drumbeats; the choir cums all over itself.

The scion emerges from backstage, donning a flowing robe in the same style as Norwood's cape. The same embroidery. The same unfamiliar symbols. Probably an expression of the church's own mythology.

"I feel my mother in this room tonight," Bennett roars.

Thunderous applause.

"Your love, your praise, and your tears have brought her back here. And I can't thank you enough. She is so touched by your outpouring of affection, as am I," he tells the crowd. "Her death comes as a shock to us. A terrible, untimely end. But she had truly risen here in the church. She had been sent on her mission. She was ready at any time."

Mills turns to Powell. "This ain't the Bennett we know."

"He's possessed," Powell says. "That's why. He's channeling some kind of entity."

Mills laughs.

"Oh no, I'm serious," Powell whispers. "Ask your friend Gus . . ."

Mills laughs again and turns to his other side. "Hey," he says to Gus, "Jan thinks the kid is possessed."

Gus shakes his head, as if waking up. "Yeah," he says.

"Yeah?" Mills asks him.

"Something," Gus says. "I think Jan may be on to something. I'm getting kind of a similar vibe. Except it tells me this whole place is possessed."

"Okay," Mills says. "I'm not sure what to do with this information."

"Me either. It's too soon."

The men turn back to the spectacle below. Bennett continues to roar, his arms stretched to the heavens. "Goodbye, Mother," he chants. "Goodbye, leader, legend, heroine, angel of the angels. Goodbye, Mother. Few earn your mission. May those in your path find your grace. May our paths cross again, Mother, friend, protector, comforter, angel of the angels."

The congregants on the floor rise to their feet, swaying. Still facially paralyzed. Under a spell. That's it. They're hypnotized. The guests rise to their feet as well, taking a cue from the church members. The posse in the skybox doesn't move. *It should be this way*, Mills thinks. They should be seen, if seen at all, as impartial observers, as staunchly indifferent.

After the ceremony, Norwood's security team escorts Mills and his colleagues one flight down to a conference room adjacent to the preacher's suite. They sit and look at each other, nascent smirks on their faces. Sarcasm and Kool-Aid don't mix, Mills has learned over the years. But shit. This place. Mythology embroidered right into the woodwork. The service, by design, did not reveal a glimpse into what or who these people worship.

Gleason Norwood enters with a flourish. He's relieved of his cape, but no less dramatic. Four people file in behind him. "I hope you enjoyed the memorial service," he announces. "Let me introduce a few members of our board of directors . . ."

There's Tucker Charles, a white man, middle-aged, clean-shaven; Christine Triggs, also white, green eyes, white-haired, a beautiful witch; Harris Goodman, African American, handsome as fuck, could play a lawyer on *Law & Order*; Misty Yee, Asian, young, barely thirty, fingernails that leave her lovers in pools of blood.

Lesson Number One: The Church of Angels Rising welcomes all the stripes of the rainbow (except gays).

"Was Jillian Canning here tonight?" Mills asks the preacher.

Norwood offers a glinty smile and says, "She was invited as a guest, of course, not a member. I don't know if she accepted the invitation."

They talk from the same mouth, these people. Without one inflected syllable, Charles, Triggs, Goodman, and Yee (like an in-house law firm) all have an enormous amount of nothing to say.

Charles: "She was a lovely lady who wouldn't hurt a soul. She had no enemies that I know of. How could she?"

Triggs: "She reached a level of angelism that eludes most of us. She was that rare. A gem. Who would want to clip those wings?"

Goodman: "She was adored. We're in shock. Complete shock. I'm sorry we can't be more helpful. But there is no one here in the church, no one in her family, no one in the community who would wish her harm."

Yee: "My sister died a few years ago. She was only fifty. She had stage four breast cancer. Viveca took her to doctor's appointments, to chemo. She stayed with her, with us, during those last days. We don't canonize people here at the church, but if we did, Viveca Canning would be a saint."

Crestfallen faces all around. Except from Tucker. Tucker just sits there staring blankly at the wall, dumbstruck, it seems, by some kind of invisible scripture there.

"I felt the presence of Viveca's husband," Gus says.

"Is that a question?" Goodman asks him.

Mills turns to the psychic, transmits a signal in his eyes to tread lightly.

"No," Gus replies to the church member. "Just an observation."

"If that's the case, we have nothing to say," Goodman tells him.

Mills leans forward to all the church members and says, "Why? Did Mr. Canning have some kind of falling out with the church?"

Gleason Norwood lets out a belly laugh and waves his hands in the air. "Of course not. They were a wonderful couple. Devoted to each other and the church. We pray their missions intersect."

"I felt like there's something unresolved," Gus tells the room.

"That could mean many things," Yee says. "And we can't sit here speculating, can we?"

Mills and his colleagues press these people further, but get very little else but rehearsed incantations of reverence. Reverence doesn't get this thick without some kind of bullshit leavening. How these people think they can fool a room full of detectives is beyond Mills, but he sees right through their obsequious smiles. Outside, he says as much. First he exhales, like he's releasing the bullshit from his adrenal glands, and he shakes his head vigorously. "Wow. Just fucking wow. That was quite a performance," he tells the group.

"The board of directors? Or the memorial itself?" Preston asks.

"Both," Mills says. "Did anybody get anything I might have missed?"

"There was nothing to miss," Powell assures him. "It was completely rehearsed."

"Or maybe they really are that catatonic," Mills says.

Preston says, "Probably."

Gus digs his foot into the pavement and says, "What is angelism?"

"Huh?" Mills asks him.

"Angelism. The white-haired lady mentioned angelism."

"I caught that," Preston says.

"Is it a religion or a practice?" Gus asks the group. "I don't think I've ever heard of it. I mean, in my line of work, I've run into lots of people who believe in angels and seem to practice it as a religion. But not an organized religion with churches and all. You know?"

"Right," Mills says. "Gleason referred to Viveca on an 'angel's mission.' Bennett said she was the 'angel of the angels.' Obviously, the whole 'angels rising' thing leads their doctrine, defined, I'm guessing, by 'angelism.'"

"Sounds like a fake religion to me," Powell says. "Like somebody dreamed this up and turned it in to a business."

"The common criticism is that the church is a cult," Preston reminds them, "but maybe Powell is right."

Mills lifts his head and looks up to the prism, lit solely now from the inside. "Or, more likely, it's both. Based on what I've read."

Gus shuffles around them, pacing, his lips moving. This makes Mills nervous, but he knows better than to interrupt a man on a psychic tightrope. Gus had once explained that sometimes it's a tightrope because often he's tethered to earth on one end and the cosmos on the other; the trip across is fraught with risk. There's plenty of opportunity to lose his grip and slip into a purgatory of the ill-defined. Which is why, he's told Mills, he doesn't use the tightrope often.

Mills notices the others regarding Gus with curious if not dubious stares. "Hey, just let him do his thing."

Gus makes one more orbit around the detectives then rejoins the circle. "As for the woman's murder itself," he says, completely lucid, "I don't think church doctrine has anything to do with it. All this angel rising stuff is just low hanging fruit. And it has the feel of a tacky façade."

"Wow, that's quite an interpretation, Gus," Powell says, her voice dusted with sarcasm.

"It's not an interpretation," he tells her. "Just an observation. I don't know if you think the church is somehow involved, but there's a tug of war going on in what I call the psychic layer of my consciousness."

"Tug of war?" Preston asks.

"Yeah," Gus says. "I think both the business and cult-like aspects you perceive here are worthy of a closer look. Her money. What she knew. What they wanted. And I think you're going to find that she was scared of doing something, but decided to do it anyway. I definitely sense fear here. Huge fear. Right there at the center of the spectacle.

Right there embroidered into the façade."

The others just look at him soberly.

"What kind of façade?" Mills asks.

Gus squints at him, says nothing.

"You mentioned a façade twice," Mills reminds him. "I know you well enough . . ."

"Right," Gus says. "Something worth probing. It's a door or a wall, maybe. But I need some time. Can I take a day or two and focus on that?"

"Go for it, Guster," Mills tells him, offering a handshake. "And thanks for coming."

The rest of them turn to their cars, but Gus calls for them to turn back. He's staring at the peak of the prism above the cathedral. "What is it?" Mills asks.

"I will say one thing about angelism, whatever it is," Gus tells them. "It was a slip."

"A slip?" Preston asks.

"That woman was not supposed to mention that word. If there is a cult to be investigated, whether or not it has any connection to your victim's death, it certainly lies beyond the door of angelism."

Then, the spell of the prism broken, the psychic turns away, leaving the rest of them to ponder murky images of doors and façades and angels.

16

I t's about noon the next day when Morty Myers appears in Mills's office.

"I'm obsessed with this woman," Myers says.

"It's about time, Morty! All grown up. Who is she?"

Myers snickers. "Very funny. She's dead. Her name is Viveca Canning."

Mills gestures for him to take a seat. "Oh. I wasn't kidding, buddy. I thought you'd finally given up the video games for dating."

"Whatever, Alex. Her story keeps getting better and better."

Mills is genuinely interested. He had been studying his notes from last night's memorial service, but now he shifts those aside and looks at Myers earnestly. "How so?" he asks.

"She revised her will. I've been digging deeper into her computer all morning, and I found a different version of the will. More recent. It was simply named 'revision,' but I was opening all the files I could find, and it turns out she'd nullified the bequest to the church. That's exactly what it says in the revision. It says, 'I hereby nullify the previous will and the bequest of my designated assets to the Church of Angels Rising.' I sent you the PDF a minute ago."

"Thanks, Morty. Where does the money go now?"

"Back to the children," he says. "The art is still going to the museum, but the value of her estate will be split evenly between her children."

Mills nods, then rests his chin into a hand. "Something must have happened to change her mind. I'm not going out on a limb to suggest that 'something' could be a critical piece of the puzzle."

"Probably so."

"And if her kids knew about the revision to her will," Mills says, "they had a motive to kill her, right? So, we have to take a more serious look at them. I think you need to call Viveca's attorney and find out which version of the will is the most recent."

"I can tell by looking at when the files were created."

"No," Mills says. "We have to find out when they were signed and dated."

"Will do," Myers tells him. "Where's Preston at with the phone records?"

"As soon as you vacate my office, I'll be calling him."

"Is that a hint?"

"Go call the attorney, bud."

Between Myers and Preston he has about five minutes to take a leak, refill the sludgy coffee with more sludge, and text Kelly.

<F-ing love you>

<You're so romantic>

<Let me try that again. I love you>

<You didn't have to edit out the f-ing>

<That's good. I'll remember that for later.>

<Please stop sexting me, Alex.>

<Okay. Talk later>

Preston's standing in the doorframe. Mills waves him in. Ken sits and describes some key findings of Viveca Canning's phone records. "I'm not done going through them," he tells Mills. "Just so you know."

"That wasn't my expectation."

Preston describes a series of unsurprising phone calls between the dead woman and her children, a few more to Jillian than to Bennett, but not a significant difference. She also made routine calls to the main phone number at the Church of Angels Rising. To whom she spoke is not clear from the records, but probably not worthy of further probing considering her relationship with the church. A series of calls between Viveca and Gleason Norwood, the detectives agree, would not be remarkable. "But then there's a few calls to a real estate development company in French Polynesia. I can't get my head around that one. We know she transferred money there, but we don't know why. I've tried calling the company."

"And?"

"Even when I've synched up to the right time of day in the right time zone, I get voice mail."

"She was probably interested in buying another home to add to the Canning list of properties abroad."

"She has other homes?"

"I'm just guessing. We need to look into their holdings more thoroughly."

Mills thanks Preston for the updates, tells him to be around for a three o'clock meeting with the squad. "I'll send out an email to the others before I split for lunch."

"You want company?"

Here Mills has to gamble with the truth. "Don't take this the wrong way, Ken, but no. I just need to think."

And that's what he does. He thinks, oblivious to the burrito, the music, and the roar of the lunch crowd at Fiesta Taqueria. He just needed to get away from the building and all the badges coming in and out of his office, passing him in the hallway, everyone expecting something. He couldn't concentrate with all the blue closing in on him. That's how it is sometimes. The blue gets in its own way. Jimmy Jimenez, the restaurant's owner, stops by with a crazy grin and a tray of samples. He does this all the time. He loves having cops around. "Hey chief," he says to Mills, "what's happening?"

"I've told you a million times, Jimmy, I'm not the chief."

"I know, man. But you should be."

Jimmy is built like a snowman on a diet, which is to say rotund but trying. The kids sure got to his face, though. When they carved his mouth, they gave him a smile so upturned it reached his eyes at both ends. The result is a man who looks elated even when he tells you about his dead chickens. It was a trend, raising chickens in the backyard and on the roof, supplying your kitchen with eggs and meat, but it all went south for Jimmy when one of his kids left the chickens on the roof all day and they fried, every single one of them, in the blistering Phoenix sun.

Smiling, Jimmy leaves the tray of samples on the table. "Hey, I see your lovely wife is on the Trey Shinner trial," he says to Mills. "Saw it on the news. You know he broke in here once."

"I did not know that."

"It was a long time ago. We came in one morning and he was sleeping on the floor of the kitchen."

"Did he steal anything?"

"Just what he could drink." Jimmy laughs, raising his chin as he does.

"He's a nutcase."

Jimmy bends to his knee and, eye to eye with Mills, says, "He's not a nutcase. He's possessed by the devil."

This is the first time in the two years that he's known Jimmy Jimenez that Mills has witnessed the man's smile disappear. "Possessed by the devil? Maybe by Jim Beam or Jose Cuervo, but the devil seems a bit of a stretch."

Mills laughs at his own joke. Jimmy doesn't. Instead Jimmy narrows his eyes and searches the detective's face. "I'm serious," he says.

"About the devil?"

"Oh yes." Jimmy's accent has the same Mexicali texture as many Mexican Americans of his generation. It's more SoCal than Spanish, more Los Lobos than Latino. "Definitely, the devil. When we found him we was lying in the middle of one of those pentagram things. He drew it on the floor with a Sharpie."

Mills snickers. "I'm sorry, Jim, but I think a pentagram is a symbol for Wiccans."

"Symbol for who?"

"A type of witchcraft," Mills says. "I'm not an expert on religion, but I'm pretty sure that witches don't worship the devil."

Jimmy peers around his dining room, as if he's suddenly concerned someone might overhear. "Look, I don't care who worships the devil, but when the cops woke Shinner up from his drunken stupor in my kitchen he was talking in tongues!"

"I think those are certain Christians."

"Well, whatever, Detective, you tell your wife to be careful. Very careful. That dude is not from this world. I'm telling you. He's dangerous."

Duly warned, Mills nods and dives into the tray of snacks. "Gotcha, man. Thanks for the tip. And thanks for the samples. What's this one?" Mills asks, holding up a fried, round cylinder.

"Chimichanga Menudo."

"What's that?"

"It's like a fried burrito of cow intestines."

Mills gags on instinct.

"I'm just kidding with you, man," Jimmy says, his smile bursting back on the scene. "It's just a vegetarian Chimi."

He walks away laughing.

They file into the conference room at three o'clock, one after the other, three of them, Preston, Powell, and Myers, clutching cups of coffee.

"I asked Jake to join us," Mills tells them.

"Why did you do that?" Powell asks.

"Preemptive strike. Better to loop him in now than get called on the carpet later."

The sergeant has earned a reputation for quarterbacking on Monday mornings. They all know it. They've all experienced his indifference give way to sudden blame and disapproval. Mills almost looks forward to it, like a kid who knows if his daddy's drunk, all is right in the world. Almost. He preempts it whenever possible.

Jake Woods enters the room, gives them all a nod, and takes a seat without saying a word.

"All right, everyone," Mills begins, "I guess we're still in that phase of the investigation when the case presents more questions than answers. But we're not without a roadmap."

He tells them about the change Myers discovered to Viveca Canning's will.

"I need a warrant to search Bennett Canning's house," he says. "With half the estate going to him, he had a motive to kill his mother. Remember, we got him taking the jewels from her house. That should help with the warrant."

"What about the daughter?" Powell asks.

"Same motive," Mills replies. "But she has no house to search here. And she's been far more straightforward with us than her brother."

"But we should question her again," Preston says.

Mills nods and says, "Yes. We should."

Myers raises his hand.

"Myers, you don't have to raise your hand. You should know that," Mills says. "The floor is yours."

"I'm still dumping data from the victim's computer, but I found something else that could be interesting," he says.

Powell leans forward and rests her chin in her hands. "All ears," she sings.

Mills clears his throat. Myers ignores them both and says, "I found a file that inventories her art collection. It's a long, boring list of paintings and painters and dates. Dates for everything. The artist was born on this date, died on this date. The painting was acquired on this date, loaned on this date, stored on this date."

"We get the point, Myers," Powell tells him.

"No you don't," Myers retorts. "She has three Dalis catalogued in this file. And one says, 'Untitled,' and in parenthesis it says 'key.' I'm thinking this is the Dali that's missing from her house, 'cause the other two say they're loaned out."

"What does a key have to do with the painting?" Powell asks him.

He says, "I don't know. But of all the artwork she has inventoried, and she has hundreds of pieces, only one has a notation like that."

"But what key is she referring to?" Powell persists.

"No clue," he says.

Mills and Preston look at each other. They share an eyeful of acknowledgement. "If I had to make a guess, maybe a wishful thinking guess, I'd say it's the key to the chest."

"What chest?" Woods asks, the question abruptly surfacing from the veil of boredom on his face.

"Something Preston and I stumbled upon last week," Mills says. "Could be anything, but we went to the gallery where Viveca stored pieces of her art collection, and we saw an old chest, an ancient chest in her vault. And it was locked. With a padlock. It was weird because you wouldn't expect to see that kind of lock on a piece of art from the 1400s."

"What's in the chest?" Woods asks.

Mills looks at the sergeant, incredulous at the man's inattention.

"Keep up, Sarge. The chest is locked," Powell says so Mills doesn't have to. "Which means it's as important to find the Dali as it is to find the killer. Though I suspect we'll find one with the other."

Mills mouths the words 'thank you' to Powell. "That's true," he says. "But let's not wait 'til we find the painting or killer to find out what's in that chest. Consider it a clue. I'll get a warrant to break the padlock."

"Be careful," Woods says. "You could destroy evidence."

"I'm aware," Mills assures him. "We'll try to disengage it first."

Then Woods rises to his feet, his way of saying the meeting's over, whether or not Mills has more to say to the squad.

Ten minutes later Mills is at his desk when his phone rings from the lobby. "You have a guest. Aaliyah Jones from Channel 4."

Right. His four o'clock meeting. He looks at his watch. It's 3:45.

He could make her wait or he could get this over with. The latter seems more practical, so he heads downstairs. In the lobby he finds a striking woman waiting to shake his hand. She comes forward and shakes firmly. "Thanks for meeting with me," she says, with a smile so blinding Mills thinks about averting his gaze to save his retinas. He has a gut reaction to her, something visceral; he senses the smile is genuine, that it conceals nothing. Mills laughs at himself. He, too, can get vibes about people. He wouldn't be much of a detective if he didn't. But there's something about Gus sending this woman to him that seems fated, as if Gus has sent him a vision to behold, not a person to talk to. "Let's go up to my office," he tells Aaliyah Jones, snapping out of his initial stupor. "I don't think I've seen you on TV before," he says on the way. "Have you worked for Channel 4 long?"

"Under two years, so I'm still fairly new."

"Sorry. That was probably rude of me to say I didn't recognize you from TV."

"Not at all," she says convincingly. "I'm not on every night. And there are five other stations in town."

"Not on every night?"

"I'm an investigative reporter, Detective Mills. I work on more time-intensive stories. So I'm not on regularly, and it's actually better that way. The fewer people who recognize me, the easier it is for me to work undercover."

Mills bristles before he can think. "Undercover? You're not playing detective on me? Or PI?"

"I don't play anything," she says.

Mills lets the conversation go quiet until they reach his office. He closes the door, offers her a seat. "It was just a joke," he tells her. "About playing detective."

She looks at him, her face finely sculpted, not a blemish on the surface, not a blemish below it either. "I can take a joke. But just in case you were serious, I wanted you to know that my work is not a game to me."

"I know it isn't," he says. "I can tell."

She's wearing a sleeveless black dress that hugs her body to mid-thigh. It's simple and uncomplicated. Gold buttons parade from her neckline down the length of her cleavage. No other adornments. "You were vague on the phone."

"Sorry. Had to be. I should have called from my landline. My cell might be hacked."

"By whom?"

"The Church of Angels Rising. Viveca Canning's church."

Mills nods slowly. "Why would the church hack your phone?"

"Because I've been poking around."

"About what?"

"About church practices. This predates Ms. Canning's murder. I've been investigating for a while."

Mills sits up, straightens his posture. "Let's cut to the chase. What are you investigating?"

"Tips I've received about abuse in the church."

"Child abuse?"

Aaliyah crosses her legs, rests an elbow on a knee. "Not exclusively. A few independent sources have come forward to tell me they were abused by the church both as children and adults. There's some kind of mandatory camp for children between the ages of six and twelve. They live away from their families. They study and do projects for the church. They reunite with their families on weekends for prayer."

His cell phone rings. He ignores it. "Okay," he says. "I think this has been reported before. Doesn't sound like news to me."

"I've got photos of injured children at the camp."

"Where did you get them?"

Aaliyah looks down for a moment and shakes her head. "I can't reveal my sources. Not yet. I promised."

His landline rings. He lets it ring, talks over it. "We're checking Viveca Canning's phone records. Was she in touch with you for any reason?"

Her eyes meet his. "Yes. It was mostly phone tag, though. Ultimately, she declined to comment."

"How old are the photos?"

"Ten years. Five years. Some are as recent as two years ago. From what I'm told, adults who fail to recruit their yearly quota of church members are subject to something they call 'Second Calling.' It's like a prison camp of forced labor. And intensive brainwashing."

Mills laughs.

"Don't laugh," she warns him, her voice unapologetically grave. "People believe so fervently in Gleason Norwood, they'll do whatever he tells them to do to stay in the church. Except for the defectors."

Mills thinks of Jillian Canning. She was banished, but she left willingly. "It's run like a cult," he says as much to himself as to the reporter sitting in front of him. "Or so it seems. One woman I know who was banished says they call it 'erasing.'"

"When people leave the church, voluntarily or not, they're called 'untouchables.' I've met with several of them. People who remain in the church can have no further contact with an 'untouchable,' therefore they call it 'erasing.'"

"Why haven't your sources come to the police?" he asks. "About the abuse? About anything?"

Aaliyah folds her arms across her chest. The high beams of her eyes turn on. "They're scared," she says. "Some of the 'untouchables' have gone missing."

He makes a mental note to check with state authorities. He stares into her high beams and says, "Do you mean they're kidnapped? That seems to be consistent with what I've been reading online."

His phone dings with a text message. It's Kelly.

<Call me>

<In a meeting. I'll call u as soon as I'm done>

"They vanish," Aaliyah replies after Mills puts his phone down. "I don't know much more. They just disappear."

At first he offers her a slow contemplative nod. Then he feels the doubt rising on his face, twisting at his mouth, scrunching at his eyes. His nod fluidly becomes a shaking head, a rejecting gesture he can't help but articulate. "That doesn't add up, Ms. Jones," he says. "How do all these people end up missing and no one reports it to the police? One person, two people, maybe. But you make it sound systematic. I just can't believe that many people can vanish and it all goes unreported."

She smiles in the warm, reassuring way that he's seen shrinks smile at lunatics. There's nothing patronizing there, just patience and understanding. "My sources tell me there is protocol for all this. If a kid vanishes, his family tells friends, neighbors and nonchurch relatives that he's been sent to boarding school. If a wife vanishes, the husband says she's on a church project in Africa. If a husband vanishes, it's the same believable explanation. The speculation is there are bodies buried somewhere out in the middle of the desert."

"Jesus Christ," Mills whispers.

"It's not that kind of church."

"Yeah. I'm beginning to realize that," he says. "But I need to remind you I'm not investigating the church, even if it is some kind of crazy cult. I'm investigating the death of Viveca Canning. I've found no evidence, so far, that her death had anything to do with the church. That could change, of course. But I hate to tell you that the nefarious activities of the church, as alleged by your sources, are irrelevant to my case. Unless I can link the church to her death. Was she an untouchable who vanished?"

"No," she says, her deflation visible. He can tell she's not easily deflated, and he instantly regrets treading on her mojo.

"Look, I think your investigation of the church matters," he tells her. "It matters a lot. It should be a good piece of journalism. And it could expose things that need to be exposed. If there is some kind of connection to the death of Viveca Canning, I assure you I'll be in touch."

He gets up. She rises, too, if a bit reluctantly. "I think you will be," she says. "Are you interested in hearing more if I get more?"

"As it pertains to the Viveca Canning case, yes," he says. "Have you tried talking to Gleason Norwood?"

"Yes, I've tried," she replies, following him to the elevator. "But I'm told he doesn't do interviews under any circumstances."

"Doesn't surprise me."

"I have a book," she says as the doors slide shut. They descend.

"What kind of book?"

"Their book. The book of their religion," she replies, removing the book from her satchel. "One of my sources gave it to me. Would you like to borrow it?"

He smiles. "Sure. When do you need it back?"

"End of the week would be fine," she says. "I'm working some other stories as well. But please guard the book. It's not allowed outside the church. Members are prohibited from removing it and sharing it with nonmembers."

"Wouldn't that make it hard to recruit?"

The ding of the first floor comes too fast.

"We can talk about that next time, Detective Mills."

"Thanks for coming by," he says as they step out of the elevator. He shakes her hand in the lobby. "This has been refreshing."

She peers at him with an odd smile.

"I mean, it was nice to meet an actual journalist for a change."

He watches as she slips out the door and into the bombardment of sunshine.

17

Beatrice has made the rare journey off the mountain to Gus's house. These days it's hard to get her to go out at all. It has something to do with the book tours she's been doing. She says her publisher has her traveling so much in support of the book that when she's home in Arizona, she doesn't want to leave the house. She wants to isolate. Which is fine, Gus understands, because she has another book to write. She's chipper, though, here in his house, his old brown couch encompassing her bum like a worn out catcher's mitt. Ivy's head is resting in her lap. She strokes the dog and says, "If you take her for a walk, you might even get me to join you."

"I'll hold you to that."

She bends her head to the side, like she's stretching, but she's not. She's taking in Gus from this angle as he sits there in the matching chair kitty-corner to her. "You sounded worried on the phone."

"I am worried, Beatrice."

"When did the worry start?"

"The minute I got the call from Billie."

"You said you don't want her to come home."

He shakes his head. "No. What I said was I wish she didn't have to fly. I'm very worried about the vision of that airplane going down."

"She's coming to visit this weekend . . ."

"Yeah. She's flying, of course. Should I tell her not to?"

"No. Different circumstances."

He plops his feet on the ottoman. "Different?"

"Yes, doll. She's not flying over water. She'll be fine."

Gus takes her at her word because that's how it works. "We'll be staying at the Desert Charm," he tells Beatrice. "You should come by for dinner."

"I have a book event in Tucson. Or Tuscany. It's all a blur these days."

Gus smiles. "I have a feeling it's Tucson."

"You two should come to the event. I'd love to have you."

He shakes his head. "We'd love to be there, but you know what will happen. Billie can't hide from the fame thing. She'll walk in that bookstore and all the attention is on her, not you."

"I don't care," Beatrice says.

"Billie does."

Beatrice shrugs. Unlike most people, she knows more about what she can't control than what she can. She likes it that way. Gus loves that about her, tries every day to live by her example. But Billie Welch is a challenge. Billie is in love with Gus, but Billie is in control of most things in her orbit. Gus is fine to spin there more often than not, but he gets restless sometimes for his own life. He has his own orbit to take care of. Which is why he knows he'll never simply walk away from Valley Imaging, pack up the house, and move to LA.

"That would take you out of your own skin," Beatrice says. "You can't survive out of your own skin. No one can."

He looks at her as dumbfounded as ever. "Wow, that's some amazing telepathy."

"Not telepathy," she says. "I've been getting these vibes from you for a while."

"Is it that obvious?"

"Only to me."

He tells her again how much he's worried about the plane crash.

"Billie's fine," she says.

"I'm not just talking about Billie," he insists. "Hundreds of people could die."

"Do you want to explore? Right now? Do you want to head to the crash site?"

He pulls at his scruffy chin. He's been growing out the facial hair for a few days, prompting people at work to call him Jesus. Never fails. "I don't know if I want to go to the crash site," he tells her. "But I'd like you to take me to the sky."

"Fine then," she says. "Let's have a few moments of silence."

Even Ivy seems to agree. Her snorting and whimpering and sloppy tongue go quiet. The only sound is the hum of Beatrice gathering the winds around her, the rustle of her skirt as she twirls the engines and ascends. And then a hush, a distinct powdery hush, and Beatrice says, "We're in the blue. There are streaks of clouds and intersecting contrails. Off in the distance I can see the edge of night. There's no danger here, Gus. Not yet."

"Not yet," he repeats. "But it's a very big sky."

"And I have a very big view. Can you see the expanse?"

His eyes closed, Gus surveys the inner pictorial as it unfolds, and he sees that it, indeed, is a huge sky, above all the continents at once, above all the energy, good and bad, all the love and the hate, the beauty and the evil, because there's a purity of perspective here. But the darkness is calling; Gus knows it. He can hear it ringing like an alarm. From here, the darkness is as wide and as deep as the sea. "Should we turn around?" he asks Beatrice.

"No. That ringing sound is your purpose."

"My purpose?"

"The reason you're here," she says. "It's a helpful signal."

"Of what?"

"Must I do all the work, Gus? It's telling you that you need to look into the darkness. It's giving you a direction."

"So we're going over the edge?"

"Be quiet and hold on."

Gus shakes his head, thinking *this is too freaky even for me sometimes.* But he clutches the fat arms of the chair and he follows. They bump over the edge of night like a ship crossing the Gulf Stream. A small but riotous hiccup and then drenching black. Soft, sharp, inkier than ink, misty and terrifying. He can't see. He tells Beatrice.

"Give it a second. Your rods and cones. Remember them?"

He'd roll his eyes if they weren't closed.

"Transcontinental," Beatrice says out of the blue, or the black, whatever, and it chills him.

"That's the airplane, the same airline."

"I know," she says, her voice velvet soft.

The logo. The colors. The shining behemoth hurtles through the night like a bullet. He can see everything now. He can see the passengers, most of them sleeping, some of them indulging in elegant wines under the dim purple light of the cabin, some soaking in luxury, some ambivalent. "This isn't it," he says, a sudden revelation.

"What do you mean?" Beatrice asks.

"I mean the airplane I saw go down went down in daylight," he says. "This is a night flight."

"No, dear. Our daytime is their nighttime," she tells him. "We've crossed the date line."

"But it was daylight. I'm sure of it."

"I know you are. But you were seeing it during your flight in from LA. You were flying during the day."

"So are you telling me that my vision is for real? That it's a doomed flight?"

"That's what we're here to see," Beatrice says. "But I don't think it's doomed."

"Why not?"

"It's just not a vibe I'm getting . . ."

Gus watches as the aircraft trembles in a pocket of turbulence, but it quickly recovers. A flight attendant splashes coffee on herself. A man masturbating in the first class lavatory knocks his head on the mirror, stops the deed, and zips up. Turbulence as God's way of saying *that's disgusting dude, not on a plane.* In a lavatory in coach, the warble knocks the cigarette from the hand of a woman who's been smoking in there despite the posted signs and all the warnings from the cabin crew. She bends over trying to find where it landed, but she can't see it. It's too late. The cigarette has already rolled to the door and set the edges on fire. The alarm screams. There's a rush of feet toward the door.

The smoker grasps for the handle, slides it back and frees herself from the slow inferno. She's met by the extinguishers of the cabin crew. And shouting. Everybody is shouting. A cyclone of smoke escapes the lavatory. It billows and wafts, moving into the cabin, down the aisles, slowly creeping toward the front of the plane. Every few seconds something sparks from the ceiling, like an electrical short, and the aircraft seems to stall. Gus knows what's next. He knows there will be a sharp bank and then a dive. He opens his eyes. He doesn't want to see it. He says nothing. He leaves Beatrice there to witness it for herself. He watches her face go from confusion to alarm to terror. She holds her hands in the air, then to her heart. And she nods a few times before lifting her head to Gus and opening her eyes.

"I sensed you got off the plane early."

"Yeah. I had enough."

"I understand," she says. "I don't think the plane crashed."

"Of course it crashed."

She shakes her head. "You're taking too much from the images."

"It's not just images. Everyone knows a fire can bring a plane down."

"You've been to Tahiti?"

"Nice change of subject."

"I'm not changing the subject," she says. "I recognized the aesthetics."

"It could have been anywhere in the South Pacific."

"True," she says. "Maybe Fiji. But I got a vibe about Bora Bora."

"No. I've never been. To answer your question."

"Then sleep on it," she says.

"Last thing I want to do."

"Funny that you think you have a choice."

Later, after Beatrice's Karmann Ghia is puff-puffing down the street, after Gus takes a quick, hot shower and hops into bed promptly followed by Ivy, he closes his eyes and inhales a deep, deep breath of air. The smell of jet fuel lingers.

Kelly doesn't look up when he comes in. "I tried calling you."

"Oh shit," he says. "I know. I meant to call you on the way home. But forgot. Sorry."

She's sitting in the living room, on the far corner of the couch, farthest from the light. Her face is lost in a shadow. "It's fine."

She's not convincing. "Really, I'm sorry. I had a reporter there and it threw me off."

"Oh, right. That reporter Gus told you about. How did it go?"

He shakes his head. "Never mind that," he says. He sits beside her, tries to see through the dark mood on her face. "What's up with you? Something with the trial? I'm guessing it was important."

"Good guess," she says.

"You're angry with me."

"Not angry. Scared."

He reaches for her hand. "Scared?"

She faces him now. "Last week I felt a lump in my breast when I was showering."

"A lump?"

"Yes."

"Last week?"

"Yes."

"And you're only telling me now?"

She takes him in from an angle. "Are you interrogating me?"

"No," he says with a pang of guilt, a kind of nonspecified guilt. He just feels fucking stupid for not knowing how to react.

"My gynecologist referred me to a place called the Central Phoenix Breast Center," she tells him. "For a mammogram and a needle biopsy. To make sure it's not cancer."

He knew the word was coming, particularly down the gauntlet of her last sentence. He lets it sink in, the word, but it can't; he doesn't have room for it, wasn't prepared for it, will have to rebuild his house for it. He has no clue what he's thinking because the room is sort of spinning. "Oh my God, Kelly. Oh my God," he stutters. "We'll do whatever we have to do. You'll be fine. I'm not going to let anything happen to you." He's aware of how freaked out he sounds but then he adds, "You should quit your job and get some rest."

She laughs. "I'm not tired. And I'm not quitting my job. I'm scared, but right now I don't feel sick or anything."

"I'm coming with you for the mammogram and the needle thing."

"Biopsy."

"Sounds painful."

"It won't be comfortable, according to my doctor," she concedes. "I'm trying to put it off because of the trial."

"You won't put it off, Kelly."

"This is not your cue to order me around, Alex."

Jesus. He doesn't know what the fuck to say, or how to say it, or when to say it, or when to shut the fuck up. How's that for being the perfect husband?

Mills's phone dings with a text from Morty Myers.

<Call me. Urgent now>

"Jesus . . ."

"What is it?" Kelly asks.

"Nothing. Just a text from Myers. It can wait."

"No. Text him back, Alex. My breast isn't going anywhere."

<Can't talk now, Morty. Family issues. Whatever it is can wait til morning>

<This is huge>

<If we don't talk now will tomorrow be too late? Think about that>

<I got Viveca's search history. It's a big deal but it can wait>

He shakes his head again. Stress always attracts stress. "Sorry," he tells her. "Let's order in."

"I cooked."

"You cooked? With this news?"

"First of all, Alex, it's not cancer news yet. I have to prepare for the possibility that it will, in fact, be cancer news. But I had to do something to get my mind off of it."

He smiles, pulls her forward and kisses her cheek. "Of course you did. Let me do the final preps and I'll serve."

"Was it important? The text message?"

"Yes. Seemed so. It was Myers. Something about the case."

"You need to call him."

He shakes his head. "No. I already debated this in my head. It can wait," he says. "In fact, if this turns out to be cancer, babe, I'm going to have to bag this case."

She laughs with a growl. "No you won't."

"No. I will," he insists. "I'll stop everything."

She gets up. She pulls his hand. "Come on, let's put dinner out. We're going to act as if everything is fine. We're going to be normal. We're not deviating from routines."

They have dinner. They watch *The Walking Dead*. They hold each other. They don't deviate from routine. In bed they open their books. But Mills can't concentrate on the mice or the men. He's read it several times, knows it inside out. Maybe that's why. That's not why. Kelly has drifted off to sleep. He stares at her, the meaning of his life. Sorrow creeps into his chest and it blooms, gently, tenderly, until a shiver of panic makes him freeze. He can't blink. He tries to drift but can't sleep. And when he finally does, three hours later, his dreams are haunted.

18

The following morning, sitting in his office, he broods over a cup of coffee. His brooding is dark. His coffee is a surprise.

When did I stop for coffee? Starbucks. *I went through the drive-thru?* Jesus.

He looks up at the shuffle of feet. Myers and Preston are hulking in the doorway. Myers is nearly foaming at the mouth. "Come in, boys. Have a seat."

Myers barely has his ass in the chair when he says, "Viveca Canning was searching the terms 'exhuming bodies' and 'autopsy after many years' on her computer."

"No shit," Mills says.

"No shit," Myers says, smiling ear to ear.

Mills reaches for his phone, texts Powell. <Come to my office>

"How recently did she do these searches?" Mills asks.

"In the two weeks leading up to her murder," Myers says. "And a little further back than that."

"How much further?"

"Maybe a month."

Powell enters the office, pulls up a chair. Mills gives her a brief update on Myers's discovery. "Whose body would she want to exhume?" Powell asks the room.

"I don't know," Myers says. "Maybe her own."

"Her own?" Powell challenges.

"Yeah. You know, maybe she figured someone would rush to bury her before we could find the truth."

"Maybe," Mills says. "But that assumes she knew her life was in danger. I think we need to stick with what we know, not with mere speculation."

"What do you mean?" Myers asks.

"You know what I mean, Morty. We have to stick to what we know about the dead people in her life."

Myers laughs. "Well, the only dead person she refers to on her computer is her husband. She saved his obituary. She emailed a cemetery, a funeral home, a florist, you know, to make all the arrangements. She saved photos of them together."

"Nobody else close to her died?" Mills asks.

"There are no files that reference anybody else who died," Myers replies.

"I'm guessing it's her husband," Mills says, aware of the annoyance creeping into his voice. "Let's go with that proposition. Maybe someone rushed to bury her husband, or maybe she was rushed to bury him. And now she regrets it."

"Wasn't it a heart attack?" Powell asks.

"It was," Preston says.

"I think I need another visit with Jillian Canning," Mills tells them.

For the balance of the meeting, Mills alternates between paying attention and imagining the lump. The lump. Kelly's lump. It sits in the corner of the room, behind everyone else, banished there on a stool. It throbs and pulsates. Sickening and sickened. Purple, veiny, and bruised. He looks at it, looks away. He looks at it a few minutes later, still there. It goes like that while they reconstruct, at least in theory, access to the Canning home. If the perp went in through the residents' lane, he'd need a remote. If the perp is a resident of the community, which just feels unlikely, he'd have a remote. If not, perhaps the perp drove in with a resident or with Viveca herself. Unless she gave a remote to someone else, like the housekeeper, a house sitter, someone. If. Unless. If. If. If not. Unless. Unless. "The Dali," Mills says. "It's gone. According to her kids it disappeared upon her death. Someone wanted it. According to the victim's own files, there's another layer of possibility. There is likely a key associated with the painting. Presumably the key has gone the way of the Dali. How are we coming with the warrant for the gallery?"

"Probably tomorrow," Preston says.

"You think someone stole the painting to get at the key?" Powell asks. "Or just took the painting for its intrinsic value, unaware of the key?"

Mills leans back in his chair, goes palms up with a half shrug. "I have no fucking clue. We don't even know if there *is* a key. But I'm curious about that old chest in the gallery and whether the key fits the lock. And I don't mean that metaphorically."

"But all you have for now," Preston says, "is a metaphor."

"A metaphor and a reporter," Mills retorts.

They look at him blankly, mystified, successfully thrown.

"I've had a reporter approach me with what she claims are big problems in the church," he tells them.

"Since when do you hang around with reporters?" Powell asks him.

Mills folds his arms across his chest and says, "We all know the church is controversial. Viveca Canning has strong ties to the church. So we really need to look there. Apparently this reporter already has."

"But you all went," Myers says.

"Yeah. We went. We saw. It's over the top," Mills recites. "The people look like they're drugged. We heard from those people on the board, which only reinforced an air of secrecy around the church."

"An air of creepiness," Powell adds.

"Look, it's not my kind of religion," Mills says. "But I'd like to talk to some ex-members."

"If you can find them," Preston says.

"We'll start with what we've got," Mills tells them. "We already found one. Jillian Canning. Bennett may be in, but Jillian is out. I'm going to head out now to sweet, old Aunt Phoebe's. Anybody wanna come?"

Myers ducks his head as if his disinterest won't be noted. Preston says he's busy with the warrants.

"Unless there's another crime scene to process, I'm good to go."

It's Powell.

Myers laughs.

"What?" Powell asks him.

"Oh, nothing," he says.

"No. Tell me."

"I'm just guessing she's hot. That's all. You seem so eager."

Powell gives him a lethal snicker and a tsk, and says, "Exactly. That's exactly why I want to go. I want to go see that hot lesbian and grab her by the pussy."

Preston sprays his coffee everywhere.

Myers praises Jesus.

Mills says, "Come on, enough, guys," rolling his eyes, shaking his head, getting up from the desk. He opens his office door so the motley crew will exit.

Belinda Garcia needs an MRI of her knees. She's forty-seven, allergic to Penicillin and peanuts, takes a multivitamin daily along with Lexapro (20 mgs), Lyrica (150 mgs x 2), Tramadol (she can't remember the dosage), Diclofenac (50 mgs), and Ativan (as needed). "The goal," she says, "is to have the surgery if I need the surgery, and get off some of these drugs." She tells Gus she'd been a runner since high school, that she'd finished marathons all over the country, often running twenty miles a day in training until her knees began to wear out, gradually abbreviating the distances she could run. "Until I couldn't run at all."

Gus feels a knock in his chest and knows it's her sorrow. These days he'd be called an "empath." And he'd wear the badge proudly. "Who knows? Maybe you'll have the surgery and some great physical therapy and be back to your old self."

"I doubt it," she says. "The operative word is 'old.'"

Her voice is husky and laden with regret. She medicates her regret with Scotch whiskey. It's just a hunch. Gus smiles and helps her onto the sliding platform. She looks up at him, at his name tag, and says, "Oh, your name is Gus. I guess I wasn't paying attention when you introduced yourself."

"That's okay."

"Gus is my son's name."

"What's it short for?"

"Gustavo," she replies. "My husband's Cuban. It was his great-grandfather's name. What about you?"

"August. I don't know where it came from. But no one has ever called me August in my life. Not my family, not my friends, nobody. I've thought of having it changed to just Gus, but never bothered."

"Do you mind if I call you August? It's a beautiful name."

He smiles again at the husky-voiced woman, a voice that's reminiscent of Billie's but less decorous, not as golden. "I'm going to need you to lie still," he tells her. "The whole procedure should take between twenty and twenty-five minutes. There's a built-in microphone, so if you need to talk to me or you need me to stop, just speak up."

She assures him she'll be fine and he slides her in. Five minutes or so into the exam, however, Gus hears a voice coming from the speaker on the console. "Are you okay, Mrs. Garcia?" he asks.

The woman answers, but Gus can't make out what she's saying through the static. This is nothing new. The system is erratic. The connection often sounds like it's coming from the far end of a tunnel, filtered through sandpaper, three times removed. "Mrs. Garcia, can you repeat that? I'm sorry. I'm having a little trouble with the audio."

Through the speaker he hears a deep breath, then a cry. Then a whisper. "They know where I live," she says. "They know what I drive."

He does a double take. He feels the blood rush from his face. He dashes from the booth to the patient's side. "Mrs. Garcia? Should I stop the test? Are you all right?"

The machine is knocking and whining and chirping, but he can hear her muffled response when she says, "I'm fine, August. I'm fine."

He looks at her through the machine. He looks at the booth. He turns again to her. Then he eyes the whole room suspiciously. It's in the air. An energy. He can't shake it. Gus returns to the booth. The exam continues.

"I think they've been here."

The speaker again.

"Mrs. Garcia?"

"They've been here, Gus. They know where I live."

The voice is certainly not Mrs. Garcia's. There's no huskiness. Where her voice is deep and resonant, this voice is lithe. It's coming through the speaker. Someone is talking to Gus, but it's not Belinda Garcia.

"Please help me, Gus. Please help me. Tell me what you see."

And then it hits him. *Tell me what you see.* Finally, he recognizes the voice. It's Aaliyah Jones. The reporter. She's in danger. And he has to warn her.

"I hope this isn't a bad time," Mills tells Jillian Canning when she greets them at the front door.

"No. Please come in."

They follow Jillian to the same room where she had first met with Mills. Powell ogles the house along the way. There's a lot to see here. The views. The craftsmanship. The art is all original, Mills guesses, like the art in Viveca's house. "Your brother took several things from the crime scene, mostly jewels," Mills tells the victim's daughter.

"Of course he did," Jillian says.

"Did you?" Powell asks.

Jillian turns to her, stares her down and says, emphatically, "No."

Mills intervenes. "Besides her artwork and jewels, is there anything else in the house your mother treasured?"

"Her books. She absolutely treasured them. You saw her library?"

"So she actually read those books?"

Jillian gives him a puzzled look. "Yes, she did. Voraciously, as I remember. She loved the classics."

"I love the classics," Mills tells her.

"Well, the two of you could have had a very nice book club." Jillian smiles, her face as optimistic as a sunflower. There's something bright and ingratiating about her, even in her grief.

"May I borrow one of them?" he asks her.

"In lieu of going to the public library, Detective?"

Mills laughs. "No. I'll be honest with you. One of my closest friends is a psychic. I understand if you want to roll your eyes. Please feel free, but I would like him to study something of hers. I know this sounds unconventional, but it can't hurt . . ."

She sits up, her face beaming. "No, no. I love it," she gushes. "Grab a book. Grab two."

"You'd have to get them for us."

"No problem."

"And we'd need to keep this off the record," he tells her.

She shrugs. "No problem with that either, I suppose."

Powell leans forward as if she's ready to pounce. "You left the church," she says.

"Is that a question?" the woman asks.

"Let me try again," Powell says, her voice serrated. "Did you leave the church?"

"The church left me," Jillian replies. "The lesbian thing didn't work for them."

"When I was here last time you said your mother couldn't completely 'erase' you," Mills reminds her. "Was she conflicted about that?"

"At first, yes, of course," Jillian says, her face kind of disappearing into a memory. "She was so torn. But less so after my dad died. I think he was the one standing between us because, to him, the church rules were black and white. But after he died, my mom and I got closer. I think I told you that last time."

"You did," Mills says.

"But even though we were getting closer, I knew something was bothering her. I asked her all the time, 'Is it me? Is it me?' But she assured me it wasn't. She said she was just distracted and I left it at that, you know, figuring she was probably overwhelmed by the estate. All the responsibilities fell on her when my dad died."

"What about Bennett?"

She laughs. "You've met my brother. He thinks of himself as the valley playboy. It's kind of pathetic, but he wouldn't know responsibility if it hit him in the face."

"Yet he put on quite a show at the church," Powell says. "We were at the memorial."

Jillian nods soberly, says nothing. The air conditioning whirs to life again and whispers through some unseen vents. It's so freaking hot outside, the system barely shuts off for two minutes. The maid reappears, offering iced tea, lemonade, and bottled water. Both Mills and Powell accept a bottle. Jillian instructs the woman to leave her a glass of iced tea on the coffee table, then thanks her. The maid drifts out of the room, but her departure fails to prompt a peep out of Jillian. Mills guzzles the water. Powell sips less enthusiastically. When the maid is safely out of earshot, Mills leans forward and says, "We think your mother may have changed her will. Were you aware of that?"

Jillian tucks her hands under her thighs and rocks gently. She conveys nothing on her face. "Changed from what to what?"

"I don't know whether or not you were aware that your mother left mostly everything to the church," Mills says. "But we found a revised will that bequeathed the entire estate to you and your brother."

"Okay . . . I didn't know that," she says. "Have you confirmed with her lawyers?"

"We're working on that," Mills tells her.

"Is that all you have to say?" Powell asks her. "You just find out you're going to inherit a fortune and you don't even blink an eye."

Jillian crosses a leg, clenches her hands together around one knee. All business. "It doesn't matter to me. I've made a life for myself."

Powell shakes her head. "Are you kidding me? Hundreds of millions of dollars don't matter to you? Certainly you don't live in a convent, ma'am."

"No, I don't, *ma'am*. Nor have I taken a vow of poverty," Jillian snaps. "But I don't want their money. I absolutely do not want their money."

Mills extends his arms between them like an umpire. "All right, ladies. Let's bring it down a notch. I think the only reason that Jan is pressing you is because this news could completely change the motive . . ."

"Meaning what?" Jillian asks.

"Meaning this presents certain people who directly stood to gain from your mother's death," Powell says evenly.

"Meaning my brother and me," the woman says.

"We have to cover everything," Mills reminds her. "I know you understand this."

Jillian shakes her head and brings one hand to her face, wipes a tear that inches down her cheek. Another tear falls to her chin, and it hangs there deciding on the weight of grief; Mills looks right through it, imagines something in the tiny orb shining back at him, flecks of gold, faerie dust, a talisman. And then the tear lets go and drops to the floor.

"I'm sorry, Jillian," Mills says.

"It's okay," she says, staring past him. "You know I was home in California when my mother was killed. You can check and double-check. But if you have more questions about me as a suspect, you can talk to our lawyers. I shouldn't be answering those kinds of questions alone. That much I know."

Mills nods. "Of course."

"What about your brother?" Powell asks. "Do you thinking he's capable of murdering your mother?"

Jillian catches her breath. Mills shoots a look of caution at his colleague.

"We're just trying to eliminate suspects," Powell adds. "You understand that, right?"

"I can't answer for my brother," the woman says. "After I left the church I was never around to witness how he interacted with my parents. But that's enough. Okay? Any more questions about my family need to go through the lawyers."

Powell starts to speak, but Mills puts his hand up. Whatever he's orchestrated here has gone off the rails. The room needs a little less percussion and a little more violin. "Okay, we completely understand," he says, as gently as he can muster. "We're done talking about the will and the family. But can we talk about the church itself, Jillian?"

"Why?" she asks.

"As an ex-member, can you tell us how the church treated dissenters?"

She reaches for the glass of iced tea, takes a sip. "What does that have to do with my mother's death? She never dissented."

"But she started having doubts about erasing you," Mills says. "Correct?"

"She kept her doubts private."

"What about others?" Powell asks her.

"I don't know what to say. I've only heard the rumors and they're not good."

"Rumors about a prison camp?" Powell asks. "Child abuse?"

"Look, I really can't," the woman pleads.

"Can't or won't?" Powell persists.

Jillian Canning puts her face in her hands and through muffling sobs says, "Just tell me what this has to do with my mother."

"Maybe she witnessed something she shouldn't have seen," Mills suggests.

"Maybe," the woman concedes. "But the real awful stuff is kept far away from the big donors. The big money never knows."

"So there *are* secrets," Mills says to her.

She pulls her head up, brushes her tear-stained face, and with a deep exhale says, "The whole fucking place is a secret. It looks like a behemoth church. It looks like a giant cathedral all about religion. At least from the outside. But it's a crazy cult. This can't be a surprise to you. It's been rumored in the valley for years. I don't want to say any more."

"Why?" Powell asks.

She says nothing. Mills yields to the silence for a moment. He and Powell have already pounced. A good detective knows when to pounce, when to pause. So much can happen in the pause. A witness's regrets emerge, anger flourishes, old wounds reopen. For Mills, this pause, unlike most, is a vulnerable place for him personally, a place where he's easily distracted by the tumors of life. Namely Kelly's. He can't fathom how she could have gone from healthy to not healthy without warning. Neither one of them could have anticipated the tumor. Apparently, neither one of them has a say in the matter. That's what impotence feels like. How the fuck is he supposed to fight an adversary like cancer? Interrogate it? Follow it? Catch it in the act? Jesus.

"You're scared," he says to Jillian Canning.

"I know they know I'm here. I'm sure Bennett told them," she says. "They have to know I'd come home to bury my mom, especially since I missed my father's funeral."

"Because he erased you?" Mills asks.

"Yes," she replies. "But also because there wasn't enough time. My mom had him buried before I could get home."

"That quickly?"

"Immediately," she says.

To Mills, the connection of dots is palpable. He pushes himself forward in the chair and locks his eyes on Jillian's, taking her eyes prisoner.

"What?" she says with a nervous flutter in her voice, her eyes still captive.

"Is there any reason your mother would want to exhume your father's body?" Mills asks her.

"What did you say?"

"We found a search she did on her computer about exhuming bodies," Mills explains.

"I can't fucking believe this. This is fucking nuts," she cries, her eyes breaking free. "If you don't mind, I just have to ask you to go now. I can't do this."

"Please," Powell says, "you said the church would know you're here. Are you worried?"

"No. I can handle myself. They can follow me all day and all night. But they will not touch me."

"Are they following you?" Mills asks.

"I think so. Probably to be sure I'm not talking to reporters and spilling secrets."

"Just tell us," Powell begs, "if you ever witnessed any form of torture in the church."

The woman gets up. She's had enough. She's telling them to get the fuck out without saying a word. So Mills rises, prompting Powell to do the same. Before they can move more than an inch, however, Jillian says, "Stop. Wait." She unbuttons her blouse in front of the two of them. Suddenly, she's brazen. She shimmies the blouse from her shoulders low enough to expose the top halves of her breasts, both of them skewered with deep, angry scars—a small but vivid 'X' on each.

"Oh God," Powell moans. "What the hell?"

"I kissed a boy at church before I turned eighteen," she replies. Then she buttons her top and says, "That's all folks. I'm done. I'll get that book for your psychic, Detective Mills. You'll have it tomorrow."

In his stunned silence, Mills knows they're not done. He will follow up. They will talk again. Here in the desert, in this scorching heat, under a blazing August sky, he has discovered the tip of an iceberg. It could blow the case wide open. Mills shakes his head without shaking his head all the way to the car.

He can't help it. He hears the sighs, but he can't stop the sighs. He's been taking deep breaths all through dinner. And of course Kelly asks him, "What's wrong with you?"

And he says, "Just a lot on my mind."

And she says, "That won't suffice for an answer."

And he can't shake the images of Jillian Canning's scarred breasts out of his head, not now, especially not now looking at his wife. It feels like a sign, a malignant sign. But it's not a sign, it's just the fucking universe taunting him.

"My case is on my mind," he says. "And you. You too."

She smiles. It's a normal smile, but that's not where his eyes take him. His eyes take him to a pained expression that's not there, to a smile that's thin and grim even though it hasn't surfaced. "The breast center can fit me in tomorrow afternoon at three," she says. "My second chair can take over for me in court. I need to be there at two-thirty. Can you meet me?"

He can't help but do a double take. "You think I wouldn't? Of course I'll meet you there."

"I don't know if it's necessary."

"It's necessary," he tells her. "In fact, let's meet here at the house so I can drive you. Sounds like an uncomfortable procedure. I don't want you driving home yourself."

Kelly says that sounds fine. She tells him to meet her at the house at two o'clock. Then she says she's going to take a bath. He watches as she rises from the table, as she drifts to the sink with her dishes, as she disappears down the hallway. Then he stares at the walls, at the clock on the microwave, then the ceiling. It occurs to him, *thank Christ*, he has some reading to do to take his mind off the doom staring back at him.

19

He's still reading the following morning at headquarters.

People live, but you rise. For Glory God made a sacred pact with his chosen followers, and as chosen followers it must be your duty to embody that pact as you practice, as you study, as you sleep, and as you wake. For these pacts inform you, instruct you, inspire and propel you to the very essence of Angelism. For you are on this path. You are rising. There is much to learn as you move down this path from one milestone to another. You are rising. For you are an Angel in training.

You are not living life, unlike your neighbors, unlike the Others who inhabit the planet. You are not living life. For you are not alive, said the Glory God. You are an Angel rising. And we will teach you. To Glory God!

Mills closes the book and calls Preston into his office.

"You look like you saw a ghost," Preston says when he arrives.

"No," Mills says with a jaded laugh. "I was just reading a prayer book from the Church of Angels Rising. The reporter from Channel 4 gave it to me."

"Anything interesting?"

"Not sure. Not yet," Mills says. "But I was thinking . . . Viveca's charming son is still in the church."

"So?"

"So, what if she was having second thoughts about the church? We know she changed her will . . ."

"I'm not sure I follow," Preston tells him.

"Maybe Bennett Canning is so indoctrinated that he wanted all the money to go to the church, so he tried to off her before the new will became official."

Preston shakes his head. "We don't know yet if it was signed and delivered to the lawyer. We don't even know if he knew about the first will. And why would he give up hundreds of millions to a *church*?"

"Maybe the money guaranteed him advancement in the church," Mills surmises.

"Advancement?"

"Power. You were there for the show. It was all spectacle. The perfect mix of power and pageantry. Obviously, there's a hierarchy at that church, and obviously Bennett is climbing. I'm sure he's angling for a seat on the board of directors. Maybe his mother's seat."

Preston rubs his chin. "And with church power, the money will come anyway," he says. "I'm sure they're sitting on hundreds of millions, between the church, the TV and radio network, and all those members sheepishly handing over their hard-earned cash every year."

"And who the fuck knows what they're doing with it? They're tax exempt, you know. As a religion!" Mills laughs and sighs. "They don't fucking file with the IRS!"

"Which means we can't exactly get a search warrant for the church's financial records. If the IRS can't get at them, we certainly can't."

"Not true, Ken. The IRS issue does not preclude a criminal case and cause to search. But here's the catch, no judge is going to sign off on a warrant unless we find a stronger connection between Viveca's murder and the church. Other than the fact that she was a big donor."

Preston pulls his chair closer. "I'm thinking Gleason Norwood was counting on that bounty from the Canning estate. I'm sure it would have bought him five or ten years, maybe more, of zero revenue growth. Like a fucking vacation, Alex."

"That's if he even knew Viveca was bequeathing everything to the church."

"You don't think he knew?"

"Maybe not," Mills says. "We can't assume Viveca told him."

"But if your theory is right about Bennett, then Bennett probably told Norwood in the interest of the kid's own advancement."

"But right now we can't establish that Norwood knew anything about the will," Mills argues. "So we can only focus on what Bennett knew."

Preston levels his eyes at Mills. In them, Mills instantly sees the wisdom. Those eyes tell the story of a career. "Bennett knew. He had to know everything about his mother's estate. With his sister banished, he was the only one left. Viveca had to have someone in the loop, right?"

"I suppose so."

"In case something happened to her," Preston says. "Myers is checking all her emails, right?"

"Exhaustively."

"Tell him to do more than check. Have him open every single attachment Viveca sent to Bennett."

"I'm sure he's doing that."

"Be specific with him."

"Thanks, Uncle Ken."

Preston smiles. "That's the kindest thing you could say."

"Don't forget to leave me in your will."

Preston is about to get up, but stops halfway. "As far as we know, that kid was the only one with access to Viveca Canning's house."

"But the sister must have access. She said she'd be getting me a book," Mills says.

"Before she came to town, Bennett was probably the only one with a key."

"As far as we know. We still need to work that. What's your point?"

Preston sits. "How else did he get into Copper Palace that first afternoon if he didn't have a remote for the residents' gate?"

Mills shrugs. "Maybe the guard let him pass considering the circumstances."

Preston says he'll follow up with the guard station. Then he bolts from the office, leaving Mills alone to read more scripture from the

Church of Angels Rising. It sounds like a science fiction spaceship that crashed at the box office.

He's somewhere in the middle of his read, in a black hole of fantasy warfare, deciphering the "angels" from the "aliens," wrapping his head around astral palaces and the dungeons of the Inner Core, when he gets an email from Phoebe Canning Bickford:

Detective Mills:

Attached is a catalogue shot of the untitled Dali taken from my brother's house when Viveca died. I'm sorry it has taken so long to get to you, but I'll have you know that I have done little else with my life but search high and low for an image to send you. After all my efforts, I sure do hope it helps your case. PCB

He opens the attachment, enlarges the image. He studies it, discerning three stick figures who look like they're dancing across desert dunes. There's something about the painting that suggests shifting sands. The hues are golden and clay and blue. An art aficionado he is not. But it's good to have the image. Mills forwards the picture to his squad. Then he sends a quick email back to PCB, thanking her for her noble efforts. He uses the word noble.

Central Phoenix Breast Center occupies a modern, three-story building across the street from Phoenix Memorial Hospital. Upon entering the lobby, Mills thinks they might have the wrong place.

"It looks like a fucking spa," he says.

"It's supposed to. For the calming effect," Kelly says.

"It's working."

"Maybe for you," she groans.

"You OK?"

"As well as can be expected."

They sit by a fountain, among a burst of bromeliads, until a woman with an overcompensating smile calls Kelly back for the procedure. Mills stares at the same magazine article for the entire hour that Kelly is gone. His eyes pace the pages as his feet would pace the floor if he were standing. He's thinking about everything, taking in nothing; he couldn't tell you what the article is about. There are words and they seem to be assembled in columns. With a few pictures. Far off in the distance, he sees a door open. It's the same door he's been watching for one hour and eleven minutes. But this time he recognizes the woman coming through. He gets up quickly, goes to her, put his arm around her. He says, "You okay?"

She says, "Yes," but sounds exhausted. She looks exhausted. Her face is void of color, mostly void of expression.

"Now what?" he asks.

"Now we go home."

"But what's next? When do we find out?"

"They say the report should go to my doctor in a few days and she'll call me."

"In the meantime we worry," Mills says.

"In the meantime we focus on our work," she corrects him.

"I'm trying to tell you it's okay not to be brave."

She punches him in the arm. "The good thing about being busy is I don't have to choose to be brave."

She has a point, as she always does.

When Aaliyah Jones returns Gus's call, he's mixing a bowl of salad while the meat cooks on the grill, two skewers for himself, two for

Ivy. His house is a mess. He hadn't noticed its descent into madness until now. There are clothes everywhere. Whites, darks, clean, dirty. Everywhere. "Thanks for getting back to me," Gus tells her. "I was wondering if you got the message."

"I got it yesterday, but I was tied up on some things," she says. "I'm sorry I didn't get back to you sooner. You sounded kind of urgent."

"I think you're in danger."

A dead pause. Like a solitary drumbeat. Then, "Because?"

"Because of the story you're working on," he replies.

"I know there's an element of danger. But I'm aware of my surroundings," she says.

He closes his eyes for a moment, sees the eyes, the eyes only, of men in masks moving clockwise in his field of vision. "You won't know until it's too late."

"Know what?" she asks.

"That they're after you."

"Is this a psychic thing?"

"Absolutely."

"May I swing by after work?" she asks.

"You may." The answer seemed to come from the ghost of him.

He eats with Ivy. She sits on the floor below him at the small bistro table in the kitchen. The lamb is scrumptious. He can tell by the way she's lapping it up. Her tongue wags with delight. He understands her satisfaction. He's enjoying it too. The news is on in the family room, but Gus isn't really paying attention. He hears a few headlines, but nothing much besides a truck accident on I-10 spilling watermelons or condoms (that's how poorly he's listening), a story about how it's too hot for planes to take off at Sky Harbor, and a break-in at a Scottsdale gallery. Then a commercial for Pampers.

He quickly cleans up the dinner plates and wipes down the kitchen. Then Gus scoops up the piles of clothes, dumps them all—without any effort to sort—in the laundry room, and closes the door. Aaliyah Jones knocks about fifteen minutes later. They sit in his office.

"What am I supposed to do?" she asks him.

He beams at her. He can't help it. "Well, if you back off the story, you lose it. But if you don't back off, I sense ugliness and danger for you."

"You have a nice smile," she tells him. "Do you know I have no idea how old you are?"

"Is that even relevant?" he asks her.

"Maybe. I'm a reporter, remember. I study people. Not quite like you do, but I study what I see. I look closely but you puzzle me."

"Don't be puzzled. I'm in my forties."

"What's your secret to aging?"

He laughs. "I don't have one," he says. "I don't think about it. Maybe that's the secret."

She tucks a leg under the other. "I know you're dating a rock star." Her eyes, now, are deep and dark and brooding like grottos where secrets hide. But she's told him everything. There are no secrets.

"Yes. I'm dating a musician."

"Billie Welch."

"Correct."

"She's an icon. A legend."

"I'm aware."

"She's lucky."

"Thank you," Gus says. "Now, about your story, and my vibes about you . . ."

"I'm not afraid," she preempts him. "I grew up in a tough neighborhood. I was always able to hold my own. And I got out."

"Right," Gus says. "And you've accomplished so much. You've transcended. And I want you to keep accomplishing. Keep climbing. Keep moving. You are destined for some great things, Aaliyah. But do me a favor. Change your driving habits. Take a different way to and from work every two or three days. Always let someone know where you're going if you're leaving the house."

She scoffs. "I can't do that. That's as bad as being intimidated by street gangs."

"Apples and oranges," Gus says.

"Look, I gotta go, Gus. I appreciate your support and your concern. I'll keep it mind, but I don't intend to be anyone's prisoner. OK?"

Gus has a sudden vision of her dancing. It's just her, alone, on a massive stage, one spotlight on her, the rest a smudge of black. She's naked, her body taut and long-limbed. Those limbs fly. She's an acrobat, a dove; she is beauty and he can't look away. He stands at the side of the stage. She comes at him, glowing in her light. She wraps herself around him. The song is familiar. He knows the melody. She curls into him and their lips graze. He's in the light. But when he opens his eyes, the woman is gone.

Kelly hangs up the phone. She'd been talking to a partner in the firm. She turns to Mills and says if the cancer doesn't kill her, the trial will. He balks at her announcement, but keeps the shuddering to himself. "We don't know if you have cancer," he tells his wife.

"Not the point," she says.

"It kind of is, Kelly. Let's cross that bridge when we get there. OK?"

"My point is Trey Robert Shinner is adding years to my age."

"How about your second chair? Can't he pitch in some more?"

"It's a she. That was her on the phone. She's doing her part," Kelly says. "But I think we're dealing with a problem that no one has really identified throughout Shinner's many, many run-ins with the law. He has multiple personality disorder."

Mills nods thoughtfully and then says, "So how'd you get this diagnosed?"

"I didn't," she replies. "That's just the thing. No one's ever diagnosed this guy with anything other than bipolar disorder. He's been in and out of state institutions, and I can't believe no one has witnessed what we've witnessed. It's like he goes in, they medicate him, he comes out, he stops taking medication, goes in again. And he's just a reoccurring patient to them, not someone who they're making the effort to study."

Mills leans on the kitchen counter. She's sitting opposite him. She had dimmed the lights and the glow is orange and anemic. "And what makes you think your diagnosis is correct?"

"Honey, he's a different person every time we see him."

"With different names? Does he introduce himself by different names?"

She shakes her head. "No. Not yet. But his personalities aren't consistent. It's like he shows up to court with a different one every day."

"He could be playing you, Kelly."

"One day he acts like an adolescent, other days a grown man. One day he talks like a gang banger, the next day he talks like a college professor."

"It's creeping you out."

"Yes."

"Who's paying his legal fees? You're not a public defender."

"It's coming out of a trust," she says. "He inherited a ton of money from his grandparents."

"Then why is he holding up bodegas? Stealing cars?"

"I'm telling you, Alex, he's possessed."

The word chills his blood. That's exactly the word Jimmy Jimenez used. *Possessed.* He says no more about Shinner. He gently changes the subject and they have dinner. He kicks her under the table and she laughs. He grabs her chair with his leg and pulls her close. "You're too good for me," he says. "You've always been too good for me."

"Oh, shut up, Alex," is her response. "Everyone in the world knows that. It's been translated into sixteen languages."

He shuts up. Somewhere else there's a language for how she's transformed him. Perhaps it's in the subtitles of their life, but he thinks it's even more nuanced than that. He won't find it in a dictionary or in a classroom. He won't find it in scripture, especially not the scripture he's reading now, the dishes cleared, rinsed, and stuffed in the dishwasher, as Kelly soaks in the tub, cleansing the impurities of Trey Robert Shinner and an afternoon of cancer screening from her pores.

Page 55
Glory God has selected you to come into the realms. You leave the living world behind when you come into our Home. You are not living here. You are rising. You are not beholden to the living world. You are not beholden to the living. You are not alive like they are. Thou shalt know the borderline between our realms and theirs! Thou shalt study the path! Thou shalt study the realms! Thou shalt worship none other than the one Glory God!

Page 101
Come now and sing with the angels. They have risen. Their wings will lift you from one realm to another. Onward and upward. Their voices will give you words for Glory God. In their radiance, you will discover your own hidden powers. In their radiance, they bequeath to you an energy. They will guide you into the light of the final realm.

> *And now we sing, responsively:*
> *(Angels at the altar)*
> *Glory God, Glory God, Glory God*
> *Without you, we do not rise*
> *Without you, we do not fly*
> *(Congregation)*
> *Glory God, Glory God, Glory God*
> *We pray for wings*
> *Your grace, your love, your Supreme knowledge.*
> *We pray to get nearer and nearer to thee, through every realm*
> *For we are your chosen, and we choose thee.*
> *(Angels at the altar)*
> *Cantara, cantra, Velpay,*
> *In the language of Angels*

We are with thee, Glory God, Glory God, Glory God
Protecting the floating ship of Taurara.
For we are your angels, and we understand our mission

Page 118
Rules of Angels Rising. Follow or thou shall perish.

That ought to make some light reading for another night. For now, Mills closes the book to an unnerving quiet in the house. It's stiller than still, as if there's a prowler padding around the perimeter. Or a death. He immediately thinks of Kelly, and the image of her lifeless body drowned in the tub propels him from the couch. Her face will be purple. Her body will be blue. She will have slipped away. He's breathing heavy, aiming for the master bath. But before he gets there he finds her in their bed. He feels like a dunce. She'd already crawled into bed and she's fast asleep. He crawls in beside her and checks her breath anyway.

20

The book is doing somersaults in his head. He can't get his mind off it. He's fascinated, but he doesn't understand a word of it. Maybe that's why he's fascinated. Whatever it is, he's so intrigued he's brought the book with him to the office. He keeps trying to take a peek at it, but he keeps getting interrupted, like right now by Morton Myers who comes busting in his office.

"Am I disturbing you, Alex?"

"No. I'd ask you to come in, but apparently you've read my mind."

"Sorry. Whatcha reading?"

"Scripture from the Church of Angels Rising."

"Any good?"

Mills laughs. "Oh yeah. It's a page turner."

"No, really. Is it, like, a real religion?"

Mills hyperbolizes a shrug. "What's a real religion?"

"You know, a major one. Like Christianity or Jewishness."

"I think they call it Judaism."

Myers sits. "I probably just had too much coffee this morning," he says. "What I meant was does the scripture sound like a real religion, you know, like something from the Bible?"

Mills shakes his head. "I don't know, Morty. Who's to say what a real religion is? If you read parts of the Bible, some of that stuff sounds as far out as the scripture from Norwood's church, maybe even more so. Maybe religion is just a state of mind."

"Oh, man. You're not thinking of signing up?"

"For what?"

"Norwood's church . . ."

Mills does backflips with his eyes. "Of course not, dumbass," he says. "Now are you here to discuss theology, or is there another reason for your visit?"

"More breaking news from Viveca Canning's cyber footprint," Myers replies. "Listen to this little morsel of information: I discovered a receipt for a one-way ticket for Viveca Canning to fly to P-A-P-E-E-T-E. I don't know how to say it, but I Googled it, and it's the airport city in Tahiti and the capital of French Polynesia."

"I don't know how to say it either," Mills tells him. "But that's good work."

"She was scheduled to leave in three weeks."

"Vacation probably."

"Maybe. But don't forget the calls from her phone records. She'd been calling a real estate developer in French Polynesia. And maybe you didn't hear me, but it was a *one-way* ticket."

"I heard you. Maybe she was actually moving to P-A-P-E-E-T-E."

"Bingo," Myers says, like he really means it.

His phone rings. It's the switchboard. He puts a hand up to Morty and takes the call. "Mills . . ."

"Can you take a call from Scottsdale PD?"

"What's it about?"

"Something about a break-in . . ."

A break-in? Why the fuck would they be calling homicide? But as a courtesy he says, "Yeah," and the operator puts the call through. The caller identifies herself as Lieutenant Liv Chang.

"Thought this might interest you, Detective," she says.

"I'm all ears, ma'am."

"I was working a break-in last night at a gallery here in town. Carmichael and Finn. The owner says you guys were just out here asking questions about a corpse."

"You mean the Viveca Canning case?"

"Right," the woman replies. "The gallery owner showed me your card. I'm headed back over there now if you want to swing by."

"Uh, yeah! I absolutely want to swing by," Mills says. "Thanks, Lieutenant. I appreciate the call."

"No problem, brother. But just so you know, there's not much to see. Broken storefront. Nothing was taken."

Mills tells her he'll take his chances and hangs up. "Look, Morty, can we pick up on this Tahiti stuff later? Aside from the spelling bee, it sounds romantic, but I gotta go."

A deflated Morton Myers turns on his heels and leaves. Mills follows immediately, texting Preston to meet him in the parking lot.

"I'm right here," Preston says, his head rising above his cubicle.

"Great. Let's go."

Gus waits inside the air-conditioned vestibule. In the distance he sees the broil of the day, the way the tendrils of heat rise, layer by layer, across the valley. The air wrinkles in the gust, and the billowing heat, clouds of it, builds an invisible prison. He hears someone say the planes are grounded. He hears another person say, "They can't take off in this heat." And he remembers hearing something like that on the news. A guy in a mechanic uniform weighs in and says the heat doesn't affect arriving flights. And the two others are relieved. They say as much. So is Gus. He's waiting for Billie. He didn't realize how much he missed her until he stands here waiting. Sure, he missed her. But here, the anticipation of her strips him naked, gets all the other distractions out of the way. It's a tangible thing, not an ephemeral notion. He feels her, feels the absence of her. He smells her, smells her absence. And the touch.

She chartered a jet out of Burbank and is due here at Sky Harbor in minutes. He watches the sky. He can easily tell the private jets from the big commercial ones. An older woman with a fedora and diamonds galore is waiting in the same vestibule. Is she waiting out the heat to board her Gulfstream for her weekend in Cabo, or is she waiting for her Gulfstream to courier her boytoy from LA for an erotic weekend in Phoenix? She's seventy-five, if not older. Gus realizes he's been staring too long when the woman curls her lips into a lascivious smile and winks. She's 75 Shades of Gray. He turns to the window again and notices a small, private jet taxiing to a space on the tarmac. He just knows it's Billie. Not a psychic thing. Maybe a psychic thing. It's bubbling in his blood. The aircraft door opens upward and outward before lowering a set of stairs to the ground. Nobody exits. He can't take it. It's his crazy heart, in love, unsure, wild, confused, hopeful, tortured. Finally, the pilot pokes his head out, then makes way for a burst of black lace caught up in the wind. It can be no other than Billie Welch. She hovers at the first step while she lowers her sunglasses against the blazing sky. There she is, curling her pup, Glinda, into her arm as she hoists her enormous shoulder bag into place. Gus watches her approach the ramp to the doorway. He watches her notice him and he sees the feisty grin appear on her face when she does. She quickens her pace. She comes in gushing, "I love you. I love you. I love you." Half singing, half laughing. She's entirely crazy. She says she has to pee. "That lavatory on the plane was so small, I could barely fit all my hair in there."

"You have a lot of hair."

"Do you think there's a restroom in the terminal?"

"Over there," he says, pointing around a corner.

"Do you mind?"

"Who am I to stand between a woman's bladder and the ladies room?"

She drops Glinda on the floor and hands Gus the leash. She's gone in a flourish and returns with a little less drama. "I'm good," she says. "Shall we?"

It's only a twenty-minute ride or so to Paradise Valley, but Billie yawns sweetly and nods off on Gus's arm. He drives her to the Desert Charm, her favorite hideaway while she's in Phoenix. After they're checked into the bungalow, she orders lunch for them and asks room service to bring an "abundance of coffee."

"Why don't you take a nap?" Gus asks her. "If I know you, you're going to stay up all night and work anyway . . ."

"Because," she says, curling an arm around his, "I want to be awake now. For you. Come on."

She escorts him out to the private courtyard. "I took the day off," he tells her.

"I know. But I hope you don't mind if Miranda stops by later just to say hello."

Miranda is Billie's younger sister who lives in Scottsdale.

"No problem," Gus tells her. They sit side-by-side holding hands.

"I'm going back out on the road," she says.

He doesn't respond right away. There's something about her that feels autonomous. And sometimes all it takes is seven words. It's nothing new. She's not aware. She's means no harm. She lives in a different world. "Wow," he says finally. "What prompted that?"

"I got a great offer to do a bunch of concerts in Australia and New Zealand," she says. "I didn't go there on my last tour, which was a miss because I have a really big fan base in both countries. And I absolutely love it there."

"I know you do."

"Wanna come?" she asks, squeezing his hand.

"For how long?"

"Three weeks."

He turns to her. "I just can't up and leave for three weeks."

"So just come for the first week."

"When are you leaving?"

"Not for another month," she says. "They're still working on the contracts."

There's a knock on the door. It's room service. She has ordered a spread of fruit and a massive chef's salad for the two of them. The waiter reveals the last plate under the silver cover; it's some kind of torte in three shades of chocolate. Billie looks at Gus mischievously. He gives the waiter a healthy tip and sends him on the way. They're about five minutes into chowing down without coming up for air or words when Gus thinks, what the hell, and says, "You came in the terminal this afternoon singing, 'I love you, I love you, I love you.'"

"So?"

"So, where's the 'I love you' in 'I'm going back on the road'?"

"Oh."

"Oh?"

"Well, come on. You know me better by now. I don't mean anything by it."

"By 'I love you'?"

She kicks him under the table. "No. Not by that," she says with a growl. "You know I don't mean anything by making the leap from one thing to the next. You know how my brain works."

"Right."

"Meanwhile, did you say you love me too?" she asks him.

"Oh."

"Oh?"

"Touché, Ms. Welch," he says impishly. "But you said it with such gusto. You said it three times. I guess my brain must have perceived that you said it enough for both of us."

"Lame," she says with a throaty laugh. "That is so fucking lame."

Maybe it is. They eye each other with a knowing smile. But there seems to be an unknowing smile just below the surface. They continue to graze the salad tentatively. And as they do, Gus tries to shoo away the doubts grazing at the edges of his intuition.

Scottsdale police have blocked off the area around the Carmichael and Finn Gallery, almost two blocks in each direction. Mills thinks that's excessive until he sees the bomb squad truck wedged into the alley beside the building. He and Preston flash their badges when they reach the yellow tape. Mills asks a Scottsdale cop for Lieutenant Liv Chang. The cop relays the information into his radio. In less than a minute Lieutenant Chang appears. What she lacks in height (she barely comes up to Mills's shoulder), she makes up for in intensity.

"Call me Liv," she says, shaking their hands with the clamping force of a vise. "I'll take you inside."

They follow her aggressive footsteps into the gallery. Mills recognizes the place, of course; nothing has changed since his first visit except for a smashed window out front, and half the door is missing.

"Brazen," Preston says.

Liv chuckles, her spastic body still in motion. They follow her back into the gallery's restricted area, into the maze of hallways that lead to Viveca Canning's vault. "We think your victim's vault was the target."

"Nothing was taken from the gallery itself?" Mills asks.

"Nothing. According to the owners," Liv says.

Mills is almost sure he spotted Jacqueline Carmichael out of the corner of his eye. She's hard to miss with that fortress of hair on her head. "All this expensive art and nothing taken," he muses.

"Which is why we believe that the perp or perps were after the Canning vault alone," Liv says.

Mills stares at the vault with his arms folded. Preston is noting the injuries to the door. "This place is obviously alarmed," Mills says.

"They disabled the first layer of protection," the lieutenant says. "That is, the local alarm here in the gallery that would have set bells and sirens off at the time of entry. Most of these galleries have secondary, silent alarms that go right to the police station."

"And these idiots thought they got in here without tripping any alarms at all," Preston says. He's kneeling on the ground examining the sliver of space under the door.

"Our sirens scared them off though," Liv tells them. "They obviously heard the sirens in the distance and snuck out the back door before we got on scene."

Mills shakes his head. "But one thing doesn't make sense. How'd they think they'd get into the vault so quickly? Did they think there'd just be a key hanging in the office? I mean, there are two locked doors, password protected, that they'd have to get through. There isn't even a lock to pick."

"It's pretty clear they had explosives," Liv says. "Not powerful ones. But the bomb squad has disarmed everything."

She leads them both to the end of the hallway. They stop just short of the back foyer, where bomb squad technicians are meticulously examining two brown paper bags and the tangled metal coils sprouting from their tops. On the floor lay a few long, thin cylinders, apparently detached from the coils. "Pipe bombs," Mills says. "This looks like someone had a serious mission."

Liv Chang laughs. "This shit couldn't blow up a cereal box."

"What do you mean?" Mills asks her.

"From what these guys are telling me, only one of the tubes shows signs of an explosive," she explains. "The perps were either in a hurry, underestimated what it would take to do the job, didn't understand the strength of the vaults, or were just plain stupid."

"I think we've already established they were idiots," Mills reminds her.

"I have a few other things to check on," she says. "Feel free to hang out."

"But how did the explosives get back here? These hallways are all locked. You can't access them from the gallery without a key, without codes."

She offers a wince. "Seems like they pistol-whipped the security guard on duty," she says. "Made him open the doors. We got a statement from him. I'll get it to you."

"What about prints? Any other forensics? Can you share when you're done?"

She smiles at him. But even the smile is quick, compact, intense, and gone in a split second. "Of course. Anything you need. Happy to help."

She's already halfway down the hallway. Mills and Preston drift back toward Viveca Canning's vault. "I guess they planned to wire up the door or something . . ."

"Or just set the explosive by the door," Preston says. "Obviously not sophisticated."

"No. In fact, the lack of sophistication stuns me," Mills says. "A real art thief is not going to break a storefront window. A real art thief doesn't plan to fail because a real art thief doesn't get a second chance. You know?"

Preston nods. "Yeah. Something ain't right here."

"You mind if I go find the braided bun who goes by the name Jacqueline Carmichael?"

"Not at all. I'll go review a few things with Scottsdale," Preston tells him. "And if you want, I can follow up with Chang. Not just here, but until her investigation's over."

Mills tilts his head, takes in his colleague from an angle. "I think she's half your age, Ken."

The guy scoffs. "Please, Mills. What do you know? She couldn't be much younger than thirty-five . . ."

"My math was in the ballpark. Have fun," Mills says as he backs away.

Jacqueline Carmichael is not in the exhibit rooms as Mills had hoped. He checks her office but finds it empty. His next stop is the reception desk, where he's met by Carmichael's assistant. Her face a bloom of hope, she says, "Jacqueline's stepped outside. Come with me. I'll take you to her."

The oven heat nearly knocks him over when he walks out the front door. The assistant points. Jacqueline is at the far corner of the building, clutching something in her hand. "Hi," Mills says when he reaches the corner. She turns. Her immediate reaction is fear in one eye, dread in the other, WTF all over the rest of her face. Not a receptive expression, but who gives a fuck anyway. It's hot. Crazy hot. Sweat-down–your-crack hot.

She's jabbering on the phone. She holds up her "one-minute" finger which, Mills notes, is happily not her middle one. He waits for the minute to pass, and then for another, and a couple more after that until she finally hangs up and says, "I'm sorry, Detective."

"This isn't my crime scene, ma'am, but is it okay if I ask you some questions?"

"That's fine," she says, her face still a smear of discontent. "But it's an inferno out here."

"I had noticed."

"Before my makeup runs off my face can we go inside? To my office?"

In her office she lunges for a bottle of water and offers one to Mills. He shakes his head and says, "I need to know if anyone has been in the Canning vault since we were last here asking about the Dali."

"No. Nobody."

"No one asking about the Dali? Or that chest? Or any part of the Viveca Canning collection?"

"Just her son."

"Well, that's somebody, ma'am. When did he drop by?"

"Yesterday," she says. "It's in the log. The Scottsdale police have it."

"Good," Mills says. "Did Bennett go into the vault?"

"He did."

"Were you with him?"

"Yes."

"Did he remove anything?"

"No."

"Are you sure?"

She flashes him one of those do-you-think-I'm-an-idiot looks. It freezes there in all its patronizing charm until he says, "Okay. Did he tell you what he was looking for?"

"No," she replies. "I think he just wanted to take inventory and see that everything was intact."

"So, do a timeline for me. Can you remember how many hours passed between his visit and when you were broken into last night?"

She pauses to reapply her insanely red lipstick, gazes into her compact, and then blots with a tissue. She must go through more makeup in a day than Kelly goes through in a year. "The alarm went into the police station around 9:30 last night. He was here probably at two in the afternoon."

"Did he touch that old chest in there?"

"Just to make sure it was still locked, I think."

"Did you tell Scottsdale cops he was here?"

Her eyes go buggy. "Uh, hello? Detective? That's why Lieutenant Chang called you!"

He sits there with no reaction until she recoils, her insult a failure. "And you gave them a log of all your other guests?"

"Just as I already told you."

"Detectives ask a lot of repeat questions. Like how do you get those braids to stay like that?"

Now she's a coquette. "You never asked that question before," she notes demurely.

"I'm kidding," Mills says. "I don't need to know."

"They're very strong, these braids," she tells him. "Want to see me unwrap them?"

He takes that as his cue to stand.

He meets up with Preston, who's loitering in the front gallery room, and the two of them head to the car. Less than a minute into their drive, his phone rings. It's a San Francisco area code, and he knows who it is. It's Jillian Canning. She says she has a book for him, a book from her mother's library as he had requested. "For your psychic," she says.

"Oh, right. Great. Thanks. If you're at your Aunt Phoebe's, we're not far."

"Actually, I'm out and about. You know Hava Java at the Biltmore?"

He laughs. "Of course I do. In a valley of iced tea, it's a coffee oasis."

Preston snorts beside him.

"I'm just heading into the oasis right now," she says. "Wanna swing by?"

"Yup. Be there in ten or fifteen."

When he's off the phone, Preston says, "Don't give up your day job."

And he says, "For what?"

And Preston says, "For poetry."

"Go fuck yourself. And I mean that symbolically," Mills tells him. "Considering your age."

21

Hava Java bustles with the cacophony of the coffee grinder competing with the cappuccino maker competing with the flatulence of the whipped cream nozzles—and the people, a cross section of valley professionals, hipsters, academics, beauty queens, and drama queens, some of them whacking away on their laptops, some in lively conversation. This is poetry, he knows. The poetry of coffee. Jillian waves them over. They sit. "Can I get you a cup of coffee?" she asks.

"Thanks," Mills says. "But we'll get our own. Department policy."

She shrugs and pulls a book out of her bag. "Here," she says. "Hope it helps."

She hands him an exquisitely bound edition of *The Secret Garden* by Frances Hodgson Burnett. "I've read a lot of the classics," he tells her. "But not this one."

"Are you taking it to your psychic or curling up to it in bed?"

"My psychic," he says. "I already have some new reading material. I'm reading a book from the Church of Angels Rising."

She stops in midsip, softly chokes. "Why?" she gasps. "How?"

"To learn more about the church and whatever Angelism is," he answers. "We know about the vast amount of money your mother had originally bequeathed to the church, on top of what she had donated over the years. We're kind of wondering what kind of faith calls for that kind of loyalty. She had changed her will, but it keeps the church in play . . ."

"So you're investigating the church?"

Mills responds with a lone-syllable laugh. "Not exactly."

"Someone should," she says.

Mills nods. "I can see why you'd feel that way. Some of this is just personal interest to me."

"But how did you get the book?" she asks. "They're not allowed out of the church. Ever."

"It was given to me," Mills says. "By an anonymous source."

She throws her head back, an eyebrow raised, her eyes cartoonishly wide. "You better be careful, Alex," she says, every word more grave than the one before. "No one, and I mean no one, is supposed to have that book outside the church. None of the church literature is public."

Mills smiles. "Thanks for the warning. But we'll be fine, Jillian. Don't worry."

"I've seen people beaten for taking it home. Never mind giving it to a nonmember."

Preston jolts his chair closer to the table. "What did you just say?"

She closes her eyes and shakes her head. "Fuck," she mutters. "Fuck. Fuck. Fuck it."

"No, really," Preston insists. "Please elaborate."

"I can't," she says, her eyes still closed.

"Please," Preston begs. "Just give me a little more."

"He took the book out of the church by mistake."

"Who?" Mills asks.

"Just some church member," she says. "There was a $1,500 fine and a three-day work camp assignment for any member caught with a publication outside the church."

"Jesus," Mills whispers.

"Jesus has absolutely nothing to do with this." She says something else, but the noise of the café chops up her words. When Mills asks her to repeat herself, she says, "He refused to pay. He refused to go."

"Was there some kind of hearing?" Preston asks.

She laughs. "If that's what you want to call it. It's a joke. But yes, he was heard before a panel of his peers. He told them truthfully he had not even made it out to his car in the parking lot when he realized he had taken the book by mistake. But by then someone had already turned him in. They sentenced him to the maximum."

Preston looks at her as if she's high. "That's some story," he says.

"It's true," she tells them. "When he refused to abide by the sentence, they beat the shit out of him."

"Who did?"

She looks away. Her face is a portrait of sorrow and anger and bitterness, each a Picasso-like shape, an angle of her, a different way of seeing her. And Mills thinks he sees her. "I can't do this," she whispers. "Certainly not here. I've said too much already in public. There could be repercussions."

"We understand," Preston tells her, his eyes sympathetic. "We need to know more, but we can wait for a better opportunity."

Mills nods, even as another approach to her occurs to him. "You ever been to Tahiti?"

"Huh?"

"Tahiti. You ever been?"

"Interesting change of subject, but yes," she says. "My parents took us there a few times over the years when we were younger. Beautiful place. One of my favorite places, now that I think about it."

"Were you aware your mother was planning a trip there?"

"No. When?"

"Next month."

"No. But she wouldn't necessarily tell me," Jillian says. "She travels a lot. And we weren't completely reconnected anyway. That's my biggest regret now."

Mills tells her that her mother had purchased a one-way ticket.

Her cup is halfway to her mouth when she pauses and says, "What?"

"Phoenix to LA. Change planes. LA to Tahiti," Mills recites. "No return."

"That makes no sense."

"That's what we said. Any chance she was buying real estate there?"

"Could be," Jillian says. "Anything's possible. But if she was getting ready to move in a month, she would have told me."

"Unless she was running away," Preston suggests.

"From?"

"From whoever wanted her dead," Preston replies.

"I don't know what to say," Jillian says. "Maybe you should talk to her lawyer. And I'm not saying that to shut you down this time. I'm saying that because her lawyer would probably know about her real estate dealings."

She's right. Viveca's lawyer probably knows a lot of things about the dead angel. If only Mills can get the douchebag to return his calls. "Can we meet again in private, someplace safe like my office?" he asks Jillian. "I will do whatever I can to protect you if you feel in danger. But I have to know more about this cult."

She exhales a catharsis as deep as a canyon. Choking back tears she says, "Thank you. Thank you for calling it what it is. You don't know what that means to me."

Mills nods, says nothing. Preston, the avuncular one, grabs her by the hand and squeezes it, and that's enough for her to recover her smile, thin as it is. Mills gets to his feet. Preston follows.

"No coffee for you guys?" she asks.

"We'll get some on the way out," Mills tells her. He holds up *The Secret Garden*. "Thanks for the book. I'll let you know if my psychic finds anything noteworthy. But tell me, how did you get into your mother's place to get it? You have a key?"

She starts to pull her things together. "No," she replies. "My brother gave me one. How generous of him."

"But how did you get through the guard gates at Copper Palace?" Mills asks.

"My Aunt Phoebe drove me."

"Does she have a remote?" Preston asks.

"I don't know," she says, her voice betraying some annoyance. "The guard just let us in."

"Only asking for your protection," Mills says, aware of the elasticity of truth. As he turns away, he says, "We'll be in touch. As I said, I'd like to meet with you again."

As soon as he starts the car, a steaming cup of coffee in the holder beside him, he dials Gus.

The "I love you"s came, at first, in panting breaths. Then they climbed the scales. The "I love you"s became more fast and furious the longer they went at it. The longer they rocked into each other, the longer Gus buried himself in her, the longer they rolled and intertwined and the further they sunk their kisses into each other's faces. The "I love you"s yielded only for the muffle of a kiss. He felt himself inside her, every inch of her pocket closing around him. Yes, he loves her. Yes, he said so. Yes, she heard him. And he heard her. It's not just the sex talking. It's the intensity. It's the way they absorb each other's skin. When he wakes up an hour later, she's still sleeping. Gus slips out of bed and quietly pads off to the shower. Then he sits out in the private courtyard donning one of those ridiculous hotel bathrobes, something Gleason Norwood would wear in the spa while waiting for his anal bleaching. Just a guess. He flips through Billie's copy of *Rolling Stone* magazine. With every page he turns, he ages a decade. He does not recognize the name of one band, one solo performer, anybody. He supposes Beyoncé is a household name. But not in his household. No criticism, he's just not drawn to her. Valley Imaging provides playlists for patients who'd rather hear music than the rattling and rolling of the MRI, and he's heard Beyoncé on those playlists and can't help but wonder why she's always in such a hurry. She sings so fast. As if she has to finish the song and go pee. There are no more Billie Welches out there. Except for the one in the bedroom. His phone rings. It's Alex.

"I've got something for you," the detective says.

"My visions tell me it's a Rolex."

"Ha ha! Once again, your visions come up short."

"Thanks, Alex. What's up, bro?"

"It's a book. From the dead woman. I need you to work your magic."

"I'll try," Gus tells him. "I'm at the Desert Charm. Bring it by."

"Oh right. Billie's in town. This can wait 'til Monday."

"Are you sure?"

"Yeah. No problem. Go enjoy."

Later, after Billie is up and showered, after she takes Glinda for a short walk in the stifling heat, Miranda arrives with her puppy and a bottle of wine. Billie pours a glass for herself and her sister and hands Gus a beer. Miranda is Gus's age, divorced, no kids. Billie worries about her sister's loneliness, her tendency to isolate. Billie doesn't seem to remember that, before Gus, she wrote hit songs about her own loneliness and isolation. Their parents are gone. So it's just the two sisters. Which is why Billie brings Miranda along for the ride as often as she can. They're the best of friends, overlapping at the core, as they should, even if it means that for Gus, sometimes, three's a crowd. Miranda will accompany Billie on the Australia and New Zealand tour. "You should come, Gus," Miranda says from her spot on the floor. Gus and Billie are stretched out on a sofa, the short part of the "L" perfectly free for Miranda, but she chooses the floor; she's ensconced on a huge pillow looted from the bedroom, wedged between Glinda and her own pup, a Maltese named Garbo.

"Billie and I have already discussed it," he says. "Maybe for one week of the tour."

"You'll need a week just to get over the jet lag," Miranda tells him.

"Not if we do what we did last time," Billie says, a twist of conspiracy in her voice. "Last time we stopped in Tahiti both ways. It breaks up the flight almost evenly. Lovely place too."

"It's paradise," Miranda chimes in. "Gorgeous. We took this tiny little plane to Bora Bora and hung out there for a few days. I love it there, Gus."

After "tiny little plane" the rest of the words were mere mosquitoes to him. Because they were all but drowned out by the roar of engines, jumbo jet engines, struggling engines, failing engines, engines coming apart. "No! No, you can't do that!" he cries.

"What?" Billie asks, sitting up, grabbing his arm. "What's wrong?"

"You can't do that," he repeats. "That's my vision. I see a plane going down in the South Pacific. I've been having this vision since I came home from LA. Please, don't go . . ."

"Go where? To Tahiti or to Australia? Or both?" Billie asks him.

"I can't let you fly over the Pacific right now."

Billie stares at him. "Let?"

"You know what I mean."

She gives him a coy grin and then says, "How do I know this isn't a ploy because you don't want me to do the tour down there?"

"Because you know it isn't. You know me. I'm not one for ploys."

"You can tell me more about the vision later, Gus. Not now. I don't want to scare my sister."

Miranda sets her wine glass on the floor beside her. "Oh no. Please scare me."

Gus describes his vision of the ill-fated flight. Miranda gasps at all the right places. He edits the most graphic of the images. Still, Billie turns away through most of his story, studying something outside at the courtyard pool, the fountain, maybe, or nothing at all. She's quiet over dinner, despite her sister's prodding. She's quiet after Miranda leaves. She stays up after Gus has gone to bed. "Gonna write in my journal," she tells him. The rest of the weekend is chilled, despite 108-degree heat. They love and they make love, and it's purely mechanical, but they don't talk about the tour anymore.

22

There's an email waiting for Mills from the OME Monday morning.

Alex—

We're done with the Canning body. We're preparing to release to family, pending your go ahead. Let us know.

Mills writes back, tells them to release the body. The quick email exchange reminds him to check in with Roni Gates at the lab. She says that tests for possible trace DNA from the shooter have, so far, come back inconclusive. But they did find a few stray hairs that did not belong to the victim, as well as fibers from a garment that were not consistent with the clothes Viveca Canning was wearing at the time of her death. "They might match a garment worn by the killer," Roni says. "Or the fibers could just be stray ones from other clothes Viveca wore around the house."

"That's going to be a little harder to nail down than the hair," Mills says.

"Yup," Roni confirms. "It will be. Let's talk again tomorrow, if we can."

Turns out they're talking again only minutes later.

Powell and Preston have skulked into his office, trying to remain marginal while he finishes his call. As soon as he hangs up, they pounce. "We've got the warrant," Preston says, "to search the gallery. Just came from the judge now."

"We can search her vault *and* open the lock on the chest," Powell tells him. "Looks like the break-in actually helped our cause."

"How so?" Mills asks.

"Convinced the judge that something isn't right over there," Preston replies. "The judge agreed the break-in could have been an attempt to destroy evidence."

"Love the judge, whoever he is," Mills says.

"She," Powell corrects him. "Judge Louise Leary."

"Love Louise," Mills says. "Now let's get some techs to meet us over there."

Which explains why he's back on the phone with Roni Gates, who agrees to meet them at Carmichael and Finn. "Bring someone who knows how to pop a lock without damaging it," he tells her.

"We're experts, Alex. Don't worry."

About an hour later, the team meets in Scottsdale, a few blocks away from the gallery. Preston and Powell have joined him to execute the warrant. Myers stayed behind, still knee-deep with the cyber forensics team. Mills watches as the young Roni Gates emerges from her van, accompanied by one of her colleagues. There's a dry breeze in the air, mildly comforting, but not enough to cool them off. "If anyone makes a scene," Mills tells the others, "it's not going to be us. It will likely be one of the owners. But we're going to execute this thing as quietly and unobtrusively as possible."

He scans the circle of faces, and the team unanimously nods around him.

The receptionist says Jacqueline Carmichael has stepped out to lunch. Ideally, Mills would like the owner there, but senses that, faced with a search, Carmichael would be the explosive type, the way she always seems to be brewing a couple ounces of crazy just below the surface. "That's okay," Mills tells the receptionist. "Ms. Carmichael doesn't have to be here to execute the warrant."

"But Mr. Finn is out of the country," the woman says. "Only those two can get you into the Canning vault. No one else has the code. We can get you into the back hallways, but not into the vault itself."

"If you wouldn't mind, then, please call Ms. Carmichael and ask her to return," Mills says. "We'll be waiting in the gallery."

The team, five of them including Mills, circulate through the main gallery feigning interest in the objects on display. He's asked the others to keep an eye out for any anomalies that beckon for inspection.

"The thing is," Preston says, "unless you live in an art gallery, how do you know an anomaly when you see one?"

Mills gives a quick laugh. "Like anywhere else, Uncle Ken, you just look for things that don't make sense."

Preston gestures to the exhibits with a sardonic smile.

"I know," Mills says. "I don't understand any of this. Especially not the modern stuff."

Powell overhears him. "Yeah, but you love your literature. That's already above and beyond the call of duty."

Mills shakes his head and turns to a sculpture in the center of the adjoining room. Three white orbs, one atop the other, stand like a snowman. The Arizona flag is wrapped around its neck, like an ascot. A sign on the floor reads: **Buttplug, A Salute to Former Maricopa County Sheriff Clayman Tarpo.** Mills doesn't know whether to laugh or cringe, but he laughs and he can't control it, and the others, beckoned by curiosity, join him, and it's a feast of laughter. Tarpo was an asshole, is an asshole, now aspires to be an asshole in the U.S. Senate. And now this human asshole has a buttplug named personally for him; the poetic justice deserves a Pulitzer, if poems get that kind of thing. Then all the revelry is sadly interrupted by the voice of Jacqueline Carmichael, who peppers the feast of laughter with her cries of disbelief. "Oh my God. Oh my God. Oh my God," she cries. "This can't be happening."

Mills turns and she's breathing in his face. "Hello, Ms. Carmichael. Sorry to disturb your lunch."

"My lunch?" the woman says, her eyes saucers of indignation. "You're disturbing my life. Can I see you for a moment in private, please, Detective?"

"We have a warrant to search the place, ma'am," he tells her without budging.

"What for?"

"You are entitled to read the warrant, ma'am."

"The whole place, or just Viveca's vault?"

"There are no restrictions from the judge."

She turns on her heels. "Give me just one second to call my lawyer," she screeches as she walks away.

Mills shakes his head at her retreat, then follows her and finds her in her office, where she's pacing with a phone to one ear. "I see. I see. Okay. Please do," she says to the person on the other end. Then she hangs up.

"I didn't ask you to come back here, Detective."

"Look, I have a warrant to execute on this place. It's legal."

"Aren't I entitled to have a lawyer here?"

"I just let you call your lawyer."

"He wasn't in. That was an assistant."

"If you're asking if we're required to have your lawyer here, the answer is no."

She winces audibly. "What if I refuse to let you into the vault?"

"I'll have you arrested."

"But I'm a good girl!"

Mills does a double take. A good girl? He's reasonably sorry to see a sophisticated, intelligent businesswoman, when threatened by authority, devolve to a sixteen-year-old debutante. "Let's begin in the Canning vault. Maybe that's all we'll need to see."

She drops her head, leads him out of the office. He calls the team to join him and, as they gather, Jacqueline Carmichael puts the code in to enter the first hallway. Security lights come on as they meander through the maze, a small mission of footsteps hitting the concrete floor. Another code, another hallway. And finally, the vault. The gallery owner enters first, flips on the lighting. Mills detects a kind of hushed admiration and awe among those who have not been in the vault before. He lets it steep. Normally he'd immediately say, "let's get to work," but the first impression of the collection back here, art posing in a macabre purgatory, speaks to the stakes. Jacqueline clears her throat, but Mills ignores her. Instead, he stares into the dull orange lights and watches as they form halos, and remembers never to forget for whom he investigates. Then he steps forward and turns to the others. He lets out a heavy sigh, intentionally, hoping to work Jacqueline's last nerve. As committed as he is to the victims, he is that apathetic to those who'd thwart his work.

"Okay," he drawls, "I'd like everything in this vault dusted to see if we have recent prints. Do the chest and the padlock first, because after that's processed we're breaking in."

"Oh no you're not," shouts a shrill Jacqueline Carmichael. "You didn't say a word about breaking into anything!"

"But I did say the warrant gave me no restrictions," Mills reminds her.

She steps forward and points a finger in his face. "I'm sure it doesn't allow you to damage possessions in my gallery."

"Actually," he says, very gently moving her finger back to a neutral place, "the warrant affidavit specifically grants me permission to disengage the lock. Would you like me to read it to you?"

"If you break that lock, who says you can't break the hand off a sculpture?"

"So *that's* what happened to the Venus de Milo," Powell says.

"No one is breaking any sculptures," he assures Jacqueline, flashing Powell a beseeching look. "Now, please . . ."

The techs have already started. Preston and Powell are snapping pictures, taking notes. The gallery owner huffs and puffs in the corner. *Let her fucking sulk*, he thinks; *she* doesn't have breast cancer. That he knows of. He steps into the hallway and calls his wife. "You okay?"

"Yeah. I guess."

"What can I do?"

"Nothing," she says. "Just concentrate on your work. Not me."

He laughs. "Don't be ridiculous, Kelly."

"The judge was great," she says. "He kept the trial in recess 'til tomorrow. I've been home ever since."

"Doing what? Worrying?"

"Laundry. Your t-shirts stink, by the way."

"It's very hot out, as you might have noticed."

"And I'm going over some financial aid stuff with Trevor . . ."

"Shit. I thought we finished that."

She laughs. "It never ends. And I thought the football scholarship would cover more than it does."

"Let me do it. You don't need that on your plate right now."

"We'll talk later," she says. "Love you."

Back in the vault, Roni says there seem to be fresh prints on the chest.

"Seriously? I didn't dare even hope for that."

"Well, we haven't found much else, but we still have a ways to go."

"Before you continue, I'd like Pablo to do the honor and pick the lock."

"No prob," she says with a smile. "You hear that, Pablocito? We need you and your tweezers."

Pablo Cruz, the other tech, approaches brandishing the necessary tool. Preston shoots video and, in less than five minutes, the padlock slips off and dunks on the floor. "Nice," Mills tells the tech. Then, donning plastic gloves, he approaches the mysterious box. He kneels before the chest and flips the latch downward; it lowers with a rusty creak. Preston shoots video over his shoulder as Mills lifts the top, it, too, creaking with the aches and pains of age. At first the bin looks empty, a black rectangle of nothing. But he lowers his hands and feels around. In the lower left corner of the box, Mills's fingers stumble upon an object, something wrapped in burlap or cloth. He can't see because his own shadow is hampering the view. He shifts on his knees. He won't lift the object, whatever it is, until he knows it won't break in his hands. He shifts again so his own figure doesn't block the light, and he can see a small fabric sack clasped closed by a rope. He lets his fingers listen for cracking, snapping, breaking. And nothing. The content of the sack feels solid enough to lift. He takes it by two hands, each end by the fingers, and raises it from the chest. Then he pivots and places the discovery on the floor.

"Still shooting?" he asks Preston.

"Of course."

"The light in here sucks," Mills says.

"I'm adjusting fine for the light."

Mills unties the thin rope at the neck of the sack. He slips his hand inside and feels for the object. It's sturdy, thick, heavy, but relatively flat. He slides his hand out with the object resting partly in his palm. He shifts again, to allow for light. He's looking at a key. A big key, to be sure, but a key. He's holding a large, vintage skeleton key. In this light, it looks antique bronze with an intricate head.

"That's an old key," Preston says.

"Or something posing as an old key," Mills says.

Roni has come close, hovering for the big reveal. "I can get it analyzed," she tells them.

"You're a key expert?" he asks her.

"I'm an expert in something different every day," she says. "Actually, I know a guy."

"A guy?"

"We come across a lot of keys in our work, Alex."

"Great," he says. "But let's bag it and get it entered into evidence. I'll worry about the analysis later."

"Analysis?" Preston asks. "I'll give you an analysis: the woman associates a key with her Dali. Maybe that key is supposed to open this chest. So we break open the chest and what do we find? We find a key. It's the universe fucking with us, Mills. What more analysis do you need?"

Mills laughs. "You make a good point. But if you're right about one thing leading us to another, in a universe-is-fucking-with-us kind of way, then we need to know where this key leads us next. I want to focus on that first, before we worry about how old the key is."

"But Alex, the origin of the key could be the thing that tells us where or what it leads to," Roni says. "You know that."

He nods. "You're right. I do know that. I concede. My head's not quite in it. Yes, of course. All of the above. Maybe the design of the head is proprietary. That would be a huge clue, no? So, again, let's start with bagging the damn thing and taking it in as evidence."

He hears the click of heels in stereo, one sharpened stiletto in each ear. "Take what in as evidence, Detective?" Jacqueline asks.

He pivots. "This," he says, pointing to the skeleton key.

She shakes her head. "No. No. You can't remove anything from the property. I can't allow you to do this. All of this is trusted to me."

"I see you don't understand how warrants work," Mills says, "and I don't have time to give you a crash course, but suffice it to say that a warrant is specifically issued to gather evidence." He points to the key. "Evidence. We're gathering it."

The demure debutante returns to her pout. "Why are you doing this to me?"

"We're not doing this *to* you, Jacqueline," he says. "We're doing this *for* Viveca Canning."

Remember to never forget. That's about the only thing that gets him through right now with a wife at home fending off a disaster. He turns to Preston and Powell. "While these guys finish up dusting in here, let's go check and make sure there isn't anything else on the premises that we need to inventory."

They follow him into the hallway, the gallery owner on their heels. "I can't be two places at once," she calls to them. "I can't be in the Canning vault and following you around at the same time."

"Then choose one," Mills calls to her without turning.

Unfortunately, she chooses to follow them. Mills asks her to name the owner of each and every vault, up and down each hallway. At first, she refuses citing client confidentiality, claiming that she has "an actual confidentiality agreement" with each of her clients. Mills gently disavows her of her notion and explains that the law supersedes any agreements she might have with her clients and that the warrant preempts her objections by assuming confidential material might be taken as evidence. "That's it, Jacqueline. Search Warrant 101 is over. Let's go vault by vault and you tell me who owns the contents inside."

"I just don't know how that's helpful to your investigation."

"The nice thing," Powell says, rescuing Mills, and it's about fucking time, "is that you don't have to worry about that. You just have to tell us what we want to know."

"And if I don't?"

"I'll arrest you with the same handcuffs I would have used the last time you refused to cooperate," Mills tells her. "But, if it will satisfy your curiosity, let me just say that the names of other art collectors could give us another path to explore. Maybe we find an intersection between Viveca and another collector here. Maybe another collector conspired to steal from her private collection. Doesn't everybody know everybody in the Phoenix art world?"

Jacqueline has not lost the art of the patronizing laugh. She offers one now and says, "I don't know if I'd say that. But, true, it's a small world."

Mills looks at her with genuine compassion for the upheaval he and his team have brought to her gallery. "Look, we aren't doing anything we don't absolutely have to do. But it is absolutely critical that we uncover anyone with ties to Viveca Canning. Even if they're completely innocent ties. Someone might know someone who might know someone, or better yet, some*thing*. You get it?"

She gives him a winsome smile. "I guess I do."

And so she leads him from vault to vault, through hallways he had not known before, reciting a list of names like, "Frida Spellman, Garrett and Jessica Wright, the Kennedy family."

"*Those* Kennedys?"

"No," she says, moving on. "Henry and Joanna Littleton, Patsy Grace, Sylvia and Merlene Tater, Ricardo del Rio . . ."

He jots down all the names. None rings a bell. He had not expected any would, necessarily. But he'll check the databases for all of them.

"Rosemary Patchett, Fran and Leo Foster, and that's it," she says. "Last hallway. Last vault."

But he sees one more doorway. "What's that?"

She laughs. "Oh, that's my vault! But you already have my name!"

"You have your own collection?"

"I do. Of course I do."

"May we?"

"May you what?"

"May we see?"

"Oh, God no!" she says. "I'm embarrassed. It's a mess in there. Nothing's organized."

He scoffs. "Oh come on, now. We're not art snobs."

"Next time," she says. "Just give me a heads up and I can put things together. Unless, of course, you're going to threaten me with your warrant . . ."

"No," he says with a snicker. "Next time."

They return to the Canning vault, where Roni tells him that she's collected as much potential evidence as she's going to get. "That is to say, very little," she tells Mills.

"Something is better than nothing," he says.

"Then we've overachieved."

And they leave, all of them, parading out of Carmichael and Finn as though they had shopped and found nothing to their discerning tastes. Except for a key.

23

He's sitting at his desk the next morning, about eight-thirty, when Gus calls. He has a billion regrets running through his head, but he answers the phone. Gus says, "Sorry, man."

"Sorry? For what?"

"Wasn't I supposed to swing by yesterday and pick up that book? From the dead lady?"

"Oh, right. No problem. Yesterday got away from me. Mondays, you know."

"I don't have to be at work 'til 1:30," Gus tells him. "I can come down to headquarters in about an hour."

"You shouldn't have to come out of your way for this. I'll bring it to you."

"You sure?"

Mills surveys the room, still sees the regrets. "Oh yeah, I'm sure," he says, an idea displacing the regrets. "But I just got in. So I need to do a few things. How about 10:30?"

"Great."

"Brew the coffee."

"No sweat. French roast or Colombian?"

"Caffeine," Mills says and hangs up.

He checks in with the squad. Myers is still mining data with the cyber experts. Preston and Powell, meanwhile, are obsessed with the skeleton key—for different reasons. Powell is comparing images of antique keys online to photos of the one found in the old chest yesterday.

"Could be that it belongs to an ancient dynasty, or a monastic order, or a medieval land baron," she says. "Or maybe a king."

Mills tightens his lips inward to stifle a laugh. But his cheeks are yearning. And the smile he cannot hide. "This is Indiana Jones's daughter," he finally says, pointing to Powell. "Indiana Jan!"

Myers howls. Preston snickers.

"Just wait," Powell insists, "I'll find a match and you won't be laughing."

Next Mills turns to Ken Preston who, convinced that Viveca Canning's killer was after the Dali for the key to open the chest, is on a quest to find the painting.

"I've been talking to all kinds of authorities on stolen art," he tells the group. "They've all been helpful and are putting BOLOs through their own channels, not that I fully understand what those channels are. But the art world is interconnected through many different ways, and the protection of masterpieces is an industry and a network all its own."

"Sounds like quite the rabbit hole," Mills tells him.

"It is. But, assuming my theory is right about the key, whoever has the painting never made it to the vault," he says. "I don't know why. But we made it first."

"Actually, we made it second," Mills reminds him. "I'm guessing whoever broke into the gallery is the same perp, or is associated with the same perp, who has the painting. If you're right about the key to the chest being connected to the Dali, then whoever stole the Dali was trying to break into the vault to get to the chest."

"I'm with you," Preston tells him. "But what a fucking mess."

"Agreed," Mills says. "Powell, when you're done with your own epic research, please help Preston with his."

Then he leaves the conference room and signs the skeleton key out of the evidence room.

Ivy's sluggish on her walk this morning. She's had it with the 100-plus-degree heat. All she wants to do is sit on the tile floor and sleep, or jump into the pool and bathe, and Gus can't blame her. "I get it, girl," he tells her. "We'll make this a short one."

She looks up at him with gratitude all over her face, as if she understood what he said.

He should have walked her around six, like most of the dog owners in the neighborhood, but he slept in and she slept in and she doesn't easily budge from the cold tile. People driving by are accusatory in their stares. Normally they smile warmly, melted as they are by the sight of the beautiful golden retriever. But this morning they're hateful, looking at Gus as if he's abusing the dog by bringing her out in this heat. As if he's committing an act of animal cruelty. He doesn't need the looks. He knows how hot it is.

But, actually, the morning did not feel warm at all. Gus can't put his finger on it. He can't quite intuit, but ever since he spoke to Alex this morning he's sensed a dark chill. Despite the blazing sky, Gus sees a horizon swirling with dark clouds. Then he stands at the edge of a black tunnel. The coolness seeps into his skin, settles in his bones, before he even steps into the tunnel. He doesn't hear a message. It's as though a vision is warning him about another vision. He can't remember if this has ever happened. He's a bad psychic that way. He doesn't take notes. He should take notes. He should do a lot of things that real psychics do but he doesn't. He returns to the house with Ivy and shrugs this whole thing off the second he hears a knock at the front door.

"Come in," he tells Alex. "How about some hot coffee to cool you down?"

"Absolutely." He's holding a book and a box.

"Gifts?" Gus asks.

Alex just taps Gus's shoulder and steers him into the family room. They sit. Ivy jaunts from her square of tiles and sticks her face in Alex's lap. "Hey, girl," he says, and gives her neck a vigorous scratch until she loses interest and retreats.

Alex hands the book to Gus and says, "It came from Viveca Canning's personal library. We got it from her daughter."

"From the library in that house? From the crime scene?"

"Yeah. Same house. Copper Palace."

"I might have to go back there. But I'll hopefully get what I need through the book. *The Secret Garden*. I've never read it. Have you?"

"No. Is that a problem?"

"Quite the contrary. Neither of us has any preconceived notions or expectations. The best way."

"Great. Now stop stalling. Get to work."

"I take Visa and MasterCard."

Mills laughs a hearty laugh with traces of "fuck you" in its contours.

Gus flips through the pages, runs his hands across the prose, his fingers stopping occasionally to trace a letter or a word. The spirit within him shakes its head, stops him, and reminds him it's not about this story; it's about her story. The book is just the conduit. So, he closes his eyes, as he often does when sifting the earth for grains of truth, and he searches. He sees patches of color. Brilliant greens first, then azure blue, and the diamond necklace of a mountain city at night. He sees a woman. She, too, is bejeweled. But then, like an ill-timed engine in traffic, he stalls. He can't move, can't push forward. That black tunnel again. No way in, no way out. He can only exit through his eyes, and so he opens them and says, "Sorry, man. I'm not getting anything. Not yet."

"But I saw your mouth moving around like you were talking," Alex tells him.

"Really?"

"Yeah. And your eyes. I could tell they were searching for something."

"They were," Gus says. "But they haven't found something yet. Can I hold on to it? The book?"

"Yes. It's not evidence. Just a personal item the victim's daughter gave us. You think it's a dead end?"

"No. Not at all," Gus replies. "But I just feel rushed. I'm going to have to get ready for work. Let me try again tonight. I'm just not getting anything now . . ."

"No prob, man. Keep it for a few days."

Gus puts the book aside. "What's in the box?"

Alex recounts the story of the gallery, the Canning vault, and the ancient chest with the key locked inside. "But if you're feeling rushed, I don't want to get started with the key."

"Can you leave it with me?"

"Not if I want to keep my job. It's evidence."

"Let me have a look."

Alex hands him a pair of latex gloves, and then, once Gus has his hands snugly inside them, Alex hands him the evidence box.

First Gus balances the box on his fingertips just to see how strongly a vibe might present. If he can get a vibe without even opening the evidence box, that bodes beautifully for a connection. He senses a minor tremble, barely noticeable on his Richter scale, but it's there, like a buzz, like anticipation. Carefully he removes the lid and reaches inside. The box balancing on his knees, he grasps the key in one hand and raises it to his forehead. He doesn't know why. This is not a ritual, not a routine. Not a performance. There is no standard practice, but something about the key informs him to bring it to his forehead and run it across his skin from temple to temple. Immediately, Gus understands this as a dangerous act. He has no idea why. But it's as if he'd been coerced, as if that one act of raising the key to his skull was symbolic of a fatal trap, a complete loss of free will. It happened so fast. And he puts the key down just as fast.

"I have no clue what just happened," he tells Alex.

"Me neither, man. It was over as quick as it started. But it looked like you were praying."

Gus nods, for no other reason than to give himself some space to consider. But he doesn't know what to consider. He'll have to handle the key again. This time he consciously fights the urge to bring it to his head or to even let it graze his skin. He just holds it in midair. "This thing," he tells Alex, "really wants to make contact with me. I can't explain why yet. But we're fighting each other. Whatever it is, it has a strong power. Over some people, but not everyone. I don't know what that means, so don't ask. I'm believing this is linked to her religion. I'm trying not to impose my own bias, but that's what I think."

"Bias?"

"I was at that church, Alex. The vibe about that place and those people was so strong. You must have felt it. You don't have to be a psychic to pick up on these things."

"Like what? That it's a cult?"

"Something like that."

"Do you think the key is linked to the cult?"

"I don't know if it's linked to the cult-aspect of her church, or just the religious aspect, whatever that is," Gus tells him. "This is very complicated and I can see many, many layers to interpret."

"Well it wouldn't be such a great leap to connect the key with the church," Alex says. "Viveca Canning lived and breathed the church. If there's something we don't understand about her life, it's probably connected to her church."

"I can't say that yet. But I am getting a vague link to religion. Can we try this again another day? I can swing by headquarters if you can't bring it back here."

Gus lowers the key to the box, covers it with the lid. The chill leaves his body, except for some residue at the surface of his skin; there's something unsettled in the atmosphere, like a distant storm. It's not about the key. The lid of the box has made sure of that for now. It's not the key. It's Alex. It's been about Alex for most of the morning.

"What's bothering you?"

"Me?"

Gus nods and says, "Yes, you. I can tell in my gut something's wrong."

"Is this a vision or a hunch?"

"I know you enough."

"Oh."

Gus smiles. It's been a while since the two of them have done anything alone together that isn't work-related. In April or May they went rafting. They double-dated with Kelly and Billie about a month before that. Gus can't remember the details, but the three of them, without Billie, went to a Coyotes game around Christmas time. Gus isn't much for team sports, but Arizona won, so that was good. Kelly enjoyed it the most.

"Are you feeling okay?" Gus asks him. "Have you been sick? Hiding something so it won't impede the investigation?"

Alex looks at him as if Gus has the emoji of stupidity stamped on his forehead. Then he squints and says, "Pardon the fuck out of me, Gus, but no. I'm fine. I'm hiding nothing."

"Just asking. How about Kelly? Is she okay?"

The silence is concussive. For both of them. Gus can tell. He can see the invisible shockwave.

"I'm not sure," Alex says finally.

"Yes," Gus whispers. "I was getting that. She's sick? Tell me . . ."

"It's her . . ."

Gus nods. Alex can't acknowledge the word. "Breast," Gus says. "Jesus . . ."

"Just a good guess," Gus tells him. "But I did sense something was going on with you. I think it's you in this black tunnel I've been seeing."

Alex looks away, exhales deeply. "Wow. That describes it exactly," he says. "Do you have a diagnosis for her?"

Gus smiles. "I don't have the medical diagnosis for her, no. But I'll work on a spiritual prognosis for her, if that's what you mean."

Alex gets up. "I mean whatever you mean, buddy. We'll take whatever insight you can give."

Gus follows him to the door, the box in his hand. "No problem. Let's get Kelly over here. I want to see her. Meanwhile, I'll work on *The Secret Garden*."

He hands Alex the box.

"I'll have you over to headquarters to do more with the key," Alex tells him. "Thanks. For all of the above."

Jan Powell's *Raiders of the Lost Key* has not yielded anything new in the past few hours. Neither has Preston's infiltration of the art world. But Morton Myers has a smile on his face. He looks like a happy, farting baby. "Wait 'til you guys hear this," he says. "Viveca's computer is a treasure tove."

"Trove," Preston tells him.

"Trove?" he asks.

"Treasure trove," Preston says, gritting his teeth. "Spill it."

They're in Mills's office. Myers gets up and walks to the window, leans there. "Well, we know the victim had booked a one-way ticket to Tahiti, right? But I just found another itinerary tied to hers. She wasn't traveling alone."

Mills spins in his chair so he's facing Myers and says, "You have a name of this other traveler?"

"I found an email to Viveca Canning from someone named Francesca Norwood," Myers answers. He removes a piece of paper from his back pocket and unfolds it. "Let me read it. 'Hi doll, this is a copy of my itinerary confirming we're on the same flight. Can't wait. We deserve this.'"

"That's Gleason Norwood's wife," Mills says.

"Was she going one-way too?" Preston asks him.

"Not sure," Myers says. "This is a one-way itinerary. But she could easily have a separate reservation coming home."

"But why?" Powell asks. "Why would the two of them be taking off and not coming home?"

Mills sits back, folds his arms across his chest. "Let's remember that one of them is dead and she isn't going anywhere at all. The other one has the answers, people. I think that's obvious."

It's time to pay a visit to Francesca Norwood. Mills seems to be the only one in the room dreading another trip to the Church of Angels

Rising. The rest of the squad are already on their feet, nearly coming to blows to be first out the door.

24

The receptionist at C-ARC, the same woman who presided there before, tells them Francesca Norwood's show is on hiatus until early October.

"Show?" Mills asks.

"She has her own TV show on the church network," the woman explains. "But it doesn't resume production until the fall. I double as one of her cohosts." She scans the visitors as if she's mugging for the paparazzi.

"Where is she in the meantime?" Mills asks.

Her starlet smile disintegrates. "I can't give out that information."

Mills flashes his badge. "Remember us? Police."

She hops off her stool and disappears down the hallway to the left. It's several minutes before she returns with Gleason Norwood at her side.

"Honored to see you again, folks," he says, his smile a forgery. "What can we do for you today?"

"We're looking for your wife," Mills says.

"My wife?"

"Yes. Can you reach her for us? We have some questions . . ."

The preacher shrugs. "I don't know what to tell you. She's in Switzerland."

"What's she doing there?" Powell asks.

"Vacation."

"Separately?" Powell persists.

"Now you're getting personal," he says, his wide smile thinning.

"So?" Mills asks him.

"A preacher preaches. We don't get much vacation. My wife has family near Lucerne."

"Please provide us with a phone number for her," Mills tells him.

"Fine," he says. "Anything you need to solve the case. Viveca cannot truly rest until you do."

Norwood pulls out a business card and writes his wife's number on the back.

"I'd like to discuss your church doctrine if I might," Mills says.

"What about it?"

"I'd like to know who originated the theory of elevations and the system of realms . . ."

Mills catches the momentary panic in the man's eyes, the rapid-fire blinking and, just as quickly, the effort to recover the snake-oil serenity on his face. "How would you know about elevations and realms?"

"I've been reading about them."

"That's impossible," Norwood declares. "Our texts are for church members only."

Mills offers a friendly snicker. "C'mon, you surely don't think that everything that happens here stays here."

The receptionist clears her throat. All heads turn in her direction. She reminds the pastor he's scheduled for a conference call. "It's in five minutes," she says. "I'd hate for you to be late."

"People," Norwood says to his guests, "I'm afraid I must dash. I'm sorry. But about the doctrine, some other time. How's that sound?"

Mills nods and leads the others outside. "If that guy has a conference call in five minutes, I have God, himself, on speed dial."

"Herself," Powell says. "God herself."

Mills half smiles, half grimaces and dials Francesca Norwood's phone number. She doesn't answer. He doesn't leave a message. They pile into his car and, as they're pulling out of the parking space, Mills turns his face to the building and says, "My skin crawls in that place. I don't know what it is. It's not churchy and spooky. It's like oppression disguised as sunlight."

"Go with that," Preston tells him. "Good hunch."

Jake Woods marches in without a knock on the door or a rap on the glass. He sits with a sigh. But Mills understands the difference between an antagonistic sigh and a collaborative sigh; this is a collaborative sigh. Jake Woods needs help, needs answers, says the media is calling all day every day. Of course they are. It's not that reporters actually care who killed Viveca Canning; they just want to be sure no one else finds out first. Some may actually be driven by curiosity, but most are driven by fear of losing their jobs if they get beat on stories. And then there are those whose raises depend on how many stories they break; those types are insufferable.

"All I'm going to say is we're following up on multiple leads," Woods tells him.

"How do you define 'multiple'?"

"More than one."

"OK. You're fine."

"Are you getting any tips at all?" Woods asks.

"Nothing actionable," Mills replies. "But I'm working a tight circle around Canning. Her family, her friends, her church."

"Yeah, speaking of that, we've heard from Gleason Norwood."

"Oh really?"

"Says you've been nosing around the church a lot."

"Only during regular business hours. Once by invitation. It's all a legit part of a homicide investigation."

Mills leans back in his chair, his posture a signal. His phone rings. It's Kelly. He tells Woods he has to pick up. "Hon? What's up?"

"The results are in . . ."

"I kind of had a feeling. And?"

"And she won't give them to me over the phone."

"Oh."

"She said she wouldn't give them to me over the phone, positive or negative," Kelly explains. "She says she'll stay late if I can make it there by five."

"I'll meet you."

"You don't have to."

"I said I'll meet you. Text me the address."

Kelly says she will, tells him she loves him, and she's gone.

A probing look occupies Woods's face. "Everything OK?"

"Yup," is all Mills says.

"Can we pick up where we left off?"

"Yup."

Mills looks at his watch. He has an hour.

"The preacher says you're scaring his members by nosing around."

"Not my intention."

"He's very upset."

"Is he?"

"He told the chief the next time you show up it should be with a search warrant or a subpoena, or don't bother coming..."

"All the more reason to show up."

Woods throws his hands up, paces. "I don't know what to say. I want to avoid a lawsuit. These people sued the U.S. government for Christ's sake."

"Not for Christ's sake, let me assure you. And they lost."

"Whatever, Mills. I don't want this to look like we're persecuting a religion."

"A cult."

Woods stops pacing, turns to Mills. "I get it. But I'm not interested in a standoff."

"We're not even close to that."

Woods makes an attempt to wave as he leaves Mills's office, but the hand gesture looks more like a slice. Mills thinks it was intended for his neck.

Dr. Eileen Gilmer sits behind her desk, her face placid, her skin unadorned by makeup, and she says, "The pathology report shows you have invasive ductal carcinoma. A clinical term for breast cancer."

Kelly takes a short breath. "I figured. I've been getting a bad vibe," she says.

Mills wants to open his mouth and scream, but it's one of those nightmares when he can't make a sound.

"Before your vibe gets any worse, Kelly, I want you to know I've been down this road with many, many patients, and most are living healthy lives today," the doctor says. "I don't want to sugarcoat it either, but let's just take this one step at a time. First, you'll go back and meet with a surgeon and medical oncologist at the breast center and discuss your options."

"Which are?" Kelly asks.

"A lumpectomy or a mastectomy," the doctor replies. She describes both procedures, comparing and contrasting the indications and the benefits. Mills wants to be taking mental notes, and he's trying, but his stomach is a kettledrum, the percussion giving birth to waves of nausea; he might throw up.

"I want the lumpectomy," Kelly says. "I don't need to deliberate."

"Spoken like a true attorney," Mills says for comic relief. "Did you know my wife is an attorney?"

The comedy lands like a lead balloon, providing no visible relief, which is to say, not comic at all, and Mills's stomach becomes volcanic. He listens but doesn't listen as doctor and patient continue to discuss, and he doesn't actually hear anything until Dr. Eileen Gilmer says, "You can go in as early as Friday."

"This Friday?" Mills asks.

"Yes," she replies. "I've talked to my colleagues over there and they have a couple of procedures postponed. They can fit her in, if she wants."

"No. I don't think we should rush it," Mills says.

Dr. Gilmer leans forward. "And I want to emphasize that there is no rush. You could wait a week. You could wait three weeks. Personally, I'd like you to do it sooner than later, but there is no immediate rush."

"What about the cancer spreading?" Mills asks.

Kelly tugs his arm and says, "Alex, could you just shut up for a minute and stop talking for me?"

Mills doesn't say anything but acquiesces by retreating physically into himself, withdrawing in the chair, lowering his head, studying the pattern of the carpet below.

"We're not worried about the cancer spreading over a week or two," the doctor explains.

"I want to do it Friday, if they really have an opening," Kelly insists. "The judge is off, so I don't have to be in court. Otherwise, I'd wait. But the timing works out."

The doctor nods. "I'll make arrangements for you. You'll probably have to go over there tomorrow morning for some labs and to meet with the team."

"Fine."

"Hon, can we talk about this later?" Mills asks as he emerges from his retreat.

"There's nothing to talk about, really."

"What about recovery time?" Mills persists. "Don't you want to know if and when you'll be able to get back to work?"

Kelly doesn't reply. A truck thunders by. Mills can hear its brakes screeching at the intersection. Taking a cue, the doctor says, "Recovery time from a lumpectomy can be anything from a few days to a couple of weeks. For you, I suspect the shorter end."

"What stage cancer is this?" Kelly asks.

"We don't really identify the stage right now," the doctor says. "We think the tumor is about two centimeters, which is not insignificant, but that will be confirmed with surgery. They'll take a sample of your lymph nodes and that'll give us the bigger picture."

Kelly asks about radiation and the doctor says her guess is six weeks. Kelly nods as if she's letting that sink in, as if she's still probing too, and she asks about chemotherapy. The doctor tells her that the team at the breast center will recommend chemotherapy if it's deemed necessary after the surgery. Kelly is braver than anyone in the room, the way she sits there interviewing the doctor. She's braver than her husband, the way he sits there imagining the worst, and as he sits there, again, on the verge of hurling lunch. He's overcome by a damp chill. His head is in his hands. He's not proud of himself. But he's proud of her. He's so fucking proud of her as she stands up and extends a hand to the doctor, as the women shake firmly with knowing smiles, as Kelly nods defiantly even though the cancer, as Mills sees it, is casting shadows everywhere.

Later, at home with Kelly, he looks at his wife and notices the first signs of affliction. She's beaten up, wiped out. She has the opposite of a sunburn on her face; it's the fluorescence of disease. Maybe he's making too much of this, but he's never seen her like this before. Never as in never. They're both on the couch reading. "You don't feel well," he says to her.

"Just exhausted," she says.

Despite the malaise of her complexion, there is a contentment on her face, a God-given rendition of goodness that she was born with. It's a sleepy contentment now, but it's there and it confounds Mills in the contradiction. If he could hold her as tightly as he craves, he'd surely break her. "I'll make dinner," he announces.

"I had planned on that," she says.

"I love you."

"Ditto," she tells him. "When do you think we should tell Trevor?"

"Whenever you feel it's right."

"I'd like to wait 'til we know more."

He leans forward, grabs her hand. "I support whatever decision you make."

As he gets up from the couch to prepare dinner, his phone rings. "Mills," he says absently.

"Detective Mills, it's Aaliyah Jones."

"Who?"

"Aaliyah Jones, from Channel 4."

"Oh right," he says. "I'm sorry but this isn't a great time . . ."

"Someone's following me," she whispers.

"What?"

"Someone's following me," she repeats. "Gus Parker warned me about this last week. And he was right."

"Are you in your car or on foot?"

"In my car," she replies. "Can you meet me?"

Mills looks at his wife. No way. No freaking way. And he doesn't feel bad about it when he says, "No. I'm sorry. I can't. I have a family issue."

"Oh my God," she begs. "Can you send someone?"

"How long have you been followed?"

"About ten minutes."

"Are you sure?"

"He's making every turn I make."

"You know it's a he?"

"No," she says. "I can't see."

"Can you identify the car?"

"I can't tell. Shiny and new, I think."

Mills knows he should jump in his car. He knows he should stay home. He knows too many things about being faced with bad choices. He can hear tires squealing on Aaliyah's end of the call. "Aaliyah," he says, "you have a few options. You can pull into a public place, like a gas station, or you could drive to police headquarters and I'll have someone meet you."

"OK," she says.

"How far are you from downtown?"

"Less than ten minutes."

"Fine," Mills tells her. "Do not go home. Go to headquarters. Park out front on West Washington. Put on your hazards."

"I'm on my way . . ."

"Stay on the phone w—"

But she disconnects. Mills dials Powell, asks her to meet Aaliyah Jones at headquarters. Powell says something about being late for a date and Mills says, "Just leave her car there and take her someplace she feels safe. Leave her with a friend or coworker. Mission accomplished."

"Fine," Jan says. "But you owe me."

"Infinitely," he tells her. "Call me if there's an update."

When he hangs up Kelly looks at him and says, "What was that about?"

"Who the fuck knows," he replies. "And let's not think about it."

Truth is, he doesn't know. Could be Aaliyah Jones is paranoid. Could be she's in danger. Powell can figure that one out. He does know one thing. The only life he can protect tonight is Kelly's.

25

Gus sits again with the book. He tries to focus not on the story, but rather on the leftover vibes of a woman who once traversed these pages. The lights are out in the house but for the one lamp over the couch where he sits. He just finished the tofu rice bowl he picked up on the way home from work. Maybe too much soy sauce. There's a salty taste in his glands. He hears the collective whir of the neighborhood's air conditioning outside. He hears Ivy breathing at the other end of the couch. He listens for more, but hears not even another heartbeat— inside or out. He'd like to hear the heartbeat of Viveca Canning. He touches the lines of *The Secret Garden*, grazing the words with his fingertips. He sees the woman. She's a familiar face, this most social of socialites. Her face has appeared on the covers of glossy magazines. She's that woman on the news, the one who's always raising money for good causes, the one with the pastel voice who enunciates her words with hope and an almost inaccessible grace. Almost. But she's accessible. People adored her. Gus can access her somehow. There she is, her hair as white as clouds. Gray streaks at her temples. Her greenish-hazel eyes stare back at him, happy, beneficent. This is not a vision, per se, just her face as he has seen it before.

A light breeze stirs. But not a door or window is open. And yet the breeze persists, softly circling him, and the pages turn. Or feel like they're turning. The wind rises, first a whisper at his neck, and then a whip, a storm, a monsoon. The pages flip furiously in his hands. There's an urgency to escape, to outrun the danger. And she's running in the shadows. But she can't outrun the storm, and there's nothing Gus can do to help her. Instead, she turns to a wall of rock, braces herself, brings her shawl to her face, and waits for the ruin to pass. She hides there behind the gossamer shield, and then she's a shadow, herself, a silhouette on the mountain. She must leave and she must leave soon. This is she and her endurance. This is she and her intensity. This is she who survives and transcends and makes this a beautiful afternoon.

Her kids are coming home from school. They're young. She's young. She throws her arms open to both of them, and they rush in for an embrace, and they stay there, holding each other close, and Viveca Canning's smile is on fire. In the house, she and her husband sit at opposite ends of the table, the children between them. And they talk about school. And about church. And they say a blessing. Gus strains to listen but can't hear the words. He sees lips moving in unison, and he hears a ring of whispers rise from the table, but nothing else of the prayer. Finally, Gus hears "Amen," and then the slamming of a door that echoes from the end of a long, dark tunnel. Again, a tunnel. Gus knows, even in this trance, that the tunnel is most likely his own, mostly represents his own uncertainty about this murder and the vast ground he must cover between the known and the unknown. He watches the family. The children exchange mischievous glances. The boy launches a pea at his sister. She kicks him under the table and he laughs. The parents barely acknowledge each other, Viveca absorbing the sight of her children, seeing them as her own salvation, her husband only looking at the food on his plate. Then the windows explode.

Gus recoils. He slams the book shut.

That man. Her husband.

Gus picks up a vibe right now as his fingers linger on the book cover. The message is ringing in his ears. Viveca Canning's husband paid for something with his life.

Mills picks up the phone.

"Your girl never showed," Powell says, sidestepping hello.

"What girl?"

"You know, the reporter . . ."

He puts a hand to his forehead. "Aw, Jesus Fucking Christ," he groans. "You gotta be kidding me. How long have you been waiting?"

"About thirty minutes."

"Shit. She should be there. Let me call her. Stand down for a few minutes."

He can't reach Aaliyah Jones. He dials her several times and gets sent to voice mail each time. Kelly is clearing the dishes. She points to the coffee maker and he nods. He calls Powell back. "Hey, can you do me a favor? Run by her house and—oh, shit, I don't have her address . . ."

"Never mind. I'll run her DL," Powell says. "Spell her first name."

"Man, I owe you." He spells *Aaliyah*. "You sure you don't mind doing this?"

"I said I'd run her DL and find her address. I didn't say I'd go over there."

"Come on, I'll make it up to you, Jan."

She scoffs. "What's wrong with you, Dude?"

"Nothing. It's something . . . with Kelly."

"Something?"

"Yeah, I can't talk about it."

"Uh-huh. Is she okay?"

"I said I can't talk about it."

"OK, Alex. Forget it. I'm already fifteen minutes late for my date. A girl needs to get laid. I'll enlist Preston for this little reconnaissance mission."

He can hear her car peeling out. "Thanks," he tells her.

When he's off the phone, he pours himself a cup of decaf and turns to Kelly. She's asleep on the couch. He doesn't know whether to throw a blanket over her and leave her there, or to gently carry her to the bedroom. He stares at his resting wife, his masterpiece, and he doesn't know what to do.

26

As usual, he sits in a conveyor belt of traffic the next morning, as the Squaw Peak Parkway slowly churns cars southward into Central Phoenix. It's 7:55 a.m. Mills stares across the valley as the morning sun chases away the long shadows of dawn, the sleepy mountains coming to life, flexing their muscles, welcoming God, or whomever they answer to. He doesn't know. He doesn't know anything. But this is how he makes it through today's commute, watching a landscape he can't control, that doesn't need his control, one which, even if he were to conquer it, would be there tomorrow unchanged and indifferent to his feat. Gus has always told him those mountains are alive, have some kind of inner pulse, something like that, and Mills has no proof the guy is wrong, but for now, for right now, the panorama sweeping across his windshield doesn't ask a thing of him. It's just there offering him a vast meditation. A constant stillness. This is an image he'll keep.

Even when his phone rings.

Even when Ken Preston says he never found Aaliyah Jones.

"She wasn't at her house," Preston tells him. "I would've called you, but it was midnight before I gave up."

"Hmm. Looks like we have a missing person situation on our hands."

"It doesn't have to be *our* hands."

Preston must be studying the same view, Mills thinks. The detachment in the man's voice sounds like the detachment in Mills's mantra.

"Okay, Ken, thanks," he says. "I'm slowly rolling down the Squaw Peak. I'll see you when I get in."

As soon as he's off with Preston he dials Aaliyah Jones. The call goes to voice mail. He calls Channel 4 and they transfer him to her extension and, again, he gets voice mail. He calls back and asks to speak to an actual person, and someone picks up and says, "Newsroom. This is Liza."

"Liza, this is Detective Alex Mills from Phoenix, PD."

"The famous Alex Mills! What an honor."

Mills smirks. "Yeah, okay, I'm actually looking for Aaliyah Jones."

"Not coming in today. Called out sick."

"Out sick? When exactly did she call?"

"I don't know," the woman replies. "I came in this morning and the note was on my desk. I'm the assignment editor, so I'm the first to see sick calls. She probably called in sometime between midnight and seven this morning,"

"OK, thanks," he says, as his car finally spills off the conveyor of the highway and onto the city streets.

"Is there a problem?" Liza asks.

Mills hesitates, knows his hesitation speaks volumes. So, he lies. "No, no problem. Just returning her call. As soon as you speak to her, have her call me."

It's 8:19.

That was one slow conveyor. So slow he has to skip the drive-thru and drive straight to headquarters, where he pours himself a cup of police-issued caffeine sludge. He makes a beeline to his desk now, suddenly aware, even without his notes, that the day is chock-full. He senses there won't be enough hours. He flips through his legal pad (he still is a hard copy guy, not enamored of digital to-do lists), and the first item is a reminder to call Francesca Norwood. It has to be seven or eight hours later in Switzerland. She answers on the fourth ring. Mills introduces himself.

"My husband said you'd be calling."

"Warned you?"

"He gave me a heads up, Detective. Anything wrong with that?"

"No. Sorry. This is not an adversarial call at all. In fact, I'm calling because I need your help—if you could find it in your generosity to help."

The woman seems to purr into the phone. After the purr, there's a lighter tone in her voice when she says, "Of course. Viveca's death has me absolutely lost in grief, you know?"

"Yes."

"She was an angel. A great lady. A great churchwoman. A great friend . . ."

"Is that why you were planning an exotic trip with her? One way?"

Dead silence. Deadlier the longer it lasts.

"Mrs. Norwood?"

Sniffling, then, "How do you know about that?"

"We know. We seized a lot of information off of Viveca's computer in the course of this homicide investigation."

"Oh my God," she moans. "I . . . I—"

"You don't know what to say? You don't know how much to say?"

"But I thought this call wasn't going to be adversarial."

"It wasn't. And it isn't," Mills insists. "I'm sorry if you're surprised by my line of questioning, but there's really no devious intent here. In the course of any investigation, if we see an anomaly, we look into that anomaly. Your trip with Viveca to the South Pacific seems like an anomaly to us."

He hears her weeping. "I can't," she says. "I'm sorry, but I just can't. If my husband ever finds out, he'll kill me."

"Kill you?"

"Or worse."

"I'm not sure I understand . . ."

"Please, please, please," the woman begs. "I've said enough."

Mills puts her on speakerphone and rubs his temples. "How close were you to Viveca?"

"You know we were planning a trip together. So that should tell you something."

"I do know that," Mills says. "But I don't know why you two were going one way or why she had invested in real estate in French

Polynesia. Unless the two of you were moving there, and that confuses me."

"It was a one-way ticket, Detective. But it doesn't mean I wasn't coming back."

"Were you?"

"Look, I really have to go."

Mills breaks a pencil in half. "Ma'am, please. If you care about your friend, about letting her soul really rest at peace . . . if your church members believe in such a thing . . . please reconsider helping me out here. Please. Your husband doesn't have to know."

Mills recognizes the silence that comes next. It's the silence of consideration. Of weighing the odds. A few moments later, Francesca Norwood says, "My husband will find out. But give me your number. I'll call you right back."

"No, you won't. But that's okay. I understand."

"No," she insists. "I will. Give me your number. I need to use a different phone."

Mills concedes to her wishes and, to his surprise, his phone rings a moment later.

"Can you meet me?" the woman asks.

"I can't come to Switzerland, if that's what you mean."

"I'm not in Switzerland," she says.

"When did you get back?" he asks her.

"I never left."

"Well, your husband is under the assumption that you're in Switzerland, ma'am."

"My husband is under a lot of assumptions, and that's okay. I'm here in the valley."

Mills feels an eyebrow arch. "Hiding?"

"I'm at the Desert Charm," she says. "In Paradise Valley. Can you meet me?"

"I know where it is. We can be there in about an hour or so. Just a few things to take care of here . . ."

"We?"

"One of my investigators and I."

"Come alone."

"But—"

"Come alone or no meeting," she insists. "I'm not comfortable with too many people. They'll buzz you in from the lobby."

"I know the drill. See you soon."

First, Mills meets with the squad, gives them an update on Francesca Norwood and Aaliyah Jones. Powell says she'll follow up on the reporter. The general consensus about Mrs. Norwood is surprised, but not surprised. The squad now seems to share a healthy skepticism of the Church of Angels Rising.

"The reporter was trying to interview our victim before the murder," Mills reminds them. "Myers, I want you to search and pull any email correspondence between the two of them from Viveca's computer."

Myers says, "No prob."

Mills asks Preston to follow up with the lab. "Check on the prints from the gallery," he says. "I haven't heard a thing."

"It's been less than a week, Alex," Preston says.

"A week that might as well be a month. And, I know, the lab's probably backlogged."

Preston says he'll check. Then Mills tells the group he'll send a text when he's ready to reconvene.

He's on his way to take a leak when he gets a text message from Gus.

<Are you around?>

<For a few minutes>

<I'm a few minutes away. The book is talking to me>

Whatever that means.

Not long after the piss, Gus arrives and explains. "This was not a random act of violence," he says to Mills. "I realize you know that, but I also got a very strong vibe that Viveca was running from something or someone. That she was hiding something. I don't know why."

"The key I showed you? Was she hiding that?"

"Of course. But why? That's what's got me stumped. I probably need to hold the book and the key together," Gus suggests to him. "Then I'd know for sure."

Mills tells him he doesn't have time to get the key out of evidence now, but they can meet again later.

"And there was something about the husband . . ." Gus says.

"What about him?"

"All I could tell is that his death was irregular," Gus replies. "I think there's more to it. The vibe says he paid for something with his life."

Mills smiles. "I'd believe anything at this point," he remarks with some sarcasm. "But, like I said, I got to run. I'm heading out to speak to the preacher's wife. Turns out *she's* in hiding."

"This is getting complicated," Gus says. His statement seems more inward than outward.

"I talked to her on the phone. She was cagey and didn't really answer my questions," Mills tells him. "But she agreed to meet."

"Take me with you."

"I can't do that."

"Why not? I'll take my own car."

Mills laughs. "Transportation is not the issue. I promised to come alone. It was a condition of her meeting with me."

Gus shakes his head vigorously. "No. No. I must come, Alex. I have to come and search for vibes. I think she's key. This is important."

"You're telling me?" Mills actually takes a pint of umbrage at his buddy's insistence. Feels like overreach, maybe.

"Where's she hiding?"

Mills puts his head in his hands. "Always off the record, right Gus? No one should know this."

Gus gets up, sits at the edge of Mills's desk, and bears down on him. "I think you know how insulting your question is, right Alex? You and I practically exist off the record."

Mills shakes his head, looks up. "Yeah, sorry."

"What's wrong with you?"

"I'm fucking distracted."

"I can see that," Gus says. "I can also see, and I'm getting a tremendous vibe right now, a vision of a rope, Alex. I see that you're very close to untying a very significant knot in the case."

"A rope?"

"Yeah. It was here, now it's gone. But it was a message. You'll be fine. All these people are connected. I know it. You know it. Soon everyone will know it."

Mills, still looking up, searches the psychic's eyes. In there, somewhere, is the anatomy of Gus's visions. Unfathomable, but it's there. Maybe the guy has an extra retina. Maybe that's how Gus's superhuman visions get to his brain. They have their own highway.

"Why are you staring at me like that?"

Mills reflexively withdraws his gaze. "Oh, sorry man. Sure, you can come. But you'll follow and wait outside. Let me set the stage and make her comfortable," he tells Gus. "And if I can make her comfortable, and if she agrees, I'll text you to come in."

"In the meantime, I'll see if I get any vibes from the outside. We'll make it work," Gus assures him.

"She's at the Desert Charm."

"I was just there with Billie."

"I know."

For a split second, Mills sees something pass across Gus's face, like the face people get when they take a wrong turn.

Maybe staring into Gus's eyes was the wrong thing to do. Now Mills thinks he's picking up on vibes. But there's no way a power like Gus's could transfer from eye to eye. He would laugh at himself, but his heart weighs heavily; there's no laughter in there. Only worry for Kelly. And the Canning case. Mostly Kelly. Almost entirely Kelly. At the Desert

Charm, safely ensconced in her bungalow, Francesca Norwood asks if the meeting can be off the record.

"You don't have to give an official statement yet," Mills tells her. "But I'll be asking you if certain things you tell me can be stated on-the-record for the purposes of determining your credibility. You can lead me anywhere you want, Mrs. Norwood, on or off the record. Just don't lead me down a path of lies."

"I'm not interested in doing that," she says. "Please have a seat."

They sit in the living room, which looks out to a private courtyard overrun by bougainvillea. Mills hears the splashing of the fountain out there, the incessant chirping of the birds. They're at opposite ends of a coffee table, their chairs facing a fireplace that's accented by copper tile and, thankfully, not burning on this 108-degree day. Mills twists his chair so he's facing more of the woman and less of the hearth. She bears a creamy white complexion and dark eye makeup, the contrast apparently premeditated. Mills had checked out her website, the one that supports her TV show on the church network, and she looks a lot tamer here in front of him. A lot tamer than those images of her online with the cyclonic wig and the forest of eyelashes. She sits here not encased in the robes of a monarch, but in what some would call a smart blazer and slacks. She has the same million-dollar dentistry as her husband.

"What do you want to tell me that you couldn't tell me over the phone?" Mills asks her.

"You were asking me about Tahiti," she says. "About the trip with Viveca."

Mills nods. "Yes. It was a surprise to see you both going there one way. I was hoping for an explanation."

She hesitates, turns her face away, and studies something on the wall. "My divorce," she says before turning back. "My divorce is the explanation." Then, looking squarely at Mills, she says, "And that is completely off the record. The church cannot know. The public cannot know."

The words come rolling at him like elegant grenades.

"Divorce," he says. "I wasn't expecting to hear that."

She sucks in her cheeks, then exhales. "We're not ready to go public. It will tear the church apart. We have a plan."

"So, your husband, he knows about your intentions to divorce?"

"He does."

"Do you have children?"

"Only one. Gabriel," she says. "But he's been banished."

"Banished? Like, exiled?"

"Most religions would call it excommunicated," the woman explains. "We say banished."

"How old is he?"

"Twenty-five."

"Wow," Mills says. "Your own son. Your only child."

She lifts her chin, narrows her eyes. She sniffles and says, "It has not been easy."

"Your husband has taken a harder line than you."

"Toward Gabriel, yes."

"Is that the reason for the divorce?"

"One of many."

Mills leans forward, his hands folded between his knees. "Where's your son now? What's he doing in his exile?"

A tear rolls down her cheek. She brushes it away. "He lives in the valley. I'm not supposed to give him money, but I do. I control part of the business, so I have access, of course."

"But he's an untouchable, and you've erased him?"

She sobs now, her hands covering her face. He yields to her misery, her torment, whatever it is that destroys her right here in her bungalow at the ultraexclusive Desert Charm. Her body is heaving, wracking. He's been this close to grief and torment before. He's seen witnesses break down. He has sat across the room from the grieving. He's comforted, he's grabbed a hand, and he's offered a mild hug. Yet he's not tempted to do any of that now. Her only child. Banished. Something ain't right with these people, with that church. Mills fences himself off from her emotion.

She coughs and says, "It's true. Technically he's untouchable. And technically I've erased him. How do you even know about that?"

He looks at her through a diamond in the chain-link fence and says, "I have sources."

"People talk," she says.

"Why Tahiti?"

"Viveca was buying property there."

Mills shakes his head. "No. I mean why were you going to Tahiti. Were you agreeing to exile?"

She laughs, her mood apparently recovering. "No. I was not. I had a one-way ticket because I would be gone for an extended period of time. That much we planned," she explains.

"To avoid a messy, public divorce?"

"And to explain my absence from the church," Francesca says. "People would be told I had gone off to the South Pacific to break ground on a new cathedral. My husband is all about image, Detective, and this avoids the embarrassment of a divorce and the horrifying scandal it would cause. But I was not forbidden from coming back to Phoenix."

Now Mills wants to laugh. *A horrifying scandal!* "But if you're getting a divorce, that's public record. People are bound to find out."

"I didn't say we were getting a legal divorce. Gleason and I are agreeing to terms. To a contract that only our lawyers will know about."

Mills just sits there looking at her. He tries scrunching his face, narrowing his eyes, shifting in his chair, anything to articulate, without opening his mouth, that he has no idea what the fuck this woman is talking about. Because that's how it would come out. What a fucking marriage of snake oil. Con artistry so exquisite it belongs in a gallery. "You said there were other reasons for your divorce, er, *contract* . . ."

"Right. And those are too personal."

"And irrelevant to my case?" Mills asks. "Because if they're relevant, you should share."

She shakes her head. "No."

"Does your agreement with your husband call for you to leave the church?"

"I'm not sure I want to answer that on the record."

"Why not?"

"My religion is personal."

"I respect that," Mills tells her. "But this indefinite excursion to Tahiti with Viveca, does it not have implications for your role in the church?"

"No comment."

"Because you don't want me to ask you why or how you'd leave the church."

"You're very smart, Detective."

But she clearly thinks she's smarter. He resists the urge to squirm. He does this by turning the tables on Francesca Norwood, by finding a way to make her squirm in her elegant way. "What sin did your son commit to get himself banished from the church?"

She goes dour and sour. A shadow passes over her face. She tosses the shade his way. "We don't really use the word sin," she says.

"Offense?"

"He stole a million dollars from a church fund."

Mills laughs.

"It's not funny," she scolds him.

"I realize. And I'm sorry. But you say you're still giving him money. I would think a million dollars would last a kid a while."

"We recovered almost all of it," she says. "And no one but the board of directors knew. He wasn't as much banished from the church as he was banished from the family. But the board of directors did, in fact, draw up papers formalizing the banishment."

"And church members never knew . . ."

"They figured it out after a while," she concedes. "The terms of his banishment forbid him from entering church property."

"I suppose you never reported his theft to the police."

She smiles. "We did not."

Mills mulls this over, kind of luxuriates in the silence. He's insistent on it to the extent that it keeps her uneasy and it gives him time to process. On one hand, he doesn't want to get lost in the weeds of church business, however intriguing those weeds might be; on the other hand, his gut tells him there's a skeletal connection between the church and Viveca's murder, that somewhere in the bones of the church resides the marrow of her death. This is not a new revelation. It's an ongoing revelation that produces more questions than answers. But the weeds. So many weeds. Gus Parker! The name goes off like an alarm. That's what he has Gus for, and Gus is sitting nearby in his car. He had nearly forgotten Gus. How to make a mental pivot a verbal pivot? Aw, fuck it. "What do you think of psychics, Mrs. Norwood?"

"I'm sorry?"

"Psychics. Would your church approve?"

The shake of her head conveys confusion. "I don't think we've ever taken up the issue. Are psychics guided by a particular theology?"

Mills shrugs. "I don't know."

"What does this have to do with Viveca's murder?"

"I have a friend. He's got the gift. I'd like him to talk to you."

She rolls her head and Mills can hear her neck crack from where he's sitting. "Are you serious?"

"Yes."

She laughs. "Does your department approve?"

"Sometimes."

"What would the taxpaying public think, Detective Mills?" she asks, batting her eyelashes a thousand flirtatious and heinous ways.

"Do you really want to discuss taxes, Mrs. Norwood?"

"Touché."

"He's nearby. He can be here in minutes."

She shakes her head. "I'm not really comfortable with this."

"Of what he might find out?"

She whips her face at him. "I have nothing to hide."

"OK. Of course not. Never mind." Mills rises to his feet. "I should get going."

"Can't you stay for lunch?"

Mills, surprised by her invitation, looks at her and sees a faraway woman, a lonely soul whose sphere is unbroken by the affection of others. She's out there, across the room, adrift at sea, and it's probably best for him to leave her this way. But he's curious. Mills is curious, as any detective would be, about what information a casual lunch would yield. If he can be honest with himself, and who the fuck can he be honest with if he can't be honest with himself, he's stumped. The tentacles are a tangled mess.

"I'd love to join you for lunch, but my friend and I had plans," Mills tells the woman. "Maybe he can join us."

"If that's the only way you'll stay . . ."

"It is."

"Fine," she says. "Let me order lunch for three."

And she does.

27

Gus notices his unruly straggle in the rearview mirror. Often confused for Jesus, Gus has to do a better job with the morning shave. The sandals don't help. People don't actually think he is Jesus, but they often do a double take and tell him he's the "spitting image." Gus laughs it off because, as far as he knows, and he knows even less than those who claim to know everything about Jesus, Jesus was several shades darker than him. Several Semitic, Arabic shades darker. Though they both have surfer bodies because Gus was, in fact, a surfer, and Jesus might have spent time surfing the waves of the Galilee which, now that Gus considers it, might explain why so many people think Jesus walked on water. Just as his ruminations are going off the rails, he gets a text from Alex.

<Come on in. Ask for Francesca Norwood>

Five minutes later he's walking through the door of Francesca Norwood's bungalow, escorted by a butler who insists on referring to him as Mr. Welch, familiar with him from his stays here at the Desert Charm with Billie. Gus doesn't bother to correct him. Alex makes the introductions and Francesca Norwood says, "Charmed," as if she was paid by the hotel to say that. Gus's arrival is followed a few awkward minutes later by a buffet lunch that rolls into the room as if it's strutting down a culinary catwalk.

"Mrs. Norwood tells me she was planning to move, indefinitely, to Tahiti with Viveca Canning," Alex says.

"Transcontinental Airlines?" Gus asks reflexively.

"I don't remember," the woman says. "But I can check."

"You must," Gus insists. "I know about an ill-fated flight."

The woman laughs. "I'm sorry," she says demurely through her chuckles, "but I'm not accustomed to prophecies outside the church."

Gus looks at her and nods, keeps nodding, studies her, this black-haired woman; she reminds him of a cobra, the position of her head and the curvature of her neck, the way she looks ready to pounce despite her fine manners.

"You're making me nervous, Mr. Parker," she says.

"Sorry," he says. "Call me Gus."

She doesn't respond. Instead she leads them around the buffet where they pick at the food. Gus has filled his plate with a conservative mound of salad and topped it with a few cubes of grilled salmon. Alex, like a defiant child, is eating chicken strips and sweet potato tots and completely confident about his choice. "Detective," the preacher's wife says, "I'd appreciate it very much if you would not share anything else about our conversation with your friend."

A tot on its way to his mouth, Alex says, "Of course. Whatever you wish."

As they eat quietly for a few minutes, Gus stealthily studies the woman again. He has a knack for knowing when people look away. Those moments, however brief, are opportunities. He conducts a foray. He does the Jiffy Lube version of a psychic maneuver. He swoops in and gets out. "You don't have a daughter," Gus says to her.

She looks up from her scoops of tuna salad. "Are we warming up with a guessing game?"

"No," Gus says.

"But it was a good guess. I don't have a daughter."

"But you wanted one. Right?"

"Also a good guess," she says.

Gus crunches into a tooth-defying crouton. "I sense a lot of fear, Francesca."

She tilts her head. Her eyes look like black pearls. "You fear me or I fear you?"

"Neither," Gus says. "You're afraid of something. A kind of fear you run from. Which explains the trip to Tahiti."

Alex clears his throat and says, "Actually, Gus, the trip to Tahiti was planned. It doesn't appear that Francesca was running away."

Gus nods. "I'm just saying what I sense." And then to Francesca, "Is there a fear dominating your life?"

She turns to a wall and ponders, then turning back she smacks her lips and says, "Isn't there always? To varying degrees."

"You won't tell me," Gus says, "so I'll tell you. You fear the church. There is something about the church that you're running from. Am I right?"

She balks. "I don't have to answer to you."

He treads lightly, relaxes his posture and says, "Of course not. I'm just trying to help you."

She points to Alex and says, "No, you're trying to help *him*."

Gus explains that he hopes to help both of them, that he's here to decipher whatever messages are in the air, that he has no bias. He says it wouldn't be the honest thing to do to deliver messages that only benefit Alex. "It doesn't work that way. I deliver whatever's in the room. I don't pick and choose."

She turns back to the tuna salad, spreads some of it on a triangle of pita. The splash of the fountain outside fills the silence. So does the hum of estrangement. Gus guesses he's the only one who can hear the hum. It sounds like an empty house where the din of the appliances and the whir of the air make up for what can't be or won't be said. Gus remembers the first years of his own banishment, when he could hear the Parker home wherever he went. A lively conversation, a clanking diner, a rock concert could not displace the hum of that place. He would always know the hum of the Parker home. He knows he has some vacant space in his heart, but with his mother dead and his father dead, it's not the void of estrangement. And Gus suspects this is not about him. He hears the longing and the separation, he hears the abandonment and the regrets, because the church is speaking and Francesca Norwood has had to make a choice, a frightful choice, a life-changing choice.

"Your son wants to come back to the church," Gus says.

She looks up, alarmed. "I did not say he ever left."

"I know," Gus says. "But I sense the turmoil and the separation. I sense he was removed."

"Did Detective Mills send you a text while I wasn't looking? Is that how this sideshow works?"

Alex drops his fork and says, "No. Gus can show you his phone if you'd like. This isn't a sideshow."

"I understand your skepticism," Gus tells her. "But did he leave? Your son?"

"Yes," she hisses. "He did."

"I'm a banished son, as well," Gus tells her. "That's probably how I picked up on it. I'm sensitive to experiences I've experienced, but not exclusively. I'm sensitive to all kinds of happenings in the universe."

Francesca eyes him, openly smirks. "I'd like to keep my son out of this," she says. "Will either of you be wanting coffee?"

Alex declines, so does Gus.

"Then we're probably through here," she says. "I have calls I need to make."

"Of course," Gus says.

Alex pushes back from the table. "Francesca, if you don't mind, I do have another question or two about Viveca," he says. "It won't take more than a minute."

She sighs, removing the cloth napkin from her lap and tossing it on the table. "What?"

"Why was Viveca leaving the church? We haven't discussed that."

She grips the edge of the table. "Viveca was leaving the church to fully reconnect with her daughter, Jillian. To finally end the banishment."

"By moving to Tahiti? That's no closer to San Francisco."

"Her relationship with her daughter was not compatible with the church. She had slowly been moving away from her role at the church without actually leaving."

"Because she was afraid to leave?"

"Afraid?"

"I'm sure you're aware of the rumors that bad things can happen to those who defect."

"Rumors!" she huffs.

"What about Bennett?" Mills asks. "If she leaves the church to reconnect with Jillian, doesn't that leave her erased by Bennett? It doesn't make sense."

The woman shakes her head and sighs again. "Those are the kinds of questions you'd have to ask Viveca. And, as we all know, she's not available."

"I think there's something you're not telling me," Alex says. "Viveca Canning was rewriting her will. She had been leaving most of her estate to the church, but recently decided to change her beneficiary."

She gets up and nervously straightens the table. "How do you know that?"

"It's all part of the investigation," Alex replies. "Were you aware of that?"

"Of course not."

Gus can see the skepticism in Alex's eyes.

"So you're saying she made a sudden decision to move to Tahiti, but you don't really know why?" Alex asks her. "Even though you were going with her?"

"Exactly."

The disbelief at this point is so palpable the curtains look embarrassed.

"When we were on the phone earlier, you said your husband would kill you if he knew about the trip with Viveca," Alex says, his eyes following her as she flits about the buffet cart, then to the sofa. "But you also told me your so-called divorce has been all arranged and you've reached an agreement. So why would he care about your trip?"

She freezes. "He doesn't care where the hell *I* go," she growls. "But not with her. Not with a defector."

"I see," Alex says. "Does he know about the change to her will?"

"I don't know," she says, flopping her arms to her sides. "You should ask him."

Gus rises. "Should we ask your husband about the key?"

Francesca trembles. He can see it in her wrists, her shoulders. She steadies herself at the edge of the sofa. "What key?" she murmurs.

Gus moves to her. "I don't know. I was hoping you could help me with this vision. I see you with a key, Francesca. And I don't know where you're going. But you're heading to a door. And the door is heavy and the light is red, and maybe there's artwork. I'm not sure. But you want to turn around and run, don't you?"

"Enough!" she cries. "I don't know what you're talking about. I don't *want* to know what you're talking about. I want everyone to leave. This minute."

Gus apologizes for upsetting her. "I'm going to leave you my phone number. Call me if anything I've said begins to make sense. Again, I'm sorry."

"As am I, Francesca," Alex adds. "It wasn't my intent to frighten you. Please remember, I'm investigating a homicide. So, I'll be in touch if I have more questions. I certainly hope you'll call me if you can think of anything helpful."

She doesn't move. She doesn't say another word. Alex, apparently, doesn't need another cue. He turns to leave. Francesca Norwood regards them bitterly and looks away and, as she gazes off into nowhere, Gus grabs her cloth napkin from the table and follows Alex out the door. Outside in the parking lot, in the sauna of a Phoenix afternoon, both men stand there shaking their heads. It's a silent debrief that says everything. Alex kicks at a small palette of pebbles on the ground. Gus twists his sandal in the pavement. A squawking bird soars overhead as if it's mocking their silence. Gus stuffs his hands in his pockets and says, "Francesca Norwood's not being straight with you."

Alex smiles meekly with a nod. "No shit."

"She's answering questions, but she's not on the level," Gus tells him.

"Yeah, I suspected as much."

"She knows much more than she's saying."

"Is that a psychic thing or just an observation?"

"A psychic thing," Gus says. "And the psychic thing also tells me that as much as you think Viveca's move to Tahiti was planned, she was fleeing, Alex. It was a planned escape."

"Duly noted," he says. "Interesting that you mentioned your vision of a key, but you never mentioned we actually have a key in evidence."

"It wasn't my place to mention."

Folding his arms across his chest, Alex says, "So was the vision for real? Did you actually see her with a key? Or were you just messing with her?"

Gus whips his head back. "What? You know I don't mess, dude. Why would you even ask?"

"I don't know. I don't know anything." Then Alex gets a text message, reads it, and says, "It's Powell. She's on the lookout for that reporter. Aaliyah Jones. Have you heard from her?"

"No. Not in a while," Gus replies. "What's going on?"

Alex shrugs. "We don't know," he says. "She called me the other night, said she was being followed. And no one's seen her since."

"And it never occurred to you she was in trouble?"

"Of course it did. But I thought we'd look in the obvious places before we put all our resources into finding someone who might not be missing. She could have convinced herself she was being followed and just took off because she was scared."

Gus shakes his head vigorously. "No, no, no. That's not it, Alex. No, the last time I talked to her I warned her that she could be in trouble. I mean, I actually warned her that she might be followed. Maybe not in those words exactly, but still. She didn't take off. She doesn't scare easily."

"What are you telling me?"

"I'm telling you not to shrug this off. She's someplace against her will."

"Your gut or your vision?"

"Both."

"Well, Jesus fucking Christ, Gus, why the fuck didn't you tell me about the warning you gave her?"

Gus backs up a few steps. "Hey, Alex, chill, okay? I've only met the woman twice. I can't say if her investigation of the church was intertwined with Viveca Canning's death. I know she had her suspicions. But *you* never said it was connected. *You* never told me otherwise. So how about you don't put this on me?"

"Buddy, I'm sorry. I didn't mean it that way."

Gus tilts his head, sees his reflection in Alex's sunglasses, sees the blistering, seething expression on his own face. "Then how did you mean it?"

With a deep exhale, Alex says, "Ah, I don't know. The thing is Aaliyah and I only scratched the surface. I have no idea if she would have led me anywhere near the Canning homicide with her investigation of the church. It was all about her sources. All about a group of people who came forward."

"Did she put you in contact with any of them?"

Alex wipes his forehead. "No. It was going to take some convincing."

"Can't you track her phone?"

"Yes. I asked Jan to get on that this morning," Alex tells him. "In the meantime, why don't you see what signals you pick up in that psychic head of yours?"

Gus shakes that psychic head of his, once again, and turns to his car. He gets in, rolls down the window. He takes a serious look at Alex. He gazes all over him. He sees Alex fidget nervously at the wordless surveillance. "You've got all kinds of crazy all around you, my friend."

"That's exactly how it feels. Is that exactly what you see right now?"

"Yup."

"I don't like the expression on your face," Alex tells him. "Is it worse than I think?"

Gus peers into the crazy all around Alex Mills. The strands of it whip in the air like Medusa's snakes, coiling tightly into a cyclone. The desert erupts. All of it, the venomous cyclone dipping to the earth and the pillars of dust rising to the sky, is coming after Alex. Gus nods. "Yeah. It might be worse than you think."

Then he drives away, eyes on the road, but he's out of his own body where there is no GPS.

28

On the way back to headquarters, Mills receives a series of text messages from Jan Powell, each one of mounting importance, too many to respond to; instead he sends one group text to the squad indicating it's time to reconvene. They're waiting for him in the conference room when he gets off the elevator. He walks in and says, "Jan."

"Good afternoon, Detective."

"Fill us in."

"The lab has completed as conclusive an analysis of prints as we can get at this point," she says. "From the residence, we have prints from the victim and the maid, who volunteered her prints when we asked. We also have two extra sets of prints that, right now, can't be identified. Nothing shows up in the databases."

"One could be Bennett's," Mills suggests. "But they could be anybody's. A worker. A visitor. Who the fuck knows?"

"From the vault, we have one fresh set of prints. It does match one of the sets from the residence," Powell says, her inflection cresting. "So, I'm guessing Bennett. We know he visited the vault the day of the break-in."

Preston says, "Right. He was legally in the vault that day. But we have no evidence he was there later that night during the break-in. Unless his prints show up on the explosives."

"I think we can safely assume there were gloves involved with the explosives," Powell tells them. "Scottsdale tells me all they could recover was one print."

"What about surveillance video?" Mills asks.

"One camera was down," she replies.

"Down? Are you kidding me?" Mills groans.

"Yes. Down. Sabotaged. But there was another camera, and Scottsdale says that once they enhance the video, they'll probably be able to make out a few plates in the alley behind the gallery."

Mills nods. "Good," he says.

"I also texted you about Aaliyah Jones," she says, as if he needs a reminder, which he doesn't.

"The floor's still yours," Mills tells her.

"The last ping from her phone was picked up around one-thirty Wednesday morning at 44th Street and Thomas. I got the registration for the car and asked the precinct over there to search the area. About an hour ago, they found a vehicle with the exact description and tag parked at an abandoned rental car lot on Thomas, just west of 44th."

"Where's it now?" Mills asks.

"I asked them to get it on a flatbed over to impound."

"Let the lab know," he tells her. "I want it processed like we would any other crime scene."

Preston says he's checked all the area hospitals. "Nothing there."

"I'll get with our friends in Missing and Unidentified," Mills says. "We need her description and her photo out there, across as many agencies as possible. And I think we're going to have to enlist the media . . ."

"You sound ecstatic about that," Powell says.

"I'm not, but we got to get this out there. I'll hit up Grady and he can push something out tonight or tomorrow morning."

"What about her own TV station?" Preston asks.

Mills cups the air. "What about them? There's no saying how much, if any, they're sharing with the other media in town," he explains. "Might be a good idea for me to drop by her station tomorrow."

Myers yawns operatically and says, "Excuse me. Sorry."

And Mills says, "Are we keeping you up, Morty?"

Myers shakes his head.

"Good," Mills tells him. "Because it's time for columns." He turns to the whiteboard and creates two columns, one with the header "Viveca," the other with the header "Aaliyah."

"What the hell does that name even mean?" Myers grumbles. He's been grumbling a lot since he's been on a low-carb diet. It's not surprising given the reddish hue of his neck that he'd be grumbling about a name that sounds more exotic than, say, Ann.

"Google it, Morty," Mills barks. "But for now, let's list what we know about the two women."

The lists look like this:

Viveca	Aaliyah
Dead	Missing
Mother of two	Family life unclear
Socialite/Philanthropist	Reporter, Channel 4
Art Collector	Investigating Church of Angels
Church of Angels Rising Member/	Rising
Board of Directors	Sources from Church
Planning to leave Phoenix	Sources fear retribution
with preacher's wife	Vehicle recovered
Changing will	
The Key	

"For all we know," Mills says, "Viveca was Aaliyah's prime source about the church."

Powell shakes her head. "Didn't she tell you that Viveca declined to comment?"

Mills nods. "Yeah. That's what she said. But reporters are rarely inclined to reveal their sources and even less inclined to divulge what sources tell them . . ."

"Even to solve a murder?" Powell asks.

"Even to solve a murder," Preston affirms. "Trust me, they have their own set of rules."

Powell harrumphs and folds her arms across her chest.

"Let's say Viveca wasn't the primary source for Aaliyah's story," Mills surmises. "But maybe she supplied her with a list of other sources. A way to get the truth out without being the one to tell it . . ."

He looks around the room. Nobody reacts. He sees ambivalence in Powell's eyes. Introspection in Preston's. Images of Twinkies in Myers's. Then Preston mumbles something as he comes back to life. "OK," he says, "if Viveca was at all involved with the reporter's investigation, it's possible the church had her killed to shut down the whole thing."

"Only if we're looking for direct cause and effect," Mills reminds them. "But it's possible we have two parallel cases. Maybe the motive to kill Viveca had something to do with the church but not necessarily something she told Aaliyah Jones."

"Well that brings us back to square zero," Myers growls.

"No, it doesn't," Mills says. "I want you to keep searching Viveca's emails. I want to see every one that went back and forth between her and the reporter. And I want to see every email that passed between Viveca and Francesca Norwood."

Mills describes his visit with the preacher's wife at the Desert Charm. He shares what she disclosed about her pending separation from the preacher and her plans to relocate with Viveca Canning to French Polynesia. "I think the biggest news flash to come out of the meeting was this: Francesca told us that Viveca was leaving the church to reconnect with her daughter. That's a big deal. But Ms. Norwood was cagey about everything else, and perhaps not fully forthcoming," he tells the squad. "There has to be more we can find out in their digital footprint."

"I'm on it," Myers says. Anything digital and the man froths at the mouth. His geekiness about cyber forensics has probably kept him securely employed in Homicide. "We can tell Mrs. Canning *thought* she was deleting all her emails, but it's been fairly easy to recover them."

Something doesn't feel right. Mills sees shadows. He doesn't understand shadows, how they form, how they drift, whom they hide. But he knows they're no different than nagging doubts, only darker; they creep instead of nag. The creep rises like a migraine, closes in like a vise. His doubt resides in the Church of Angels Rising. Would Norwood's organization be so brazen as to conspire to kill? The church would have to be desperate to do something so reckless. What's confusing about the shadows is that sometimes they reveal just a glimpse of the obvious—yes, the church is in on it—while sowing insidious doubt at the same time. Like an abuser. This is the classic domestic call. And, as usual, it comes down to the wife and her bruises, the visible ones and the ones killing her from within.

As if he's reading Mills's mind, Preston says, "I don't care what Francesca Norwood tells you about the agreed separation. She was fleeing her husband. Or the church. Probably both."

"I'm guessing Norwood paid her a lot of money to shut her up," Mills says. "I'm sure she signed a nondisclosure. She has dirt on the church."

"Of course she has dirt on the church," Powell says. "She is the church."

Powell's not wrong. Mills turns again to the board. He creates a third column. It looks like this:

Church of Angels Rising
Gleason Norwood
Francesca Norwood
Gabriel Norwood (excommunicated)
Viveca Canning (dead)
Husband (dead)
Bennett Canning
Jillian Canning (excommunicated)
Sources for Aaliyah Jones story

Mills draws the lines of certitude from one column to another. As these lines often do, they form a web.

29

Gus spent most of last night in his office with Francesca Norwood's cloth napkin. You would hardly know it had been used but for the imprint of her burgundy lips against the white fabric. He draped it over his hands. He listened to it at one ear, then the other. He brought it to his nose and smelled it (fresh, bleachy, crisp, and clean). Taking a deep whiff, he felt a faint stirring of vertigo. He attempted to steady himself in his chair by grasping the armrests. But it was too late. He was spinning. Madly spinning. His hands and feet, arms and legs, like Da Vinci's Vitruvian Man, a perfect circle spinning through the universe. Gus tried to steer the thing, but he could not steer. He tried to flap his arms and fly away, but he could not fly. This felt more like a dream than a vision, more like vapor than a vibe. But as he came skidding to a stop at the opening of a dark tunnel, he realized, of course, he had been here before, at this same spot in the universe. It was a recurring vision, not a dream. The dark tunnel had been forbidding and ominous; there was no way to know how long to the other side, what lay between the openings, how thick the darkness, how dangerous the path, and how tangled the footing. There was no way to know if it was a trap. But as he stepped closer to the opening, here, as he approached with caution, each step more resolved than the one before, he arrived at the truth; this had never been his tunnel. It did not belong to him. He had assumed since the first sight it was his. But it wasn't. It was hers. Glowing red, now, from one end to the other, the walls amber, this tunnel belongs to Francesca Norwood.

He had seen her heading to a door, a heavy door.

Her path had been paved by a reddish glow.

And then she asked them to leave her bungalow.

The dark tunnel that had haunted him is dark no more, is his no more, will likely lead them all to a place where the secret is unearthed.

He rose from his chair, sweating from head to toe. But it was a good sweat. It was a workout sweat. Every damn muscle was on fire. He stood under the showerhead until he out-drenched the sweat, and he then fell into a dungeon-like sleep. He didn't remember drying off. All he remembered was sliding between the sheets and pulling the covers over his head, smelling something like fresh linen envelop his body as he slipped away into the thickest night.

Waking now, a mere four hours later, to an alarm clock piercing through the forest of his sleep, he swats at the day as if the day were a flea. Swatting, it all comes back to him: the visions, the vibes, the vertigo, Da Vinci. He laughs, pulls himself up, and sits at the edge of the bed. He shakes his head, happy to be alive, but woozy from his psychic hangover. Gus steps into drawstring pants and sandals. He shakes the leash and Ivy comes running. She had woken before the alarm and, perhaps annoyed by Gus's snoring, had gone into the living room to watch the birds from the glass doors. Donning a baseball cap and a pair of shades, Gus leads her outside. He waves to Elsa, the neighbor's housekeeper, who's arriving for work. It's 6:07. He has to be at work at 7:00. He'd like to write down some notes about last night's psychic activity, but he has no time. Ivy barks happily at her winged companions, and they chirp back at her with their own renditions of camaraderie. For no reason at all, he bends down and squeezes her. And yet that's all he has to do to understand the reason.

Later, on the way to work, the morning still pink from the waning dawn, he calls Alex Mills. Reporting for duty. That's what the call feels like. He's hoping to report all the psychic activity around Francesca Norwood, but he gets Alex's voice mail. Gus is about to hang up without leaving a message, but hearing Alex's voice gives him a tremble. It's a quick spasm of a vibe, but it tells him something viscerally: the Viveca Canning case is much bigger than Viveca Canning.

The missing Dali is the ending, not the beginning. Go beneath the surface.

"It's Gus. Call me."

Mills calls Aaliyah's boss precisely at 9 a.m. But he's told the boss begins the morning news meeting at precisely 9 a.m. "Why don't you call back at 10:15?" the woman suggests. Mills has a better idea. At 10:15 he and Preston roll into the parking lot of KARI-TV, Channel 4, a building with all the charm of a state prison. It sits on Central Avenue near Indian School, nothing more than a box of concrete with a panel of glass windows above the entrance. A cluster of cacti adorns the pathway on one side, while a team of soaring palms adorns the other, all the botany probably a zoning requirement. Mills tells the receptionist that he's there to see Sam Robatelli.

"Do you have an appointment?" the woman asks from behind a partition of Plexiglas. She's sporting a string of pearls and a minor, but noticeable, facial tic.

"No," Mills tells her. "Tell him he has visitors from the Phoenix Police Department."

For a split second she frowns, peeved, it seems, at the men who arrived without an appointment. "I'll try to reach him," she says. "Have a seat."

They don't have a seat. They loiter near the entrance. A television is on in the lobby, the obligatory narcissism of a TV station playing its own programming, but that doesn't surprise Mills. What else are they going to have droning in the background? At 10:15, the station is running a talk show obviously produced somewhere else and syndicated to the poor souls across the country who are at home watching midmorning TV.

"You think Robatelli is fleeing out the back door?" Preston asks.

Mills laughs, but before he has a chance to respond, a door opens from beyond the Plexiglas and out into the lobby steps a short, wiry guy with an eager stride and an extended hand ready to press the flesh and press it heartily. Sam Robatelli has the face of a thirty-year-old and the scalp of a sixty-year-old; that is to say he's a baby-faced bald man and makes up for it with his manly handshake. "I'm glad you guys showed up," he says. "We were just debating in the morning meeting whether to contact you."

"May we talk someplace privately?" Mills asks him.

"Of course. My office."

Robatelli leads them inside the penitentiary to a large chasm of a room that offers even less warmth than the prison walls outside. It could be for the lack of windows or the lack of color or the reluctance of the fifteen or so people sitting at assorted pods to look up from their computers. The news director leads them into his glassed-in office and asks them to sit. "What can I do for you guys?"

"We want you to know we're releasing information to the public regarding Aaliyah Jones's disappearance," Mills says. "We're alerting the media today."

"Good to know," the man says. "That's partly what we were debating this morning, whether we should be putting a story out there before the police says she's officially missing. But it sounds like it's OK for us to report something..."

"Correct," Mills tells him.

"I don't suppose you'd want to do an on-camera interview with us, to give us an official statement."

"I'm afraid I'm not authorized," Mills replies. "I'll put you in touch with Josh Grady, our public information officer. If there will be interviews, he'll likely be doing them."

The man nods his head, but not happily. He's kind of a corporate version of the reporters Mills sees in the field. They want everything, and they want it on their timeline. They don't like when they don't get it.

"We're also going to put you in touch with our Missing and

Unidentified Persons Detail," Preston tells the news director. "I think they'll ask you to file an official report. Be prepared to give as much detail as possible."

Robatelli puts both palms on the surface of the desk. There's a hint of drama when he volleys between Mills's face and Preston's. "Level with me," he says. "Is she in danger?"

Mills is surprised the guy has to ask. "She could be," he says.

"Do you have evidence to suggest she is?" the man persists.

"Circumstantial," Mills says. "But that's off the record."

He sighs. "We're very worried about her. Should we contact her family?"

"I would have thought you had already done that."

The man shakes his head.

"Yes," Mills says, "you should do that."

"Her colleagues are starting to freak out," Robatelli tells them.

"I'm sorry," Mills says. "We'll do whatever we can to find her. We did find her car."

"I didn't know that," the man says, jolted.

"The information will be in the news release," Preston says.

"We're going to ask that you don't report what Aaliyah was working on at the time of her disappearance," Mills adds.

"She was working on a few stories," Robatelli says.

"Her investigation of the Church of Angels Rising," Mills advises him.

"Really? That's such a great hook," the boss says.

"Hook?" Preston asks.

"You know, a great angle," Robatelli explains.

Mills and Preston enter an unspoken agreement to stare the man down. They sit there, Mills with his arms folded across his chest, Preston with his chin resting in a hand. Robatelli shifts in his chair. He looks at his watch. He scratches a temple. Then he shrugs and says, "Well, maybe that's a little callous."

"A little," Mills says. "Besides you really don't want to tip off the competition that Aaliyah was investigating the church. You don't want to broadcast that. Next thing you know all your competitors will be going after a story that could have been yours exclusively."

Robatelli nods thoughtfully. "True," he says.

The news director excuses himself while he dials a few digits on the phone. "We're running an Aaliyah story tonight," he tells somebody. "Be on the lookout for a news release. Start putting together coverage. Hey, on second thought, let's do a quickie for the noon newscast, before everyone else in the market knows about this . . ."

The man hangs up. "I apologize," he says. "I wanted to alert my assignment desk before I wander off to my next meeting."

"Is that a hint for us to leave?" Mills asks him.

Robatelli claps his hands and smacks his lips. "Not exactly. Is there something else?"

"We'd like to listen to Aaliyah's voice mails."

"Voice mails? I don't know. I would think that's something we have to run by our attorneys."

"Why?" Preston asks. "We're trying to find her."

The man shakes his head. "Yeah, I get that. But there's this thing called reporter privilege, and I don't think we can—"

"We know what reporter privilege is, sir," Preston says. "I guess we're asking you to waive it since it involves the reporter's own safety."

Now Robatelli stands, smacks his hand to his forehead, paces the length of his small office. "OK, OK," he says. "But let me at least talk to my general manager first. He'll probably want to check with the attorneys. But either way, I can't give you access to what you want without his permission."

"How long would that take?"

"I'm not sure. Could be an hour. Could be the rest of the day or tomorrow if we're calling Legal."

"Every second counts," Mills warns him.

The man says, "I know," in such a grave, inner voice that Mills believes him.

Gus spends most of his waking hours looking beneath the surface in one way or another. When he's involved in psychic activity, his visions lay far beyond the layers of human consciousness. He explores the realms of realms. There's an international date line quality to the experience, as well, where today is always yesterday or tomorrow, and if he digs deep enough, he can see the continuum of time all at once. Dizzying, to be sure. The hangover is the result of a cosmic jet lag that's more profound than any time zone shift he's experienced hopping the globe with Billie. Then, there's Valley Imaging and his earthbound job where, during most of his working hours, he peers through human flesh into the bones and organs of strangers.

Going beneath the surface. Gus had been stuck on that notion, if only transcendentally, since earlier this morning. So far today he has peered at two knees, a hip, a pelvis, and a lower lumbar spine. And that's just before lunch. There was something about Mrs. Bloomstein's hip that gave him pause. Nothing serious. Her hip actually looked great for a 75-year-old hip. But there was a shadow there. Not a physical shadow. A shadow of doubt. It all becomes clear to him when he gets a call from Billie during his lunch hour.

"Hello, love," she says.

"Billie!" His heart seems to flip. She still has that effect.

"I just woke up."

He looks at his watch. "Of course you did. All good?"

She hums. "Oh yeah. Miss you."

"Likewise," he says. He moves to an unoccupied corner of the lunch café and sits. "Have you been recording?"

"Rehearsing. Until almost four o'clock this morning."

"I don't know how you do it—"

"But the band was off. They were playing like imbeciles." Her laugh sounds more like a growl, a sweet growl.

"That sucks."

"We'll be back at it tonight," she insists. "Hey, you coming to LA this weekend?"

Something goes thud in his stomach. He can feel a wince on his face. "Is it my turn to come to you? How did I forget this?"

"The last time we were together was when I was in Phoenix. Sorry if it wasn't memorable."

He scoffs. "No. Of course it was memorable. Always is. It's just these days go by so fast. It's hard to keep track."

"Don't worry, Gus. It's all good. I just found out I'm having company. I thought I'd check to see if you'd be here as well."

He shrugs. "Well, I can certainly come. Or I can make it up to you the following weekend."

"Yeah," she says, waking up fully. "Let's do that. I haven't seen Cam in years. We wouldn't want to bore you with all the catching up."

"Wait," Gus says, his shoulders high and tight, fight or flight. "Cameron Taylor? *That* Cam."

"Yes."

"Oh."

That Cam is Billie Welch's former on-again/off-again boyfriend, lover, drummer, arranger, burden. They finally called it off ten years ago, if you listen to Billie and the tabloids tell it. They had been living together, and he had insisted on drinking and drugging even after Billie decided to get the drugs out of her life. He would not change. She would not tolerate it. She threw him out. But their emotionally bruised relationship had made headlines for years. Her early music regularly reported the status of their heartache. Some songs were no more than anger bombs, f-bombs, coordinated sorties to attack Cameron Taylor.

Besieged
After the Fall
Shadow of a Man
Battlefield
Black and Blue Heart

The two of them have since reconciled their anger but have kept their distance. And that was fine with Billie, even more fine with Gus. But a couple with that much history looms large. Occasionally his name comes up. Occasionally a tabloid would speculate on a renewed romance, despite Billie's full disclosure about Gus, despite the fact that Cam hasn't stepped foot in Billie's house in more than a decade. But Cam is stepping foot into Billie's house this weekend.

"Is he staying with you?"

"I said I was having company."

"That's a yes?"

"Yes. Is that a problem?"

Trick question. Whether she intends it or not, it's a trick question. If it weren't a problem, then why is Gus too jittery to answer? He can hear his inner voice fluttering. Like a child. He won't answer like a child. So, yeah, it's a problem. It's a problem because he doesn't like the way it was presented. But it's not a problem because he's a grown-up and he respects Billie's history and all the strange pieces that make up her puzzle. The respect thing. That's the thing. He respects her, but how respectful was it of her to put him on the spot? To assume he'd be okay with a lover from the past?

"Gus?"

"Yeah . . ." he says, stretching the word like a downward dog.

"You're cool or you're not cool."

He laughs. "I'm always cool. Can I trust Cam not to put the moves on you?"

"No," she says, to his confoundment. "But you can trust me to resist him."

He says nothing. He lets that sink in. *Trust. Resist.* Why should she have to resist him?

"Besides," she adds, "I'm an old lady. I don't have the energy for multiple lovers."

"You're not an old lady," he tells her. "And I'm not sure your energy level has anything to do with it."

"Gus, I can tell you're not thrilled with this. But Cam was a big part of my life."

"As am I."

"Right," she says. "But it's not like we're joined at the hip."

There it is! The hip! Mrs. Bloomstein's hip!

The shadow of doubt.

"What's that supposed to mean?" Gus challenges her.

"It's supposed to mean that as long as we live long-distance, I gotta have a life."

Gus groans. "Oh, God, of course you do. As do I. I think we're doing it pretty well without hosting old lovers for the weekend."

"Okay, Gus. I didn't call to have a fight."

If he had a dime . . .

Worst line in history.

"No, you didn't. There's no need. We're adults. Do as you wish. Have a great time."

She was going to do what she wished anyway. She always does.

"You know, with Cam, it could be a great time. Or it could be a nightmare," she says. "He's been clean for six years now. So I'm optimistic."

Gus could not care less about Cameron Taylor's sobriety. He doesn't say so when he says, "Oh, damn, gotta get back to work, love you!" and hangs up.

He looks at his watch. Twenty minutes left.

There's no way they can get a search warrant to listen to Aaliyah's voice mails. Not at this point. Not unless they can convincingly and materially tie her to Viveca Canning's death. Right now they just don't have that. The Missing Persons detail might have an easier time getting the warrant. Mills coordinated a meeting after lunch with Missing

Persons and Josh Grady, and they all mapped out a strategy for publicizing the Aaliyah Jones disappearance. Grady had already drafted a news release, and Missing Persons signed off on it with little alteration. The story hit Aaliyah's station at noon. They didn't have to wait for a news release from the PD. But the story will be in the hands of the rest of the media shortly, and it'll be all over the Internet by the end of the day, on the evening news tonight, in the morning headlines tomorrow. It should be a tweetstorm, a Facebook frenzy; reporters everywhere will be salivating over the proposition that one of their own has been victimized. *See! It's not an easy job!* Mills has no fucking sympathy for media types, but oddly he feels an attachment to Aaliyah, like an older brother who shirked his responsibility, whose DNA is a helix of guilt and betrayal. He should have gone and found her that night. But he punted. He fucking punted and sent Powell to go find her. Every second counts. Write that one on the board a hundred times. If he ever had a burden of shame to carry, he earned this one. And he knows his squad knows it.

He plans to sit here and wallow in the misery. Because he can. Because what's the alternative? Pound the desk? Throw a chair? This fuckup was uniquely his. He puts his head in his hands and squeezes his temples. Then his phone rings. It's Powell.

"What's up?"

"I'm at the lab," she says. "They've been working on the Aaliyah Jones car. The reason we're not getting a signal from her phone after the location where we found her car is because the phone remained in her car."

"Oh?"

"Yeah. They found it in plain sight."

"How plain?"

"It was on the floor of the passenger seat."

"Great. Tell them to get what they need and then I'd like you to enter it as evidence so we can take a look," he instructs her. "That is if it's her personal phone."

"Whose phone would it be?"

"Her employer's. It could be a station-issued phone, in which case we might have a problem. Not a huge problem, but perhaps a delay in inspecting it."

"Why?"

"First Amendment stuff. Reporter privilege."

"Does the same thing apply to a thumb drive?"

"What thumb drive?"

Powell snickers. "Time to make your day," she says. "We found a thumb drive in the car as well."

Now, who's salivating? Mills is salivating. "I'm surprised whoever snatched Aaliyah didn't also snatch the thumb drive."

"Well, it wasn't as easy to find as the phone."

"Where was it?"

"Wedged between the seat and the center console, down deep, practically on the floor," she replies. "I'm not sure what it's doing there."

"I am," Mills tells her. "She knew she was being followed. She sensed she was in danger. She slipped the damn thing down there. On purpose. They might take *her*, but they weren't going to take *it*. It's her gift to us."

"You want me to bag it also?"

"Yeah. We'll have to figure out, again, if it's hers or the property of her employer."

Powell groans.

"No. This is all good news, Jan. This is the best news of the day."

It's only now, when he disconnects from Powell, that he sees he missed a call from Gus earlier in the day. From first thing this morning. He calls back, gets voice mail, leaves a message. "You're it," he says.

His computer dings. Email. Myers.

Alex—

Attached is the first in a series of emails between Viveca Canning and Francesca Norwood. There are many. I can only get to a certain amount at a time because of how they're partitioned off in the cache.

So this is the first. Happy reading. I'll probably have more tomorrow. MM

Homework.

Turns out Kelly has homework too. The Trey Shinner case wrapped up today. Closing arguments will likely begin Monday. Lately, their evenings have been characterized by good books and good wine. Tonight, it's homework and good wine. Kelly pours.

"You sure you'll be up to the closing Monday?" Mills asks his wife. "That only gives you two days to recover from surgery . . ."

"How many times are you going to ask me?"

"I don't know. How many times have I asked already?"

"Forty-four."

"Then forty-five."

"I'll be fine. I told you what the doctors said."

"You did?"

"Alex, you are in such a fog. What's wrong with you?"

He puts his head in his hands. "What's wrong with you is what's wrong with me."

She scoffs. "If you had been at the appointment yesterday you would have heard the doctors yourself."

"I already feel guilty for not going. Don't remind me."

She scoffs again. "That's not what I mean, dumbass. I mean, they sat there and told me some women go to work a day or two later. I remember we had a 77-year-old paralegal at the firm who had a lumpectomy and went to jazzercise class the very next day. I hate the thought of jazzercise. So I'll work all weekend and prepare for the closing."

Alex shrugs. Fine. Whatever. He's not going to fight her. She's a warrior. She doesn't know how to lose. Good. She can be in charge.

Maybe she's always been in charge. Mills married a fiercely independent woman. Nothing's changed. Some fucking spidery mass of tissue, or whatever the fuck the tumor is, isn't going to change that.

"If worse comes to worst," she adds. "Deb can do the closing. She's preparing as well."

"I really think we should call Trevor."

She shakes her head and sighs. "I told you, I think it's best we wait until I'm recovering over the weekend. No need to worry him."

"And I told you, that's not the point."

"Alex, you're working my last nerve."

He says, "Sorry," and goes back to work.

To: Vivican@mymail.com
From: Mtnladyphx@suncast.com
Re: What flight number?
To: Mtnladyphx@suncast.com
From: Vivican@mymail.com
Re: What flight number? Re: 2021

To: Vivcan@mymail.com
From: Mtnlady@suncast.com
Re: New email
Viv, this is my new private email address. Fran

To: Vivcan@mymail.com
From: Mtnlady@suncast.com
Re: somewhere in the world
It's the best plan, Viv. I can't believe I forgave him!!! How could I be so stupid?
It's all about the money, always about the money.

To: Vivican@mymail.com
From: Mtnlady@suncast.com
Re: attorney
I know a good real estate attorney who's done lots of international transactions. He's discreet. Won't say a word.

To: Mtnlady@suncast.com
From: Vivican@mymail.com
Re: Stuff
How did he know I was changing the will?

To: Vivican@mymail.com
From: Mtnlady@suncast.com
Re: stuff
I think Bennett told him. You know Bennett thinks of himself as second in command now that Gabriel's out of the picture. Gleason's like a second father to him.

To: Mtnlady@suncast.com
From: Vivican@mymail.com
Re: stuff
Gleason better hope Bennett never finds out what happened to his real father. I'm still researching all about exhuming.

To: Vivican@mymail.com
From: Mtnlady@suncast.com
Re: Stuff
I don't think we have time to exhume.

To: Mtnlady@suncast.com
From: Vivcan@mymail.com
Re: Stuff
I have to. If there's something to prove, I have to prove it. I can't go to

the police with nothing.

To: Vivican@mymail.com
From: Mtnlady@suncast.com
Re: Stuff
I think we just have to get away before it's too late. Clark didn't know what was coming. But you do.

To: Mtnlady@suncast.com
From: Vivican@mymail.com
Re: Stuff
I never should have sent Gleason that email. I tipped my hand.

To: Vivican@mymail.com
From: Mtnlady@suncast.com
Re: Stuff
At least you didn't threaten to go to the police. You'd be gone by now. And I don't mean Tahiti, darling.

To: Mtnlady@suncast.com
From: Vivican@mymail.com
Re: Stuff
Right. Which is why I'm trying to put together the perfect dossier. I'll have it couriered to the Phoenix police just hours before we hop on that plane! It would be a whole lot more convincing if I could get Clark exhumed and include some kind of report with proof!

To: Vivican@mymail.com
From: Mtnlady@suncast.com
Re: Stuff
I actually think you need the cops or somebody to sign off before you exhume a body.

To: Mtnlady@suncast.com

From: Vivican@mymail.com
Re: Stuff
I'm still researching.
Do you want a ticket to the Heart Ball next weekend? You can come as my date?

To: Vivican@mymail.com
From: Mtnlady@suncast.com
Re: Stuff
I hope you're trashing all your emails, Vivi. And you should delete all your browser history.

To: Vivican@mymail.com
From: Mtnlady@suncast.com
Re: whereabouts
Vivi, I'm staying at the Desert Charm until this whole thing gets settled and we take off. XO

To: Vivican@mymail.com
From: Mtnlady@suncast.com
Re: time
Is running out. I don't know how he's going to do it. But he's consumed with anger. Frothing at the mouth, practically. I just don't like what I see. Can we move up the departure date?

"Jesus Christ," Mills hisses. "These people are a whole new brand of crazy."

Kelly coughs up a laugh, her head sinking in paperwork.

There are many more emails between Viveca and Francesca, most of them out of order and out of context. But a story is emerging. Some of it with flashing lights and sirens, some of it with whispers and innuendo. One thing is clear: he'll be questioning several people again, bringing them in for their callbacks, a second audition. Another thing is clear: "I never should have sent Gleason that email." He needs to see that email. He texts Myers instructions to search for correspondence between Viveca and Gleason Norwood first thing in the morning.

"You shouldn't be on your computer and your phone so close to bedtime," Kelly warns him.

"So now you're the boss of me? A digital cop looking over my shoulder?"

"Something like that," she says. "I think it poses more risk than eyestrain, Alex."

"Like what?"

She pushes her papers aside. "We spend so much time in front of these screens. You know, laptops, phones, TV. Maybe the radiation causes cancer."

"Oh, I see what's going on . . ."

"What?"

"Hon, you can't necessarily find the culprit for cancer. Yeah, there's smoking and sucking on BPA plastic, and you've done neither. That I know of."

She laughs. "You know what I mean . . ."

"I know you want to know why, how, and all that. It could be genetic. But, in the end, you might never know the why or the how, and you better prepare for that."

"Where's my sympathetic husband?" she asks. "And who are *you*?"

He moves to her and pulls her to his shoulder. She rests her face there. "I've been here all along, as sympathetic as you'll ever need me to be, but also realistic. I don't want you going down that rabbit hole, OK? It's a bad place for you. I'm here to keep you away from bad places even if you pretend you don't need me."

She looks up at him. "I need you. There I said it," she declares. "But it's no different now than it's ever been. I don't need you any more or any less today or tomorrow than I did last week. That's the amazing thing about us. We're a constant."

He is on the verge of tears. "Can we go to bed?"

"Best idea I've heard tonight."

Resting beside her, the night whispers anxiety in his ears, zaps him with doubt. The hum of night is not benign, not safe; it's serrated and cruel. He says, "You scared for tomorrow?" When she doesn't answer, he listens for a moment until he hears her breath. He looks over and sees the rhythm of her chest rising and falling, and he concludes that she's fast asleep.

30

What gets him first are the sounds. Like an orchestra warm-up that won't cease, the hospital is a cacophony of tones and rings and dings and beeps. Monitors, IVs, phones, elevators, carts. Everything. And they haven't even made it beyond the pre-op suite.

What the hell are those things dangling from her ears? Feathers? Tassels? Dr. Susan Waxler pulls her untamed curls behind her ears and says, "I'm glad we could fit you in. The sooner we can get this done, the sooner you can move on. That's the way we like to think about it around here."

Oh, they're peacocks. The surgeon is wearing peacock earrings. And she just announced Kelly is going to die. No. She did not announce that. She made an announcement, for sure, but it sounded like a list:

- birth date
- left breast
- lumpectomy
- procedure forty minutes
- sentinel node dissection
- pathology
- overnight
- recovery three days to a week

"Will you be taking off the peacocks before the surgery?" Mills asks her.

"Excuse me?"

"The earrings? I'd hate for you to lose one inside my wife."

The doctor laughs out loud, stopping abruptly to tilt her head. "You're serious," she says. "If it would put your mind at ease, then yes, the earrings come off."

Kelly giggles. "Have you met my husband?" she says from the gurney, her words sluggish from a mild sedative. "Alex, this is Dr. Waxler . . ."

The surgeon nods and acknowledges him. "Yes, I have. Are you waiting?" she asks.

"Of course," he says.

"Have you met your wife's oncologist?"

"He came by earlier, when we first got here."

"OK. Just make sure her case nurse has your phone number in case you have to leave."

"I'm not leaving," he insists.

"Then just say goodbye for now," the doctor tells him. "We'll let you know as soon as she's awake."

He leans over and kisses his wife and says, "I love you."

She smiles and says the same. Then he watches as they wheel her away. And he waits. And waits. And he studies his watch. And he studies the ceiling. And he ignores a call from Gus. Likewise a call from Powell. Then he thinks twice and calls Powell back, gets her voice mail. He stares at the ceiling again. He imagines Kelly's breast. And the knife. The incision. Everything. An hour later, not forty minutes, not forty-five minutes, not fifty minutes—an hour later, someone comes to fetch him and says, "Everything went smoothly. She's awake and doing fine."

It's Dr. Susan Waxler without the earrings.

He goes to see his wife, who looks up at him from the bed with a sleepy smile on her face. She says, "Hi."

He says, "Hi."

And he holds her hand. And she says, "You know I'm spending the night, right?"

"I know."

"Just one night. I come home tomorrow."

"I know."

"So why don't you go to work? Are you playing hooky?"

Mills laughs softly. "I'm not leaving you. You know that."

She rests her head to one side. "Actually, Alex, I'd like to sleep," she says. "I don't think I can sleep knowing you're here brooding. Go to work."

"I'm not brooding."

"Yes, you are. Go to work. I really want to sleep."

He hears a desperation in her voice, and that's what makes him acquiesce. "I'll be back for dinner. I'll even eat hospital food with you, so you won't feel so bad."

"The only thing I want to eat right now is a Pop-Tart for some reason."

"Can she eat a Pop-Tart?" he asks a nearby nurse.

"Nothing right now," the nurse replies.

"Goodbye, Alex."

He kisses her forehead and her cheek.

For the first few minutes in his office, he sits with the door closed. He can't believe life can actually go on. Out there, everybody lives. They go to work, they do their food shopping, they sit in the barber chair, they fill their tanks, sit in traffic, meet for lunch, they plan weddings, they worry about money, they celebrate birthdays, they make deals and break deals, they head to the gym. They do this all day. Nothing stops. The machine doesn't have a pause button for Alex Mills and his anguish. The machine is so fucking noisy with its laughter and traffic and airplanes and joy. No one notices the burdened or the grieving. No one notices the darkness or the shadows, especially not here in the Valley of the Sun. No one gives a shit. Not one shit. He has to screw on his working head now. He has to take off the husband head. This is going to be one fucking impossible transfer. He wants to throw up. He sees Kelly staring back at him from the photo frame and he gets that thing in his chest, that swelling of despair, that inflammation caused by the broken pieces of his heart—he feels it now, the fist in there beating him to a pulp. But nobody gives a shit. They're pissed off the drive-thru is backed up. They hate their bosses. They need an oil change.

Fuck!

His phone rings. Gus.

"Perfect timing," he tells his friend.

"Good. We've been misconnecting."

Mills swallows hard. "I know."

"You OK?"

As he describes the latest news on Kelly and her cancer—there, he said it—he feels, with every word that leaves his mouth, better adept at breathing. The swelling of his chest has gone down. The words are practical, informational, tactical even.

"It's a process," Gus tells him.

"Exactly!" he cries. "If you were here I'd give you a big, fat kiss."

"Really?"

"No. Probably not. But I love you, man."

"You too, Alex. And Kelly too. I think she's going to be fine."

Alex stands up. Stares out the window. "Is that Gus, or Gus the psychic?"

"Both," he replies. "My gut tells me this will be ugly for a while. She will not be feeling well. But I don't think this thing will take over her whole body."

"Metastasize?"

"Right."

"You're an imaging expert and a psychic. How can we go wrong?"

Gus laughs. "It's actually more simple than that, Alex. I've been around Kelly long enough to pick up vibes. I just don't see her body as metastatic."

"Oh, come on, man. That sounds far-fetched, even for you."

"I know," Gus concedes. "But I'm just giving you my vibes.

Speaking of which, do you have a second to talk about Francesca Norwood?"

"I do."

Gus tells him about some kind of tunnel and says Mills should ask Francesca about it.

"That's not a lot to go on," Mills says.

"I know. But I think it will open a new conversation."

"Don't worry. I have a lot for a new conversation," Mills says. "Like a treasure trove of emails."

He describes the back and forth between Francesca and Viveca.

"Wow. That is a treasure trove. Can you forward me a few of the emails?"

"I can't, Gus. They're evidence, so I can't send them to an unauthorized person. But we could meet somewhere, say, your house, and I could pull 'em up on my laptop and show them to you. Besides, they're out of order and somewhat out of context."

"Understood. We'll set up a time," Gus says. "Now get back to your day, Alex. I mean really get back to it. You can stare at the world like you're peering in from the outside, or you can go join the world and get some stuff done. Roll up your sleeves, man, and dig in."

Alex shakes his head to nobody or nothing in particular. "You really have to stop this, Gus. You know, this mind-reading thing."

And Gus says, "Goodbye, dude. I'm out."

Mills stands there holding the phone for a few moments after Gus is gone, letting the adrenalin surge.

Gus is like lightning in the desert.

How do you thank a fucking storm?

You thank a fucking storm by gathering your squad in the conference room and adding another column to your whiteboard, which already looks like some kind of flight chart produced by the FAA.

Mills starts with a debrief about the emails between Viveca and Francesca.

"I have to talk to Francesca again," Mills insists. "She obviously knows more than she's telling us. I need to find out what she's hiding and why she's hiding it. What about emails between Aaliyah Jones and Viveca Canning?"

"Still looking, Alex," Myers says. "I'm sure they're here somewhere."

"And the reporter's phone?" Mills asks.

"Company-issued," Powell says.

"Fuck," is Mills's response. "I think we're going to have to go for a search warrant for her voice mails on her newsroom landline and the cell phone."

"Based on what?" Preston asks.

"She's missing!" Mills hisses.

"Then it's a Missing Persons thing," Preston reminds him. "Let me partner with them. They'll have a much easier time getting the warrant. We'll get it done."

Mills paces. "What about the thumb drive?"

"There is no way to tell unless we open it," Powell says. "Catch-22."

"Nothing on the exterior to indicate it's company-issued? A small engraving?"

"No," Powell says, moderately annoyed, it seems, that she needed to clarify.

"Then we might be OK," he says. "Let me check with Woods."

The room goes quiet. Mills can hear the quaint murmur of the fluorescence. Probably carcinogenic. Everybody seems to be pacing, seated as they are. Pacing with their minds.

"Do you think *we* should have Clark Canning's body exhumed?" Preston asks, shattering the silence.

"The thought has crossed my mind," Mills says. "If the county attorney goes before a judge with the emails, he'd probably get a green light to exhume. But not yet. That calls too much attention to itself. You know, a big, dramatic thing. I don't want to tip anyone off."

"But you'd consider it?" Preston persists.

"Yes. But first, there's supposedly that email between Viveca and Gleason Norwood. I'm thinking that's key. Before we go exhuming any bodies, we need to exhume that email."

He glowers at Morty, who stares back slack-jawed.

"Wake up, Morty! Are you following me?"

"Yeah," he says. "You want me to find that email between Viveca Canning and the preacher."

That was like scolding a child for a crime he did not commit. And Mills instantly regrets it. "Thanks, Morty. I really appreciate all the hard work you're doing."

The guy nods like a puppy dog, half no prob, half fuck you.

The new column:

Follow up

Mills: Reinterview Francesca/Jillian/Bennett, See Woods re: Thumb drive

Preston: With MP for Aaliyah voice mails

Powell: Lab/Car, Lab UI fingerprints, other prints, Scottsdale/gallery security vid

Myers: Cyber/email GNorwood<->VCanning, AJones<->Viveca Canning

"I know it's a Friday," he tells the squad. "But for the rest of the day act like it's a Monday. We have more work ahead of us than behind us."

He then takes his own advice and drives out to Paradise Valley, where he hits the drive-thru at a taqueria and continues on to the Desert Charm. If best-laid plans were truly best, this would have the element of surprise. But this was more of an impulse than a plan, and Francesca Norwood is nowhere to be found. This was not best, nor laid, but it was worth a try. The front desk won't tell Mills whether she's coming back or whether she's checked out. Then he flashes his badge, which technically is useless in PV, and a manager comes forward and confirms that Ms. Norwood is still a guest. "We don't have a check-out date on record for her."

Back in his car, sitting there in the shadow of Camelback, he knows he should continue his worst/unlaid plans and drop in on Bennett and Jillian Canning. Instead he calls the family attorney (he's lost track of how many times he's called the asswipe) and leaves another message requesting a meeting with both of Viveca's children. Then, though he has more work ahead of him than behind him, he drives straight to the hospital and stands by Kelly's bed. It's a good thing she's sleeping. He can hover with impunity.

31

Gus paces all weekend. Not physically—he doesn't pace his living room or his kitchen or the cul de sac outside. He doesn't swim laps in the pool either; rather, he goes back and forth down the hallway of his psyche knowing she's with Cameron, knowing Cameron represents everything rock 'n' roll that she loves, that she's lived for, that he hates. She will be immersed. She will not call Gus. He will not call her. For the weekend, she'll be under some kind of spell that no psychic powers could break. They'll go to a Hollywood party or two, Cameron and Billie, and they'll laugh, maybe even sing a song. Maybe they'll smoke a joint. They'll probably smoke a joint, Cam wink-winking at his sobriety. She'll say pot is harmless. It won't be a glamorous party. It will be old-school and simple. There will be wine and breezes on somebody's incredible balcony.

He doesn't want to break the spell.

He wants to figure it out. Whatever *it* is. It is something, this departure Billie has chosen, however brief. Searching that hallway, pacing from end to end, he doesn't find an answer. He doesn't find a clue.

Kelly was home by noon on Saturday. She dove into her notes and files and began to prepare for closing without stopping for lunch. Mills forced her to eat. He slapped together a sandwich, poured a bowl of soup, and put it between her and her stacks of paper. She ate and studied without missing a beat. She was on fire. Mills understood the fire as her way to boldly reset the agenda: trial now, cancer later. So he sought to find a way this weekend to give her another distraction. During a pee break, when she made a rare retreat from the notes and the laptop, he handed her the prayer book from The Church of Angels Rising.

At first she had said, "Are you serious? You want me to read this nonsense? While I'm peeing."

"I think this so-called religion will be at home in the toilet."

"Really?"

"It would be a big help to me. I can't make heads or fucking tails of it."

Then he couldn't get her to put it down. She brought it to bed with her.

"Captivating?" he had asked.

Kelly had nodded intently, too intently to even open her mouth.

Now, on this lazy, idyllic Sunday morning—the coffee is on, the house is still, Mills hasn't shaved all weekend—Kelly comes tottering out of the bedroom, the book in hand, and says, "Did you read the last section?" Accent on "read."

He looks up and smiles at his lawyer in PJs. "No," he says. "And I can't believe you did either. The book's, like, 700 pages long."

"Six hundred," she corrects him. "And I skipped to the last part."

"Of course you did," he says. So like her to not suffer the foolishness of the filler and to get to the conclusion. He motions for her to sit on the couch beside him.

"The whole thing is a scheme," she says.

"Yeah, Norwood feels very snake oily. It's the typical megachurch, televangelist hoax. His flock hands over all kinds of money so he can live in a megamansion and fly a Lear Jet."

"He has a Lear Jet?"

"I don't know. Just speculating."

"Well, this definitely is not Christianity he's pushing," she says. "It's like a religion he just sat down and wrote one day."

"As have many before him," Mills says. "Maybe all of them before him. What did you find?"

She's not exactly on fire again, but there's purpose and conviction written all over her face, and a quiet resolve burning in her eyes. "A schedule of fees."

"Fees?"

"Yeah, like you see at the DMV," she replies. "It's very straightfor-ward, nothing disguised."

She opens the book, snuggles into him. He puts a hand on her lap. "Go on . . ."

"'First realm: no charge. All welcome. Prepare for Interview. Interview. Advancing: $500. Study. Prayer. Coaching. Review. Test. Second Realm: $1,000. Study. Prayer. Coaching. Service to Others. Personality Encounter with Committee. Review. Test. Third Realm: $3,500. Legion Wings. Study. Prayer. Sweat Equity. Work Assignment. Coaching. Review. Truth Analysis. Test. Fourth Realm: $7,500.'"

"Stop."

"What?"

"What the fuck does any of this mean?" Mills asks his wife. "Per-sonality Encounter? Truth Analysis?"

"I can read you the descriptions," she says. "A personality encounter is a series of sessions with those on higher realms to determine if the pathway is clear for the lower member to move onward and upward to the next realm. The encounter, and I'm quoting here, babe, is a 'robust, high-energy, volatile experience that identifies your inner core to you and, more importantly, to the church.'"

"Holy fuck."

"I don't think that's what they have in mind, Alex, but yeah, this shit is nutballs."

He squeezes her, suddenly grateful for everything, but grateful mostly that they've been spared the madness that sucks so many people into the wilderness of idiots.

"Can you define Truth Analysis?"

She mocks a groan and says, "If you insist. 'The Truth Analysis audits how honest your inner core has been during the Personality Encounter in the Second Realm. Before you rise to the Fourth Realm, you must pass multiple Truth Analyses in the Third Realm. It is a safeguard for you and the church. It strengthens the filaments we will use for your wings . . ."

"OK! Enough! I can't take it," Mills begs.

She tosses the book on the floor below them, and it lands with an ominous thud. But Mills laughs. He laughs his ass off, the effect of which is apparently contagious, because now Kelly too is roaring. And she collapses on him. She says she's a little sore in the armpit from the surgery but otherwise feeling good. He doesn't know if she's saying that for his benefit or not, but it doesn't matter; they're staring into each other's eyes and cracking each other up. They writhe there on the couch. He knows they could seamlessly slip from laughter to tears, but for right now, anyway, they've boldly reset the agenda. And the coffee's ready.

Beatrice Vossenheimer greets him at the door with a smile as wide as the valley. He realizes that's hyperbole, but her face is worthy of the hyperbole. She's wearing a beret and a lacy shawl. He eyes her, amused, but he doesn't ask. Beatrice already knows what Gus is lamenting. He can tell. It's in the soul of her eyes. He kisses her on the cheek and brushes past her. They sit in the room she calls her study, the one with a wall of books on one side and a wall of glass that looks out to Camelback on the other. Gus appreciates the vast light in here. Part of it is the spill of sunshine through the window; part of it is the optimism that comes with learning. He hands her *The Secret Garden*.

"Viveca Canning's daughter gave it to Alex," Gus explains.

"What a strange selection."

"It was random, I think. She has an impressive library."

"I see . . ."

First Beatrice flips through the pages, pausing here and there to read, as if she's sampling the goods at a bookstore or library. Then she closes the book and runs her hands all over the front, the back, the spine, making a tactile kind of assessment of her vibes. "Wow, there are a lot of secrets here that have nothing to do with a garden."

"Yeah. I've been getting the same kind of vibe. Not just from the book. But from the woman's house as well . . . and her life in general."

Beatrice peers across the room, beyond him. "I would say she was afraid of the secrets."

"Good guess."

She clears her throat.

"You know what I mean, Bea."

She nods. "She knew things that she wasn't supposed to know. Yet she was still obsessed with unearthing the truth."

"I'm confused," Gus admits.

"She discovered things she wasn't supposed to discover, and she wasn't done. What she discovered only forced her to look deeper."

"I keep seeing tunnels," Gus tells her. "Strange tunnels that lead somewhere, but I don't know where."

"There are tunnels."

"You saw them too?"

She nods slowly, then she takes a deep breath and gets up. She crosses the room to the windows and says, "Yes, I saw them."

"But you attribute them to Viveca?"

"Yes," she says. "To whom do you attribute them?"

"I thought Viveca, at first. But I get a stronger vibe about Francesca Norwood, the preacher's wife."

"The Church of Angels Rising?"

"Yes."

Standing there at the glass, still in her beret and shawl, Beatrice is a street urchin in silhouette. "Well, it is the church."

"You say that so matter-of-factly."

"It is a fact," she says. "You don't need to be a psychic to know that the church looks suspicious."

"That's what the cops assume," Gus says. "So what are we doing?"

"Validating those assumptions."

Gus shakes his head. "I don't know. The pieces don't add up for me yet."

"You told me about a painting, the Dali, right?"

"Uh-huh."

"Has it been recovered?"

"Not that I know of."

"The Dali is key," she says.

"Right. I kind of assumed that. The cops kind of assume that. I think we're going around in circles."

In silhouette, she twirls in front of the window. "Don't begrudge a psychic her circles," she says and returns to her chair opposite Gus. "I'm sorry I don't have all the answers right now."

"I wasn't expecting you would."

"Maybe the Dali is in a tunnel."

"Or buried underground," Gus says.

"But how would that benefit the killer?"

"Burying the evidence?"

"I don't know," Beatrice says. "Unless Viveca Canning hid a message in the painting..."

"And destroy a masterpiece?"

Beatrice shakes her head, closes her eyes. "No, no, no. Not in the painting. Maybe under the painting."

Then he too closes his eyes, feels his head roll. He marches down a hallway of possibilities, searching. "No, not in the painting. Not under the painting. Behind the painting."

"Behind the painting..." she repeats.

"Yes," he says. "Definitely behind the painting." He opens his eyes. "Thanks for the prompt, Bea. I have a really good hunch that it's not the painting that has something to do with her murder, it's something behind the painting. I was there. I was staring at the wall."

"In your visions?"

"Yes. But also in the house. I stood right in front of the spot where the painting hung. Maybe there's a secret in the wall."

"In the wall? Or on the wall?"

"In the wall. I would have seen something on the wall. Maybe there's some kind of secret note, or map, or weapon stashed inside the wall."

"Then why steal the painting in the first place?" Beatrice asks.

"Oh, damn," he says. "You're right. Then maybe there's a note or something attached to the back of the Dali. Or instructions scrawled across the back of the frame."

She smiles her valley-wide smile again. "Yes. That's it. I think you're getting closer."

"*We're* getting closer."

"To dinner."

It's only about 5:00. So, it'll be an early dinner. Gus drifts into the kitchen after her. She's pulling vegetables from the refrigerator. "What are we having?" he asks.

"It's too damn hot to cook," she says. "So I bought some grilled chicken this morning from AJ's. I'll put it on a salad."

"Sounds good."

He sets the table. He peers out the windows of the dining area at the changing colors of the valley. It's too early for sunset for this glow of orange and pink. Gus searches for the wind and, sure enough, he sees it out there scooping up dirt and dust in curvaceous funnels, creating a racket of pebbles on the patio and against the glass. "I think a dust storm's coming," he says.

"I got caught in a dust storm a couple of weeks ago and it almost blew me off the road," she tells him from the kitchen. "It's been an active monsoon season. Wine with dinner?"

"Nah, just water for me."

"Put on the news in the family room. Maybe we'll catch the weather."

Gus doesn't see the point in catching the weather. Either there will be a dust storm or there won't. There's not much they can do about it anyway. It's not like in LA where you can stand under a doorway during an earthquake or hide under a table so you won't get crushed. Unless the table collapses. Which it probably will. But they don't tell you that. They just tell you to get under a table. Because there's only room for so many people under a doorway. Earthquakes never bothered him. He thinks it's a good thing to be shaken to the core.

"Gus, are you obsessing about something?" Beatrice calls to him.

"Obsessing? No. Why?"

"You've gone awfully quiet in here," she says, entering the room, carrying a huge glass bowl of salad. "Sit."

They dig in. The newscast in the next room babbles on about nothing. The windows sustain a punch of wind and Beatrice nearly jumps from her chair. "It'll pass," Gus assures her.

"Look at the sky," she says.

He can't really see the sky. But that's her point. All that's out there is a billowing wall of dust. "It's a good thing they had caves out here."

"Who?"

"The ancient tribes of the desert."

She smiles. "Always looking out for others, Gus. Even when they're ancestral."

He laughs.

"Aaliyah Jones remains missing tonight, and her family here at Channel 4 is asking for your help. If you're a frequent viewer, surely her face is familiar to you. If not, please watch the following images as we tell you what we know."

Gus turns to the television, craning his neck.

"What is it?" Beatrice asks.

"That reporter. She's the one you referred to me."

"I referred her?"

"Well, Hannah did. Same thing," Gus says. "She's the one who was investigating the Church of Angels Rising. She hasn't been seen in about a week."

"Phoenix police first announced her disappearance on Thursday,"

though she had failed to report to work several days prior," the anchor-woman continues. *"We've learned that her car has been recovered at a vacant business near Thomas and 44th Street. Police are not offering any theories about Aaliyah's disappearance, and we cannot speculate about the reasons behind it. As you can see, she's an African American woman, about 5-7, brown eyes, and shoulder-length wavy brown hair. She sometimes wears it pulled up and sometimes she applies gold highlights."*

Beatrice pours herself another glass of wine. Gus likes the gulping sound the wine makes when it sloshes into the goblet. He doesn't know why. He thinks it reminds him of Billie, maybe, the way she pours wine with abandon, like it's a way of life, not a ceremony.

"It's chilling," Beatrice says. "I heard about it a few days ago, but I didn't make the connection."

"Billie?"

"No," she groans. "The woman on the news."

Gus shakes his head vigorously, coming back to the moment. "Right. Aaliyah. She came to me. I connected her with Alex. And then she disappeared."

"The church," Beatrice says, shrugging.

"Yeah, the church. Or anyone else who felt threatened by her investigative work."

"I'm going with the church."

"Please, if you have any information regarding Aaliyah's disappearance, we urge you to call Crimestoppers at 1-800-555-1177, or call us here at Channel 4 at 1-800-555-4444."

Gus pushes back from the table.

Beatrice looks at him, a sagacious gleam in her eyes. She knows what's coming next.

He turns his chair around, away from the approaching storm. "Now I'm getting something," he says to Beatrice. "I'm absolutely getting something."

"Where are you?" she asks.

"I don't know. I don't know yet. But it's strong, this vibration, whatever it is."

"Close your eyes, Gus."

"They are closed."

"No, they're not."

"Oh." He does as he's told. He closes his eyes. He lets the vibration rise the full length of his body, and inside this vortex he sees her. *I see her.* "I see her now in a dark room," he tells Beatrice, "on the floor, in the corner. She's weeping. She's beautiful, but frightened—I don't know. I don't know. She and I . . . she and I . . . There's something deadly calling. I have no effing clue what this means . . ."

"She's dying?" Beatrice asks him.

He feels his foot tapping the floor. "She will die. They have her."

"Who?"

"The church, I think. That's my gut more than my vision."

"But did they know about her investigation?"

"Of course they did. They know everything."

"Can you see where they have her?"

"No."

"Go back to your vision."

He does. There's that amber light again. The amber light of the tunnel. But he looks to the left, and then to the right, and he can't see her. He doesn't know which way to follow. He tries to get back to that room where she's sprawled on the floor but he's lost. His visions are getting crossed, as they tend to do: the tunnel, the room, her fear, his apprehension, her beauty, his darkness, and the inevitability of everything. He feels something land in his hands. He recognizes it. It's the key Alex had taken into evidence from Viveca Canning's vault. He knows viscerally that this key, this old brass key, is the tangible link between Viveca Canning and Aaliyah Jones.

"She's in prison," he says aloud.

"Who?"

"Aaliyah."

"Prison? Like a criminal."

He opens his eyes. "No. Not criminal. A hostage." He tells Beatrice about the key.

"Now all you have to do is find the door, Gus. Find the door."

"Jesus," he mumbles. "Maybe it's all a metaphor. I think the vision's a metaphor. She's already dead, I think. But the key. It unlocks whatever it was she was looking for."

Beatrice rises. She comes to his side. She cradles his head in her arms. And she rocks him. "So much, Gus. It's so much. Why don't you just call Alex and step back?"

"I don't know," he says. "I don't think so."

"I have a big event in Atlanta next weekend," she tells him. "A book signing and a workshop. You should come."

He gets up, starts clearing the table. The wind outside is crazy and disorganized. "I can't, Bea. I'm heading back to LA for the weekend to pick up where we left off."

"What does that mean?"

There's no wriggling out of a conversation with Beatrice, so he tells her about Cam Taylor's visit with Billie.

"She's not sleeping with him, if that's what you're worried about."

"Is that a psychic thing, or a woman thing?"

"It's both," she replies.

"That's not even the point. Whether or not she's cheating on me, she'll always be married to her music. She'll never marry me."

Beatrice turns on the disposal and it starts to ravenously chew. "Is that what you want, Gus? Really?" she asks as the discarded remains scream for dear life.

He shrugs and says, "I think so."

"Then you don't know so . . ."

"What?"

"You wouldn't just think so if you knew so. There would be that voice inside you that just says, 'Yes, Gus, this is what I want.' It affirms."

"OK."

The disposal grinds to a stop.

"Marrying her won't change the dynamic. It won't remove the other lover."

Gus returns to the dining area where he wipes down the table. "I don't want to remove her music. Her music is everything. And I love it. It's really the only thing she knows to do, and she does it well, and this is who she is. She is that and nothing else. And I get *that*. I get who I'm with."

Beatrice approaches from behind. "You want to be a husband?"

"I . . . the voice inside me says . . . I've been a lone adventurer for a long time."

"But you two have been together for a couple of years."

He faces her. "Right. You know, I don't want to talk about this, Bea."

"OK. How about you help me rehang a mirror in my gym?"

"Sure."

"Maybe you'll get a good glimpse of yourself."

He shakes his head. "You don't have a mirror to rehang, do you?"

She drifts away without answering.

"And let's get back to Buck Aaron at Severe Weather Center 4 for an update on the destructive dust storm passing through the valley at this hour. Buck, should people still be sheltering in place . . . ?"

32

They're finally burying Viveca Canning.

Jillian had texted Powell this morning, and this is the news waiting for Mills when he gets off the elevator. "One o'clock. Valley Vista Memorial Gardens," Powell tells him.

Mills is familiar with Valley Vista, the luxury cemetery and crematorium serving the valley's ultrawealthy and ultradead; it figured briefly into a case last year when bodies started turning up at area graveyards, the victims forced to dig their own plots before they were bludgeoned to death.

Nice memories. Around every corner.

"Let's leave at 12:30," Mills tells her. "I'll let Preston know. Myers can stay here on cyberpatrol."

In the meantime, Mills drinks a cup and a half of municipal coffee, wincing with every sip, and meanders to the office of Jake Woods, where he asks the sergeant about Aaliyah Jones's thumb drive.

"Fair game, I would say," Jake tells him. "It's all done in the interest of finding her."

"Are we going to have a turf war with Missing Persons?"

Jake laughs out loud. "Aw, come on, Mills, don't be a drama queen. Of course not. Share it with them. End of story."

Drama queen? Mills grits his teeth. "OK, Jake. Thanks."

"I take it you're not making much progress to date?" the sergeant asks.

"I don't think that would be a fair assumption."

"Care to explain?"

Mills looks at him squarely. "Go down to the conference room, Jake, and take a look at the whiteboard. That's our progress."

Then, with a nod, he exits the sergeant's office.

The thumb drive contains thirty-four folders. Mostly document files, some photos. Just looking at the folder names he can tell Aaliyah Jones used the device for both personal and professional storage. *Charter School Investigation. Lt Gov Travel Expenses. Head Shots. Resume. Angels Rising. Blog. Peru Plans. San Diego pics. Hawaii pics. Animal Charity Investigation.*

"As much as I'd like to see a Hawaiian sunset, open the Angels Rising folder," Powell says. She's sitting beside Mills at his desk. He is very conscious of the two of them gawking at the screen.

"Thank you, Captain Obvious," he tells her. Then he clicks on the folder. About two dozen files pop up. He opens the first one.

Ruth Adams
602-555-1919
Won't go on the record. Says she married into the church twenty years ago before it became a megachurch. Thought it was a cult. Claims she was beaten during a Truth Analysis for questioning origins of church. Husband beat her too. She fled. Filed for divorce. To save marriage, husband renounced church, reported Norwood to sheriff's office and contacted newspaper. Then husband disappeared. "I know they lock people up. Because I know people who've been locked up and let out. But I think they silence the true dissenters. I think they kill them. I have no proof."

Agnes
Adm1970@mymail.com
Will not meet in person. Refuses phone interview. Says she grew up in child camp. Not so bad. Treated well. Some discipline. As adult, joined church staff as a bookkeeper. Left the church as adult, claims she spent time in a "dungeon" for giving IRS financial data.

JP
602-555-1688
jpmarcophx@phxnet.com
Email: "Hello Ms. Jones. Ruth Adams said I should get in touch with you about construction work I did at the church before I left . . .you can reply to this email or call me at . . ."

Karl
480-555-0227
Won't go on record. Left church two years ago. Says he ran out of money and could not pay to go to a higher realm. Says church tried to pressure him to stay, promised a higher realm if he earned it through sweat equity at the children's camp in Sedona. Says he tried working there but he saw counselors and guards beat the children. Children separated from parents at early age to study nothing but church doctrine, views of the world as seen through Angels Rising. Says parents are instructed to tell neighbors, nonchurch friends and family that children have been sent to boarding school. They lock dissenters up if they can. "If you can flee, great. If you can't, you get locked up, maybe killed. And your family goes along with it if they're true believers. They're instructed to tell outsiders that you're on a permanent mission overseas. It's totally fucked up."

Mills clicks out of the folder. "I think most of the files here are probably similar," he says. "We can check the rest later."

"We can call these people," she says.

"We have to be careful about that. They're anonymous sources to a reporter. It would be different if we were investigating her death."

"We might be."

"I'm not saying no. But one death for today," he says. "Viveca Canning."

After Powell is gone, Mills chows down on leftovers for lunch. He dials Kelly to see how closing arguments went.

"Better than expected," she said. "I'm surprised."

"I'm not," he tells her. "How are you feeling?"

"Great. That's the strange thing."

"Don't question it, hon. If you feel great, you feel great. I'm proud of you."

"Wait until the verdict."

"I said I'm proud of you. I don't need a verdict for that."

"The case will go to the jury this afternoon."

He tells her he loves her, then he hangs up and heads for the elevator, where he meets up with Preston and Powell.

The chapel at Valley Vista Memorial Garden overflows in unruly tentacles of black and tears. Mills and his colleagues manage to squeeze into the last row, and he looks with great sympathy at the mourners forsaken to the outdoors. The heat alone is enough to make you cry. The socialites have flocked to the service in their royal fascinators as if it were a freaking fashion show. He recognizes a few of them, the friends and fellow philanthropists he interviewed earlier in the investigation. Both Bennett and Jillian stand front and center in the hall, guarding the casket with eyes full of protracted sorrow. The kind of sorrow that comes to visit and can't seem to leave. Her eyes notwithstanding, the rest of Jillian's face is stone. Bennett looks drunk with misery, his face sagging from the weight of grief. The officiator, notably not Gleason Norwood, enters from a side door, his white robe trailing behind him. He welcomes the mourners. Mills can't hear much of the eulogy or the blessings because the sobbing around him is so boisterous. Clutching roses, Bennett Canning bends over the casket and howls. His body shudders, and his sister goes to him with a tentative caress on the shoulder. Even in the tenderness, the estrangement is obvious. As her brother backs away, Jillian lays one hand on the casket and the other on her heart, her lips moving as if in prayer. This lasts about a minute, then she pulls back, stoic again.

A woman approaches the podium. Mills recognizes her. Doesn't remember her name. But as soon as he hears someone say "Liz," he remembers her as Viveca's best friend, Liz Livingston. One of the first people he interviewed. Through the yelps of sorrow, he strains to listen to this woman's version of remembrance. He hears a few vague strands of her tribute, her words greeted by the vigorous nodding of ladies in black, by some of the men too, though most of them seem fairly aloof to the funeral happening around them.

"My life was not the same because of her. My life will never be the same without her," Liz Livingston concludes, then steps down.

After the service, the black amoeba creeps over to the Canning family's marble mausoleum, where Bennett offers sincere clichés of no surprise. "And here she will join my noble father, Clark. And here they will rest together for eternity."

A harpist harps. A flautist does whatever a flautist does. There's a keyboard. A woman sits behind it and plays. And then she opens her mouth and she sings "The Greatest Love of All" with the fullest conviction, indifferent or oblivious to the cliché. She belts it out as if she's trying to rouse Whitney Houston from a nearby grave. Mills doesn't understand it, finds himself stifling a laugh and nudging Powell to stifle hers.

The three of them, Mills, Powell, and Preston, pull back from the crowd as the service ends.

"That's Francesca Norwood," Mills says, pointing to a svelte woman in black standing by a palm tree in the distance. She's wearing huge black sunglasses and a massive hat that, while sporting a floppy brim, still exposes her face. "Follow me," he tells the others.

The woman offers a wan smile as Mills approaches.

"Hello, Detective."

"Francesca . . ."

"I take it you're not mourning," she says.

Mills shakes his head. "No. We're investigating."

"You really think your killer would be so brazen as to show up here?" she asks.

"It happens," Powell tells her. "So we have to be here just in case . . ."

"Find anybody?"

"Not yet," Powell replies.

"But we need to talk, Francesca," Mills tells her. "We found more emails on Viveca's computer. She knew something. Maybe about the church. About your husband. And we know she shared it with you."

Francesca folds her hands, stares downward, freezes for a moment. She's a sculpture, posing here among the other statuary. She and the marble deities line the promenade, all of them whiter than the sun, as still as their secrets, as majestic as their powers would convey. Mills thinks of ancient Greece. This section of Valley Vista Memorial Gardens looks like Athens had too much to drink and threw up its mythology all over the place.

"She didn't share anything with me," Francesca says suddenly. "Not the details. She said she wanted to protect me."

"Like I said, we need to talk," Mills prods her.

She makes a sweeping gesture with her arms. "Here? You can't possibly be serious. Let's have some dignity."

"Right. Dignity," Mills says. "I assume your husband's not here."

"Correct. Under the circumstances. Knowing that Viveca was leaving the church and all . . ."

"Then why the big show at the church for her memorial?" Powell asks her. "All that drama, all that spectacle."

"That's exactly what it was. It was a show. All for the sake of the members," Francesca says. "It was my husband's way of showing that nothing was awry. That Viveca was still very much a part of the church."

"Even though she wasn't . . ." Mills says.

She turns and watches the lingering crowd. "What did I just say? I don't want to be seen talking to you people here."

"No, you said it was a matter of dignity."

"Well, both, then," Francesca snaps. "Tomorrow morning, Detective Mills, you can meet me at the Desert Charm."

"I'll be there."

"And one more thing," she says, stepping away. "I thought I could blend in here today underneath this hat, behind these sunglasses.

Obviously, I wasn't successful, since you people found me. But please, if he doesn't know already, I don't want my husband to know I'm in town or where I'm staying."

Mills assures her that's not a problem. He watches as she walks away.

When Alex walks in the door, he can sense from the light in the house, or lack thereof, the malaise that has beset his wife. She's not a cave dweller who lives with just a single source of illumination. Typically, her house is a bright one. An optimistic one. The curtains are open in the daytime; prior to bedtime, the bulbs, all of them, are bright, the utility bills be damned. So, when the house goes dark, as it is now, when the dimmers are one notch from the "off" position, and when the only real source of light is the feeble yellow glow over the stove, Mills is not surprised to find his wife curled up in bed at 6 p.m., her hair matted against the pillow, her skin sallow and clammy.

"Hon, you awake?"

"Umm, hmm," she murmurs.

"You don't feel well?"

She hasn't lifted her head. "No," she says with a labored breath.

"Do you need to go to the doctor? Should I call the doctor? Take you to the ER?"

She's still looking at the wall. "Not so many questions, Alex. I'll be fine."

He sits on the bed at her side. "You have to tell me what's wrong. Are you in pain? Are you nauseous?"

She reaches for his hand. "Nothing like that. Just exhausted."

She's more exhausted than he's ever seen her for a Monday, and he can't imagine how she'll make it through the week. "Did the case go to the jury?"

"Yup," she says.

"You went back to work too soon. We have to get you better for the verdict."

She squeezes his hand.

"If you'd like me to pamper you, I will," he tells her.

"Let me take a rain check. I'm going to need it."

He asks what she wants for dinner, but she says she's not hungry. He goes through the lecture of how she has to eat, needs to eat, must get stronger, but she says she's too tired to eat. He says he'll put on some soup for both of them. She murmurs something that he can't understand.

"It's canned soup," he says. "But it's better than nothing."

Then he's in the kitchen. He turns on the news and rummages through the pantry. Puts the soup on the burner. The label says, "do not boil," but it boils. He can never catch it before it boils. Someone at Campbell's will probably issue him a violation. Mills relates this to Kelly when she shows up at the table, but all she offers is a meager smile, a kind of shrug of her bare shoulders, not even a syllable of a laugh.

"Phoenix police say they have no leads in the disappearance of TV reporter Aaliyah Jones. She was last seen about a week ago before failing to report to work. Police aren't commenting on their investigation at this point, but Jones's news director at Channel 4, Sam Robatelli, provided a brief statement.

'At this time our focus is on Aaliyah's whereabouts. If anyone has any information that could help police find her, please call the Phoenix Police Missing Persons detail, or call us by dialing the main number for Channel 4. Someone will be answering the phones 24/7. Aaliyah is an important member of our family. Her work is some of the best we've ever produced. We'd like her to come back to her family and the work that she loves. Whether you're a friend, a relative, a viewer, a fan, please help us find her.'

Robatelli would not take questions. At times like this we don't feel like Channel 4's competitors. We feel like family. Aaliyah has many friends at the other media outlets in town. We all pray for her safe return."

Kelly puts her spoon down. "That's so scary," she says. "I'm worried for her."

"So am I."

"What does your gut tell you?"

He hesitates for a second, recalibrates his optimism, and says, "I think she's alive. I do. But I think she's in trouble. I don't think she has a lot of time."

"That's rather concerning."

"But whoever has her wants information. She's a reporter. That has to have something to do with her disappearance. She won't be killed until she gives them the information they want."

"Do you think she will?"

"I don't know her well enough."

They slurp in unison. The soup tastes more like can than soup.

"In other news, valley socialite Viveca Canning was laid to rest today at Valley Vista Memorial Gardens. The 62-year-old philanthropist was murdered in her Phoenix home earlier this month. Police have no suspects in her death, but Josh Grady, a spokesperson for the department, says the police are focusing on her life at her church . . ."

"What?" Mills pushes back from the table. "What! What the fuck?" He lunges for the phone and calls Grady. "What the fucking fuck, Josh? I just watched the news. What were you thinking?"

"Hey, I'm out having dinner, dude. Chill the fuck out."

"'Focusing on her life at church'? Really? Why not just let the media into the conference room to take a shot of our whiteboard?"

"Look, I only gave that information because Woods told me it was OK."

Mills's next call is to Jake Woods.

"It was time to say something. Anything. We have to at least look like we're doing something tangible and not just sitting around on our asses."

His forehead pounds. "We're doing lots of something tangible, but nothing public."

"You think this will spook the church." Not a question.

"Damn right, it will spook them. I'm going to need a warrant, like, tonight."

Woods scoffs. "We simply said we were focusing on her life at her church. That doesn't say we're focusing *on* her church."

Now Mills scoffs. "You expect the church to appreciate that nuance? Really?"

Woods says, "I think you're getting a little carried away, overreacting. 'Her life at church' could mean anything to anybody."

"To the preacher, it means the church. Period." From the corner of his eye he can see Kelly rise from the table and drift toward the bedroom. "You know, man, I got a sick wife and I don't need this stress."

Oh. Shit. It just came out.

"A sick wife? Is Kelly OK?" the sergeant asks.

"No. But I don't want anyone in the department to know. She has breast cancer. She had surgery on Friday."

"This past Friday?"

"Yes."

"You should at least tell your squad."

"Because?"

Woods does a wireless sigh and says, "Because they need to be ready to jump in. You know, cover for you."

"They've already jumped into the case as much as they'll need to," Mills tells him. "I don't need anyone to cover for me."

"All right, just a suggestion," Woods says. "Give Kelly a hug for me. I'm sorry to hear the news. But I know she'll pull through."

And you know this how?

He doesn't say that. He just says, "Thanks. Goodnight."

Then he goes into the guest bathroom and throws up.

33

As he glides down the long driveway of the Desert Charm, Mills sees a family of crows circling overhead like a warning. By the time he reaches the entrance, one of the birds has swooped from the sky and is sitting on a stucco wall by the guard booth. The crow leers at him but doesn't leave his post as Mills, cleared by the guard, rolls forward. The bird's animosity could not have been as bad as Mills imagined. He dials Gus Parker.

"It's Alex . . . You up?"

"Yep. Just came in from a walk with Ivy."

"I'm on my way in for a talk with Francesca," he says. "You got anything I can use on her? Any vibes? Visions? Anything?"

"Yes. I've had time to contemplate and conjure . . ."

"The napkin you stole?"

"The napkin I stole."

Mills laughs. "And?"

"I'm coming up with wild experiences."

"What is that supposed to mean?"

"I don't know, exactly. But I've been having these visions of tunnels. Dark tunnels. Mysterious tunnels. And there's been a lot of movement, me spinning through the universe. Like from one tunnel to the next. But then suddenly it came to me, in my gut, that these are not my tunnels to decipher. These are Francesca's."

Mills grumbles. "But you're the decipherer."

"Not here. I can't tell you what they mean until you ask her about them. And hers are amber, not black."

"Amber what?"

"Her tunnels have an amber glow. They're not black like the ones I had been seeing. Once I got a hold of that napkin, the light came on. Ask her about the tunnels."

"Ask her about the tunnels," Mills repeats. "OK . . ."

"Then get back to me."

With that, Gus is gone.

At first Mills doesn't get an answer at Francesca Norwood's door. Immediately it occurs to him that she's hightailed it to French Polynesia because seeing him at the funeral was enough to rattle her cage. But it's just a fleeting reaction, not based on a reasonable instinct, so he knocks again. He wonders if the water in Tahiti is really as blue as it looks from the images he's seen online, if it really is Ty-D-Bol blue. His next knock will be his last. He's about to turn away when he hears a shrill voice calling, "Be right there, be right there."

The door opens about ten seconds later. Francesca Norwood stands there freshly coiffed. He can smell the hairspray, the perfume, the nail polish, a mix of vapors that should, realistically, cause the bungalow to explode. A woman stands to her side. "This is my stylist, Contessa. She's just leaving now."

The stylist nods, smiles, and slithers past him.

"I hope you weren't getting all gussied up for me," Mills says.

She laughs. "Oh no! Don't be silly. My lawyer's coming for lunch. Come in."

He follows her to the living room area where they sit. She looks at him but says nothing; there's something passive-aggressive about her silence, calculated, as if he must grovel for her attention, as if groveling is the only thing that would please her this morning, here in her luxurious bungalow, in her understated statement-making hideaway. "Clark didn't know what was coming. But you do," he says instead of groveling.

She stiffens, as if her chair is electric and she's strapped to it. "What did you say?"

"I was reciting one of your lines from an email you sent Viveca. Can you explain?"

He almost feels bad for making her squirm, but he doesn't. Good detectives can make a corpse squirm. She puts a hand to her forehead and rubs. There's pain clamoring there, or stress, or both. He sees a tiny suggestion of a tear. "I think Clark had something over my husband. I'm sure of it."

"Like what?"

"I don't know," Francesca replies. "Really, I don't. But Viveca and I had been talking a lot lately about Clark and the key."

Just the mention of the key gives Mills a detecterection: that's a word he made up for a detective's erection. You'd think that's something the forever-adolescent Morty Myers would come up with, but it's all Mills, when the important discoveries, when the hint of conquest, still feels as satisfying as sex. Stupid, yeah, but come on. The key!

"What key?" Mills asks, because a little subversion hurts no one.

"Before Clark died, he mentioned something to Viveca that really frightened her. He said 'if I die, make sure no one knows you have the key,' and then he showed her a key to some padlock. And then she asked him what it was for, but he wouldn't tell her. He said it wasn't safe for her to know. Not yet. That he'd tell her when he had all the answers. He said he needed to confirm things. But if he ever got around to confirming his suspicions, he never got around to telling her anything else."

"So, what does this have to do with your husband?"

She gives Mills a bitter laugh, really like the laugh of a pit viper, and says, "Well . . . I remember Gleason getting very upset. He said Clark stole something from him. Something very important. He wouldn't tell me what, but Viveca and I put two and two together and we realized it had to be the key. Gleason was absolutely crazy mad. I mean, flipping out. Said Clark would have to be banished. And I remember saying 'you can't exactly banish a member of the board,' and Gleason said, 'I can banish anyone I want. I own this church. I own this religion.'"

"Do you think your husband killed Viveca Canning?"

The woman coughs hard, almost chokes. Mills waits. "No. Not

at all," she says finally. "But I know he told the board of directors and they were just as upset as he was."

"About a key?"

"About some kind of leverage Clark, and then maybe Viveca, would have on the church. . ."

"So then anyone on the board of directors could have a motive to kill her . . ."

"Maybe."

"And Clark Canning dies without telling Viveca what he suspected or what the key was for," Mills persists. "I take it she found out."

Francesca nods emphatically. "Oh yes. She did. She didn't spend a whole lot of time at the gallery where her vault is. But a few years after Clark died, she had loaned a rather large collection to a museum in LA, I think, or Chicago, I can't remember, but after the collection was removed from the vault, she was in there, and all of a sudden she realizes some old chest in the back had a padlock on it. And she knew. She just knew. So she went home, grabbed the key Clark left her, and went back to the gallery—"

"And opened up the chest. And found some deep, dark secret inside?"

Been there, done that, he's thinking. Why not get her version?

"Not exactly, Detective," she says, her eyes sadistic slits. She is fucking enjoying her new role as Minister of Information. She's getting off on it. "Viveca said her discovery was 'confounding.' I think that's what she called it. She says the only thing in the chest was some kind of ancient key. A bronze key."

"And then what?"

"And then nothing," the woman says with a smile. "She had no idea what to do with the bronze key. Had no idea what it meant. How could she?"

Mills pushes his seat forward. "And then she died. Just out of the blue?"

Francesca throws her head back as if she's about to laugh, but she doesn't. She holds it there, bent, and Mills can see the pools brimming in her eyes. The angle of her face calibrated to defy the gravity of her tears. "No," the woman whispers. "She did find out a couple of months ago what the bronze key was for."

"How?"

"From what I understand, that reporter from Channel 4 dug up some guy who'd been on the building crew of the church almost twenty years ago," she says. "I guess he knew things."

"What things?"

"I don't know. Viveca didn't want me to know. She said it would be dangerous for me to know," she tells him. "The reporter arranged a meeting with Viveca and this construction guy, or contractor, and he led her to the truth. Whatever Viv saw or whatever she found out, it shattered her faith and scared the shit out of her, if you'll pardon my language."

"And then she died for it . . ."

Then Francesca howls. "I can't believe this!" she cries.

"You're safe, Mrs. Norwood," Mills assures her. "I'm a cop. I can protect you."

She whips her face to him now. "I don't care about my safety," she hisses. "I care about my reputation."

Mills does a shake of his head with bulging eyes, a kind of "you're-shitting-me" telegraph.

"I mean I care about Viveca, of course. But she's dead and she doesn't have to worry about reputation. I've had to give up everything. My TV show. My life. Everything!" the woman begs. "But yes, she found out what the key was for. She threatened to go to the cops. She wrote a letter to Gleason, attached it to an email, and told him she was leaving the church and changing her will and that the church would never get a dime from her."

"But she never told you what the bronze key was for?"

"No."

"Really?"

"Really."

"Aren't you curious?"

"Of course," Francesca replies. "But I sure as hell wasn't going to ask Gleason about it. He certainly looks suspicious now. Doesn't he?"

"But you don't think he killed her. You said so."

"He didn't. He wouldn't risk it."

"Does anyone really know what he'd risk to protect the church?"

She doesn't answer.

"Viveca obviously never went to the cops," Mills says.

The woman gets up and walks to the kitchen where she removes tissues from a box on the counter. Dabbing her eyes, she says, "No. But she was preparing a dossier for the police. And she was planning to leak the story to that reporter. It was all a part of her escape plan. Viveca was devoted to the church. I had never seen someone so devoted or, God help me, brainwashed. When she told me she was cutting the church out of the will, I knew she had learned something horrible. I knew I had to leave too. I wanted to escape with her."

Mills rises to his feet now too. He walks toward the kitchen, stopping short and leaning against a wall opposite her, the formal dining table between them. "You know, Francesca, it does seem a bit disingenuous when you talk about *learning* horrible things about the church. People have been saying horrible things about the church for years. Do you mean to say you never believed there might be a kernel of truth, or that you never actually witnessed a kernel of truth?"

She seems to buckle. But then her fists, by her side, go tight. Everything clenches. Her face, her neck, her shoulders. "How dare you imply that I'm some sort of accomplice, Detective? I'm here talking to you of my own free will. I don't have to do this. I don't have to do this ever again."

"And I could have you deposed. Based on the emails we found alone," he retorts. "In fact, I will probably have to depose you at some point if we ever make an arrest of someone connected to the church."

She starts to sob. "Are we done?"

"No," Mills replies. "Did Clark Cannon die of natural causes?"

She looks up from her sobs and her tissues and says, "How would I know?"

"You and Viveca were emailing back and forth about exhuming Clark's body . . ."

"Oh, Jesus. Yes. Viveca suspected something. Remember Clark had told her that he had some kind of leverage over my husband."

"Again, the key . . ."

She turns away and drifts to the refrigerator. "Something cold to drink, Detective?"

He shakes his head, declines the offer. She pulls out a bottle of Evian and sips. Elegantly. She's all affectation, not unlike her husband. But she's alone now. A pageantry divided by two, and she does appear somewhat forsaken to Mills, as he stands there gazing, staring, sizing her up. Gus sometimes talks about aura, about what he sees radiating from the outlines of a person; to Gus, at least, aura is truth, a mix of brain chemistry and soul that seeps out. But here, studying Francesca Norwood, Mills either can't detect an aura or can't interpret whatever it is that radiates. So he defers to his gut, a tool that sometimes proves more effective than forensics. His gut tells him this woman is telling the truth and, at the same time, is full of shit. She's full of shit in the way she's revealing the truth. She loves the drama. She loves the intrigue. She loves getting on a midnight plane and fleeing the scene. She can't wait.

"What kind of leverage?" Mills asks her.

"I told you. I don't know," she says.

"But it's fair to say someone at the church might have had him killed."

"That's not what I'm saying."

"But with Clark dead, the secrecy of the key was safe. If the key, in fact, was the leverage."

"Well, yes, assuming Viveca didn't know about the key, its whereabouts would remain a mystery," she says. "I guess no one knew that Clark told her about it at the time."

"He died of a heart attack. Officially," Mills says. "But there was no autopsy."

"The church forbids autopsies."

"Why? That sounds like there's something to hide. You know, like the church can do away with dissenters and leave no trace . . ."

She approaches him, stops just about a foot away. "That's horrifying of you to say," she chides him. "It's church doctrine. You don't understand our religion. We are not like the living souls outside the church. We have already been blessed with the afterlife and we are here simply waiting to rise as angels."

Mills does a singular, perplexed shake of the head. "Huh?"

"We're technically dead already," she says. "That's the basic tenet of our religion. While the rest of you walk around in this miserable life, we float through the world awaiting our calling to rise . . ."

She's in his face. He looks down, averting. Technically dead already? How do you follow that up with a serious expression? Really? Mills has toured the fun house called the Human Condition. He's seen the reflection of humanity in the house of mirrors. He thinks the universe is one big fucking theme park where God, or someone in power, has the last laugh. Mills has been doing this a long time. But this is a first.

Slowly he looks up. "OK, so you forbid autopsies."

"Yes. Because it's like double jeopardy. We were already autopsied when we left the world of the living. To do it twice would be an imposition on the angels."

"Clark Canning was buried quickly?"

"From what I remember, yes," she says. "No one suspected foul play. Not then, anyway. And certainly not outside the church. We're pretty insular, if you hadn't noticed."

"It's the first thing I noticed," Mills tells her. "Don't you suppose the church wanted the key back, Francesca? And if someone at the church wanted the key badly enough to kill Clark, wouldn't the same be true for Viveca?"

"I think we're talking in circles, Detective."

Mills can feel the steam rising. "What would you prefer, rectangles? Hexagons?"

She spins on her heels and sits at the table. "Don't be flippant with me."

"I'm sorry," he says, though he's not. "But don't you think the motive to kill Clark and Viveca might be one and the same?"

"I'm not a detective," she says. "But yes. It has vaguely occurred to me. But nobody but me had proof she ever knew about the key, that Clark ever told her about it. At least that's what Viveca said."

"Except your husband, once he received her email. Then he knew she had the key, and he knew what she found."

The woman weeps. The tears segue to sobs. Mills watches and listens. There's a depth to her despair that sounds as if she's crying from the hollows of a basement. He's reminded of tunnels, something Gus said about tunnels. He asks her.

She looks at him confused. "What do you mean?"

"Do you know anything about tunnels?"

"What kind of tunnels?"

"The psychic is seeing images . . ."

"Oh, please. Are you serious?"

"I guess the images don't mean anything to you."

"Nothing," she says with a dismissive laugh. "Nothing at all."

"OK, Francesca . . . you've had enough of me for one day. I'll get out of your hair. I really do appreciate your time. Can you do me a favor?"

"What?"

"Two actually. One, please don't leave the valley without letting me know where you're headed. And, two, please call me if you think of anything else that might be helpful."

She nods. "You'll understand if I don't walk you to the door."

"Of course."

From the door leading him out of Francesca Norwood's bungalow, down the pathway, across the parking lot, he can think of only one thing. In reverse, in drive, on the road, on the ramp, he can think of only one thing. On the highway, the desert blowing by him, the browns and reds striping the walls of the valley, he is as single-minded, as laser focused as he's ever been. There's a thumb drive in his desk. Within the binary code, as daunting and impenetrable as any religion, lies more truth. He'll unearth it from the digital realm. He will scour that thing until his fingers bleed. Because somewhere in the valley, there's a construction worker who might hold the only key that matters.

He's in this zone of anticipation when his phone rings. "Hey, babe," he chirps to his wife.

"Hey."

It's not her usual "Hey," or "Hello," for that matter. One cold, gaunt syllable can change everything.

"What's wrong?"

"I just got off the phone with Dr. Chambers."

A flutter in his chest. "Which one is that?"

"The medical oncologist," she replies. "I need more surgery."

He hears her, but he says, "What?" It comes out like exasperation.

"I know. I was surprised too," she says. "But four of my lymph nodes came back positive for cancer."

He wants to smash the dashboard but he doesn't. He wants to scream at the fucking valley but he doesn't. He is going to hover the fuck all over her. He's going to stand guard. "So they have to get rid of those lymph nodes."

"Exactly. But it'll mean chemo in addition to the radiation."

"Chemo . . ." He repeats. No. Not in his house. Not in their house. This is a drive-by shooting. "Aw, shit, Kelly. Aw shit."

"I'm going to get pretty sick," she tells him. "Not from the cancer. From the chemo. And I'm going to lose my hair."

"Why don't you sound more upset?"

"You mean, why am I not hysterical?"

"Yeah, that . . ."

"'Cause we can't control this, babe. And the doctor says after the surgery and the treatments, I should be cancer free."

He almost runs off the road, overcorrects, and nearly careens into a truck. The truck makes a hostile honk and Kelly says, "What's that? You're driving?"

"Yes."

"I'm sorry. If I had known . . ."

"Never mind," he says. "We're going to fight this? Right? We're going to fucking fight."

"Right, Alex," she says. "The surgery is Friday."

"What? This Friday?"

"Yeah."

"It's that urgent?"

"No," she replies. "It's not that urgent. The doctor made that clear. It can wait a few weeks, but it's a scheduling thing. If I don't go in Friday, I'll have to wait five weeks."

"You're not a wait-five-weeks kinda gal, are you?"

She laughs. "You know me."

"I take it there was no verdict today."

"Correct," she says. "And I'm hoping we get one before Friday."

"And if you don't?"

"We don't."

"I'm proud of you," he says, as he swerves to avoid another vehicle. The other driver gives him a pumping middle finger, a truly aggressive, road-ragey gesture, and a protracted honk.

"You need to get off the phone, Alex, before you kill yourself," his wife tells him.

She's right. He tells her he loves her, that he'll see her at home.

34

Gus's client arrives at 7:30. The man has the fierce baby face of The
Incredible Hulk and boasts a similar physique as well, though
not green. He's a new client and his name is Diego Gladstone. Gus
leads him into the office, asks him to sit on the futon. Gus notices that
the fabric covering the mattress is wearing thin; it will only be a matter of time before it rips. He supposes he should grow up and buy a
sofa for the office, but that would be like getting rid of his surfboard.
Which still hangs in his garage. In the middle of the desert. "So, Diego, it's nice to meet you. Relax and let me know when you'd like to
get started."

"I don't know how this works."

The man has bright blue eyes and the kind of unshaven shadow
you see on a young movie star who's between projects. Unlike the
messy, harried growth on Gus's face, this guy's shadow is a style. "It's
actually a fairly loose process," Gus tells him. "Let me ask, how old are
you?"

"Twenty-seven."

Diego Gladstone is wearing gray shorts that stop just below the
knee, a bright green polo shirt, and sandals that Gus admires. "What
can I help you with?"

"I found you through that lady Beatrice," Diego says. "I went to
one of her classes. You know, a workshop she did at a bookstore, and
she was amazing, and she helped out this guy because he was scared
and having a hard time being who he was. And I wanted to talk to her
afterward, and she was great but she didn't have a lot of time. Which is
why she referred me to you . . ."

"I see. So, you are, maybe, having a hard time being who you are," Gus says. "You identified with that other man. Right?"

"Right."

"This isn't psychic of me. That was easy to infer from what you described," Gus tells him. "I sense that the guy at the bookstore had some issues with his sexuality, and I sense the same for you."

Diego nods. "I overdo it at the gym to compensate. Is it obvious?"

"That's not the first assumption I'd make. In fact, I don't do assumptions. I do vibes and hunches and visions."

"That's so cool," the man whispers in a manner that's cool itself.

"Again, not psychic, but I'm guessing you're gay. And I'm also guessing this isn't news to you."

Diego laughs. "No. It's not. I came out a few years ago to my friends. They're OK with it. But my family doesn't know. They suspect, I think. But I haven't told them because I don't know how they'll react, and I don't want anyone to get upset."

Gus leans forward. "None of us wants to get anyone upset, Diego. But that's not how life works."

"I was told to go see a shrink about this," he says, "but then I heard Beatrice Vossenheimer speak that night, and I got really excited about talking to someone like her."

"Am I correct to assume that one part of your family is Latino? I'm guessing because 'Gladstone' sounds Anglo, 'Diego' sounds Spanish . . ."

"Correct."

"You're worried most about your Latino side."

"I don't know. I really don't," he says. "But I really don't want to be, you know, thrown out of the family."

"Would they do that?"

He shrugs, leans back, and sinks into the mattress. "Not the family I know, but they've never had to deal with something like this before."

Gus sits up straight again. He opens his chest, shoulders, and he takes a magnificent yoga breath. He says, "OK, Diego. I'm going to sit here and look at you for a few moments. I'm going to stare right into you. If that makes you uncomfortable, feel free to close your eyes. That's perfectly fine. But I am going to read you as long as it takes me. I'm not sure I'd want someone staring at me for that long either."

The man nods. "I'll keep them open as long as I can," he says. "This is kind of amazing."

Gus studies his client's face, looks for the openings, the opportunities to go beneath the skin; he hopscotches from pore to pore. Then he observes the man's hands, the wide hands from which Gus infers a softness, an abiding need to touch with care—to a fault, perhaps. Back to the face, to the full lips that speak a message of kindness and love; Diego's face articulates the exquisite geometry of love, loss, and loneliness. Just like Billie's music. It's uncanny. It's almost as if Diego Gladstone could break out any minute in song.

"I'm going to close my eyes now," Gus tells Diego. "I'll be back with you shortly."

The darkness lasts only a minute.

And then a dove swoops into view. Against a placid, blue sky, the dove flies and loops. This is not the caricature of a dove with an olive branch. This is not a cartoon. This dove is real and she flutters like an angel, as if her movement inscribes a message in the sky, like billowy skywriting. Gus tries to read. At first he doesn't understand the language. It looks like an ancient text, like Hebrew or Aramaic, but as Gus follows the trail of the white bird, he sees her message morph into a language he understands.

"Do not be afraid. Do not fear."

"Are you talking to me?"

Gus hears a voice, then watches as the dove lands atop a soaring saguaro. "Do not be afraid."

"Mr. Parker?"

Gus opens his eyes. "Oh yes. That was for you. That was a message. I trust the angels. Do you?"

"Huh?"

Gus shakes his head vigorously. "I'm sorry. That was a very vivid vision. Very real. And it came to me as if it were coming from an angel. I don't know why. All I know is that your family loves you, adores you. Regardless of their strong Catholic convictions, they will embrace you, Diego. I know they have strong faith, but they will use that faith to accept you for who you are, not to fight you and try to change who you're meant to be."

"I never got around to discussing their religion with you . . ."

"You don't have to."

"It's fascinating."

"Are you asking me how to come out to them, or when to come out to them?"

Diego shakes his head. A huge smile emerges on his face. "Not really. But I welcome any psychic suggestion you have . . ."

Gus laughs. "You don't need a deadline, Diego. You do it when it feels right. Now that the angels have told you not to fear, you are free. I know this all sounds kind of ridiculous, I do, but trust me, I would rather say nothing than give you a load of bull. I really feel you have some lovely souls watching over you, taking you by the hand, walking you through this . . ."

A solitary tear spills from Diego's eye and slides down his cheek.

"It will all be fine," Gus tells him. "Have you thought about writing a book?"

Diego shudders, a quick spasm of his shoulders, and says, "I *am* writing a book."

"That was an instant vibe. It was like filling in a blank."

"I don't get it."

"Don't worry," Gus says. "I think it's great. I see you doing really well with the book. I mean, I see you writing for life."

"I don't know what that means."

Gus smiles. "You will."

"It's a coming out story," Diego tells him. "So much of it is still unwritten."

"Finish it," Gus says.

"Wow. Can I come back for more?"

Gus nods gently. "Of course. I can put you on the calendar," he replies. "But one more thing."

"Yeah?"

"I'm suddenly getting a vibe about something else."

"What?"

"Part of the reason you're here has to do with Billie Welch. Isn't that right?"

Diego Gladstone fidgets, smiles coyly. "I don't understand."

"You're a huge fan and you know I've been dating her. It's not exactly a secret these days."

Diego puts his head in his hands. "I'm so sorry. I'm not going to lie. It was a factor in coming. I was curious."

"You're hoping I'll introduce you to her, that you'll meet her through me."

Diego's bronze skin turns red. "I'm so embarrassed. But yeah, I'm a huge fan. I grew up with my parents listening to Billie Welch. She's, like, everything to me."

"I see," Gus says. "But it doesn't really work that way. My practice here doesn't really intersect with my private life. I hope you'll understand."

"What if I gave you something for her to autograph? Is that something you might do?"

Gus takes a deep breath, inhaling, in a way, Billie's stardom and the omnipotence of her music; it's all too much. Too much. In the exhale comes something cruel but true. He can't articulate it, but it comes out like sorrow and grief and sediment. "Yeah, sure. I can probably do that," Gus tells his client. "But we can talk about it next time."

Later that night, curled up on the couch with Ivy, he's watching the National Geographic Channel and sipping a glass of red wine. Rising ocean waters threaten the Maldives. Islands of plastic are floating across the seas. The earth is choking itself. But the next show features the Emperor Tamarin monkeys in the Peruvian Amazon, so that's uplifting. Except their habitat is disappearing due to development, so that's alarming. Still, these little creatures with their huge white mustaches and their humanlike faces are fetching Gus's affections, and he shoots a guilty look at Ivy, because it's clear by the look on Ivy's inquisitive, if not interrogating, face that she's jealous. "Come on, they're on TV, girl. It's not like I can bring one home."

The program cuts to commercial. Alex Trebek is selling some kind of insurance. Charmin is softer than ever. Hilton invites you to stay three nights for the price of two. Flights to Australia and New Zealand on sale now! With Transcontinental Airlines!

The name hits him in the chest with a singular drumbeat.

It rocks him like an earthquake, like a sudden tremor, and he feels something else coming on. Like a wave of affirmation, or in the case of this sudden seismic event, a tsunami.

He puts the wine glass down on the coffee table and sits back, closes his eyes, and there it is—the same plane, the same livery, the same flight, flying high above the Pacific. The aircraft is deceptively steady in this inky sky, in these hours before disaster; the passengers lulled into their safe bubble at 32,000 feet. The only difference he sees from the other visions of this flight is two passengers seated in first class whom he had not seen before. They might have been there, but he's not sure; his auditing of the manifest had been fleeting. But they're here now: Viveca Canning and Francesca Norwood. They're sitting side by side, lounging under duvets, their lie-flat seats half-extended. Viveca grasps a magazine in one hand, a teacup in another. Francesca wraps her fingers around a svelte glass of champagne. Gus shakes his head. There's nothing more to see.

He gets it.

They've been on this flight all along. For the plane to go down, they will have to be on this flight together. And they won't be. They can't be. Viveca is already gone. Her death has already altered the fate of the flight and its passengers. The foiled premonition gives Gus a chill, then a cold sweat. Viveca Canning's death has completely changed a future reality. She, in the context of his vision, has been a salvation. Could it be that she really was an angel rising?

He bends to grab the glass of wine from the coffee table, but as he does he's propelled in another direction, crashing, it seems, through funhouse doors and down a long tunnel until the ride comes to a stop in front of an elegant dining room where two couples hold their goblets high and toast to something fortunate and celebrated. Gus can't hear their words. But they're living charmed lives, or the masquerade of charmed lives. One woman, in fact, hides behind the veil of a crepe hat, the kind you'd see on a 1930s starlet. She tips her neck back, but that's all you see, a long porcelain neck and ruby red lips. Down goes the wine, and they're all smiles and insouciance. Except for one of the men. He turns away from them and points a finger, his whole arm, actually, further into the funhouse tunnel. He wants the strangers to move on, to get away, to get out. He shakes his head. He mouths the words. Gus reads his lips.

Death has come and you must go.
Death has come and you must go.
You will survive the Madeira.

What the f—

Then Gus hears a phone ring. A funhouse of phones. The rest of it fades away, and Gus comes crashing back through those doors and lands on the couch, with just a little bit of whiplash and a little bit of nausea, the turbulence of his visions so severe. Ivy tilts her head and gives Gus a bewildered look, as if to say, "Will you answer the damn phone, you psychic freak?" He swears she's crossing her eyes at him.

It's Billie.

"Darling I do want you to come on the tour to Australia and New Zealand, but I know it's a lot to ask. I know . . . and I know why you can't come . . ."

"Uh-huh."

"Were you sleeping?"

He shakes his head just to check. "Uh, no. Just staggering out of a few visions."

"Oh. Cool."

Not necessarily cool. "What's up with you, Billie?"

"Nothing," she says, her voice sailing at him through the night.

"I know I've been so self-absorbed lately, but if you would consider coming with us as far as Tahiti, that would be great. We're doing the stopover on Miranda's insistence. We'll land in Tahiti and then charter a plane over to Bora Bora. We won't go 'til the end of September, but come. And we'll spend four days, maybe five there."

He tells her he'll think about it. He tells her he'd really like to go. "I'll see if I can get Beatrice to watch Ivy, if I can get off work, you know the drill . . ."

At the mention of her name, Ivy raises her head. Gus pets her, pulls her close.

"Of course," Billie says. "But it's paradise there. I promise you."

They chat for a few minutes. The words, his words, anyway, are a patchwork of uncertainties, and he can't seem to stitch the patches together. He ricochets off her and she him. He looks at the time on his phone. He tells her he needs to get to bed. She says, "I love you. I do. Sleep well, angel."

And he says something similar, but different.

Then he turns to Ivy, who takes his regard as an opportunity to have a wish granted, her eyes begging, hopeful. He tells her it's late. But she doesn't give a shit. She wants to go for another walk. That's the least he can do, she hints with a particularly sly look, for making her sit through another crazy night of visions and verbal contortions. *Fine*, he indicates to her with a nod of the head. *We'll go, girl.*

Mills had copied the files from Aaliyah's thumb drive onto his laptop before leaving work earlier in the day. Now, after a dinner for dinner's sake, he and Kelly are both sitting at the table, their laptops open, their eyes glued. She's doing some kind of research for another case. Mills worries that moving from one case to the next might create an undue burden for her as she faces another surgery and the treatment ahead;

he also worries that if she doesn't stay engaged in work, then all she'll think about is the cancer. He thinks the latter would have a more withering effect. So, he just keeps his mouth shut. He realizes, looking at the files on his screen, that his attempt to open and read each and every file is proving inefficient and, well, he'll admit it, stupid, so he'll try what he should have tried first. He'll run a search through the batch of files all at once.

C-o-n-t-r-a-c-t-o-r
No results found.
B-u-i-l-d-e-r
No results found.
C-o-n-s-t-r-u-c-t-i-o-n
Three hits:
Church of Angels Rising
Constructionworker(s).docx
ConstructionUnderground.docx

He clicks on the last item and finds a file of notes similar to the ones he had exhumed earlier from Aaliyah's thumb drive:

Unconfirmed reports of underground construction
See architectural plans/zoning/permits >> phx planning & development
Project completed: 11 Feb 2003
Mulroney Construction Company: 602-555-2221 >> out of business/ closed >> sec of state
Sec of State: MCC dissolved 2018

LinkedIn profiles (3)
1)Salvador Reyes
Sun Valley Construction (current) Mulroney Construction (prior)
2)Helen Destille

Royce Engineering (current) Mulroney (prior)
3)David Patrick
Patrick Construction & Design (current) Mulroney (prior)

Reyes: ~~left message at Sun Valley 2/24, 3/2, Reyes calls back 3/3,~~ will not comment
Destille: Will not comment 2/28
Patrick: ~~left message at Patrick Construction 2/24, 2/28, 3/4,~~ Meet on 3/11

Mills opens the second file that came up in the search, constructionworker(s).docx, and finds the digital equivalent of scrap paper.

David Patrick
480-555-1818
Owner, Patrick Construction and Design. Previously worked for Mulroney Construction contracted to build C-ARC.
3/11 Meeting at station. DP says he worked the entire C-ARC project in various roles, says I'd have to get architectural plans/blueprints from city or the county. Confirms underground construction. Not unusual for a facility that large. Figures it's used for storage. Unfinished walls, doors, floors, just basic drywall, beams, etc. Large area. Half a football field. DP left Mulroney in 2012, started own company. Never saw anything unusual at C-ARC through construction process. "It's all just a building to me. Just floors and doors and hallways. And a ton of windows!"
Update 5/1: DP says he'll meet with VC

Mills has what he needs for now. He closes out of the thumb drive and dials David Patrick. The phone rings and rings before the automated message finally kicks in. It's the universal message that just won't quit. "Please leave your message after the tone. When you are finished you may hang up or dial 1 for more options. To send a fax, press 7." Like, who the fuck needs instructions on how to leave a voice mail these days? He puts the phone down without following instructions, without leaving a message. This is classic Mills, he knows, getting impatient with what he calls the "mediocre condition."

And who the fuck sends a fax?

"What's wrong, babe?" his wife asks.

"Nothing," he says, clenching.

She looks at him, nodding slyly, as if to say "yeah, right."

"I'm just stressed, that's all," he says.

"That's enough," she says. "How about a nice hot shower?"

"With you?"

"No, with Mary Finkelstein, head of paralegals at the firm . . ."

"Oh, I'm so glad you're being funny again. And sexy."

"I was always sexy," she reminds him.

He can't believe she's in the mood. "I'll go run the water. Meet me in there."

The hot shower, as a setting, is not what it's cracked up to be. At least not for Mills. There are only so many positions to assume without falling over or getting a nozzle up your ass. And while that might feel pleasurable to some, it does not to him. Nor does bracing his ass against the cold tile. And then there's all that steam. They laugh because this used to be romantic when they were a lot younger. But now they're older and it's not as romantic or sexy or even steamy, despite the steam. It's satisfying, yes, but a lot of work and a lot of mechanics.

He dries off, puts on his drawstrings, and returns to the dining table, where he puts another call into David Patrick. The man answers on the second ring. He's tentative, at first, can't understand why a detective would be calling him. Mills tries to explain, but David Patrick gets defensive, says he spoke to Aaliyah Jones on the condition of anonymity, that his name, as a source, would not be revealed.

Mills needs something from this guy. And he needs it badly. So he's congenial and understanding, apologetic even. "Under the circumstances, I was hoping you'd help us out, sir."

"What circumstances?"

"Uh, Ms. Jones, you know, has gone missing . . ."

"What?"

"She's been missing for about a week," Mills tells him. "We have a Missing Persons Detail on her, but so far nothing."

"Jesus," he whispers. "I don't watch the news. I had no idea."

"That's OK," Mills assures him. "But she didn't betray your confidence or reveal your name to us. We found your name when we were reviewing her work files. You know, we were hoping someone or something would lead us to her."

"Well, I don't know nothing 'bout that," he insists. "I wouldn't have a clue where she is."

"Right. But I'm calling you about your conversations with Aaliyah Jones and Viveca Canning about the C-ARC," Mills explains. "I know this is all confusing to you, but I'd like to know more about those conversations and about your work at the cathedral. Would you be willing?"

The man scoffs. "Do I have a choice?"

"At the moment you do," Mills replies. "But if we gather information that indicates your cooperation is critical, you might not really have an option. That's not a threat. That's just an explanation. I think we can have a very enlightening discussion, you and I."

He hears hesitation on the other end of the line, a kid or kids in the background. But that's OK. Silence and consideration is OK. In the meantime, Mills sees a text come in. It's from Kelly. In the bedroom. **<Come to bed>** He laughs to himself, and then David Patrick says, "When would you want to meet with me?"

"At your earliest possible convenience."

"OK, well, then why don't you give me a call midmorning tomorrow, and I'll see what my afternoon looks like."

That's risky, not to confirm something. Too much latitude for the construction guy to change his mind or think of the perfect blow off. But, fuck it, it's better than nothing. "Sure. I'll call around ten," he tells him, then hangs up and joins Kelly in bed. They don't say a word.

A thin layer of moisture from the recent shower lingers. They lay close, absorbing it from each other's skin.

35

God, or whoever controls the weather, has blessed the valley with a milder morning. Ninety-seven degrees. Dry. Doable. Window down, even, if he wishes. He doesn't wish, but he appreciates the relief. Gus calls as Mills exits the Squaw Peak.

"Some mornings you just want to throw your arms around Mother Nature and give her a big, fat kiss," Gus tells him.

"Oh, so that's who controls the weather?"

"I think so, yes."

"Well, you better be sure it's okay with Mother Nature. Unwanted advances can backfire big time. Just ask Cosby."

"That's not funny, Alex."

Gus tells him about some strange vibes he's been getting again about those tunnels. Gus is insistent. He keeps repeating their names. Aaliyah. Viveca. And he jumps back, now, to the visit to Viveca's home in Copper Palace, when Mills let him stand in front of the blank wall where the Dali had hung. Gus says there's a message either in the wall or behind the painting itself. He's not sure. But he's sure there's a message, or a code, or something they're missing.

Mills smiles. It's a strange collective effort. A camaraderie he can't put a price on.

"I know this a little confusing," Gus says. "But that's what I get."

"That's fine," Mills tells him. "Your confusing vibes, mixed with a little old-fashioned police work, usually gets the job done."

"I don't know if that's a compliment."

"It's not an insult."

This red light is as stubborn as a toothache. He's going to be late, but fuck it. He rolls down the window and lets the fresh morning air circulate. It's a soothing kind of warm, and Mills is tempted to cut the A/C. But he doesn't. He lets the warm stir with the cool, and the capricious mix reminds him of those first few months dating Kelly. He was unsure, unsteady all of the time. He had never been so enchanted or so mowed down by desire for another. He confesses to Gus how scared he is for her, though he doesn't say scared.

"Of course you're freaking out," Gus says.

"I don't know how I'm going to make it through Friday."

"You will, dude. Anything I can do?"

"Nothing I can think of."

"I'm on standby."

"Good to know."

The light finally turns green. Mills takes this as a cue to let Gus go. Gus says, "It's another day for constructing theories, dude. Good luck."

Mills shakes his head with a smile. Constructing. Pure Gus.

Once he's off the phone he realizes how good it was to be on the phone, for distraction, if nothing else. Now, the rest of the way, he can't shake it. The image hovers, a dark, spidery mass of tissue and fibers on the horizon, like a web waiting to ensnare. And it does ensnare. He drives right toward it, right into it, to prove what? That he has no fear? He has fear. That he's not to be fucked with? It fucks with him. It settles on his shoulders. He carries it into headquarters, into the elevator, into his office, and then it lands on his desk and sits there like an ornament: his business cards, a paperweight, a framed picture of Trevor in his football gear, and Kelly's tumor. He takes a sip of coffee.

As planned, Mills calls David Patrick promptly at ten o'clock. Mills would not be surprised if the guy had decided not to answer his phone. Some people play like that. They won't cooperate but they don't have the balls to tell you they won't cooperate. They just go dark. Unfortunately for those uncooperative types, Alex Mills and the Phoenix Police Department have some very bright, insistent lights. Turns out he won't be needing the incandescent muscle quite yet. Patrick answers on the third ring.

"Mr. Patrick, it's Alex Mills from Phoenix PD."

"You can drop the formalities. My name's David. Call me David."

"So, David, you asked me to call this morning. Have you thought about meeting with me?"

The guy's outside. There's noise in the background, the maddening backup beeps of a truck, then a whistle, then a horn. "I've been too busy to really think about it, Detective," the man says. "But yeah, it's fine. You free around one, one-thirty?"

"I can be."

"I'm at a work site. I'll text you the address. You'll find me in the trailer. OK?"

"I might have a partner with me," Alex tells him. "See you then."

After the call, Mills wanders down to the Missing Persons folks. He briefs them on the contents of Aaliyah Jones's thumb drive.

"Thanks for sharing, Alex," one of them says. Mills can't discern whether there's sarcasm in the woman's inflection.

"It's in evidence," he tells them. "Sign it out if you want."

"Thanks," the woman says. He's never met her. Her desk is such a cluttered train wreck he can't even read her nameplate.

"We got the warrant for her phones," the other one says. Mills knows him, peripherally. Nate Sharpe.

"Oh?"

"Yeah. We're still going through them," Nate says. "That woman didn't destroy a voice mail."

"That's probably a good thing," Mills says.

"There's a bit of crossover," Nate adds. "Some of the same people calling her on both phones."

Mills shrugs. It's a classic detective shrug, an in-house shrug. "That doesn't necessarily surprise me," he tells them.

"Sources," Nate specifies. "Some of her sources were calling her on her personal phone as well as her work line."

Mills offers a more affable nod. "They trusted her. She trusted them."

"Viveca Canning was increasingly calling her on her personal phone, like she was avoiding Aaliyah's work phone on purpose."

"Scared of it being traced, maybe, or not entirely in Aaliyah's control. That's my guess," Mills tells them. "Do me a favor. Send me over whatever you log when you have a chance."

"Of course," the nameless woman says. "Give us another day or two."

Mills says that'll be fine and heads back to his office. He calls Kelly, gets her voice mail. There's another call he has to make, but he's been dreading making it. He reaches for the phone again, but the dread overcomes him. Not yet. He pictures his son, Trevor, equal parts jockish and studious, equal parts sensitive and brutish, a child of dichotomies, a twisted helix of Kelly and Alex and the remnants of ancestry. Trevor settled so well into college life it caught Mills by surprise. How had the kid taken the detachment so seamlessly? And why had he taken it so enthusiastically? They had been good parents. Trevor had had a good upbringing. There were bumps in the road, but the road is bumpy. All roads are bumpy. Children and parents alike make stupid choices. Trevor is only down the road at U of A, and he comes home to visit every other month or so, for birthdays and holidays, but the kid decided to stay in Tucson for the summer and work at a local bookstore. At least he'll be around books. Maybe some part of Alex rubbed off on his son. He needs to tell Trevor about his mother's illness. No one prepares you to make this kind of call.

So he doesn't make it. He'll do it later. He'll meet with the squad instead. Get some updates. Then he'll grab Preston and go meet with David Patrick.

Don't get him started on development in Phoenix. It's out of control. The growth. The sprawl. Today's valley is not the valley of Mills's youth. And while he doesn't begrudge the modernization of the skyline and the infrastructure, and while he does, in fact, enjoy living in a more cosmopolitan city, he thinks the growth is unsustainable. If there is an inch of land, there's a developer waiting to build. It will be a "mixed-use" project. Which means whatever they can shove in there to make the most profit. Every inch of available land. Politicians turn a blind eye as the desert disappears, and it's easy for them to do that as the developers line their pockets. Mills gets mad about this, because once you destroy the desert, you can't get it back. It's gone, along with the beauty of isolation. Soon there will be no place left to build but the medians of the highways, and Mills suspects that the vampires of the valley are already taking bids. He's trapped in this mental riff because, as it happens, he's approaching the work site of DP Construction. It's a small lot near the corner of East McDowell and 52nd, but there are backhoes and excavators and bulldozers. And it's too damn close to the neighboring buttes. He drives past a sign that says "Magic Creek Townhomes, Coming Soon!"

Preston is riding shotgun.

They park, approach the trailer, and Mills raps hard at the door.

"Hey there," comes a voice from behind them. "You Mills?"

"I am."

The man in the hardhat steps up to the trailer and offers a hand-shake to both of them. "David," he says. "Why don't we do this inside so you don't have to wear the hats?"

Inside, blueprints hang from the walls, as do other mechanical drawings and engineering renditions that Mills doesn't understand. The place is also strewn with OSHA posters warning of work site hazards. Otherwise, the trailer is neat for a temporary office, more upscale in décor than Mills would have imagined. David Patrick sits in a smart, black chair behind a glass and steel desk, while Mills and Preston sit opposite him in matching seats. The pendant lighting above is shaped like Saturn, and Mills is taking mental notes for some home renovation projects of his own that might never happen. Odds are fifty-fifty. "Thanks for meeting with us," he tells David.

"Like I said, I have no clue what happened to Aaliyah Jones, but I can tell you about my work at the cathedral. Just don't use my name. I don't want, you know, bad publicity."

"Right now, we'll keep it off the record," Mills assures him. "But you should know that if you provide information the county deems material, you might end up as part of the official proceeding."

"Shit," the man says.

"Why don't we cross that bridge when we get there?" Mills says.

Then Preston leans forward and says, "So, what are you building here? Townhomes, is that right?"

Uncle Ken to the rescue. Just the perfect pitch to put the man at ease.

"Yeah," David replies. "It's a small project. Only twenty-two units. The lot is only zoned for eighteen, but the developer got a variance for an extra four. It'll be a tight squeeze."

"But ain't that the story of the valley," Preston says.

"Guess so."

Okay, enough warm, fuzzy, avuncular lubrication. "While we understand you don't know anything about the missing reporter," Mills intervenes, "we do want to know why she was asking you about construction of the C-ARC in the first place. Can you help us understand that?"

The man tosses his head back and forth and says, "I suppose. She said she found me through LinkedIn because she searched Mulroney Construction, the company I used to work for."

"Yes, we know that," Mills tells him. "But why? Why was she looking for construction workers or contractors?"

"Oh. Okay, I understand," David says. "She told me she was looking for people who had built the cathedral, because some of her sources told her about hidden rooms and vaults and, like, stairways to nowhere. That sort of thing. It sounded like fantasy to her. And she wanted to confirm. She said her sources, some ex church members, were telling her about rumors of a secret underground."

"Were you able to confirm any of this for her?" Mills asks.

"I was."

That familiar wave of affirmation rises in Mills's chest. It floods him with anticipation. "How much of the building did you work on?"

"I did framing mostly. But there were dozens of us. The place is huge, you know."

"We know," Preston says. "But did you get a good sense of the whole project?"

"Of course," David replies. "There were zones, and different workers were assigned different zones, but we were free to be wherever we wanted to be. Though, I will say, that preacher guy and his wife liked to stop by and watch us like hawks."

The guy laughs, then shrugs.

"And what were you able to confirm to Aaliyah about those rumors?" Mills asks. "Do you have firsthand knowledge of any unusual deviations from normal construction and why that would have alarmed anyone?"

Another shrug from David Patrick. "All I can tell you is that there is an underground beneath the cathedral. It doesn't fill the entire acreage of the structure above it, but it's a large underground area. Kind of like a crawl space, but you mostly don't have to crawl."

"Did you work on it?" Preston asks.

"Yes. Mostly."

"Did you see it finished?" Mills asks.

"Not exactly."

"What does that mean?" Mills persists.

"Well, we did some of the finishing, but then we were told that church members would come in and do most of the painting and flooring themselves . . ."

"An underground in Phoenix sounds like a big effort," Mills observes. "I mean, with the rocky soil, mostly rock, you know. Most people don't have basements for that reason."

The guy leans back in his chair, suddenly relaxed, self-assured, in control. "Well, Detectives, this is the same desert where Mexican traffickers dig tunnels to move their drugs. They build complete underground operations. This can't be news to you."

Suddenly, Gus's vision resonates. "So you built tunnels?" Mills asks.

"It seemed that way. They were really just hallways with low ceilings. But you know, when you excavate, it does sort of look like a drug trafficking operation."

Preston says, "It seems kind of sinister when you put it that way, but did you actually have any idea what you were building?"

David sits there blinking, his mouth closed. He tilts his head the way people often do when they're perplexed. "I'm not sure I understand the question."

"Based on the design of the space, based on the plans you were following, did you have a sense of what the space would be used for?"

Lightbulb. It's all over the contractor's face. "Oh! I see! Right, well, I don't really know for sure. But it seemed to me like underground storage space. For supplies, maybe. Or tables and chairs for big functions. I mean, most churches have to put that stuff somewhere."

"Can you remember how the rooms were divided?" Mills asks him. "How many rooms? How they varied in size?"

David rubs his chin, shakes his head slowly, thoughtfully, "Oh, God. This goes back a while. I can't be sure. I never really gave it much thought until the reporter called me out of the blue. But, let's say, maybe six to ten rooms. One really big room with several smaller ones surrounding it. Like maybe an office plan. With workers in the middle and managers in private rooms all around them. Something like that."

"I can't think of many offices that are completely underground," Preston says.

David leans forward, now, rests his arms at the edge of his desk. "I realize that, Detective, but I was just trying to describe the space, which is what you asked me to do . . ."

"I'm sorry," Preston says. "You're right. We know it probably wasn't used as an office. But do you have any idea of its intended use? Did you ever ask? Did anyone ever mention during the course of construction what the use might be? Either the contractors or the church people?"

"I can't really remember. Except storage. I don't think I reached that conclusion on my own. Someone must have said something about storage." The guy takes a deep breath.

"We're exhausting you," Mills says. "We're sorry. Our work is exhaustive."

David shakes his head. "No. No, it's fine. I'm just not sure what the construction, itself, has to do with anything."

"Ah," Mills says. "I get it. This all seems very broad to you. Indulge us. The construction is important, because if we have to, let's say, search the place, it helps to have an insider who can help us understand all the nooks and crannies, if I may borrow a stupid phrase from an English muffin."

David laughs. "Oh, right. A search. Of course. Maybe you should give me a little more time to really focus on my memories. I might be able to remember more details of the floor plan if you give me a few days to think about it."

"We're not saying a search is imminent, and you must not even discuss that possibility outside of this trailer," Preston cautions him. "But yes, focus. See what you can remember. If and when we need your assistance, we'll let you know."

"In the meantime," Mills begins, "it's time to talk more specifically about Aaliyah Jones and Viveca Canning."

The guy looks at his watch. Mills realizes David Patrick has a building to build, twenty-two tightly squeezed units. But Mills's clock is ticking too. Instead of Mickey Mouse on the face of his watch, it's a scowling Jake Woods.

"Do you have a few more minutes?" Mills asks him.

"I think so."

"Just tell me if Aaliyah Jones ever saw the so-called underground of the church," Mills says.

David's shoulders pop up. "I doubt it. But I can't say for sure. Not to my knowledge."

"Viveca Canning?" Preston asks.

"Yep."

"Yep, what?" Mills asks him.

"Yeah. She saw the underground space," David replies. "Aaliyah introduced us. Viveca paid me to show her what was down there."

"How much?" Preston asks.

"Is that really relevant?" the guy asks back.

"We can decide that once we have all the facts, David," Mills answers.

"Fifteen hundred dollars. I felt really weird taking the money, but she insisted."

A plane whizzes overhead into Sky Harbor.

"If you showed her the underground, why are you so sketchy about the details?" Mills asks him.

"I don't understand."

"When did this meeting with Viveca take place, David?" Mills asks.

"About a month ago, maybe a month and a half."

"Since you showed her the underground fairly recently, why are you still relying on your memories from the construction phase?"

David waves his hands in the air. "No, no. I'm sorry. I didn't physically show it to her. I couldn't go in the cathedral with her," he explains. "She said they wouldn't let nonmembers in beyond a certain point. So I waited outside. But I told her how to get there."

"How do you get there?" Preston asks.

"It's weird," he says. "You get there from, like, this elevator thing in the stadium. It's in the middle of the stage, and it goes down two floors. First, to the main floor, and then to the underground."

"From the stage?" Mills asks.

"Yep."

It's the hydraulic lift that elevates Gleason Norwood to stage level. Mills is sure of it.

"Was she carrying a key?" Mills asks.

"I'm not sure. She had a big pocketbook."

Mills's phone buzzes. It's a text message from Lt. Chang in Scottsdale. <call me>

"Do you need a key to access the underground area after you get off the elevator?" Preston asks.

"I think so," David says. "We installed doors. I imagine they had locks, but I don't remember."

"What happens when you get off the elevator?" Mills asks.

"You just end up in a long hallway with a low ceiling," he says. "And, yes, I think it leads to a door. But it's a while before you hit the door, 'cause it's a really long hallway."

"How long was Viveca in there?" Mills asks him.

"Twenty or twenty-five minutes, I guess," he replies. "But I was just waiting in the parking lot. I didn't time her, you know . . ."

Preston shifts in his chair, goes avuncular again, this time all posture; he folds an arm across his stomach, bends the other so his chin can rest inside his hand. And nods. So Uncle Ken. "We know you didn't time her, David. That wouldn't be our expectation. But what did she tell you when she came out? We'd expect you to remember that."

"Right," he says. "I do. She was totally freaked out. She came out shaking."

Mills sits up. "What did she say?"

"That's the thing—she didn't say much."

"Aw, come on, man, she had to have said something," Mills insists.

"I know. I know. But this was very recent. So I remember it exactly how I'm telling you. She came out of that place like she had seen a ghost or something. I thought she was going to have a heart attack."

"And that was it? Did she drive off and never see you again?" Preston asks.

The guy nods. "Yeah. She paid me," he says. "And then she walked over to her car. I got out and followed her and asked her if she was okay to drive, 'cause, you know, she didn't look okay. I even asked what happened in there, and she just kept shaking her head and saying she couldn't talk about it, and I was getting freaked out just because she was freaked out. She said someday Aaliyah Jones would expose the whole truth. And that was it. She got in her car and drove away. There was not a whole lot more I could do after that."

Mills rises from the chair. Preston follows. "Thank you, David," Mills says. "You've been a tremendous help. It might not feel that way, but you have." He hands the contractor his card. "Call me if you think of anything else."

David Patrick walks the detectives back to their car. The outside greets them with a glaring sun. Handshakes all around. "Good luck with Magic Creek," Mills tells the man.

"Oh, that's just some stupid name the developer came up with."

Mills laughs. He figured as much.

They're only in the car for about thirty seconds when Preston says, "We have to get into that basement."

Mills nods, but doesn't reward Uncle Obvious with an obvious affirmation.

With a ball of lead in his stomach and butterflies in his chest, displaced from his stomach by the lead, Mills dials his son. And immediately understands his fret as pointless. You can fret, fret, fret, and fret, and then get voice mail. He gets voice mail. Doesn't leave a message. He can't qualify the anticlimactic sensation; it's just there, relief and protracted dread. He tosses his phone on his desk and that seems to be the cue for his landline to ring.

"Mills."

"Hey, Alex? It's Liv Chang. From Scottsdale PD."

"Oh, right. Sorry. I got your text . . ."

"No prob. Got a sec?"

"Or more . . ."

"We have an ID on that license plate from the Carmichael and Finn break-in," she says. "Not an easy task. We had to do enhancements of the enhancements to read the tag and get the right make and model. Sorry it took so long."

"I've been there, done that many times. No problem. Who's your driver?"

"The owner of the vehicle is a Ralph Waters, thirty-two, lives in South Scottsdale."

"You find any connection between Mr. Waters and the Cannings?"

"Only that he wanted to break into their vault," she says. "Other than that, no. We're headed over now to execute a search warrant, probably to make an arrest. Meet us there, if you'd like."

Mills looks at his watch. 2:41. He tells the detective he can be there shortly after three.

"No rush," she tells him. "I think we'll be there a while."

She gives him the address.

He sends Powell a text <busy?>

Powell replies <Yes/No. What's up>

<Arrest Carmichael Finn breakin>

<Not 2 busy for that>

<Not us, Scottsdale. But let's go talk to perp>

<k>

He hates "k." <Meet in 5 in lot>

After a quick but powerful whizz, Mills is in the driver's seat, Powell shotgun. The house in South Scottsdale is one of those rectangles on a slab, a 60s-style ranch with zero curb appeal and a driveway laden with so many cracks it looks like a concrete jigsaw puzzle. They meander an obstacle course of Scottsdale cruisers and enter the home. It's a clusterfuck of cops. They find Lt. Liv Chang questioning her suspect at a kitchen table that, for reasons unknown to Mills, is sitting toward the back of the house in the formal living room. Kind of deformalizes the room.

"So, how is it that you have no connection to Mrs. Canning but you happened to know where she stores her art?" Chang is asking the suspect.

Ralph Waters is wearing a white t-shirt and, from what Mills can see under the table, grey cargo shorts. Ralph Waters must like to gamble. Poker or blackjack, Mills assumes. That would explain the heart, the spade, the club, and the diamond tattooed up his forearm.

He placed a bad bet on the Carmichael and Finn Gallery, to be sure. "I told you I was just helping out a friend."

"But so far your friend doesn't seem to have a name," Chang says. Then, noticing Mills and Powell, she makes the introductions. "Detective Mills and Detective Powell are investigating the murder of Viveca Canning."

Waters stiffens. He sits up from his languid position, eyes Mills and Powell nervously, as if the two have already framed him for the crime. "I certainly had nothing to do with that," he says, the emphasis on "I," which Mills knows is highly significant.

"I was just about to have him taken in for more questioning," Chang says to Mills. "Glad you could swing by. He's been Mirandized."

Mills looks at Ralph Waters and says, "Since you're suspected of trying to break into her vault, you're a person of interest to us."

"Great," the guy says. He sounds yawny, as if he'd been woken from his three o'clock nap.

"You're facing some serious charges, you realize," Chang says. "I'm thinking you'll do better with the county attorney if you cooperate. But that's up to you . . ."

"Don't I get my own lawyer?" Waters grumbles.

"That's up to you too," Chang replies. "But we asked you if you wanted a lawyer present a few minutes ago, and I think your exact words were, 'I got nothing to hide.' You're free to change your mind."

The guy pushes at the chair and slides it away from the table. The chair scrapes the tile floor and makes a screeching sound that could pierce an eardrum or curdle blood. Mills can now see Waters's handcuffed wrists resting in his lap. "Going somewhere?" Mills asks him.

The guy makes a spitting sound. "I just need more space," he says.

"If you're a guy who needs more space," Chang says, "you won't be all that comfortable in the county jail. You have a lawyer?"

Waters shakes his head. "No."

"I'm going to ask you one more time. Want us to get you one?"

Waters shrugs.

"That's not an answer," Chang says. "And you're trying my patience."

Waters studies the floor, and Chang yields to the introspection in much the way Mills would; pieces of the truth often emerge during these interludes, usually starters like, "I can tell you this," or "You should be talking to . . ."

The noise of the search warrant, meanwhile, fills the house: the opening and closing of doors, cabinets, and drawers, a swarm of footsteps, the snap of rubber gloves. Uniforms everywhere. Serious voices. *It would intimidate the fuck out of me,* Mills thinks. For him, it's always about empathy, at least to the extent of knowing where the suspect's head is at. He knows so many hardened, crusty cops who bristle at the idea of empathy, who equate it with sympathy, and that's why few of them can make it as detectives. He likes the way Chang works too. He sees something in her, a steely intelligence that transcends her job; he guesses she's smart about the whole world.

"All I'm gonna say is this," Waters begins. "I don't know Mrs. Canning. I never knew Mrs. Canning. I don't know nothing about her art. Except I know she's really rich. I'm not going to answer any questions about her murder. But I'll tell you what I did that night at the gallery."

Chang checks that her recorder is still rolling.

A cop ducks his head in. "We've got drugs," he says.

"Aw, shit," cries Ralph Waters. "Really?"

The cop nods. Chang closes her eyes for a second and shakes her head. Everyone sort of defers to her frustration. "OK. One thing at a time. If there are additional charges, we'll deal with those later," she says. "What kind of drugs?"

"So far pot and some pills," the cop says.

"How much pot?" Chang asks.

"I don't know," the cop groans. "It's a lot, but it's not like I've weighed it, Lieutenant."

"Keep me posted," she says, as a means to dismiss her colleague. She turns back to Waters who sits there pouting, an aging slacker in a shitload of trouble. "You were saying, Ralph?"

He pushes his screeching chair back to the table so he can rest his elbows there and cradle his stubbly chin in his hands. "I was saying that we used my car. You obviously know that. And that we were supposed to blow open a vault in the gallery. With very *low grade explosives*."

The emphasis on "low grade" nearly prompts a burst of laughter from Mills, as if somehow the weakness of the explosives minimizes the crime. Powell snorts aloud and Mills nudges her.

"But there was a guard on duty and he clearly saw my face," Waters continues. "So there's no denying that, right? But then we heard all the sirens and we fucking hightailed it . . ."

"What was in the vault?" Chang asks.

"I don't know," the guy says. "We never got in."

"What was supposed to be in the vault?" Chang repeats.

"I just told you, I don't know. My friend wanted to get something out of there. He said it was important."

"But he didn't tell you what it was?" Again, Chang.

"No."

"You guys took off in your car. Then where did you go?" Mills asks.

"I dropped him off at the AJ's near Thompson Peak. In the parking lot."

"And what? He walked home?" Chang asks.

"No. He got in his car and drove off. I don't know where he went."

Mills looks at Chang, tries to transmit a kind of holding pattern in his eyes, just enough of a moment to make the suspect squirm. It seems to work, the silence. The eyeballing. The way Mills makes a *tsking* sound with his tongue until it almost becomes a song.

And then, "What was in it for you?" Mills asks. "Why do something so colossally stupid and dangerous for a friend?"

The guy doesn't say a word.

"Huh?" Mills persists.

"Do I have to answer him?" Waters asks Chang.

Chang leans in. "He's investigating the murder of Viveca Canning, as I've already made clear. You tried to break into her gallery vault. So, he has interest in the case, and yes, he has a right to question you . . ."

"And, yes," Mills interjects, "you have the right to have an attorney present. We can re-Mirandize you if you'd like."

Waters looks at Mills, then at Chang, then back to Mills, as if the two detectives are playing at Wimbledon. "I owed my friend money . . ."

"For?" Chang asks.

"What do you think?" he says. "Drugs."

"Nice," Powell whispers. But everybody hears her.

"So, you owed this guy money for drugs and, what, he was going to forgive you the debt if you helped him break into a vault?" Mills asks.

Waters looks down, probes the floor again, shakes his head at his own stupidity and says, "Yeah."

Chang leans in again. "Look, I can't make any promises, Ralph, but I'm thinking the county attorney might consider dropping or reducing the drug charges if you cooperate. Assuming we find enough drugs today to charge you . . ."

Waters shrugs. "Whatever. But I need protection."

"Protection?" Mills asks.

"Yeah," the guy says without making eye contact.

"Can you elaborate?" Chang prods him.

"I said I need protection because this guy is dangerous, OK? I mean, he's a dealer. He supports himself by selling drugs. He associates with bad people. And he threatened me . . ."

Mills takes a seat at the table. Powell leans against a wall.

"With?" Mills asks. "What did he threaten you with?"

The guy turns his palms upward with another shrug. "I think he said, 'I'll fucking kill you if you ever say a word.'"

"People say things," Powell chimes in.

The guy sneers at her. "He was serious," he says matter-of-factly. "I know he's done some other damage in the valley, so I don't doubt him. Can I have protection?"

Chang interjects and says, "Obviously, we'll consider that, depending on what you tell us. But it's more complicated than just getting you a 24-hour babysitter with a badge."

"What do you do for work?" Mills asks him.

"I'm a waiter."

"You share this house with anyone?"

"Another waiter and bartender where I work," he says.

"He works at The ScottsView," Chang says.

The ScottsView is an aging golf and tennis resort that has seen better times and bigger crowds. Its elegance has faded along with the paint and the carpets. It's still popular with tourists, but not the upscale type. Ralph Waters at The ScottsView is typecasting.

"So, you owe this secret friend money for drugs. The money's forgiven if you help on this art gallery caper," Chang says. "Have you ever worked with explosives before?"

Waters nods. "I've built fireworks. Legal ones. I've built some for him."

That's bullshit, Mills observes. Homemade fireworks are not legal.

"Are you by any chance a member of the Church of Angels Rising?" Mills asks.

"What? No. What does that have to do with anything?"

"Viveca Canning was on the church's board of directors," Mills tells him. "You were breaking into her vault."

"Well, I know nothing about that," Waters insists. "This was just a favor, an arrangement, rather, between me and my dealer to settle up."

The guy fidgets, and then he starts bawling. The breakdown took longer than Mills had expected, but it's happening. A pure collapse. A cyclone of overwhelming fear and overwhelming dread makes landfall and the suspect loses his shit. Mills, weirdly, senses a cyclone of his own in his gut, and suspects it has something to do with Kelly, Trevor, and the barometric pressure of disease.

"Can I make a deal?" the suspect says between sobs.

"Not with us," Chang says. "With the county attorney. But we can get that ball rolling, if you want . . ."

"Would I get off?"

"Doubt it," Chang replies. "You're facing some serious charges. But if you plead to lesser, I'm sure there'd be reduced sentencing . . ."

"The minute I end up in jail his thugs get to me," Ralph says, evidently an avid viewer of Netflix and HBO.

"Is this guy in a gang?" Chang asks.

"Nah," Waters says. "But he has a circle."

"I'm beginning to think you're full of shit," Mills says. "You'll pardon my language. But I just don't think you did this for a friend. I think you did this for you. I think you had something to do with Viveca's murder, and I think you're trying to distract us."

"Me too," Powell says with an oomph in her voice.

"And me too," from Chang as well.

The guy looks up and shakes his head vigorously, so much his cheeks look they're pulling Gs. His mouth, too, the way its stretches across his face like a fat elastic band. "What the fuck?" he cries. "I just told you everything. I told you I did it for a friend to pay back a drug debt. What else do you want?"

"We want his name," Mills says, pounding the table once for each word.

"Or we're back to square one, Ralph," Chang adds. "You said you had nothing to hide."

"Without his name, you're just a punk liar," Mills says.

"And not even a good one," Powell tells him.

"Without a name, you have no credibility," Mills persists. "Good luck with the county attorney. Good luck with the judge. Good luck with the jury. I see you like to gamble."

"Huh?"

"The tattoos."

"So what? The Indian Casinos. Poker. Blackjack. Whatever."

"Well, you're taking a big gamble with your life."

"You don't know nothing about me."

"I know a slacker like you isn't going to hold up in prison, buddy," Mills says. "You think your friend's thugs are dangerous? Wait 'til you meet your cellmates."

Ralph slams his head on the table and sobs again. Between the wretched tears, he coughs up a name. "Gabriel," he says. "I don't know his last name. But it's Gabriel."

Mills wants to shut his eyes and let that sink in. He wants to let the truth bubble in his veins until he gets high off the drip. But he doesn't. Instead, he sidles up to Ralph Waters and says, "You're lying. You know his last name. But that's OK. I know it too."

The man lifts his head from the table, his face a red, snotty mess. "What?" he snarls.

Mills sits there and nods, does nothing but nod. That's when Ralph Waters, still handcuffed, thinks it's his cue to leap from the chair and make a run for the sliding glass doors at the opposite end of the room. Mills is on him in seconds and tackles him to the floor. "I wouldn't try that again, idiot. You're handcuffed. Remember?"

Lt. Chang asks a colleague to sit with Waters while she confers with Mills and Powell in another room. They walk into a bedroom that smells of weed and probably hasn't seen sunlight or a vacuum since Christmas. "Who's our guy?" she asks Mills.

"Gabriel Norwood," Mills replies. "Son of Gleason Norwood. Church of Angels Rising."

Chang's eyes go wide and stay that way. "Seriously?"

"Yep. I'm not quite sure how or why he fits, but that's the only Gabriel who comes to mind," Mills says. "I think we need to get before a judge tonight. Tomorrow morning, latest. You've read this guy his rights, so everything he told us sticks and the judge needs to hear it. I want to search Gabriel's place ASAP. Can your squad handle the surveillance video from AJ's?"

Chang nods.

"We're never going to pull all this shit together tonight," Powell says. "I doubt we'll get our warrants before the morning."

"So be it," Mills says. "But the sooner the better."

"Between both our resources, we'll be fine," Chang says. "I can get one of my guys before a judge in the morning. Can you spare anyone?"

Before Mills can answer, Powell says, "Me. He can spare me."

"Perfect," Chang says. "In the meantime, we'll bring Waters in, get him processed. I'll have someone call over to AJ's."

Mills thanks her. "Great work," he says. "And great working *with* you."

"You think it's him?" the lieutenant asks. "You think that Gabriel kid is your perp?"

"I'm not a psychic," he says. "But I'm a damn good guesser. And if he didn't kill Viveca Canning, he knows who did."

On the way back to headquarters, Powell is fidgety and spastic, her nerves jangled. Mills says she should go home and drink a bottle of wine. She says she'd rather arrest Gabriel Norwood first. She's afraid he'll flee.

Mills shakes his head. "You're just being neurotic. He has no reason to flee. Ralph Waters's arrest isn't public record yet. Waters's one call from jail isn't going to be to Gabriel Norwood."

"But still . . ."

"But still nothing," Mills insists. "We can't go arrest him on the basis that Ralph Waters gave us a first name. But if the surveillance video shows Waters dropping Gabriel Norwood off at AJ's after the break-in, well then, bingo, we're in."

"And if it doesn't . . .?"

"You're worrying for the sake of worrying," he chides her. "If it doesn't, there are other ways to convince the judge. Plenty of dots we can connect between Gabriel and the Cannings . . ."

That seems to mollify her, and she's quiet the rest of the way back.

Mills needs the quiet. Back at headquarters, he grabs a few files from his desk and heads home in the muted dusk. Until now, it's been a noisy day. The city has barked and whined and rumbled, all of it baking like an urban casserole under the Phoenix sun. The construction site, as well, was a hot, heavy metal concert of excavation. Which reminds him about exhumation. And the body of Clark Canning. But this is supposed to be a quiet ride home.

And . . . shit. Just shit. It's 11:30 p.m., and Mills is chastising himself for forgetting the one thing he was supposed to remember. He needs to try Trevor again. All day he had put off making another call. He had found excuses and delays and distractions. He was not acting like a father. He was acting like a fucking chicken. He had come home, taken a nap, gotten up for dinner with Kelly. He had read a chapter of *Don Quixote*, and then he had taken a shower. Now he stares at himself in the bathroom mirror and says, "You, shit-for-brains."

He dries himself off, slips into a pair of sweats, and dials from the couch in the living room.

"Hi Dad," his kid says, like it's noon.

"You're up?"

"Just eating dinner," Trevor says.

"At 11:45?"

"I know what time it is."

Mills knows what age his son is. And Mills tries to imagine himself at nineteen. Reckless is all he can come up with.

"Look, Trev, I've been needing to talk to you about something serious. Is this a good time?"

"Good as ever. Should I be nervous?"

"That's the whole point of this phone call. You should not be nervous," Mills tells him. "Mom is sick. But we have everything under control. We felt we owed you a call before her surgery on Friday. We want to keep you in the loop."

Mills can hear the kid's television go mute. "Wait. What? Mom's sick? What do you mean?"

This is what it's like to go through these things.

This is what it's like when the abstract becomes concrete.

This is what it's like.

Here, telling his son, rolling out the details, part clinically, part parentally, this is what it's like when shit becomes real. He explains Kelly's diagnosis. He tries to stay as faithful to all the medical and scientific terminology, while also explaining and interpreting it for his son. He didn't expect this would bring as much pain as it's bringing to his chest. He didn't expect the stubborn lump in his throat.

Trevor is silent, interminably. Just muted, like the television. Mills hates this, having to imagine the shockwaves and how they rattle his only child. He listens to Trevor's unabashed silence and understands that his son can't think of what to say, or how to react, or what comes next. And Mills says, "Look, we think she'll be okay. She has these great doctors who are very optimistic. We just wanted you to know because we don't like secrets."

"But you kept a secret, Dad. You just told me she had surgery last week. Why was that a secret?"

"We didn't want you to worry."

"I'm worried."

"We didn't have enough to tell you," Mills says. "We had more questions than answers."

"Should I come home for *this* surgery?" Trevor asks. "It's not a problem getting off from work, you know."

"Honestly, kid, I don't think that's necessary. She'd love to have you there, but she's going to be in surgery and recovery all day. You'd only get to see her for a minute," Mills explains. "Maybe just head home for the weekend. Spend the weekend with her."

"I'll drive up Friday night," Trevor says. "Maybe I can at least be there to say goodnight after her surgery."

"That'll work," Mills tells his son. "You doing well? Still liking the job?"

Then the kid becomes a kid again. Mills can hear it in the shaky straining of Trevor's voice and the sniffle back of tears when his son says, "She's not going to die, right?"

"She's going to be fine, Trevor."

A sharp breath from Trevor. "OK. OK. I'll be home this weekend."

"Feel free to call her tomorrow. Wish her luck on the surgery," Mills suggests. "I'm sure she'd love to hear from you."

"Yeah. OK."

It's 12:21 when they hang up. Thursday morning.

Mills contemplates angels as he crawls into bed and curls up to his wife. She's one, for sure. But he's thinking more about the angels of faith and mythology. He's compelled to consider them because he wishes one to intervene and take the cancer away. He's compelled to reject them because the Church of Angels Rising has made a sham, a scam of the divine. He's rolling around the world, tossing and turning in bed, beckoning angels, battling angels, from one gallery to another. Today he'll meet an angel. If there's a God, he'll meet an angel and he'll arrest an angel. The angel, Gabriel Norwood.

All that has to happen is that everything has to fall into place and it has to happen like clockwork.

That's all. No wiggle room. No room for error.

He's running scenarios through his head, screening different versions of Gabriel's motive. None make sense. The film loops over and over again, and in each loop Gabriel bears a different face. He transforms. He morphs. And, here, in this cloud of exhaustion, Mills remembers that he's not met the son. So, these versions of him are shifting hybrids of Gleason and Francesca. Gabriel Norwood had been excommunicated from the church. Maybe Viveca had been the one to call for his ousting. Maybe it's revenge. Maybe this. Maybe that. He can't sleep.

36

That was easy. The sleep deprivation notwithstanding, the morning was judicial butter. Judge Marielle Santos-Schwartz granted warrants like she was handing out door prizes.

"I'd like you all to come with me," Mills tells the squad. "Gabriel is under surveillance. Scottsdale will call when they're ready. I think we all need to be at the scene. We can assist in the search, maybe observe Gabriel, maybe chat with him."

Faces around the room are nodding and eager. Mills recognizes the look; the rattle of adrenaline shines through their eyes. This is what a team looks like when it anticipates winning.

Judge Marielle Santos-Schwartz had attached one condition to the arrest warrant: the successful identification of Gabriel Norwood getting out of Ralph Waters's vehicle in the AJ's parking lot, as detected by the supermarket's surveillance cameras.

At twenty-two minutes past noon, Mills's team gets this confirmation from Liv Chang in Scottsdale:

Surveillance video provided by AJ's shows Ralph Waters's car pulling into the lot and idling five rows in. This coincides with precise travel time between the gallery and supermarket. The video catches a man emerging from Waters's car and walking a few paces before the lights of another vehicle indicate the man has unlocked it. The man, who can't be identified, then gets in the vehicle and backs out. But the tag of that car matches a registration coming back to Gabriel Norwood. The judge likes it. We like it. Give us another hour or so. I think we're close.

He reads the email aloud to the squad, and Powell rubs her hands together as if she's about to dig into a twelve-ounce porterhouse, cooked rare with extra blood on the side.

"It's going to be a long fucking hour," Preston says.

During that long fucking hour, Mills dials Jake Woods to bring him up to date and to discuss some cross-jurisdictional issues. Woods sounds both sufficiently relieved and magnanimous when he tells Mills he'll "take care of everything." During that long fucking hour, he also dials his wife to see if there's a verdict yet. There isn't. If her voice is any indication, her nerves are jangled. "I really expect one this afternoon. This isn't rocket science."

"Are you scared?"

"About the verdict? Are you serious?"

"About tomorrow."

"I don't want to talk about tomorrow until tomorrow."

"Good enough," he says. "But can I tell you I love you today?"

"You just did."

"And?"

She groans. "I love you today too. Bye, Alex."

Twice during that long fucking hour he almost dials Liv Chang to say: "Hey Liv I'm running out of people to call just to keep my mind off waiting for your call. Could you hurry the fuck up?" But he doesn't.

The long fucking hour turns into an hour and forty-five minutes. But who's counting? The squad had dispersed, and now, for the love of Christ, he finally gets a text from Chang.

<we're good to execute in 15 mins. He's been at the Desert Charm all morning. He's back at his house. 6779 East Pinnacle View Dr, come along when you can>

And then they're out the door, Preston riding with Powell, Myers with Mills.

The drive will take about thirty-five minutes. Even breaking the speed limit. The address is fairly far north in Scottsdale and out to the east.

When they get on scene, the idea is to blend in. Norwood only needs to know they're additional law enforcement. They're extra sets of eyes, more shuffling feet. He doesn't need to know anything else for now. Phoenix? Scottsdale? What's the difference? They blend in. While Preston and Powell assist tangentially with the search, Myers begins the task of taking notes. Mills wanders through the home, a McMansion with a stone front, dark hardwoods, leather and granite everywhere. Essentially, a clone of every other upper-middle-class home in this pretentious but not quite affluent neighborhood. He finds Chang and two officers in the family room toward the back of the house. There's a fireplace, more leather, and a view of the sparkling pool.

"I'm telling you I wasn't there that night," the suspect groans.

"We have surveillance video that suggests otherwise," Chang tells him. "How do you think we got our warrant?"

"Why would I want to break into her vault?" he asks. "I got enough money to buy art. I don't need to steal it."

Chang notices Mills leaning in the entranceway. "Gabriel Norwood, please meet Detective Alex Mills . . ."

Mills steps forward, extends a hand. The men shake. Mills assesses Gabriel Norwood, this son of religious quackery. He's not bad looking, but the dark circles and the bags drooping in sad half-moons from his eyes make him look like a much older person. Mills has seen these eyes before. These are the eyes of a drug dealer. Maybe a coke addict. The kid's hair is a golden tousle of curls. There's no hint of the Phoenix sun on his face, instead the kid's face bears a sallow complexion; Gabriel Norwood needs a good night's sleep. In this shape, he looks like neither of his parents, though his Colgate smile does suggest they all share the same dentist. The smile lasts about three seconds before Gabriel sinks back into the couch beside Chang and folds his arms across his chest. Mills sits opposite them.

"How many more detectives have to show up before I change my mind and call a lawyer?" Gabriel asks.

"Is that a rhetorical question?" Mills retorts.

"No."

"You're welcome to call a lawyer at any time," Chang tells him. "But we haven't arrested you. Yet . . ."

Norwood rolls his eyes. His insolence, Mills guesses, is genetic. He's wearing a crisp pair of linen trousers and a crisp V-neck t-shirt that fits him like the tightest hyperbole in the drawer. His shoulders, pecs, and biceps burst from the fabric. Mills is surprised by the man's physique given his obvious affection for drugs. Ah, yes, drugs . . . steroids are probably on the menu as well.

"He told us he was out of town on the night of the gallery break-in," Chang says. "Says he was with his mother in Switzerland. When we asked about his passport to prove his whereabouts, he told us he'd already returned it to his safe deposit box at the bank."

"Wow," Mills says. "What do we do with all these lies?"

Norwood scoffs. "If it weren't for your damned search warrant, I'd kick you out of my house this minute."

"I thought we'd wait for you, Detective Mills, to disprove his alibi. Since you might be the only one in the house right now who can," Chang says.

Mills begins with a bitter laugh. "I'm just wondering, Gabriel, when did you return from Switzerland?"

"Day before yesterday . . ."

"Did your mother come back with you, or is she still in Switzerland?"

"She's still there."

"She isn't."

The kid snorts and Mills wants to punch him in the face. He hasn't punched anyone in the face in a long, long time, and never a suspect, but he's tempted to make an exception for this little shit. "I would know where my mother is," Norwood says.

"I would know where she isn't," Mills counters. "Because she's at the Desert Charm, and she had been there a while before Viveca Canning's murder."

"That's bullshit."

"Surveillance spotted you at the hotel. And I've met with her there. Twice," Mills says. "Did she not tell you?"

"She did not," Norwood says, impatience in his voice. "And what makes you think she didn't jet off to Switzerland for a few nights? She might have been gone with me the night of the so-called break-in."

Chang leans closer and says, "OK, Gabriel. If you were in Switzerland with Mom, tell us who was driving your car that night. If you give us a name we can verify, that changes the situation . . ."

Not a peep.

They all sit there looking, not looking, nodding, not nodding. Sure, they can hear the sound of the search warrant, but the riffling through the life of Gabriel Norwood has become a buffering white noise.

Powell enters the room. She surveys the silence and seems to take a special joy in breaking it. "Nothing conclusive yet," she says. "But obviously there are plenty of fingerprints here, so Scottsdale will try to match the prints found at the gallery. We should know very quickly."

Then she leaves the room with efficiency.

"Told you," the kid actually says. "Nothing conclusive."

"Yeah, I wouldn't hold on to that hope much longer," Chang tells him. "So, again, who was driving your car the night of the break-in while you were in Switzerland?"

"I don't name names."

"Even to clear yourself?" Chang asks him.

"Right."

"Dude, you sound like an amateur," Mills says. "It's best to cooperate. I think Francesca in Bungalow 18 West would agree."

Norwood sits up, pushes himself to the edge of the couch. "Leave my mother out of this."

Mills admires the guy's nerve even if he mocks it at the same time. "But I'm really surprised she didn't tell you about my visits with her. It's a huge case, and Viveca was so close to your family."

"Look, Detective, my mom and I are just, kind of, getting reacquainted," Gabriel says, suddenly even and amenable. "So she's guarded. Still keeping her distance."

"That's right," Mills says, as if he's just remembering, "you were excommunicated for embezzling money from the church."

The guy laughs. "I think 'embezzling' is an embellishment."

"You stole a million dollars from the church."

"I was never charged!"

"Because your parents never reported it to the police!"

This brings back memories for Mills. Not that his son ever stole a million dollars from anyone, but back in high school Trevor did sell pot to an undercover cop, and the disappointment and the anger and the embarrassment raged through Mills like a virulent disease. So, here he is, years later, in a fever, yelling at Gabriel Norwood. He hears his own words, doesn't understand the relapse. Mills has forgiven his son and they've moved on.

"Why don't you take responsibility, Gabriel?" he hammers. "Huh? Because that would force you to fucking grow up? Why don't you fucking grow up? You're twenty-five, not fifteen."

"You can't talk to me like that!"

"Don't fucking try me, buddy. Or it'll get much worse."

Gabriel jumps to his feet. Mills gets up instantly in response. They stand there like wrestlers before a match, and Chang clears her throat, as if to signal a timeout before the match has even begun. Now she's on her feet, one hand to Mills's chest, another to Norwood's. "Guys, come on," she says. "You both sit down now. We're all on edge. Nothing about this is pleasant."

Mills takes a bird's-eye view of the whole scene and sees his own embarrassment, the redness in his face. He mutters an apology to Chang and sits down. To her other side, she pushes Gabriel to the couch where he sinks. She's about to retreat as well when Jan Powell enters with one of the Scottsdale cops.

"We've got a crime scene here that looks like something out of Anne Frank's diary," she says.

"Nazis?" Mills asks. Nothing would surprise him these days.

"No," Powell replies. "A bookcase that hides a hidden stairway to an attic."

"We found drugs," the Scottsdale cop says. "Pills, probably Fentanyl, and what looks like cocaine."

All eyes turn to Gabriel Norwood, whose face is taking on the purple of a bruise. It's as if he's holding his breath and banging his head against the wall at the same time. But he's doing neither. He's just sitting there quietly imploding.

"Oh, Jesus, I'm going to have to arrest you on more charges than I thought," Chang says.

"Plus, a pet cobra and two little monkeys," the cop says. "I think tamarins."

"Come on, Norwood," Chang says. "Is there a crime you haven't committed?"

"No, there isn't," Powell says. "We found even more . . . Preston?"

Moving like a human easel, Preston comes in from around the corner carrying a painting. He's walking backward, then spins around. The painting, even to the untrained eye, looks an awful lot like a Dali.

37

Dalis are distinctive. You just know. There doesn't seem to be a doubt in the room. Mills pulls up his inbox on his phone, searches for the email from Phoebe Canning Bickford. He studies the photo she attached, then the painting. He volleys back and forth like that to confirm, to reconfirm, to re-reconfirm. Stick figures on a desert landscape. Sand dunes. Sky. It's obvious. It's the same image. It's the painting taken from Viveca Canning's home.

"I guess this is my cue to arrest you for the murder of Viveca Canning," Mills tells Gabriel Norwood, as he cuffs him and chants his Miranda. "Let's go, dude. There's a cruiser waiting for you outside."

Gabriel apparently doesn't grasp the right to remain silent.

"You don't understand! You don't understand!" he cries.

"What don't we understand, Gabriel?" Mills ask him.

The guy is curled up on the couch, nearly fetal, his eyes full of tears. "I didn't act alone. I promise. This wasn't my idea."

"What wasn't?" Mills reaches for his phone again, turns on the voice recorder.

"Any of this."

Mills takes a deep breath. He braces himself for a desperate fantasy, but he also braces himself for the truth. He'll know the truth. "Maybe you'd like to explain when we take you in for questioning . . ."

Gabriel sits up. "You're looking at the wrong Norwood . . ."

"Are you sure you don't want a lawyer present?" Mills asks him.

"When you hear what I have to say, I won't need a lawyer."

Mills shakes his head, not so much to caution Norwood, but to dismiss the kid's stupidity. "Whatever you say, Gabriel. I think we should continue this at headquarters. Let's go."

"No! Wait! Please take off the handcuffs . . ."

"I can't do that," Mills tells him.

"But when you hear what I'm going to say, you won't need to arrest me."

"You're already under arrest," Mills reminds him. "But I'm listening."

According to Gabriel, the break-in at Carmichael & Finn was an attempt to locate an ancient key that Clark Canning stole from Gleason Norwood. The key represented some kind of leverage, and Gabriel's father wanted it back.

"What if I told you the key you were looking for was locked away in a chest?" Mills asks.

"Then we would have just taken the chest . . ."

"Really?" Preston asks. "Then what's this?" He nods to the Scottsdale officer who holds up a small gold key. Mills isn't wearing gloves, so the officer brings the key to his face. It's a Schlage.

"Interesting, Detective Preston," Mills says. "That looks like the key that might have fit the lock on the chest. Hmm. How did you come by this?" he asks Norwood.

The kid starts to shake. "Someone gave it to me."

"Who?" Mills asks.

"I don't remember," Gabriel sputters, his body nearly convulsing.

"Well, I can certainly help jog your memory," Powell says. "The key has adhesive residue all over it, as if it were stuck to something or taped to something. Curiously enough, when you turn the painting around . . ."

She gestures to Preston who spins the exhibit, like a game show host, to show the audience the backside of the Dali.

"You'll find a patch of rough adhesive on the back of the frame," Powell continues.

Preston points.

"The key came from the frame of this painting," Powell says. "A painting that was taken from the home of Viveca Canning."

Gabriel's head is in his cuffed hands. He speaks to the floor when he says, "I told you it wasn't my idea."

"Then whose was it?" Mills asks.

"I'm dizzy," Gabriel says.

"Would you like some water?"

"Yes."

Chang crosses the room to the kitchen where she grabs a bottle of water from the fridge. On her way back she opens the cap, says, "hope this helps," and hands Gabriel the bottle.

He gulps. He's saving his own life. He drowns. He flails. Mills doesn't know what he's watching. Then Norwood comes up for air and says, "Eventually you're going to find out that I did this for my father."

"Did what?"

"I'm not making a full confession."

"Then I don't understand you," Mills says. "Let's go, Gabe. I'm taking you in."

The man sobs. "Jesus Christ," he roars between choking tears. "Let me have my laptop."

"I'm pretty sure it's been seized as evidence," Mills says, then looks to Preston. "Could you leave that masterpiece with us and go check with Myers on the laptop?"

Norwood gulps the rest of the water, wipes his mouth with the back of his hand. Mills is beginning to smell the guy's fear, not figuratively; the guy really is beginning to stink. His sweat glands must be working on overdrive as they secrete his dark, compromising secrets.

Preston returns with a MacBook.

"I'm going to show you something on my computer," Norwood says. "I'll read it to you. And if you want it, I'll forward it to you."

"You can do this with handcuffs on?" Preston asks, opening the laptop.

"Watch me."

"Wait," Mills says. "You need to put on gloves even if it is your own device."

The Scottsdale cop provides the gloves, and the handcuffed suspect types away. Then he reads.

"'Gleason, I do not appreciate the way our conversation ended today. I know what I know. And I've seen what I've seen. No amount of threats can undo this. I just came to you with questions and you threatened to have the police remove me from the church. That was hurtful and ugly. No one has supported you more so than Clark and I have. We have essentially built that church for you. And, trust me, you do not want the police at that church . . .'"

Mills stops him. "If that's some kind of communication between Viveca and your father, we should also have it. We seized her computer."

Gabriel stares at him. "You won't find it," he says. "Nope. I hacked into both her computer and my dad's and removed all incriminating emails. He told me to. But I saved the best ones."

He's now smiling deviously.

"Just so you know, we would've found this one eventually, despite your hacking," Mills tells him. "I have an expert who's recovering pretty much everything Viveca ever did on that computer."

Gabriel shrugs. "And that can take forever 'cause there are hundreds of emails. But now you don't have to waste your time. You can have this if you let me go."

Mills laughs, despite himself. It was a visceral reaction, instinctive. "First of all, we're taking it. It's evidence. It's already ours. Secondly, we don't make the deals. That's for the county attorney. And I promise you, the county attorney is going to want a whole lot more from you than one email to even consider negotiating a plea deal. I really think you'll want a lawyer if this is any indication of your judicial prowess."

Chang claps her hands. "Nicely said, my man."

Mills smiles at her, but also winces.

"Let me finish," Gabriel insists, and then reads, "'This is my official resignation from the Board of Directors from the Church of Angels Rising. This is also my notice that I will be leaving the church and denouncing my membership. Effective immediately. I have everything documented, so if you try to punish me for my defection as you have others, you will not prevail. I will live my untouchable life in peace and serenity. I will be leaving Phoenix. You will soon find that I'm changing my will and leaving my full estate to my children rather than the church. The art will go to the Heard. My legacy will not be a legacy tied to a church of horrors. I told you what I saw. You know I know the truth. I don't yet know what I will do to expose you and your church. I don't yet know how law enforcement will react to my discoveries. But you shall soon find out. You are a despicable man, Gleason Norwood. You have ruined people. You have destroyed the minds of innocent people. You have engineered a pathological, devious program of brainwashing and punishment. It will come out. I promise you. You will pay the price. I'm sorry it has come to this, Gleason. I'm deeply hurt and disappointed. Please don't contact me. If I need to I will get a restraining order. One more thing . . . I suspect you're behind the death of my husband. Sincerely, Viveca Canning.'"

Mills lets that sink in. He lets the room take a collective breath. On the exhale he says, "So, it seems Viveca confronted your father in person about something she saw at the church. Maybe he threatened her, and then she went home and composed her farewell. Poor woman, though. She had no idea she'd be making a fatal and permanent move."

"What did she see at the church?" Powell asks.

According to Gabriel, Viveca saw everything. In the blabbery that comes next, Gabriel describes a maze of rooms and hallways underneath the church, through a door that can only be opened by that ancient key. He says there are chambers behind that door where the worst of the church's activities take place. "That's all I'm going to say. If you want to know what Viveca saw, you're going to have to get a search warrant for the church . . ."

"With enough time for you to tip your father off?" Powell asks him.

"I'm in custody. Remember?"

She sneers at him. "Don't be a smartass."

"So, your father decides that he needs to eliminate Viveca Canning?" Mills asks the suspect.

"Originally, I was only supposed to get the key from Viv," Gabriel says. "But then her confrontation with Gleason happened . . ."

"So you killed her to silence her?" Mills asks. "This doesn't add up, Gabriel. You'd been excommunicated from the church, cut off from your parents, why would you turn around and protect the church that banished you?"

Gabriel closes the laptop. Tears fill his eyes. He shakes his head, wipes his nose with the bottom half of his designer t-shirt. He's cornered. Decorum is a moot point. "My dad promised to reinstate me in the church if I got the key and got rid of Viveca Canning."

Again, the room comes to a hush. In the void, Mills's suspicion coalesces. He knows the answer to the next question, but he asks anyway to prompt it on the record. "Why would you want to be reinstated in a church that banished you?"

Handcuffed as he is, the guy gets up and walks to the window; he rattles his forehead against the glass. "I'm broke, man. My mom pays for my house. But I got no money. Which might explain the drugs you found . . ."

He's all sniffles. Sniffles of cocaine and despair.

"Your fall from grace," Mills says.

"If you insist on clichés, yeah," Norwood says. "My dad offered me a full salary if I came back. I couldn't turn it down."

"And now you see all that money slipping away. You see the church slipping way. So, that's why you're cooperating with us," Mills says.

"He said if I got Viveca out of the way and personally handed him the key, he'd deposit a million dollars in my bank account," the kid explains.

"Tempting," Mills says.

"You should get my father," Gabriel says.

With that statement, Mills understands the situation as not only criminal, not only tragic, but just fucking sad, a whole ward of self-inflicted injury.

"You're selling out your dad pretty fast," he says to the kid.

"Look what he did to me."

"You're the victim?"

"In part," Gabriel says. "But I'm aware of my role. And the roles of others."

Mills approaches him, asks him to sit. Once Gabriel is on the couch again, Mills pulls up a chair opposite him. "There are others?"

Gabriel laughs bitterly. "Of course there are. My father doesn't do the dirty work."

"I'm assuming if you name names, the county attorney will be more inclined to offer a deal."

"Tucker Charles."

"Who?"

"He's on the Board of Directors."

"Right," Mills says. "I met him. What about him?"

"He's responsible for the death of Clark Canning."

"Seriously? Who doesn't the church murder? And how is that an act of faith?"

"Ha ha! Detective, you're hilarious. This isn't about faith. It's about money and power and what they'll do to protect it. Tucker poisoned Clark Canning after my father found out that Clark had stolen that key. They figured with Clark dead, the key would never be found."

"They didn't figure on Clark telling Viveca?"

"My father told Clark he'd kill him if Viveca found out about the key," Gabriel says. "But then he had him killed anyway, just as a precaution."

"And he knew he had to kill Viveca once she sent him that email," Mills surmises.

"He knew someone had to kill Viveca," Gabriel says. "And that's all I want to say for now. I won't answer any more questions. I'd like a lawyer."

As far as Mills is concerned, Gabriel Norwood has answered plenty of questions, but now come the jurisdictional issues. He and Liv Chang agree to have Gabriel taken to Phoenix police headquarters to be processed for the more serious charges of murder, conspiracy to commit, and whatever else fits the crime. Chang will also arrest him here on the break-in charges but will postpone the process of booking until Gabriel's disposition is reached in Phoenix. All will be referred to the county attorney, so for now it's simply procedure.

Back in Phoenix, Gabriel gets chatty again. Mills loves chatty but, at this point, his head is throbbing with too much information, too many dots connected for one day, too many personalities implicated, too much of humanity, of the people here on this planet with no sense of truth: there's gravity, you stay on the ground, you do not rise above others, you do not rule them, you do not harm them, you do not betray them. It's been a long day. Tomorrow will be longer. This case isn't over. In a way, it's just begun. Funny how the walls of the valley sometimes make you feel safe and protected, and sometimes they make you feel like they're closing in. They're sitting in the interrogation room, videotape rolling, waiting for Gabriel's lawyer. Preston and Powell are already preparing to go before a judge to get a warrant to search the church.

"How long before this makes the news and Bennett and Jillian find out?" Gabriel asks.

"I don't know, Gabriel. I don't run the news."

"But I'm sure this will be released to the media. You know, my arrest will be announced . . ."

"I have as little to do with the media as possible," Mills tells him. "It's not my job."

"Sensational case," the kid says.

"You want to be a media star?" Mills asks. "Is that it?"

Gabriel sulks. "No. That's not it. As soon as the news breaks, my dad will probably take off."

That's not going to happen. Mills will put surveillance on Gleason Norwood and will try to keep the arrest of Gabriel under the radar for at least the next twelve hours. He rubs his chin, takes a visual journey back to the house in Copper Palace. "Was it common knowledge that the Cannings' had hid the key behind the Dali?"

Norwood's son curls his lip and shakes his head. "No. That would be stupid."

"So, how did you find it?"

"I'm not proud of this, but I put a gun to her head. You'd be surprised how easily people cooperate with a gun to their head."

Mills has to clench his fist in order to restrain the backside of his hand from smacking this piece of shit upside the head. "Are you proud of killing her?"

"No comment."

"There's something confusing to me, Gabriel. Why did you take the Dali? You could have just removed the key and left the painting where it was. I mean, you not only gave us a lead, you put it right there on exhibit by leaving an empty space on the wall."

The suspect shakes his head. "Because I'm an idiot. All right? They had the key stuck there with so much tape, like a whole wad of it, or Krazy Glue, or something, and I couldn't get the key off the back without destroying something. So, I was like, I have to get out of this house . . . so, I took it."

"How come we don't see your car going through the visitor's lane at her subdivision?" Mills asks him.

"Because I wasn't in my car," he replies. "I Ubered over there. Told Viveca I needed to see her about something urgent. Then I borrowed her car to go home. It's parked in the big garage behind the church in case you can get a warrant."

Mills leans back, clears his throat, and says, "Now, tell us about Aaliyah Jones . . ."

"Who?"

"We don't have time for you to be coy, Gabriel. We need to know what happened to her."

The guys flips his hands upward. "I have no idea what you're talking about."

"Aaliyah Jones, the reporter," Mills thunders. "She was investigating the church and now she's missing."

"Oh her," Gabriel says.

"Yeah, her."

"I have no idea what happened with her."

"And now you're trying my patience, Mr. Norwood," Mills says.

"And now he'll say nothing else in the matter until we have a chance to talk alone," declares a man in one of those fancy designer suits and expensive hair weaves. He strides in as if he's striding into a *Law & Order* courtroom, the double doors held open for his arrival by two deputies. Unfortunately for him, there is only a single door to the interrogation room and no deputies to exaggerate the flourish of his entrance.

He says his name is Kelton Summers, Attorney-at-Law. He says it just like that, the full suffix and everything. He, at least for now, will serve as Gabriel Norwood's lawyer.

Mills is already on to the next thing. Kelly undergoes surgery tomorrow. It will be the second assault against the cancer. It will take the cancer by surprise. The surgery will be a declaration of war. So, he assumes, will be the raid on the Church of Angels Rising.

Just when he thought he had had enough of lawyers, he goes home and finds Kelly who, with one simple smile and peck on the cheek, redeems all the other lawyers on the planet—if that's possible. She's sitting on the couch, her feet up on the coffee table. "We won," she says. "Trey Robert Shinner: Not guilty on all counts."

"Amazing," Mills says. "I didn't know the verdict came down."

"About four o'clock."

He's still leaning over her on the couch and says, "I was locked in an interrogation room. Wish I could have been there to celebrate."

She winces. "There's nothing to celebrate."

"Of course there is. You won. You're one of the few lawyers to keep this goon out of jail."

She sighs deeply. "That's not something to be proud of," she says. "In a way, that makes me responsible for the next crime he commits. And you know he will commit another."

He sits beside her, rubs her shoulder. "That's not your problem, Kelly. You've been doing this long enough to know that."

"At least the verdict came down before the surgery," she mutters.

"Not a moment to spare . . ."

She turns her face to his, kisses him. Their lips touch at the ridges, they graze each other softly there, lingering just for a moment, but long enough to give Mills a lump in his throat, and to remind him that love is often this simple.

38

Billie calls it a surprise. Gus isn't so sure.

She's calling from Sky Harbor, says she's just landed and will limo over to the Desert Charm. "Why don't I just come pick you up?" he asks.

"The limo will save time. Besides, I thought you might have a client."

"I did," he says. "About an hour ago. What brings you back to Phoenix?"

"I told you," she flirts. "I just wanted to surprise you."

"I'm surprised. I think."

"Besides, Miranda is back here and we have more work to do on the tour. She can't stay with me in LA full-time."

"Right."

"Can you come by tonight? I'll order room service."

He tells her "sure," and they're off the phone. Gus scratches at his scruffy chin. He didn't get many breakthrough vibes with his client earlier—it was a woman thinking about changing careers, from what to what he can't remember, maybe sous chef to firefighter; it was something ironic—but he's getting vibes now. He doesn't recognize them, doesn't understand them, but they prick at his skin, faintly at first, and then, like the march of pins to a cushion.

He walks out to the pool. Ivy follows. He dives in and stays under as long as his lungs will allow. This is Zen, here at the bottom, his arms crossed over his chest, his breathing acquiescent. This is Zen, floating but not floating, the silence of water, the absence of a tide, no pull of the moon. So he loiters there in his vessel of solitude until he hears the frenzied barking of Ivy crashing through the depth between them. He opens his eyes. Through the wobbly water he can see her frantic at the edge of the pool, her big golden face leaning over the edge, looking for Gus. He soars to the surface with a straight-line push off the bottom. She's still barking when he breaks the surface, still barking when he pulls himself from the pool. Still barking when he towels himself off and hugs her close.

He showers, changes, heads to the Desert Charm. Billie opens the door in a white gossamer blouse, untucked, and a flowing pair of linen pants, the color of burlap. A lightning bolt pendant hangs from her neck. She smells musky when he leans in and kisses her. "Gus, come in," she says.

He follows her to the living room. She stretches out on the couch. He sits at her side, squeezing in. "You tired?" he asks.

"I'm always tired. Exhausted."

"I guess telling you to slow down is pointless."

"Pointless."

"But you are stopping over in Tahiti on the tour."

"Yeah," she says, no more soliciting him to come.

Someone has to break the ice. It might as well be him. He's feeling chilly enough. "How was your visit with Cameron?"

She smiles. "Oh great! That old guy! After all these years he's still the same old pain in the ass. But I guess you could say he's mellowed a little. Enough to join the band, that is."

"What do you mean?"

She pulls herself up a bit. "Just for the Down Under tour," she says. "He'll replace Glen 'cause Glen has a conflict."

Glen is Billie's bass player.

"So, that's it. All decided?"

She laughs. "Between Cam and me, yes. But then there's the agents and managers and lawyers."

"What about boyfriends and girlfriends?" Gus asks. He's not laughing. He's not smiling. He's not pouting. He's just looking at her with a thin expression.

"You mean, you, right?"

"That's what I mean."

"That's one of the reasons I came to Phoenix. I thought we should talk about it."

He nods. "We're talking about it."

The pinpricks are back. He's the cushion.

"It's not what it looks like, Gus," she tells him. "We're not getting back together."

"But you're not necessarily staying apart," he says. "How long is this tour between Australia and New Zealand? A month?"

"Three and a half weeks, so yeah, a month," she says. "And that's kind of what Cam's visit to LA was all about. You know, if we could be in the same house for forty-eight hours and not kill each other, we could probably survive a few weeks overseas."

"Probably."

"And you'd still be welcome to come along, the whole time, if you wanted," she insists. "But I know you have priorities here."

"Responsibilities."

The earth seems to shift below his feet. There's a tremor.

"Did you feel that?" he asks her.

"What?"

"The ground move . . ."

She laughs again. "C'mon, we don't have earthquakes here."

He tilts his chin and narrows his eyes. "Maybe you brought one with you from LA."

"Oh my God, I love that! Can I use it in a song? So dramatic!"

He puts his head in his hands and rubs his eyes. "Sure, use it. I don't think you'll forget it."

She grabs his arm. "What is that supposed to mean?"

"I don't know. I think I'm getting some strong vibes. The tremor was just the beginning."

He stands and crosses the room. He leans against a window looking out to the splash pool in the courtyard. He can't see his reflection in the pool from here, but he imagines his reflection in the pool, and that's all he needs to see. The rest is crystalline. They're in separate hemispheres, on either side of the equator. They're on opposite sides of the international date line. Just finding each other's longitude and latitude is daunting, and they haven't even left home. They're here. In the same room. Something shakes inside him, the rattle of an uninvited epiphany, perhaps, or instant grief, like the sudden news of death.

"I was supposed to be coming to LA this weekend, but you don't want me there," he says, still peering through the window. "You want me here. This is the weekend we're breaking up, right?"

He hears her gasp. "Don't say it like that."

"You gasp at what it sounds like? What do you think it's supposed to sound like, Billie?"

"I don't know."

"I think I do. You think it can't be happening unless it happens in a lyric," he says, turning to her.

She gets up. She walks to him her arms extended, a helpless waif. A helpless waif has never been so powerful. "You sound hurt, Gus. I'm sorry. I thought we could spend a few days and talk about it. But who am I to compete with your psychic vibes? I should have known you'd pick up on something before we even ordered dinner. Should we?"

"Should we what?"

"Order dinner?"

He looks at her, shakes his head. "Whatever, Billie. I don't care."

She grabs him by the shoulders and rubs him there, then pulls him closer into an embrace. "I'm too old for this," she whispers in his ear. "I'm too old to go down this road much longer."

"What road?"

"I've never been married. I will never marry. It's too late for me to learn how to do that. And trust me, I have no clue. There's a whole line of casualties behind you, Gus . . ."

"But when you love someone," he hears himself say.

"But this has nothing to do with love . . ."

"Oh, yes it does," he tells her.

She shakes her head, pushes her hair behind her neck. "I'm not saying I don't love you. I do. I do love you, Gus. Whatever pain I cause you, I promise I will cause myself double. I just know that life gives you as much freedom as you want. Some want less than others. Some want more. I don't think it's possible for me to ever have enough. The universe is too big. I need the freedom to inhabit the universe."

Ok.

So.

Hmmm.

He looks at her. He stares into her eyes, seeking what, he doesn't know. There had always been solace there. But now he's looking for something broken. Like a shattered bulb, a short circuit, a fucking broken mirror, anything. Maybe he hopes to find confirmation of their denouement.

Instead he sees Aaliyah Jones staring back at him.

"Aaliyah . . ." he says.

"What did you call me?" Billie asks him.

"Huh?"

Again, the other woman in her eyes. It has to be Aaliyah Jones.

"You said Aaliyah. Who's that?" Billie asks. "What does that mean?"

He apologizes, explains he's in a bit of a trance, asks for her indulgence. Aaliyah, strong but tormented, will not look away. She will not budge. She will not depart Billie's eyes. Trapped there, like a spirit, like a possession, Aaliyah tells Gus she's in prison. This does not surprise Gus. This should not surprise anyone. It's a good thing she's alive, but she's obviously being held against her will. Gus can't see where she is. He tries to ask her. He begs, "Where are you? Do you have any idea?"

"Gus, please . . ." That's Billie pleading.

Aaliyah shakes her head. "No, I was blindfolded."

"But you're in prison? An actual prison?"

"Figuratively and literally," Aaliyah whispers. "I can't let them know we're talking. All I know is I'm in a small room, like a shoebox, and I can't get out."

"I'm going to help you," Gus tells her. He doesn't know how. Has no clue. But what is he supposed to say?

"C'mon, Gus . . . This is freaking me out." Again, Billie.

"Any chance you're in a bunker, Aaliyah?"

"Could be. But I don't remember going underground . . ."

Billie begins to sing. At first, gently, softly. Then she begins to climb the scales of rock 'n' roll. Her voice goes from ethereal to mighty, from sweeps of sand to a percussive tsunami. Then Billie twirls around the room as she sings, like she's performing, like she's at the center of the stage under the lights, glowing like a phantom angel.

And Aaliyah disappears.

"Aaliyah . . ." Gus calls.

"It's me. Goddamnit, Gus!"

"I'm sorry, Billie. I was having a visit."

"A visit or a vision?"

"Both. This vision came in the form of a visit." He tells her about Aaliyah's disappearance.

"Oh, God. That's awful," Billie says.

"Yes. It is."

"And you know where she is?"

"No. I don't. I can't get there. At least not yet."

"Dinner?" she asks.

"No," he says. "I don't have an appetite. I think I need to leave."

She nods, smiles weakly. Her eyes, fully her own now, not Aaliyah's, turn sad and almost mournful. She comes forward and grabs both of Gus's hands in hers, as if she's asking him to dance. But she's not. She stands there holding him. Her hair falls forward, tresses of it cascading. "I don't know what to say," she says.

"Don't say anything. There are no words that need to be said."

"OK."

"OK. I love you."

"I love you."

He promises to be in touch, nothing else. She promises the same. Then he leaves. And he leaves most of it all in the room. With her.

39

Today is Friday. Either the beginning of the end. Or the end of the beginning. The morning Mills dreaded, the day he resisted. The clock and the calendar are ruthless. They go through the familiar maze of administrative nonsense: main registration, surgical registration—

Do you have a living will?
A healthcare surrogate?
Repeat your date of birth.
Please sign this form.
And this form.
Are you allergic to latex?
Please sign this form.
Please repeat your date of birth.
And initial here.

Now, here, in the pre-op room, they're facing different faces. It's as if the hospital called in a different crew. Different nurses, different techs, different people probing, all except Dr. Susan Waxler, who's already come in to say "hello." The dress under her lab coat was a gauzy free-flowing Sahara desert thing that fell just below her knees. It cinched at the waist with a thin piece of rope from which dangled tiny bronze bells. She ring-ringed softly as she came and went.

Mills's phone rings. It's Powell. They have the warrant to search the C-ARC.

"The judge looked at the gallery break-in, the Canning homicide, even the Aaliyah Jones details, and signed off," she says. "With some limitations."

For whatever reason, the warrant prohibits the removal of any religious texts, as well as the removal of religious ornaments or artifacts from the walls or displays. Peculiar. But fine. Ornaments and artifacts are not exactly within the scope of the investigation. With the exception, perhaps, of the old skeleton key.

"I'm taking it out of evidence," Powell says. "I'm happy to bust down doors, but I'd rather see if this key fits."

"Of course," Mills says. "What time?"

"Sooner the better. I was hoping by noon. Maybe even 11."

"Shit. Let me get back to you."

"Don't leave your wife," Powell says. "I'll never speak to you again if you do."

"Like you have a choice."

"You do," she says and hangs up.

Yeah. The choice. How can there even be a choice? Kelly in the bed next to him, the two of them in this box of a room, not even a room, a large cubicle with a curtain. It suddenly feels, even though Mills knows this can't be true, that all the questions of life and death must be answered here. He can't think straight. She doesn't look like a victim. She's very much alive, with her sparkling eyes, her indomitable smile. She's not wearing makeup and she is so much more beautiful as herself, just like this.

"The church warrant?" she asks him.

"Yep."

"Ready?"

"Yep."

"You going?"

"Of course not."

He's sitting in a chair as close to her bedside as he can without colliding. "Of course you are," she says. "You're no help in the operating room."

"That's not the point."

"What is the point?" she asks, like the tough attorney she is.

"I would never leave you here. What if something happens?"

"Nothing's going to happen," she insists. "You don't die from cancer in the OR."

"You don't know that," he says.

"I'm pretty sure," she argues. "Besides, even if I did die in the OR, what use would you be then? You'd rush in to revive me? Come on, Alex . . ."

He grabs her hand. "Could we not talk like this? A husband doesn't leave his wife alone in the hospital."

"She's not alone," says a nurse who comes through the curtain. She's a husky woman with a husky voice. Contrary to what her profession might suggest, she obviously smokes. She has red hair pulled back into a frizzy ponytail, evenly pink skin, and a generously distributed constellation of freckles. She must be sixty.

"I'm Nancy," she says. "I'll be your pre-op nurse. Everything good?"

"Fine," Kelly replies.

"Good. Everything good with you?" the nurse asks Mills.

"Yes," he answers, nervous. She's a good interrogator, this nurse named Nancy.

"OK," she says. "I just thought I heard the sound of two lovebirds arguing . . ."

Kelly laughs. "My husband's a cop. He has an important case he's working on. He needs to leave but he won't leave."

"Really?" the nurse asks, her eyebrows skyward.

"She's crazy if she thinks I'm going to leave her."

Hands on her hips, the nurse says, "Well, you'll be here a while. The doctor's backed up. What time was your surgery scheduled for?"

"Eleven," Kelly says.

Nancy offers an ironic smile. "OK, sure. We're looking at 12:30 or 1."

She has an accent. *Shoowah. Wehyah lookin' at twelve-thuhrty aw one.*

Mills looks at his watch. Ten forty-five. "I can't execute a search warrant in two hours."

"Two hours is conservative," the nurse says. "If the surgeon is running behind now, he'll continue to run behind."

Ow-wahs. Consuhhvative. Suhhgeon.

"Where is that accent from?" Mills asks the woman.

"Boston. Can't you tell?"

"Yeah. I was thinking maybe New York or around there."

"Boston. Not New York," she says with an emphatic nod.

Nurse Nancy adjusts something in Kelly's IV. Then she attaches something to Kelly's fingertip and watches a small screen. Pulse, maybe. Mills can't keep up, and he doesn't care to ask. This stuff all looks routine. The scary shit happens in the OR. Nancy pats him on the shoulder. "If I can get you to move for a sec. I need to get in here . . ."

Mills shuffles the chair back and watches as Nancy changes out a tube attached to Kelly's arm. "What are you putting in her veins?" he asks.

"Just electrolytes for now. She'll get the heavier stuff later."

As Nancy backs away, Kelly turns to her husband and says, "Now, you need to leave, Alex."

He shuffles back. He addresses both of them, as if Nancy is an older sister or an aunt. "Look, I have perfectly capable people who can execute this warrant. My team is the best. I do *not* need to be there, especially if it means leaving you here alone with all your anxiety about the surgery."

Kelly rolls toward him. "What if I told you that you were making me more anxious?"

Nancy bends forward, intervening. "I've seen that."

Mills says, "No."

"If you sit here worried about the search, you're going to drive me crazy."

Nurse Nancy leans in again. "Forgive me for meddling," she says. "But when you come into our house, you're family. So, I'll make a deal with you, Mr. Mills. You go. Give me your cell phone number. I will personally call you and text you when she's ready to go."

Mills shakes his head. "I'd need a thirty-minute warning, at least."

"Fine," Nancy says. "Thirty minutes."

"And in the meantime, she's just going to lie here alone and worry?"

"Who says I'm worrying?"

"Of course you're worrying," Mills tells his wife. "You're human. Yes, you won your case yesterday and that was a superhuman feat. But today you're here, babe, and it's OK to worry."

"Get him out of here," Kelly tells the nurse.

They all laugh, though Mills hears a resignation in his.

"If it makes you feel better," Nancy says, "I'm going to draw the curtain, and I'm going to give her something to relax anyway. A mild sedative. And she won't give a hoot where you are. She won't even notice you're gone . . ."

Kelly says, "I don't need a sedative for that."

Mills says, "Very funny. Are you OK with this?"

Kelly says, "I'm more than OK."

And Nurse Nancy says, "Give her a kiss. Tell her you love her. And get out of my way."

Mills gets up, leans forward, brushes her forehead with his hand, and plants his lips on hers for a kiss. He says, "I love you beyond reason. You are my everything of everything."

Then he leaves the room with an ache in his chest.

Gus wakes as if from a fever dream. A morbid sense of dissolution covers him like sweat. He eyes the ceiling. It's real. It's permanent. There will be no passage. Next, he takes in the four walls and the thump of his heartbeat. At the same time, a loneliness descends. *No.* He wills the mortality of love away from him, back into the ether. He swings his legs over the side of the bed and resolves to snap out of it. And yet he walks in a cloud, barely steady on his feet as he steps into the bathroom, feels the coolness of the tile against his feet, the rest of his body pasty and damp. He looks in the mirror and recognizes the simplicity of who he is, just a man, a mortal, a living breathing sentence of subject, verb, predicate, and period. Everything has an expiration date.

"Snap out it, August!" he says to the mirror.

There is no response, but his reflection disappears. In its place, Kelly Mills. She's weeping, sobbing really. A flood of tears washes over her face. There is blood everywhere. Rivers of blood. The vision startles him from head to toe. As his body convulses, it convulses with the recognition that he must go. He showers quickly, towels off, dresses. He runs Ivy outside. Then he's off. He's in his car, still in a trance. He's racing a demon. His phone rings.

"Dude."

"Morning, Gus."

"Everything all right with Kelly?"

"That's why I'm calling."

A chill swirls up his spine. "Oh shit."

"No, no, it's nothing," Alex says. "But today's the day. And I've had to make the worst decision."

Alex tells him about the execution of the search warrant at the C-ARC, how he had to leave Kelly alone at the hospital. How he's worried beyond belief. "It's a huge favor, man, but if you could head over there and, you know, just be there on standby, I'd be indebted to you, like, forever."

Gus laughs. "I'm heading there now."

"To the hospital?"

"Yes."

"Why?"

"I just had a vibe. Like a vibe that I was needed."

"Are you serious?"

"Yes. I am. I'm calling in sick today and I'll be there with Kelly. Now you can go focus fully on your job, Alex."

"I just love you, man."

"I know you do."

Alex lets out a cascade of "thank you"s, and Gus tells him countless times not to worry before hanging up and watching for the hospital exit. In an instant, his arm squeezes tight. Something jabs his shoulder, the pain radiating down his back. He tries to stretch out his arm to release the tension, but the movement only ignites a fire. He supposes if he's having a heart attack, he's heading to the right place.

Mills takes the 10 to the 202. All he sees in the rearview mirror is angst and a towering hospital. Both loom. The billions of regrets hover. They're following him, mostly asking him why he can't fix Kelly. He's used to fixing things. He wants to get under her hood and rewire her insides, rearrange the blood cells, give her a transfusion if that's what it takes, but he doesn't have the tools; he has to admit that. No tools and no words. He can't even conjure up the right words to comfort her. Everything he says comes out sounding like *Grey's Anatomy*, clichéd, cue the violins for fuck's sake. The regrets sit in the backseat as he drives, second-guessing his every move. Truth is, uncertainty is uncertainty; there's no way around it.

At least there's Gus. Gus to the rescue. Better than a brother.

GPS has him at the C-ARC in thirteen minutes. He passes one of those signs on the highway that reports the time and temperature.

11:07 a.m.

101 degrees.

They'll all be indoors by the time the heat reaches 108 as forecasted by the local meteorologists, most of whom are still engaged in that frying-an-egg-on-the-sidewalk sideshow. Mills has called Powell to mobilize the squad and the additional units needed for the search. They'll meet him at the C-ARC by 11:30.

He dials Kelly's cell phone. He gets her voice mail, doesn't leave a message.

When Mills pulls into the C-ARC parking lot, he finds his squad and six officers, a photographer, and a service van, which will be used for whatever might be seized.

"Morning folks," he says. "Let's get out of the heat."

The others follow him into the lobby. He hears a flute, a violin, doesn't remember the piping in of pacifying music here in the soaring atrium, but he appreciates the irony. He tells the receptionist that his team has come to execute a search warrant.

"I'll call the pastor for you," she says.

"No need," Mills tells her.

Mills advances for the main sanctuary/auditorium with the others in tow. The receptionist shrieks, "You can't go in there!"

She is uniformly ignored. Inside the massive hall, Mills choreographs the search, telling the others what to cover. Some will take the administrative offices; others will search the study and library areas. The rest will follow Mills to the underground described to him by the contractor, David Patrick. "Good luck," he tells the team.

As he's approaching the expansive stage, Mills can hear a voice thundering in his wake, "Wait just a minute! Wait! Stop!"

He turns and sees whom he expects to see. He sees the elegant Gleason Norwood racing down the aisle toward him. The man is wearing a shiny silk shirt with diamond cufflinks, the diamonds refracting the overhead light in a shower of shooting stars. Gone, however, is the diamond smile. "Just exactly what do you think you're doing?" he bellows.

"We're executing a search warrant," Mills replies. "Exactly."

"For what?"

Mills hands him a copy of the warrant. "Read it. It explains everything. We have work to do."

"Just because my son's in custody doesn't mean I've done anything wrong."

"Doesn't it?"

"How dare you implicate me!"

Mills gives the man a hard stare, a fierce meeting of the eyes, and says, "I'm not the one implicating you, Gleason. Apparently you need to have another conversation with your son."

Mills climbs the stairs to the stage.

"You can't go up there," Norwood insists.

"Read the warrant," Mills tells him again and crosses the stage. It occurs to him to look out to the audience and he can hardly believe his eyes. From this perspective, the place is cavernous. This is a stadium for believers, faithful, followers, or fools. Who knows? Who knows what brings thousands of people here to pray? He can't fathom.

Something squeezes the pit of his stomach.

When the others are on the stage as well, he tells them to look for a break in the floor, a cutout, perhaps, a lift that rises from below.

"Who's your supervisor?" Norwood demands to know.

"Just call the chief," Mills replies without turning back to the preacher. "You've done it before."

"Found it," the photographer says.

Mills drifts her way, finds her pointing her finger in a circular direction to the floor. Sure enough, there's a large oval cutout there, about five feet in diameter. He can't begin to guess the circumference, and there's no need; he can see that only one person at a time can ride the lift safely. At the front of the oval lay a button about the size of a taillight. "I'm going down first. I'll send the lift back up. One at a time please. Take it all the way to the bottom."

"You absolutely cannot go down there," Gleason shrieks. He's now on the stage, pushing away the officers.

"You touch one of my officers again, sir, and I'll arrest you," Mills warns him. "If you don't think this search will end in your arrest, don't tempt your fate."

Mills is proud of that remark. He doesn't know if it means anything, but he quite likes the way it stops the preacher in his tracks. He probably has enough to arrest Norwood now, but he has a hunch that Norwood, unlike his son, will clam up after Miranda. He needs Norwood talking, blabbing, frantic enough to implicate himself. Mills taps his foot on the button of the oval cutout and down he goes. He's in a grey cylinder tube. He's whooshed one floor down. Then he taps the button again, and he's lowered to the bottom. When the tube slides open, he exits into a narrow hallway which is dimly lit and dark at both ends, like a tunnel. He feels as if he's much deeper below the earth than he actually is. It's the reddish orange glow down here that gives this passageway a far-below-the-crust kind of feel. He reaches into the lift with his foot, touches the button and sends the thing upward.

Mesmerized, Mills can't imagine who conceived this underground and why. Certainly, he'll find out soon, but right now in this dead silence he can sense the tremors of discord. Suddenly he's Gus Parker. He's feeling the feeling of things. He's picking up vibes. He's not Gus Parker, but in this amber light, in this forsaken tunnel, he believes that Gus has been here. Not physically, of course, but Gus has been here in his visions.

Officer Steph Pullman arrives. Two more to go.

"What the f is this place?" she asks Mills.

"Hell if I know," he says. "Or maybe just hell."

The others, Officer Ron Robbins and the photographer Hailey Gibson, arrive next. They ask essentially the same question, to which Mills offers essentially the same answer. "Hell if anyone knows."

They gather around him.

"Look," he says. "I don't have a map to this place." He points to both ends of the hallway. "I don't know what's down either end. Flashlights please."

Then, somewhere along the hallway to the right, a door opens and slams shut with a thick metal echo.

Gleason Norwood emerges from the shadows. "We also have a thing called stairs," he says with a gleaming smile.

Mills ignores him, pushes past him with the others. Their flashlights illuminate a dead end. There is nothing here but a wall. They back up to the metal door. It's locked.

"Open it, Gleason," Mills says.

The preacher does a bit of a sashay and says, "Certainly you don't think you can order me around, do you?"

"Did you read the warrant?" Mills asks him. "You are working my last nerve, sir. We have a lot of ground to cover."

"It's just a stairwell, but if you insist . . ."

Gleason inserts a key into the lock and swings the thick door open. Indeed it is nothing but a stairwell, amber and empty. "C'mon, everyone," Mills says. "Other end."

Mills can feel the fire in his bones as he backtracks down the hallway, a kind of angry resolve to, once and for all, close this fucking case. He knows he's closing in. Sometimes the anger helps. Orbs of lights bounce off the walls as the team heads down the long hallway, much longer to this end. The tunnel turns a corner and they follow. Another corner. Another hallway. A maze. Mills could not have pictured this. The flashlights continue to lead, to scope out the turns, to crisscross the walls, the ceiling, the floor. They might as well be excavating.

"This is it," Pullman says. "The end."

The orbs meet on a massive wooden door, detailed in bronze, a barred window at its center. Mills can't see through. The flashlights don't help.

"Gleason, what is this place?"

"None of your damn business."

"Gleason, do I have to warn you again? If you refuse to answer you are impeding the search."

"Storage," the preacher says.

"Seems like a long way to go for storage," Mills says.

"Unfortunately, for you and your search crew, the door is locked and I don't have the key."

Mills grabs a flashlight from Pullman's hands and points it at the preacher's face. Gleason balks at the sudden light, his face squirming. "We can knock the damn door down," Mills says. "We're equipped."

"You had better not destroy our property."

"Or," Mills says, pulling the skeleton key from his pocket. "We could try this . . ."

Gleason lunges for the key. "Where in hell did you get that?"

Robbins blocks him. "No sir," the officer says. "You don't touch a thing down here. And you don't touch one of us."

Mills slides the key into the lock. He lets it sit there for a moment. He lets it sink in. He wants this moment to echo forever in the chambers of Gleason Norwood's soul, assuming he has one. Mills rattles the key just for dramatic effect. Then he turns it just slightly to the right and the door pops open. The pop sends Gleason over the edge. He jumps forward and slams the door shut. Mills grabs the man by the shiny silk shirt and pushes him against the wall. "One more move like that, Norwood, and you're in handcuffs. Just like your son. Pullman, the door."

The officer complies and swings the door outward.

Beyond the threshold, blackness. A hazy, static darkness, like night. The orbs can't penetrate.

"Norwood, the lights," Mills orders.

The preacher steps forward, enters the space, resigned, it seems, to the exposure. He reaches to the left, and as Mills hears the plunk of a lever, the lights come up.

Well. This is not what Mills had expected.

He had not expected to see a modern day catacomb. The sight takes his breath away. Pullman, to his right, gasps as well. Robbins mutters, "What the actual fuck?"

Before them are stone cases, the size of people, stacked four high, six across on metal racks. Racks that reach far back into the darkness of the chamber. Like an archive of death. Each case on each rack has a name crudely scrawled across the side. *Thompkins 2017. Walton 2013. Bayer 2001. Bayer, R. 2001. Lippinpool 2002. Hart 2018. Marx 2007.* And on and on down the line. Rows and rows.

Hailey immediately snaps pictures.

"What is this place?" Mills asks Norwood.

"I don't have to say anything."

"Fine," Mills tells him. "Pullman, would you please go grab the sledgehammer from the service van and bring it down here so we can crack a few of these open . . ."

"You can't do that!" the preacher cries.

"We certainly can," Mills says. "If I have to ask you to read the warrant one more time . . ."

Then, with a flourish, the man with the diamond-encrusted cufflinks says, "They are exactly what they look like."

"Burial vaults?" Mills asks.

"Yes. A sacred burial ground for our church members."

"Do you have a license for this, Norwood?"

"We don't need a license," he replies defiantly. "We're a church. This is no different than a church cemetery."

"A church cemetery needs a license to handle bodies, to operate in general. And you need to notify authorities about the deaths. Always. Who's buried here?"

Norwood hesitates, stutters, and says, "High-ranking members who wanted to stay close to the church. Former members of the board."

"So, if I were to match the names I see down here with church records in your office, I would be able to verify the high rankers and the board members?"

"Yes."

"Because we're searching your office right now," Mills tells him.

"I demand an attorney!" the man cries.

"Call one," Mills tells him. "We've never stopped you from calling your attorney. Take your time. We'll be here a while."

Norwood puffs out his chest. "You can't do this to me. Don't you know who I am?"

"You are so full of shit, there's not enough Charmin in the world to wipe you up. That's who you are, Gleason Norwood. Call your lawyer. You're going to need one."

With a huff, Norwood backs away, and as Mills listens to him make a call to his lawyer, he understands just how a life of fraud defines a man. The conversation is ardent and imploring. It is also fake. No one has a cell signal down here in this dungeon.

"You have a signal, Pullman?"

"Nope."

"You, Hailey?"

"Nah. I lost it when I came down the elevator."

"Thought so."

Robbins calls to them from the back corner of the room. Mills can't make out exactly what he's saying. Something about a hallway.

"You've found another hallway?"

"It's like another tunnel, I think," the officer says. "I think we should check it out."

The rest of them follow the sound of Robbins's voice. "Mr. Norwood, you'll need to come with us," Mills tells him.

"My attorney will be here any minute."

"I'm sure he can find you down here."

"There's nothing else to see back there. More storage."

"Of bodies?"

Mills insists that Norwood move in front of him as they make their way to the rear of the catacomb. "The tunnel's not that deep," Robbins says when they get there.

Mills tilts his head and nods in that direction. "Let's go."

"I'm going no further without my attorney," Norwood insists.

Mills turns to him, nearly unhinged with impatience. "As you wish. But this place is crawling with cops, so don't do anything stupid."

Norwood huffs but says nothing.

Mills joins the rest of his team and they enter the tunnel, Robbins in the lead, his voice and the orbs of light blazing their trail. In less than two minutes they reach a stone archway that surrounds another wooden door, the same design, the same thickness, it seems, as the door that led to the catacomb. Mills assumes the same key will fit the lock. He hands it to Robbins and his assumption is affirmed when the key slides in and the door creaks open.

The opening yields a sucking sound and a putrid smell.

Please, no more dead bodies.

Just urine. Maybe feces. Hard to tell.

Mills sweeps the walls of the dark space with his hands, feeling for a switch or a lever. He finds nothing on the right hand side, but knocks against a lever on the left. He pulls. Overhead lights come on. Discs of light hang from the ceiling in rounded cages; they resemble old-style catcher's masks, and they emit a feeble glow. That's it. The rest is murk and shadows. But the design of the room is clear enough. It's an open space of tables and benches, surrounded by a horseshoe of walls. Lining each wall, three or four doors to smaller rooms or closets. Mills waves them all to the center of the room. Hailey starts snapping pictures.

The place looks like a cellblock out of the county jail.

Crash.

"What the fuck was that?" Robbins asks.

Thud.

"Hello? Anybody in here?" Mills asks.

Then another thud, and it sounds like it left a dent. That makes Mills jump back, and it startles the others as well. The doors surrounding them have come alive, pounding like kettledrums, a whole percussion of desperation.

"Who's in here?" Mills shouts. "We need a key. We need a fucking key."

Robbins, examining the doors with a flashlight, says, "There are no locks. So there can't be a key."

"Jesus," Mills snaps. "What the fucking fuck . . . ?"

He turns to the lever for the lights and sees a smaller switch protected by a plastic cover. He tells Robbins to smash through the cover with his flashlight. The assault takes maybe thirty seconds, and the busted cover falls to the floor. Mills pulls the small lever and then turns his head when he hears the sound of the doors cranking open. They open in unison. Behind two of the doors, a woman and a man on their knees. Behind another, a man sitting against the wall; he's beaten and filthy. At another door, a man stands, his fists clenched. He's cleaner than the other three, a more recent arrival, perhaps. Behind still one more door is a tall, skinny man, revenge in his eyes.

"Who are you?" Mills asks them.

The woman begins to bawl. The man on his knees crawls out to comfort her.

The filthy one says, "We're dissenters . . . among many."

"We're the ones who've threatened to go to the cops," the man with the fists says. "Finally, the cops have come to us."

"But I thought if you were banished, they just make your family erase you and send you on your way," Mills says. "What's this about?"

"Banished," the woman says between sobs, "is for those who are no longer compatible with the teachings of the church. They go away peacefully and their family erases them." She gasps for air. "But a dissenter is someone who starts trouble from the inside. Or threatens to start trouble on the outside." She gasps again.

"OK," Mills tells her. "That's enough for now. Catch your breath. We'll get you to safety and get your full statements."

Some of the "dissenters"—well, fuck, they're prisoners—look too weak to move on their own. He tells Robbins to call for ambulances. "Go on out to the front. Meet the EMTs there."

Then he turns to the prisoners. "We can't risk any of you trying to walk out without supervision, whether you feel up to it or not. You'll be transported to an area hospital where you'll be checked out and questioned."

The man with the fists pounds the door. "It's not like we have anywhere to go," he says. "Our families disowned us. Just like Gleason preaches."

Mills is flooded with disbelief or, rather, too much all at once to believe. "How long have you all been down here?"

The man who's cradling the woman on the floor says, "I'm not really sure. Eight or nine months . . ."

The filthy one says, "I've been here almost three years."

The woman sighs and says, "I don't know how long I've been here. It's so confusing. They feed us twice a day. That's all we have to count the time."

The filthy one bends to the woman. "You've been here almost three years too. We came about the same time."

"Right," she says. "Your time's up after three years . . ."

"What do you mean?" Mills asks.

"I mean that they put you down here for three years to see if you'll overcome your dissent. You know, they try to program you back to the cult," she says. "They beat us. They terrorize us. They want us back as angels rising, not dissenters. But if you don't concede within three years you go next door . . ."

"Next door?" Mills asks.

"The fucking funeral parlor," the skinny one says. "Didn't you see it on the way in? It's our own private graveyard."

"Yeah. We saw it. It wasn't exactly described that way to us," Mills says with a heavy sigh. He tells Pullman to stay with Norwood's prisoners. "I have an arrest to make."

The chamber goes silent as he turns to leave. And in this silence, Mills detects a whimpering from one of the open cells. At first, he wonders if the prisoners had been allowed to keep a kitten down here, a gesture of normalcy or comfort; the whimper is that subtle, that weak. Yes, almost a purr. But then, the skinny guy says, "there's one more with us . . ."

And Mills realizes there's a cell from which no one has emerged.

He asks Pullman to shine her flashlight into the dark shoebox. In it, Mills can see the light reflecting off amber eyes. He can see the scared whites, the desperate, dark ovals, and he can see the copper skin glowing. He recognizes the face, but he has to move closer to the edge of the doorway, where the thin line separates bondage from freedom. It's her. It's Aaliyah Jones.

40

He wants to reach for Aaliyah, hold her, but all he can do right now is say, "Aaliyah, you're safe. We're going to get you out of here. But you're safe." And then he has to dash back down the hallway into the adjacent room.

"Gleason, has your lawyer showed?" Mills asks, entering the tomb.

"He'll be here shortly," Norwood shouts from a distance.

"I'm sorry. I can't wait," he says, unlatching the handcuffs from his belt. "You're under arrest for the—"

"Glory God will never!" the preacher cries. That's when the room goes black.

Mills hadn't realized that Norwood was loitering close to the lever that controls the catacomb lighting. It's like a fucking maze in here, and Mills can already hear the dash of feet, like the scurry of a rat, bolting from the room. Mills hears a gunshot. A warning? Who the fuck can tell in the dark? The sound of the gunfire has prompted more footsteps, more confusion. He hears Pullman's voice as the officer rushes toward him. "Just hang back, Steph," he instructs her. "Stay with them. I'm on the preacher."

His flashlight illuminates a pathway, around one stack of burial vaults, then another, around a corner, then another row of vaults, then two more after that. He smells rubbing alcohol, or formaldehyde, or maybe that's his imagination. "Mills to everyone on scene," he says into the radio, unsure if the thing will even work down here, "we got shots fired by suspect, suspect running... block exits if possible."

"Received," Preston says. "You still underground?"

"Yeah, he's either coming up the elevator on the stage or a stairwell behind the auditorium," Mills says, racing.

"OK, man. We're on it."

Mills flies into a wall, hears his nose crunch. "Fuck!"

In the rush of it all, he's disoriented. Norwood must have cut all the hallway lights leading back to the elevator. And Jesus Christ, the corners! Mills's flashlight gives him a decent field of vision, but not wide-angled enough to avoid the switchbacks of this maze. He runs a hand between his lip and his nose. He's bleeding. "Norwood!" he shouts. "Norwood!" Then, another "Fuck."

Mills dashes as fast as his feet will move and the light will guide, as careful as he can be not to smash his face into another wall. A door slams with a *thunk*. The stairwell. "Suspect is coming up stairwell behind stadium," he says into the radio. The responses pop into his radio as if he's taking attendance from the others on the scene. He reaches the steel door to the stairwell and, to no surprise, finds it locked. He backtracks for the elevator, finds the controls, and enters. It lifts him with a shudder to the stage. Once on the stage he leaps off the edge and races up the stadium stairs. Near the exit he runs into one of the officers he assigned to Preston.

"Where's Ken?" he asks the officer.

"In his car, blocking the driveway."

"Any sign of the suspect?"

"No."

"See if you can get behind the stage from this level," Mills tells him. "If you can, check the hallways all the way to the upper stadium."

"Will do," the officer says. It's Hall, basically the best all-around cop you could ask for.

As Hall sprints away, Powell calls Mills on the radio. "I'm in the back of the complex," she says. "We got Viveca Canning's car. It's under one of those car covers, here in a garage . . . This place is as big as a damn airplane hangar."

"No shit."

"Yeah, we ran the tag and the VIN. It's hers. And there's blood. Not obvious. But there are stains on the side of the seat, the shift, on the back of the steering wheel."

"OK," he tells her. "Standby."

He steps out into the front atrium, then the parking lot. He peers down the driveway and, yes, Preston is sitting in his car blocking the exit. Then, oh shit.

"Preston," he says into the radio. "Good idea, but you're going to have to move. We got responders on the way. Multiple ambulances."

As he's giving the warning, he can see Preston shift into reverse and back up over the curb, turn and position the car on the dirt, facing forward to the exit. Then he dials Powell.

"Let the techs do the prelims with the car," he tells her. "Then I want it on a flatbed to the lab."

"On it," she says. "Where are you?"

"In the parking lot," he says. "No sign of Norwood here."

"Here either."

"Is that garage the only garage?"

"Don't know."

"Shit. He probably has his own helipad," he says. "And I'm not joking."

He shields his eyes from the sun and looks to the sky, trying to locate where the C-ARC would stash a chopper. There's obviously no helipad atop the pyramid of the cathedral, but there might be one on another building on the campus. The shrill scream of sirens brings his eyes back to street level, where he sees an ambulance surge into the driveway and race toward the church entrance. Then another ambulance enters right behind, the sirens dueling insanely for the finish line. And then, as if he planned to use the commotion as camouflage, Gleason Norwood storms down the driveway, nearly hitting the second ambulance, his tires squealing, his engine roaring; it has to be him in that bright red Ferrari—shiny, glamorous, sexy, but a terrible camouflage after all.

"Lemme get back to you, Jan."

Then he radios Preston. "Follow the Ferrari, Ken. Let the department know we have a pursuit. I'm right behind you."

Mills runs to his car, running backward to keep his eyes on the

Ferrari. Norwood's car races past Preston. Preston falls in behind. Mills can hear Preston on the radio sending out the bulletin. "We're pursuing a red Ferrari, late model . . . it's getting on the on-ramp to the 202 eastbound from Forty-Fourth." Preston is reciting the Ferrari's tag number as Mills reaches his car and jumps in. He peels out as a third ambulance rushes down the driveway toward him.

In a flash, he's on the 202. He can't see Preston. Can't see the Ferrari. They had just enough of a jump-start. He gets on the phone with Powell.

"Put a call into the OME. I'll tell you more later, but we found where the church has its bodies buried."

She laughs.

"I'm not kidding, Jan," he says. "There's a huge room down there, like a catacomb. Or a mortuary. Something. Get down there. It's as fucked as anything I've ever seen."

"Jesus," she whispers. "Will do."

He hangs up and immediately calls Preston. "You still have eyes on the Ferrari?"

"Barely," he says. "The guy's clocking 130."

"Stay on him. What's your location?"

"I'm just getting on the 143, heading south," Preston replies breathlessly. "I can see him. He's about a quarter mile ahead of me, had to slow down to get off the 202. From here he can get on the 10 in either direction."

An affirmation crashes against his chest like a rogue wave.

"Or not," Mills says. "He's not going to the 10."

"OK . . ."

"Norwood's heading for Sky Harbor. Has to be," Mills says, his voice staccato. "Don't lose him. I'm guessing General Aviation. He's probably already summoned his pilot."

Then he dials the hospital. No one knows where to route his call. He slams the dashboard. He has to repeat "surgery" twice, "oncology" three times, and "breast cancer, breast cancer, breast cancer . . ." Finally, he reaches the nurses' station in the pre-op room, where someone fetches Nurse Nancy. Nurse Nancy apologizes for the "wicked bad" communications in the hospital and says Kelly is doing just fine. She's on a mild sedative, Mills learns, and he wants to ask Nancy to save a little for him. "She's still a good *ow-wah* before *suhhgehhwehhy.*"

OK. That's a relief.

He thanks Nurse Nancy and floors it. He blows by the other cars on the freeway. It's a beautiful day for flying. He peers into the clear Phoenician sky, into the valley of blue above, and he searches for somewhere to land his prayers. He doesn't know whom to ask. He's not best buddies with God. He's an acquaintance. This is what happens when you lapse, when you really have no claim to grace. But that's all right. Up there, there has to be hope. That sky is too fucking huge to not accommodate hope. So he prays to the sky. "Save her. Just save her, OK?"

Then, "Damnit, save her."

His phone rings. Preston.

"Yeah?"

"He's getting off at Sky Harbor," Preston says.

"Knew it!" Mills shouts. "Stay on him. I'll call in reinforcements. I'm betting General Aviation."

He hangs up and calls headquarters, as well as the precinct at the airport, for backup. He tells the precinct to get word to the tower to hold all private flights.

"That fucker," he says to his empty vehicle. "That fucker thinks he's going to fly away . . ."

He utters a full tirade of expletives, creative expletives, like "fucking fuckhole" and "holy cuntface" and "holy rolling fuckhole cuntface." He can't believe his ears.

His foot is practically through the floorboard. He swings down the exit ramp, his tires squealing all the way.

Thank Christ for red lights. That's probably not what Norwood's thinking, but the great thing about getting off the freeway is surface street traffic. The red Ferrari is about eight cars ahead of Mills, about four cars ahead of Preston. They're all sirens now, and the Ferrari is trying to get around the one car in front of it at the red light. Sirens. Persistent sirens. Persistent Ferrari. That fucking fuck actually pulls onto the shoulder, sideswipes the car ahead of him, and takes off through the intersection, nearly t-boning another vehicle coming from the opposite flow of traffic. Preston is right behind him. The other cars are yielding nicely to Mills. The light turns green, but the other drivers clear a path for Mills to bust through first. The Ferrari heads away from the terminals, keeping to the surrounding surface streets that will eventually double back to General Aviation. Another red light. No cars in front of them. Norwood runs the light, followed swiftly by Preston, followed nearly as swiftly by Mills. Mills hears the blaring of additional sirens; they're behind him, backup. Good. With any luck, they'll be coming in the opposite direction too. But they're not. Not yet. And Norwood is heading to the northwest, looping around toward General. In less than a minute, the Ferrari careens through the General Aviation gate and comes to a mild crash in a parking spot. Norwood hops out, carrying a briefcase, and sprints into the lobby. Preston is on him, several paces behind, but he's on him. Mills thunders into the lot, ignoring all parking etiquette, slams on his brakes, and jumps out of his car in the middle of the place, aware he's blocking anyone who might want to leave. He can hear the backup swarming closer. He follows Preston into the building, then out the other side where he can see his colleague pursuing Norwood. Wearing a fancy schmancy linen suit and that shiny silk shirt, Norwood looks like a cross between a cocaine kingpin and a shuffleboard player, and his run is jaunty and ridiculous. Preston orders him to stop. Mills, now shoulder to shoulder with Preston, does the same.

"We got you, Gleason," Mills howls. "Put your hands up, now!"

Preston and Mills have drawn their guns. Behind them, there's a burst of commotion, the rumble of feet. Mills can't turn, but his ears estimate about eight officers closing in. Looking ahead, Mills sees a sleek cylinder weaving a path in their direction. The sun is shooting serious streams of reflection off the roof of the aircraft. A Gulfstream. On its tail, the design of an angel. Scripted down the length of the fuselage, like the name of an airline, are the words "Rising Like an Angel."

Norwood ignores them. He's running toward the plane, which comes to a shaking, sharp stop.

"Gleason Norwood, we know exactly what you did," Mills yells to the suspect. "We know exactly what you're doing at that church. There is no escape. You cannot evade us. Put your hands up. Now!"

It's unlikely Norwood can hear him with all the aircraft noise around them, but ten cops in pursuit, weapons drawn, should be a fucking hint. Still, Norwood continues his race to the plane, Mills and Preston on his heels. Fuck. It has to be 107 degrees. Hot as fuck. But it's a dry fuck. He has to come up with a better description and he knows it. Preston surely will drop dead here; this harrowing combination of heat and age has little mercy even on the hardiest. He checks his colleague. Preston is breathing, but his face is ashen. *Jesus.*

Now the pilot is lowering the aircraft's stairs to the tarmac. Damnit, they're going to scoop that fucking preacher right up and steal him away. Mills can feel the heat of the tarmac through his shoes; ten more minutes of this and his soles will melt. Mills wants to give Preston a nudgeful of wordplay here—soles will melt—but he knows better. His feet slap the ground, followed by a cavalry of more feet. Then, out of nowhere, sirens. Their big, beautiful, sweet sirens blaring, three cruisers speed into the aircraft alley ahead of him, putting the Gulfstream and Norwood in the middle. It's the Sky Harbor precinct. With these sirens, evidently, comes the pilot's recognition that something might just be awry because, before they even touch the ground, the stairs begin their hydraulic lift upward without Gleason Norwood aboard.

Mills yells, "You're going nowhere, Norwood. Hands up!"

Norwood drops his briefcase, which Mills takes as the first sign of surrender.

Mills is wrong, as the man simply stands there waving his arms madly at the plane, waving and waving and waving, incensed that the pilot is not following orders. He actually stomps his feet, rips off his ridiculous blazer, and throws it to the ground. His back is to the cops as he gesticulates to the Gulfstream, this little boy and his little tantrum on the broiling pavement. He turns now, but it's too split of a split second for Mills to notice the holster or the gun before Norwood begins to shoot.

Preston and Mills return fire.

"Drop the gun, Gleason! Drop the gun!" Mills shouts at the preacher.

Pop. Pop. Pop.

"Drop the fucking gun," Mills repeats.

Pop. Pop.

And Mills is hit. A bullet strikes his left shoulder. *Fuck of all fucks!*

A blinding light. A piercing pain and a white flash of disbelief.

"Aw shit, aw shit, I've been hit . . ."

41

Gus sees a doorway. That's all he sees. He expects anyone at any moment, though he can't say whom. But it's a doorway, and on this side there are expectations. Gus is waiting for Kelly to come out of surgery. The door is real and it's not. He's there and he's also in a vision. When someone emerges, it will be somewhat of a triumph. He doesn't understand why. But at this same moment, the figure materializes: a woman, a gown, the beam of salvation. Something. Maybe this is about Kelly Mills. Maybe it's about Billie Welch. It's not about Billie Welch.

Billie Welch has already walked through the door. Going the other way.

She's made her exit.

There's a long hallway on the other side taking her far away.

And that's okay. He has felt, for a while, his heart dividing. There is someone else. And he always thought it was about Billie, that the someone else was Cam Taylor; but it's not. There's someone else for Gus. He knows she's close. She will drift through that doorway. He should have known before this. Something tells him that he knew all along. They've connected before. Gus feels a sudden pinch in his neck, a spasm, then heat radiating down his arm again. He tries to ignore it, but the pain wraps around him like tight coils of rope, burning, choking. He wills himself to snap out of it, but he can't and so he tries to intuit; all he can see is a speck of dark matter, a black puddle of blood, and the tributaries that run from it.

Is the sky above spinning? Or is it just the angle of Mills's face? Is he losing lots of blood, or does the pavement always get wet at this hour? Hard to tell.

Preston rolls to his side, covers Mills. The backup has advanced and continues to shoot. With one cheek against the scorching pavement, and one of his eyes free to witness, Mills sees Norwood's gun go airborne. It does a couple of revolutions and hits the ground, as does Norwood. Cops are all over him, guns still drawn. "I need to make this arrest," Mills whispers to Preston.

Preston, who's just called for an ambulance, says, "Don't be an idiot."

"Bring that asshole over here and let me arrest him."

"He's been hit," Preston says. "Not badly from what I can tell."

Blood is seeping through the preacher's pants in the thigh region.

"Drag his ass over here."

Preston shouts something to a nearby cop. A few moments later, it could be several minutes, Mills can't tell; time is slipping through him as if he's the sieve and God the sifter. Or something like that. Whoever God is.

"Mills, open your eyes . . . Mills?" It's Uncle Ken's voice.

Mills complies and sees a haggard Gleason Norwood a few yards away on his knees, his hands cuffed, blood still seeping. Sirens. Ambulances. "We got you Gleason Norwood. For the murder of Viveca Canning. And a whole lot more. We're shutting you down. Now . . . say goodbye . . . say goodbye."

Then Norwood disappears.

"I read him his rights," Preston says.

Mills feels like he's falling asleep, suddenly withdrawing from the day.

"Mills?"

"Tell the ambulance to take me to Phoenix Memorial," he tells Preston. "I have to see Kelly."

"OK."

And then he lets himself let go.

Gus watches as Trevor paces the room. The kid showed up, kissed his mom, and held her hand as she was wheeled out of surgery about twenty minutes ago. She's been dozing on and off ever since. Right now she's asleep. The TV overhead plays the murmurs of a daytime talk show hosted by a table of women. The nurses have shuffled in and out. One is here now adjusting an IV. Trevor furiously taps his phone.

"Everything all right, buddy?" Gus asks.

"Fine. I just have a bunch of asswipes pissed off that I'm missing scrimmage."

"Surely they understand with your mom in the hospital . . ."

"That's what I'm trying to explain to them now," Trevor says. "But even though I'm sending them a group text, they're all responding to me separately like they're a bunch of morons."

"Ignore them, Trevor. The game will go on with you or without you."

Trevor drops his phone to his side, stops pacing, and says, "You know, you don't have to hang around, Gus. I'm here now. I can handle things."

"I made a promise to your father."

"Right. But he'll understand. He wouldn't want you here wasting your whole day."

"Are you asking me to leave, Trevor?"

The kid shrugs. "No. Not really."

"Then how about I go get us something cold to drink," Gus says. "What do you want?"

Trevor asks for a bottle of water. It takes Gus maybe ten minutes to find the cafeteria, grab water for both of them, and return to Kelly's room. As he approaches from the hallway, he senses commotion, an intervening factor, an extra voice. Entering, the first thing he sees is a uniform from behind on a frame that isn't Alex's. The man turns. It's the sergeant. His face is grave.

"Sergeant Woods?"

"Hey Gus."

"Everything all right?"

"I was just telling Trevor there's been an incident." His voice is hushed, apparently so Kelly can rest undisturbed.

"Where's Alex?" Gus asks.

"My dad's been shot," Trevor says, his voice trembling.

Gus takes a deep breath; he wills it to calm his jittery nerves. "How bad?"

"He lost a lot of blood," Woods says. "He's in surgery now."

"I want to see him," Trevor insists, heading for the door.

Woods gently pulls him by the shoulder and says, "I told you that's not possible. You can see him after surgery."

Trevor sniffles. He's on the edge of tears. Gus approaches. "Trevor," he says, "The sergeant will make sure you're the first one to see him when he gets out of surgery."

"It's not up to me," Woods says. "But the minute the doctor gives us the okay, I'll bring you up. I promise."

Trevor pushes past him. "No! I want to go up now!"

Woods grabs him by the elbow. "You're going to have to man up right about now, Trevor, and do what's asked of you. Right now we're asking you to stay with your mother. Someone needs to be here for her when she wakes up."

"You want me to tell her the news?" Trevor asks him, his eyes brimming.

"Yes," Woods replies. "You're an adult. I can trust you with that."

Woods winks at Gus and says, "If you want to hear the latest, change the station. All the local channels are live with breaking news . . ."

As Woods leaves the room, Gus reaches for the remote and flips through the local stations. There's live video from Sky Harbor and live video from the C-ARC. There are reports from reporters live in the field. The operative word is "live," as it is plastered across the screen from one channel to the next. All the channels share a fever pitch.

"A story that's gripping the valley!"
"A dramatic scene unfolding..."
"A shootout at Sky Harbor!"
"An officer rushed to the hospital!"

Gus settles on Channel Four. Aaliyah's channel.

"... The search at the C-ARC led to a shootout at Sky Harbor International Airport and the arrest of megachurch pastor Gleason Norwood who, police say, was trying to flee.
'We placed Mr. Norwood under arrest for the murder of Viveca Canning. He will face charges of conspiracy to commit murder, extortion, racketeering, along with a whole host of other crimes currently under investigation.'
That was Phoenix Homicide Sergeant Jacob Woods, interviewed in the past hour. In another shocking twist to this story, the preacher's excommunicated son, Gabriel Norwood, has also been arrested for his alleged role in the Canning murder. Police say Gabriel Norwood fired the shots that killed the 62-year-old woman, but that he was acting on behalf of his father. Still more startling news is coming out of today's raid on the church! With more on that and the rescue of Aaliyah Jones, Marco Hidalgo-Suarez is live at the C-ARC."

Gus sits up. His flesh prickles all over. Blood rushes from his face to his feet, then back up again.

"Marco, what's the latest?
Well, this is just one of those startling stories that really shocks you! I'm standing in front of the Church of Angels Rising Cathedral, which

today could be called the 'Church of Fallen Angels.' Police say they have discovered what they call the 'unlawful burial of bodies' in an area underneath the church. Officials won't say how those bodies ended up in the church's basement graveyard nor will they identify the dead, but they do say pastor Gleason Norwood will likely face charges related to this discovery and is already facing charges related to the alleged kidnapping of our own Aaliyah Jones. Jones, who was working on an investigation of the church, went missing about a week ago. She was found alive this morning in that same underground area beneath the church. She was taken to an area hospital for observation. Police say they also discovered several other individuals who were held against their will. In a rare media conference, the chief of the Phoenix Police Department spoke about the grisly and gruesome discoveries.

'We believe the individuals discovered today were being held against their will in accordance with some kind of church doctrine concocted and enforced by Gleason Norwood, the founder of the Church of Angels Rising. Doctrine or not, these actions were illegal. They amount to kidnapping and false imprisonment. In addition to the other charges Norwood is facing, he will be prosecuted to the fullest extent of the law.'

News Four has not been able to determine the condition of Aaliyah Jones or the other individuals freed from the church. However, since Jones is an employee of our station, you can expect the first exclusive interview with her once she is released from the hospital. Stay tuned. It's sure to be riveting. Back to you in the studio.

Thank you Marco Hidalgo-Suarez. Great job reporting out there. We're looking forward to that riveting interview.

Authorities are not commenting further on the murder of Viveca Canning, a former church member herself. In still another shocking twist to this story, authorities say the dead woman's husband may also have been the victim of murder, and have placed Tucker Charles, a member of the Church of Angels Rising board of directors, under arrest. At this time, police are not commenting on motive or evidence behind any of these alleged crimes. The county attorney has not returned our calls so far *today. We will keep pressing for a response as we break into programming to bring you these live reports.*

As we reported earlier in our coverage, a Phoenix police officer was wounded during today's incident. News Four has now learned that homicide detective Alex Mills was shot in the shoulder while attempting to apprehend pastor Gleason Norwood at Sky Harbor. Police would only characterize the wound as serious, but say the detective is expected to survive. No word on his condition from Phoenix Memorial."

42

t was supposed to be the other way around.

He was supposed to be at Kelly's beside. He was supposed to be bent over her, fawning. But no. Here she is. She's sitting in a wheelchair, a portable IV towering above, leaning to him at his bedside. She's fawning. He's barely conscious. "I'm sorry," he says.

"For what?"

"I should have been there for you," he tells her.

"You are here for me," she says.

"How did it go? The surgery?"

"You need to rest."

He turns to her. "How did it go?"

"Fine."

They're whispering. She's exhausted. He can tell. His whispers are drug-induced. He has an IV of Demerol. He was rushed into surgery to remove the bullet, which came out, according to the doctors, without incident. The bullet, however, had already done some damage to the surrounding tissue and muscle. He should be getting out of the hospital in a few days. He'll need physical therapy. The chief has been by; so has Woods. They've told him not to worry, to take all the time he needs to recover. Or maybe he dreamed that, or hallucinated. Who the fuck knows? It doesn't really matter. He'll get better when he gets better. Gleason Norwood is going to fry, that's all that matters. Gabriel Norwood will likely fry too, but perhaps not quite as crisply if he cooperates. Speaking of fathers and sons, Mills thinks he spies Trevor out of the corner of his eye. Maybe a hallucination, because everything is a bit fuzzy now.

"Son?"

"Yeah?"

"Just checking. Not sure if you were here . . ."

Trevor laughs. "I've been with you for an hour, Dad. We already talked."

"Oh."

"Your father's hopped up on drugs, Trevor," Kelly says.

"So, Dad, can you spare a few hundred dollars?"

"Trevor!" Kelly begs.

"I'm kidding," he says. "I just thought this would be a great time to take advantage of him."

Someone enters the room. Mills can barely make out the figure or even the outline of the person. But as the person nears the bed, Mills recognizes the uniform: it's a cop. Mills has an officer assigned for security, and the man, Hall, leans over and says, "You have a visitor. He's insisting on coming in even though we told him you're having no visitors."

"Who?"

"It's your pal, that psychic guy."

"Gus. Gus Parker?"

"Yeah."

"Let him in."

"You sure?" Hall asks. "The doctors said you weren't supposed to have visitors. And those were my orders from the chief as well."

"I said let him in. He's been here all day with my wife."

Hall nods, shrugs, and retreats. A moment later and in comes Gus Parker, striding toward the bed. "Are you okay?"

"He's going to be fine," Kelly says before Mills can answer.

"Thank God," Gus says. "This could have been much worse . . ."

"Is that a psychic hunch or just a cliché?" Mills asks him.

"When have you ever heard me utter a cliché?"

Mills lays his head to one side of the pillow, grins, and closes his eyes. He hears Kelly say, "Looks like he's dozing off. He's been doing that off and on since surgery."

Suddenly the room is cold and still as Kelly begins to weep.

"Jesus," Gus says. "You've been through a lot today."

"Yes," she says.

"What can I do?" Gus asks. "Can I get you two anything?"

"We'll be fine," Kelly says. "You've already gone above and beyond."

"Come on, there must be something I can do."

"We have Trevor here. This is his chance to prove what a good son he is."

Mills hears Trevor clear his throat, and this brings another smile to his face. Swirling through his drug-addled brain is the soft, cushion-like assurance that all of his best friends are here in this room, surrounding him, and with that assurance, it's as safe as it's ever been to drift away.

A few days later, Gus and Beatrice meet for dinner at Paradise Grill. She's about to leave on the next leg of her book tour, and Gus tells her he'll be missing her. Like a doting aunt, she grabs his cheek between her forefinger and thumb and pinches. "You can come join me, if you'd like . . ."

"I'd like to very much," he says. "But I need to stick around. Alex is supposed to get out of the hospital today. Trevor's going back to Tucson. I think I ought to help out."

"You're a good friend."

He turns his palms up. "I guess. I know he'd do it for me," he says. "Maybe I'll meet up with you in a couple of weeks on tour. Where you headed?"

"New England. I have to get out of this heat."

"I'd like to visit New England."

"Then it's settled," she says.

"It's unsettled."

"How do you mean?"

He's not sure. But, quite suddenly, it has occurred to him that all is not settled. There are threads hanging, tugging at him actually. One of those threads has a name. Aaliyah Jones. For some reason he's drawn to her. He says her name aloud, "Aaliyah," unaware for a moment that he has an audience.

"She's the one coming through the door," Beatrice says. "Toward you."

Gus jolts back. "I told you about that?"

"You did. The day it happened."

"Oh," Gus says. "And you think it's her."

"I do."

Aaliyah Jones is supposed to be giving her first interview tomorrow about her kidnapping ordeal. Gus will be sure to watch. Then he'll be sure to call her.

43

Thank Christ August is behind them. September still swelters, but it's not the incinerator of August, which explains why Mills and Kelly are meandering through the 25th Annual Tempe Art Festival, alternately admiring and mocking the displays. They roll their eyes at the ubiquitous dreamcatchers. There's always a painting of a huge pink lily that bears a striking resemblance to the vulva. Always. It's an art cliché. It's standard fare. Consistently, there's also faux Southwestern art and jewelry, silver and turquoise galore. "Did you feel that?" Kelly asks him.

"What?"

"The breeze."

"Ah, I think you're right," he says. "Congratulations for surviving summer."

He's been out of the hospital for a few weeks, faithfully going for physical therapy, and he's been back at work part-time. Kelly tells him he's rushing it. And he says the same thing to Kelly, who's been back at work herself for two weeks, but full-time. She'll start her third week of radiation tomorrow. Then chemotherapy. She dreads chemo, and Mills dreads chemo on her behalf, but her prognosis is good. She may have to cut back some work hours during chemo, but her doctors believe she'll survive more than the summer, that there'll be many more seasons in the life of Kelly Mills.

Gus will meet up with Beatrice Vossenheimer next week in Boston. He's never been to Boston, and he's looking forward to seeing some of the places where real history was made. He's already conjuring up visions (tourist visions, not psychic visions) of cobblestone streets, sailboats, and Kennedys. He'll spend about a week with Beatrice as she promotes her book throughout New England.

It's almost 5:30 p.m. He's watching CNN. But he'd better get showered. He told Aaliyah Jones he'd pick her up at 6:30. He had reconnected with Aaliyah not long after her release from the hospital. He had watched the interview she gave her own station about her kidnapping and, in studying her closely, watching the way her mouth moved around her words and the way her eyes stared through the camera into his, he could tell she was sending a message specifically to him. She needed to see him, to talk this through. And so, he called her, and she came by. She wasn't generous with details; he had to do most of the heavy lifting, but he was able to see her experience as both harrowing and defining. It defined her strength and resolve. They fed her and her fellow prisoners once or twice a day. She was locked away in that box of a room, in the dark, on a sheet upon the floor. She was given one hour a day to come out and talk to the other prisoners. She thought she might go mad. But she didn't go mad. She wrote poetry in her head to keep her head busy. She knew she'd forget most of it, and she has, but poetry served a purpose. She willed herself to see images of hope and light. And she saw images of hope and light. She willed herself to hear the music of her life, and she heard the music of her life.

She says she never doubted she'd survive in a "big picture" kind of way, but she often felt she would not survive the day. At one point she hoped death would come, only to rebel against her own self-pity. And now Gus is drawn to her more than he had expected to be, more than he imagined. Her resolve does something to him, betters his own. They're having dinner tonight. It will be their first real date. Tentative, but real. He doesn't know what to expect. But that's okay.

"The FBI has confirmed to CNN that it has rescued thirty-seven children from a labor camp-like setting in Sedona, Arizona. The camp is

linked to the embroiled Church of Angels Rising, which is said to separate church members from their children for a period of six to eight years for intense study and so-called 'field work.' Unnamed FBI sources call the conditions of the camp 'inhumane' and 'abusive.' In fact, the embattled pastor of the megachurch, Gleason Norwood, already facing murder and kidnapping charges, is set to face additional charges stemming from the Sedona raid."

Damn. Alex Mills has opened a can of worms that can't be contained. The world could use a little more Alex Mills, and a little less cable news.

"And Gleason Norwood is not the only member of his family making news today . . . Just in to CNN, a jumbo jet carrying Norwood's wife, Francesca, and 410 other passengers plummeted more than 15,000 feet during a flight over the Pacific last night. Early reports indicate the plane depressurized midway on Flight 1010's journey between Los Angeles and Papeete, Tahiti. Also on board, we're told, rock 'n' roll legend Billie Welch, her sister, and a few members of her band . . . "

Sweat trickles down his forehead, from his temples and down his neck. His skin goes clammy, cold. He sinks to the couch. Closes his eyes. He's tossed around in the surf, like a rag in a washing machine, a huge wave pummeling, having its way with him. He's slammed against the rocky bottom.

Had Viveca Canning been on that flight, Gus is sure it would have gone down in the ocean. Her murder had changed the course of events. At least in his psychic mind it had. He has to pull himself to the surface now, wipe off the debris, and survey the damage. Billie must have been scared to death.

"Some passengers were treated for serious injuries, but none of the injuries are considered to be life-threatening. The aircraft was able to make it to its final destination after this terrifying incident."

They purchased a few pieces of pottery. Nothing too extravagant. Just three matching pieces that eschew the whole Southwestern theme and go deeper south for inspiration, across the border into Mexico. A local artist, Brava Torres, created these pieces to evoke the Day of the Dead celebrations. Kelly says the pottery, which feature intricately carved elements of whimsical skeletons and colorful celebrants, gives her the last laugh over cancer, and that's all Mills needed to hear. He told her she could buy all thirty pieces, but she said that'd be too much to pay for irony.

He has one hand on the wheel, another hand holding hers. There is something squeezing his chest he can't explain. It's not a heart attack. But it has a hold of him, a sort of bittersweet pounding in there. Love, loss, love, fear. He's not sure but he's convinced that heartbreak, either of love or of sorrow, is real.

They pull onto their street and Kelly says, "You feel like Rosita's Place for dinner?"

And he says, "I always feel like Rosita's Place for dinner."

And she says, "Good. Let's drop off the merch and head out . . ."

"Any chance we can take a steamy shower together first?" he asks her.

"There's a chance," she says with a cluck of her tongue and a lascivious wink of an eye. "The new bald look is quite sexy on you."

He runs his hand over the stubble of his unfamiliar scalp. "It's the least I could do."

As they swing into the driveway, Mills can see the profile of a man on their front doorstep.

"Who's that?" he asks his wife, as if she's supposed to know all things domestic.

She peers. They're almost parked before she says, "Oh, shit, what's he doing here?"

Mills parks and gets out of the car. As he moves closer to the man, he recognizes the demonic smile of Trey Robert Shinner.

"Trey?" Kelly says. "What are you doing at my house?"

The guy rises from the doorstep. Shinner's pasty skin and greenish eyes give the impression he's percolating with vomit. "I can't think of how to thank you for winning my case, Attorney Mills," Shinner says. "I'm indebted to you for life."

She shakes her head. "No, Trey. As you know, your trust fund paid the bill."

"That's not what I mean," he persists. "You know how if someone saves your life you're supposed to be their servant forever more . . ."

Mills scoffs. "Well, that's the stuff of legend, Trey . . ."

Shinner's eyes begin to well. Tears are brimming. "No, no," he begs. "It is not legend. I shall forever be your servant, Attorney Mills. I will spend the rest of my life repaying you for my freedom. What did you buy today?"

"Some art from the Tempe festival," Kelly says with a wary smile. "Let me pay for it."

"Absolutely not," Mills says. "Enough with this nonsense, Trey. Go home. Where the hell is your car?"

The man skulks away. "I'm not allowed to drive because of my meds," he says. "I walked."

"Call an Uber," Mills tells him.

"Goodbye, Trey," Kelly says.

"It's not goodbye," Shinner insists. "I will repay you for all you've done. Your enemies should be trembling."

"Jesus Christ," Mills mutters.

"Come on, let's go inside," Kelly says. "He's a sick man. I tried to get him the help he needs. No one will take him unless he commits himself."

Shinner is almost at the edge of the lawn when Mills turns and calls to him. "She doesn't have any enemies, Trey. Just stay away from us."

Shinner flashes one last smile, this one exposing teeth that hang from his mouth like broken windows. And then singing, "I can't do that. I can't do that. I can't do that," he skips away into the dusk as if he's about to join a gang of ghouls who haunt the valley.

ACKNOWLEDGMENTS

A s always, I thank my family for their outstanding support of my work. That includes my in-laws, as well. I lucked out on all sides. I've lived many places and have met a lot of people; thank you to my friends wherever you are. A special thanks to the Soul Team in Boston and my pals in Phoenix for always giving me the kindest welcome and the loveliest support. My biggest regret is that we don't have more time to spend face-to-face.

Again, I owe a big thanks to Sergeant Jon Howard and Sergeant Vince Lewis of the Phoenix Police Department. Their input has been a huge help, and they've been generous with their time. I extend my gratitude, as well, to Chelsea Janicek, a crime scene specialist at the Phoenix PD for all the details about CSI technique and practice, including the blood and guts. I, alone, am responsible for any mistakes or detours from official police procedures and CSI processes. Thanks to Kim Krigsten and Adam Alperin for helping me find Chelsea.

I'd like to acknowledge the people at Seventh Street Books/Start who have helped bring this book to life, particularly my fantastic editor Dan Mayer. And finally, last but certainly not least, a major thanks to my agent, Ann Collette, for being a great mentor, coach, critic, and friend.

ABOUT THE AUTHOR

Steven Cooper is the author of *Dig Your Grave* and *Desert Remains*. A former investigative reporter, Steven has received multiple Emmy Awards, a national Edward R. Murrow Award, and many honors from the Associated Press. He has lived all over the country and has traveled all over the planet. Currently, Atlanta is home.